A Grey Man

A GREY MAN

Choi In-hoon

translated by
Chun Kyung-ja

Si-sa-yong-o-sa, Inc., Korea
Pace International Research, Inc., U.S.A.

Published simultaneously in KOREA and the UNITED STATES

KOREA EDITON
First printing 1988
Si-sa-yong-o-sa, Inc.
55-1 Chongno 2-ga, Chongno-gu
Seoul 110, Korea

U.S. EDITION
First printing 1988
Pace International Research, Inc.
Tide Avenue, Falcon Cove
P.O. Box 51, Arch Cape
Oregon 97102, U.S.A.

ISBN: 0-87296-032-3

This book is a co-publication by Si-sa-yong-o-sa, Inc.
and The International Communication Foundation.

Preface

Choi In-hoon's *A Grey Man* is a relentlessly realistic depiction of the dilemmas and disillusionments inherited by the generation of Korean intellectuals who came of age in the late 1950s, a generation born before the country was liberated from Japanese imperialism and who as adolescents endured the irrational obscenities of the Korean War.

The main character of the novel, Tokko Chun, is born and raised in the North, exposed to the black-and-white world-view of a Communist education and to the inflated expectations shared by most refugees who fled South in search of safety and freedom. Once in the South, torn from his family, the lonely protagonist, neither hero nor antihero, neither ruthless knave nor self-martyring fool, is confronted with a painful liberty. For the freedom he obtains is a freedom to become an iconoclast, to pierce the hypocrisy and the confusion around him in an attempt to understand when traditional values lay bared to the corrosive winds of world history.

Black-and-white Western modes of thought, the values of Christianity, of technologistic "Progress", of historical materialism, of Rousseauean democracy, all seem to Tokko Chun to distort the task of forging an authentically Korean nationalism founded on an enlightened recovery of indigenous traditions. The most powerful parts of this book are the ruminations of Korean traditions—on Buddhism, Confucianism, the deeper truths in ancestor worship—and the reader who attends to Choi's profound reflections on ancient ethical thought will come away from this novel with a new respect for non-Eurocentric systems of social ethics.

Grey is the color of hypercomplexity, of an attitude that rejects black-and-white oversimplifications, a worldview prepared to recognize that history imposes insurmountable constraints but which nevertheless refuses to surrender either to quietistic resignation or to naively self-destructive heroism. At the same time, grey is the color of self-deception, of suspended decisions between religion and irreligion, or between political and artistic vocations. These are universal modes of skepticism, but in *A Grey Man* the author succeeds in presenting them in a uniquely Korean perspective, and the result is more concrete and more educational than the reveries of the superfluous men of European existentialist fiction.

The astonishing sweep of *A Grey Man*, which ranges freely over domains as diverse as Buddhist metaphysics and Western philosophy of history, is more astonishing still when we remember that the book was published in 1963 when Choi In-hoon was only twenty-seven years old. The reach of the author's learning, both bookish and practical, is often in evidence in these pages, and it is difficult to name a Western novelist whose command of Oriental history, religion and philosophy compared with Choi's knowledge of Western intellectual history. The depth of reflection in *A Grey Man*, to be sure, imposes demands on the reader, and those who are looking for an action-packed pot-boiler will do well to amuse themselves elsewhere, for this is a work devoted less to entertainment than to education.

It is sometimes said that the best literature is passionate autobiography, suitably masked, and the author of *A Grey Man* certainly was in a position to know first-hand about the subjects of which he treats. Choi was born in 1936 in Hamgyŏngbuk-do, North Korea, and came to the South during the

Korean War, at the age of fourteen. He studied law at Seoul National University in the mid-1950s, hence when this novel, set in 1958 and 1959, touches on the political decadence that culminated in the ouster of Syngman Rhee in the student revolution of April 1960, Choi is a particularly well-informed narrator. The political turmoil of 1958 to 1963, the years in which Choi wrote his highly regarded first novel, *The Square*, as well as *A Grey Man*, was a period of soul-searching about the deformation of democracy into plebiscitarian autocracy, and this work sheds a great deal of light on Korean political consciousness and student dissent in the intervening years as well.

A Grey Man, then, is a novel in which the dilemmas of Korean nationalism are interwoven with more personal dilemmas —subjective dilemmas encountered by all Korean intellectuals of the post-Korean war generations. For the social situation is a spontaneous resultant of countless individual decisions very much like the choices posed in this book—choices whether to embrace Western ideologies, whether to study abroad, whether to interpret Korean spiritual and social malaise in Christian terms, and so forth. These are issues of the 1980s, too, decisions that still have an immediacy twenty-five years after Choi wrote this book. *A Grey Man*, like few other modern Korean novels, furnishes direct insights into these ongoing processes of consciousness formation.

Unsurprisingly, a novel of ideas which probes the contemporary significance of Korean traditions often touches on historical events and on Korean classics unfamiliar to Western readers. Several references have been briefly explained by parenthetical translator's notes interpolated directly into the text. Many others could have been added, but it was thought best to keep them to a minimum, on the assumption that the intrigued reader might be induced to do a bit of independent inquiry. One recurrent reference, to the traditional story of *Ch'un-hyang-jŏn*, may be briefly noted here.

Ch'un-hyang-jŏn is an anonymous work, first transmitted

as an oral tradition in the eighteenth century. In this folk epic, a lowly daughter of a *kisaeng* (courtesan), Sŏng Ch'un-hyang, falls in love with a young aristocrat, Yi Mong-ryong. Their love crosses the rigid class line between *sangnom* and high-born *yangban*. After great trials, Ch'un-hyang, a paragon of chastity who goes to prison rather than gives herself to another abusive *yangban*, is rescued by Master Yi, her true love, and the two live happily ever after. What *Romeo and Juilet* depicts as a star-crossed love affair doomed a blood feud here assumes the form of a sublimated image of peasant revolt against a social hierarchy attributed to hereditary fate.

Along with prior English translations of Choi's novels *The Square* and *One Day in the Life of the Writer Ku-Bo*, the present translation hopefully will procure well-merited international recognition for the author. Choi In-hoon's uncommon grasp of the sociohistorical forces that weigh so heavily on modern Korean life makes his work significant not only for his fellow Koreans, but for people everywhere who care about the grey ambivalences of accelerating "modernization".

Chun Kyung-ja

CONTENTS

I

'Tis a joy indeed to receive a friend from afar.

One rainy evening in the fall of 1958, Kim Hahk paid a visit to his friend Tokko Chun, bringing with him a bottle of Chillo soju and a couple of dried cuttlefish. Hahk was already drunk. As he veered into a dark, gloomy alley, he muttered to himself, "Well, this guy sure picked an odd corner for his nest". His friend's face came before his eyes, a handsome face with melancholy eyes that seldom shone with excitement.

The owner of the nest was in. Judging from his beaming face, a rarity for him, he must have been bored to tears.

"Welcome."

"You mean it?"

"Never believe anything, do you? Ought to be more literally minded about life. When I say good to see you, I mean good to see you."

"Wow, since when?"

Both of them laughed loudly.

A host in spite of himself, Chun mumbled something akin to an apology as he spread out some newspapers and set up a little drinking table with the stuff Hahk had brought.

"Now, let's have a drink."

Hahk handed out an empty glass for Chun to fill, then abruptly withdrew his hand. He raised the glass close to his eyes and studied it.

"What's wrong?" Chun inquired.

"What's this? Stained. . . ."

Chun craned his neck for a better look at it, then said,

"Ah, that, that's probably toothpaste. It's my tooth brushing cup."

"Some friend you are."

Hahk said as he rigorously rubbed the rim of the glass with a paper towel.

"Stop being such a fanatic about cleanliness. After all, you yourself are a concoction of germs and illusions."

"Don't change the subject. Dirt is dirt."

Once again they both broke out laughing.

"Ah, by the way. . . ."

Out of a manila envelope Hahk removed a thin pamphlet and handed it to Chun.

"Your article appeared in this issue. Might be some typos. . . ." Hahk said as he filled Chun's glass.

"The members of our circle praised it. Sure you have no intention of joining us?"

The academic circle in question was called "Imprisoned Generation". It had been founded by students in the department of political science, Hahk's own major. Chun had contributed a guest column, at Hahk's suggestion, and it was appearing in that month's issue. Chun gulped down what was left in his glass and thumbed through the contents. His piece was listed last.

It would have been grand if our nation had had colonies. First of all, the outrageous number of college graduates now infesting the ranks of officialdom could be reduced by dispatching many to the various colonies. The anxiety and tension now current in the younger generation would thus be greatly abated and the social atmosphere in general would accordingly become far more congenial. Those who keenly compete at home, once outside, soon would lose their interest in fighting with one another. Instead, they would nurture genteel hobbies, leisurely surveying the cultural relics of their respective locales.

No matter how bellicose the National Assembly can be with its ins and outs, once the agenda concerns colonial rule the opposed parties will forthwith suppress their disagreements and exhibit excellent examples of how the race is a bond of common interests in spite of everything. All things said and done, there's nothing like a married woman's philandering, they say. Likewise, no life is more delectable for a race than one spent applying the screws to other races. Such past-times provide breathing space from domestic political quarrels. A dog to kick around in case of boredom, so to speak.

For instance, if a great fire broke out in the capital city of Seoul, turning it into a living hell, we could always unleash the members of patriotic groups like "The Scarab" or "The Death's Head", having them spread a rumor that the fire was deliberately set by certain people. By "certain people", of course, we would mean colonials. Then the livid crowds, with everyone clutching some weapon in hand, would swarm into the streets to aid in the maintenance of law and order.

Thus, the old proverb "A household prospers from accidental fire" is proven true. Even the laborers would not be taken in with talk about some international labor organization, talk that's not too palatable. Instead, they would engage in a rather moderate strike to demand a full stop to the influx of cheap labor into "the homeland" from our colonies. Economic conditions in our nation couldn't be too dire. By exploiting the ignorance of farmers in the colonies and the inefficacy of its laws, we easily could confiscate enormous parcels of farmland. Then farmers from the Korean heartland could emigrate to the colonies for permanent settlement. Under circumstances in which all aspects of colonial interests are within our sole control, we would hardly need to rack our brains to make ends meet.

Once living became a breeze, men of taste would gather

together to form a circle, perhaps called something like "Animal Lovers", and newspapers would deck themselves out with photos of protestors engaged in sit-down demonstrations in front of restaurants that serve dog soup. What is more, if the police should ever harm even one hair on the head of a citizen, the most stinking scandal would immediately erupt. In the universities, Korean Studies would become the most thriving speciality. It would be proven that Hŏ Kyun (1569-1618, Yi Dynasty scholar and statesman) was a great precursor of Jonathan Swift and teacher of Thomas More. Also clarified would be the ways in which the philosophy of T'oigye (1501-1570: leading Yi Dynasty Confucian scholar, famous for developing Chu-tzu's Theory of the noumenal and phenomenal principles of material structure and atmospheric energy) had actually taken the first steps toward modern nuclear physics.

Suppose our colony is called, say, Napaj. Then we would proudly proclaim that "We'll not trade Chŏng Song-gang (1536-1593: pen name of statesman and poet Chŏng Ch'ŏl) for all of Napaj".

Lest the colony unify itself through a quest for shared spiritual traditions, we would exploit the old ruling class as our watchdogs, throwing them a few bones and instigating factional strife by segregating them along lines of locality, pedigree or astrological indices.

At the same time, in order to forestall any rebellion due to overharsh treatment, our policy naturally would include some "civilized" administrative initiatives. The sense of mission among the younger malcontents could tactfully be channeled into a drive for rural enlightenment, which would furnish a cathartic outlet for them. In addition, branch temples of the Chogye order of Korean Buddhism should be established in every locale. Through such vehicles we could indoctrinate the people to accept wishy-washy policies reflecting the transience and voidness of life.

The superiority of Koryŏ celadon ought to be widely propagated, and all called upon to recognize the reality that a race capable of creating such art is entitled to rule by the intrinsic justice of history—everyone should accept this proof of legitimacy. The living will enjoy an existence so easy and comfortable that the complaints of the angry younger generation will certainly mark the world of literature, a delightful world worth seeing.

Speaking of literature, the population of sophisticated readers will grow, a flood of cheap editions appear, and a surfeit of classics will be in astonishingly ample supply. On foundations as rich as these, the most exquisite and magnanimous prose will reach full blossom, prose taking either the form of human biography or of racial history. The history of the Korean language will be thoroughly explored and an extensive Korean lexicon published in great quantities. A witty writer is sure to appear who will say: "The spirit of Korean literature is firstly, elegance, secondly, elegance and thirdly, elegance".

The development of music will be so breathtaking that people will refer to Vienna as the Seoul of Austria. Korean traditional music, with its melodies that seemingly die only to revive *ex nihilo*, melodies magically drawing the soul into a dancing reverie of abandonment, will certainly captivate music lovers around the world.

My thoughts having reached this point, I heaved a long sigh. Now that the idyllic age is forever gone in which imperialism could serve as an international policy even as democracy was invoked as the national ideology, we live now in an age in which new trumpets are blasting, calling for international aid and for betterment of living conditions in the underdeveloped states. Where on God's green earth could we possibly seize a colony for use as an essential fertilizer for the growth of democracy? Democracy without a colonial dominion certainly imposes great risks.

Unable to face the agony any longer, at last I called upon a female friend for whom I entertained a deep respect. I plumbed the particulars of the issue at hand, inquiring whether she knew of any ingenious solution. She first praised my patriotism and then proceeded with her advice.

"You've got to find a surrogate for a colony."

"A surrogate?"

"Right. Now is no time to secure a colony, so you must search for something else to take the place of and function like a colony."

"Where do you suppose we could uncover such a thing we are free to rob and tread upon with impunity?"

"There is, though."

"What?"

"Love and time."

Utterly flabbergasted, I remained silent for a good ten minutes before responding in a feeble voice.

"Woman, thy words are beauty."

And then I showered her with kisses.

"Not bad at all."

So spoke the writer himself, Chun. He replaced the Journal on the desk.

"Yes, I admit it. Now, what do you think of what I said before?"

"What do you mean?"

"Will you join our circle? That's what I mean."

"Would it not be a bit peculiar for political science students and an aspiring novelist to be members of the same circle?"

"It's unlike you to say such a narrow-minded thing. Naturally, the idea among the political science students is to learn from each other, thus cultivating a certain spiritual solidarity. After reading your essay, they asked me what department you were in. I told them your major is Korean literature. They said that you're not bad at all, for a descendant of 'while your parents are still alive'. They found a sense of politics in your writing."

"What do you mean by 'while your parents are still alive'?"

"Why, you know, there's a poem that begins: 'While your parents are still alive, observe filial piety to your heart's content', remember?"

"So?"

"What the circle members meant was that it's not art. All Sijo (a classical three-stanza form of Korean verse) are more or less the same, don't you think? What kind of art is it if all one does is fix the number of syllables according to the traditional order and simply follow the rules of form without even changing level?"

"You have a point there. But Sijo does not exhaust Korean literature. Prose is superior to verse in our literature, anyway."

"We are no authorities and wouldn't know that. All we know comes from the old Korean we had to learn for the college entrance examination, plus what little we learned in freshman studies. What my friends said may have gone too far, and our understanding of modern Korean literature is also rather laughable. The space-time coordinates are lacking, nobody seems to be able to tell the age or the country in which we live. The spiritual climate in Korea is like a ship without a compass. There's absolutely no difference in time. When I happen to read a novel, it never reaches me. Maybe it's just that I have no talent for literature, anyway, it's been ages since I gave up modern literature, especially poetry. What do you make of this? After all, we belong to the class of highly sophisticated readers, don't we? No matter how difficult the artistic world has become, the difficulties should be borne by the artist, and when the work is produced, I think it should emerge with a recognizable face. Or, has modern literature already reached the place where nobody but the writer himself and the specialists in literary history can understand the work standing alone? If so, then literature has contributed to making a closed society, am I not right? I don't mean that modern writers should write pop-songs. What I mean is, their work should at least be intelligible to their contemporaries who share the same space-time with themselves. I don't know how they rank in the history of Korean literature, but to me Yi Kwang-su is far better than Kim Tong-in. There is no historical sense at all in Kim Tong-in. That he wrote historical novels is itself proof of this failing. Apparently, he grasped history only a narrative, as already fossilized. No dates are impressed on the reader in his modern novels. The characters would as readily fit in the Yi Dynasty, in the Japanese colonial period or in the present, wouldn't they? His novels are not historical epitaphs but melodies of nature. They are like wind or water. You recall his short story "Toes Alike", don't you? So what if the toes are alike? With our three thousand *ri* between mountain and river looking more Japanese every day, what's so special about toes resembling toes? Does he not confuse history with nature and mankind with a herd of swine? Kim Tong-in must have misunderstood the Japanese incursion as merely a bad cold. Compared to him Yi Kwang-su was great. Apart from all his other works, "Earth" alone qualified him as the greatest Korean writer. He portrayed the typical Korean intellectual of his period with unsentimental objectivity. Whether his project at Salyŏul village was a success is beside the point. What he managed to do was to portray the dreams of a native romantic living at that time. He possessed the insight to divine the course of the mainstream. We call upon you to write such a novel. What Hŏ Sung, the hero of *Earth*, would have done had he lived today, that is what we ask you to write about. It is because we judged you capable of writing such a book that we've invited you to join our circle. You still decline?"

Hahk had started drinking early and by now was growing more visibly intoxicated. Chun, who had been chewing cuttlefish tentacles, broke into applause at the close of the supplication.

"What do you think about going into literary criticism? And earn a testimonial from Lukacs."

"Lukacs?"

"Yes, he's a Hungarian, how shall I say, a sort of romantic Marxist. Ah, I'm getting loosened by these drinks. . . ."

"I'm not joking. Stop being difficult, why not save face for me?"

"For me to join your circle would save your face?"

"That's right. I've been charged with persuading you."

"What's the point of joining such a circle?"

"My god, how many times must I.... I've already explained, haven't I? The goal of our circle is...."

"No, it's not that I forgot what you said. What will be accomplished by participating? It's useless. Besides, I'd be joining total strangers and might not get along with them."

"They're all good guys."

"I'm sure they are. That's not what worries me. But the fact that somebody is good from one person's point of view doesn't necessarily mean others will agree. Besides, I don't believe in organizations at this point in time."

"That's where you are wrong. There may be differences of scale but in the end men can act only through organizations. Look here, one never can tell. For all we know, those in our group may someday be Cabinet members. Then the law would not prevent the post of Minister of Education from falling to you."

"Political science students are certainly different. Your methods of persuasion are realistic."

"So, after all, you are refusing?"

"Can't this be enough, just you and I drinking together like this? Instead, why don't you drop political science for literary criticism?"

"Ha, ha, ha. So it's my turn to be persuaded. Do you find anything worth listening to in my opinion?"

"There's an element of truth in it, certainly. The problem of Korean literature you raised is in my opinion embedded in Korean conditions in general. Korean literature lacks myth. In that respect, it's like politics in Korea. When a Western poet uses the word "Venus", the reader grasps not only the object signified but a rich meaning that is missing for us. There are countless examples where the radiant poetic diction of the West has degenerated into whorishly vulgar usages in our hands. For instance, 'The Bells of Nikolai', 'Sacred Mother Maria', 'Rose of Lamentation', 'Camels and Mirages', 'Arabia'. These are symbols with a strong suggestive power over there because history lies behind each one. When one says, 'The Bells of Nikolai', the orthodox churches of Byzantium, Greece and Russia and the rise and fall of the Eastern Roman Empire come to mind, no? As for 'Sacred Mother Maria', need I add anything more? Do not the Bible, the crusades of medieval Catholic knights, and hundreds of millions making the sign of the cross all underpin this single name? 'The Rose of Lamentation'? To discuss Western literature without mentioning roses is like discussing the masterful Chinese poet Yi T'ae-baek without speaking of the moon. Words like 'Desert', 'Camel', 'Arabia' are the same. Without the history of European adventures and mercantilism it is impossible to understand these images. A strange concoction of Arabian Nights and Lawrence of Arabia. Myth disembodied from its people and their environment is not myth but merely philosophy. Myth is a spiritual erogenous zone that emanates from humanity and environment, from time and space. It's a zone that when touched makes you cry, laugh, become aroused, bury your nails in skin. Without such erogenous zones, a caress is but an unnatural attempt at play, a discourtesy, a mere perversion, and readers can not awaken from the slothful slumber of frigidity. Modern Korean poetry and its readers resemble an awkward married couple. What's more, there is not even a tradition worth going back to. No, we do have one, but that tradition in nine out of ten cases turns out to be a trap from which there is no escape.

The aesthetics of our ancestors, who danced like pathetic birds to their mournful chants, was a flood of pitiable sorrow. For us, their enlightened descendants, that aesthetic might lead us to trade our short hair for top-knots, but it will cost us even what souls we've gained. For us, the West is like a prostitute, and our ancestors are like clutching ghosts of the drowned. Not all ghosts are bad. The progeny of the Sirens and of the witches of Walpurgis have shot themselves to the moon, but the children of Son Oh-gong (monkey wizard in *The Chronicle of the Western Voyage*, a Classical Chinese novel) have not succeeded so, is that not the difficulty? The flying carpet and the songs of the Sirens live on, but what became of the magic wand of Son Oh-gong? For them, the present is continuous with the past, but for us time is severed. For us the words 'progressive' and 'conservative' have a double meaning. In our minds progress has to be somehow Western, but in actuality it has two faces, the conservatism of the West contrasts to the conservatism of the East. They joust with windmills planted on solid brick foundations, but we fight against phantoms hanging upside down in the air. We cannot even be Don Quixote. They raze the old myths and poetize to erect new myths, but we have no myths to demolish. Western myth will be destroyed by Western poets, but Eastern myth cannot be destroyed for it is already in ruins. We are a defeated race. The circumstances are simple. We have been colonial denizens for centuries. The East has been pulled before the light of world history as the slave of the West, not as an equal competitor. This fact explains everything. Is this why what is inevitable for Picasso is not necessarily so for us? Think about it. Even if we try to Koreanize the word for airplane by calling it 'flying frame', what would this conceivably change? To appropriate an aircraft as ours, we would have to build them ourselves and our bodies would have to become familiar with the peculiar vibrations of airplanes. The problem lies not in the realm of words but in the space of history. Judged from the standpoint of language itself, we are not badly off at all. In times gone by, language was to us existence. Language itself was the purpose. For the Westerners, however, it was a code. Language provided indices for work and a record of gains. The form of art known as 'calligraphy' is good evidence of these differences. When language ceased to be a code and was promoted as being, we lost our being. Therefore, Chinese characters, the richest system of symbols, have become the language of the impoverished, while the simplest phonetic alphabets have been the vehicles of abundant history. The absence of myth in fact marked the absence of history. Language produces nothing, only history—action—is productive. Language merely records this. The nuances of the term 'Elizabethan Age' are never generated by the mechanical production of syllables, but by a quite concrete expression of cultural history. 'Elizabeth' is not essential, a bulldog would do. The image created would be identical whether the age is known as 'The Elizabethan Age' or 'The Age of the Bulldog'. Even if a daughter of a wealthy family happened to be named 'Thunder', we would gather that the name possesses both humor and paradox. If she were the daughter of Shim Pongsa (character in an old Korean story, who restored her father's sight by risking human sacrifice), being named 'Princess Sŏn-hwa' would have mattered not at all. It is precisely for this reason that it is pointless to frequent the fortune-tellers who claim to read the future from one's name. Speaking this way, I might be accused of neglecting the creative function of poetry as an oracle, but as long as creation or prophecy concern themselves with man, an intervention of destiny is inevitably implied and that in turn inevitably takes the form of a counterstroke of history. Our irrationality lay in having leapt straight to Paris or Sŏrabŏl, without letting them filter through the present. Both Paris and Sŏrabŏl, capitals of Western and ancient Korean culture, are alien to us. Up to now, we have misunderstood. How could such a phenomenon be unique to literature? Is it not a general predicament for Koreans? In other words, it would be too harsh to cast the responsibility on literature alone."

Hahk listened as he moved the glass away from his lips. Rainwater could be heard dripping off the eaves. The sound, like a dog's tongue lapping soup from a plate, bespoke the depth of the night. Hahk suddenly seemed to remember something and said,

"Mustn't we act, then?"

"That's why I shall not act."

"That's some logic, huh?"

"Aladdin's lamp is nowhere to be found. We can't expect a palace to appear before us."

"Then what?"

"Love and time."

"A cowardly escape, that."

"A brave defeat would be the same."

"People grow through being vanquished."

"Enough irresponsible talk. Not to mention the personal damage, how could you make up for the harm inflicted on others?"

"That's like saying sit quietly and starve yourself to death."

"Overextended similes readily lead to error. What I meant was that the Korean predicament leaves no possibility of revolution. Things are far more complicated than talk about absence or presence of personal courage supposes."

Once more the conversation paused. This time the silence was of longer duration. Hahk, his face buried in his hands, spoke slowly,

"That too is a lie. At no juncture in history was revolution possible. Therefore, revolutions occurred. This paradox of theory has been overcome only by human will. Hesitancy at setting such will in motion I can only call cowardice."

"Maybe so."

Chun replied in an angry tone.

Hahk looked at his friend for a long while, then pressed his palms to the floor and lifted himself to his feet. He swayed as he rose. Why, asked Chun with his eyes.

"I'm off."

"It's raining. Stay here tonight."

"No, I shouldn't, not today."

"Really?"

Chun no longer protested against his friend's exit and followed him out of the room. Outside, the rain was not as heavy as the pattering from the eaves had led them to expect. It was an autumn rain, a bit heavier than mist and very cold.

"Sure you want to go?"

Chun asked once more, opening his palm upward to feel the drizzle. But Hahk walked straight on to the gate. Before he went out, he said in a low voice,

"Perhaps what you said was right."

There was nothing abrupt about this remark, for Hahk seemed to have been meditating on it for some time. Still, it struck Chun's heart like a blow.

"Take care."

That was all Chun said.

Chun returned to his room and laid down flat on his back. Suddenly he felt lonely. A bottle of soju between the two had been a lot for Chun's constitution, but he felt not at all drunk. The same amount of alcohol may or may not make you drunk, it depends on the circumstances of drinking. That explained Chun's present state.

Chun wrapped the empty bottle and what was left of the cuttlefish in a newspaper and set it outside the door on the wooden floor, cleaned up the room a bit, and spread out his blanket to lie down. The patter of raindrops from the eaves grew louder.

Drip, drip, drip. Listening carefully, you could hear the water falling at regular intervals into the tin basins beneath the roof.

Drip, drip, drip, plop, drip, drip, drip, plop. The constant sound, endlessly recurring, slowly transported his mind to the distant field of memories.

The house in the North. A small village near the port city. In the area, the refinery smokestack visible from far off and down to the left the coastline of Y Bay where the land is gathered like pleats of lace. The family orchard stood by his old house. The white smokestack rose into the sky in a perfectly drafted line amidst the soft curves of the landscape. On summer days that pale white smokestack had been an astonishing mystery to a second-year middle school boy. On hot days it shot up into the towering cumulus clouds like a pillar of blinding light. It was less a smokestack than a huge idol of the road. Dark grey smoke incessantly belched forth from the very top. Chun thought of the smoke as the road idol's hair. On the way home from school he always used to climb an old apple tree at the edge of the orchard to gaze at the smokestack and sea, even though if caught at this pastime by his brother he would be sure to be scolded. Not wind alone, but colors and smells came from the sea. With that smell, apple flowers blossomed, and in those hues, Chun's boyhood ripened. His family situation was not very happy, in contrast to these romantic yearnings as a boy.

The orchard and rice fields were mostly lost to the family in the land reform. Left with but a tiny orchard and a couple of hectares of rice paddy, the six mouths in the house could barely feed themselves. His older brother was the householder, living with his wife and their two year old. His sister was a sort of widow. Mother and Chun. It was an odd family. They rarely spoke, even at the meal table. Mother and Sister were less like a mother and daughter than like two widows commiserating in their sorrows. A year after Liberation, which was also a year after the land reform, both their husbands fled south of the demilitarized zone. That Father went South was only natural. He had studied in Japan, thanks to his parents, and thereafter had run this orchard in the countryside. In the eyes of the Communists, then, he was a typical feudal landlord. Upon his return from school in Japan, Father sided with the peasants against Grandfather when a small rebellion broke out, but this episode was of no help to him. One day in late spring when the moon was ringed with a halo, Father disappeared from home. For several months Chun was told that Father had gone to visit relatives in W City. As time passed, Chun gradually realized that Father had gone somewhere he wasn't allowed to ask about. That was how Father had taken leave from the stage on which his boyhood was played out.

The case of his brother-in-law was a bit different. He didn't go South until six months after Father departed. He was one of those self-styled fellow-travelers so frequently found in the North right after Liberation. His identification was merely subjective because he saw himself as a fellow-traveler of the Communist regime, though the Reds would not accept him as a comrade. That he entertained such outrageous illusions was not totally irrational. He had gone to war as a student soldier but deserted the Japanese Army. That incident he considered as his struggle. The Communist comrades, however, would not treat that as any fight at all. To them, the mere fact that one was in a position permitting such a struggle itself was objectionable. The privileged status of student-soldier they saw as illicitly grounded in an unholy union between the Korean feudal stratum and Japanese imperialism. Brother-in-law floundered about. Only then, he realized.

In this way, the family got another widow of a sort. The truth is, Sister and Brother-in-law had never actually had a wedding ceremony. They had been high school steadies in W City. Before Liberation, when Chun was in third or fourth grade, he used to tag along on their outings. Come to think of it, they probably thought having him along was like walking a pointer, but the treatment he received wasn't bad, it was fun. Another thing was that, whenever the three of them went out, his sister was unusually attentive to Chun. Not that she normally mistreated him, but before the man came along, she had been more preoccupied with Chun. I wonder, does even the mind of a woman grow tenderer in the presence of her beloved?

Anyway, Sister had become a different person with the departure of Brother-in-law. Haggard and silent, she uncomplainingly labored in the orchard or the fields all day long, dressed in the baggy pants most women wore during the Japanese occupation.

As for Brother, although he had been a fellow student with Brother-in-law, he was dull and his thoughts inaccessible, very different from his handsome and talented alumnus. Sister-in-law was a country maiden, graduate of a nearby grammar school.

In a way, these circumstances were not all that bad. In a family in which everyone had their own burdens to bear, rarely did anyone interfere with Chun's conduct. When Father was around, there were occasionally scoldings and at the end of each semester he had to account for his school record, but now nobody was around to do the scolding.

When nights were deep, a ritual known by not a soul used to unfold in this house. It is fair to call it a "ritual". In the backmost room of the house was a radio. It was of Japanese make, with five little lights, and the brand emblem was a dog sitting before a microphone. It was, so to speak, a shaman delivering oracles. They listened to broadcasts originating from the South that were aired in the deep of the night. Under their breath. . . . With pounding hearts. . . . Deeply moved by compassion. . . . A night ritual, hearkening to the beautiful voice of a woman carried through the air electromagnetically. . . . The woman's voice, beginning "Dear Countrymen in the North", was among the most beautiful poetries embroidering Tokko Chun's boyhood. The melody of the national anthem that always accompanied that voice used to fill his heart with an indescribable feeling between joy and sorrow. His house, standing off by itself where a hill rose from a corner of the field, was almost perfectly safe. Nevertheless, they needed extra assurance to reduce the anxiety of being insecure. The post of lookout was usually taken by Mother or Sister-in-law. On the wooden floor of the hall leading to the radio room, they usually had ironing or some other work laid out to block their way. The woman's imploring voice brought amazing news across the airwaves every night. The propaganda of leaders in the North is all lies. . . the North is a prison. . . it's a horrible prison where freedom and happiness have been taken away and the people all enslaved. . . the people in the North are prisoners locked in that prison. . . the South is counting the days until salvation of the Northern people will be undertaken. Democracy. Freedom. Blossoming culture. Life open to the world. A happy nation of free men. Three thousand *ri* embroidered in gold between mountains and seashores. Dr. Syngman Rhee. Mr. Kim Ku. Democracy. Freedom. The oppressors will meet ruin. They extract from us our national soul and in its place impose the spirit of Red Imperialists. They confiscated the property of good men under the name of 'land reform' and created a land of tenant farmers with the Communist party as lords. With tanks and weapons supplied by the Soviets, they mercilessly cut down our young at Shinuiju and Hamhŭng. Everyone! Don't lose hope! Your motherland will not abandon you. Your parents, your brothers and sisters, await the day when you will cross over the devil's 38th parallel and receive our embrace. A free nation. A democratic state. Utopia. . . . That was Father's voice, the voice of one's beloved. Not a single member of the family could doubt the messages delivered by that voice. To Chun, it was something beyond truth. It was a beautiful fairy tale to him. They were whispers of warm dreams emanating from the Southern realms where flowers bloom and beautiful birds sing beneath a rainbow vaulted sky.

Though Chun was unaware of it at the time, in those days the same nightly ritual was performed by multitudes throughout the North. Rumors spawn rumors, and in the pure hearts of those people South Korea was a paradise of unattainable prosperity. For someone who never shared the experience, it is nearly impossible to comprehend how such an illusion arose not in individual minds but in the collective mind of a whole generation. Since coming to the South, Chun often thought over the problem of expressing this state of things, and at last an idea occurred to him. The only method was analogy.

The outrageous zeal, almost lust, with which modern European intellectuals were drawn to Italy. He discovered an identical counterpart in that nostalgic struggle evocative of the immortal "Song of Mignon". The power of this fantastic longing for Italy in the hearts of the elite of the time—Byron, Goethe, Hölderlin and Nietzsche. Anyone with the chance to read their biographies will soon see that their spiritual residences were in Italy. After Liberation and before the Korean War, this resembled the image of the South in Northern minds. A little boy living in a society in which such beliefs were dominant naturally was profoundly influenced by them. And the impact was still deeper when the desperate situation of the family strengthened the will to believe. This ambience clung to Tokko Chun as time went by. And indeed what is the ambience of an age if not a complex verity like a woman's erogenous zones. It is something that for contemporaries has a real, immediate existence. But to capture it expressively one can do no more than plod about it with words. Thus, the voice issuing from where Father lived made us a family of spiritual exiles. At an early age, therefore, Tokko Chun tasted the melancholic ennui, the angst of an exile.

Though only a boy, Chun had more than his share of ordeals and persecution. At school, whenever the Boys Corps met, he was assigned the role of a heretic sent before the Inquisition. Petty transgressions in his daily routine, such as being tardy, falling asleep in class, negligence in cleaning after class, were invariably attributed to his reactionary family background and severe self-criticism was demanded of him.

One teacher had the job of monitoring the school for the Communist Party. In his role as guide of the Boys Corps, he directed the key students, his little heroes, the eggs of the future Communist vanguard, to attack Chun as the meetings proceeded. It was like a hunter unleashing a pack of hounds to harry an innocent creature.

It was during history class one day. A new history teacher had arrived, and the student felt tense during the first class. The young teacher, just graduated that spring from Teachers College and still wearing his student uniform, called the roll, looked over the class, and then said,

"What is history? Can anybody tell me?"

The students were taken aback. They rolled their eyes. No response was immediately forthcoming.

"You may freely say what you have in mind."

Students evidently were encouraged by this and hands went up here and there.

"Sir, history is what happened long, long ago."

"History is a class where we learn about things past."

"History is a science with which we look back into the past and use it as a guide for the future."

That was Chun's answer. The teacher was smiling and shaking his head at every answer. When everybody felt quite exhausted, he finally opened his mouth.

"Comrades, all of you are very cute bourgeois historians."

The students were utterly disheartened at this ominous term "bourgeois".

"History is not what happened in the old days, nor is it a case of looking back to predict the future. These are all lies concocted by bourgeois historians to trick the people. History is a process of class struggle. The bloodshed between the ruling and ruled classes, and the process of this war, this is history. History is the science that studies the forms of exploitation under various rulers in different ages, the means employed in class war, and the modes of culture imported to conceal exploitation from the people's eyes. This is the methodological approach to history long ago established by Marx and Engels. Namely, this is historical materialism. This alone is the true method of understanding history. From this class on, you will study the history of people's rebellions against their oppressors."

Considering that the students were only in the first year of middle school, this was a bit too much. In fact, in those days, only one kind of truth was acknowledged in the land of the North. No allowances were made in quantity of truth—children, adults, the educated, the uneducated, people with great responsibility, people with little responsibility, everyone alike was measured by the same compulsory truths. But things were taken too far at the Boys Corps meeting that afternoon. Out of the blue, the classroom section leader of the Corps denounced Chun.

"Comrade Tokko Chun, you have demonstrated insufficient enthusiasm in your work and today in history class your bourgeois remark revealed an erroneous comprehension of the true nature of history. We demand self-criticism from you."

The boy was reading off from a sheet of paper. It obviously had been written by the teacher in charge of the Boys Corps.

That day Chun was under torture for more than an hour. From then on, similar episodes occurred quite frequently. He became more and more of an exile.

Before the apple trees blossomed, in the rainy season when the cherry trees bloomed, he used to stay up late reading in the main bedroom. The room was full of books that Father, Brother and Sister used to read. Now they all belonged to Chun. Most of Father's volumes were old Japanese law books, long since superseded. To Chun, they were worthless wastepaper. Brother's and Sister's books were mostly novels. Those he voraciously consumed. As Sister exiled herself into work in the fields, so Chun exiled himself into these books. His favorite, which he read over and over, was *A Dog of Flanders.* A beautiful love, friendship and trust between man and dog, the worthless ostentation of grown-ups, and a boy's ambition. A tragedy founded on coincidence. He was touched by the tale of a kind and handsome boy, living righteously and courageously, but confronted with ruination. Another book that pleased him was *Sans Famille.* Unlike *A Dog of Flanders,* it was a story of a man whose courage and righteousness led in the end to victory. Together with the boy Remy, he traveled to all corners of France. When the monkey caught pneumonia Chun was awfully sad. He sympathized and shed tears at the part where Remy misses his foster mother. Stories of adventure and battle caused his young heart to soar with joy. But his reading was not limited to such simple fare. He also secretly read the bulky *Nana.* How could such a story of a lazy and debauched woman have been so interesting? His heart pounded violently as he read how Nana warmed her naked body before the fireplace.

There was yet another world apart from that of *A Dog of Flanders* or *Sans Famille.* It was a more dazzling and pungent world. *Nana* he read in secret. Somehow he felt embarrassed to read it within view of others. In Mother's presence, however, he boldly opened it and read. For Mother knew only scraps of Korean and Chinese, she never learned to read books. Whatever book Chun held in his hands, Mother always assumed he was studying and she would warn him not to ruin his health. At such times he felt he was a cheat. Perhaps it was his first clear encounter with guilt.

Though it was a guilty pleasure, the world of stories retained its charm for him. In a way, it was a world turned upside down, a land inverted in one's soul. It had an order that made the stories seem real and the real world seem fictional. In time he had to pay for these guilty pleasures. On rainy days, the sound of drip, drip, drip, plop, plop, filled his ears. For a long while he would pause to listen to the sound before turning to the next page. While reading, the sound would disappear, but it would sneak back as soon as his attention wandered.

At the sound of somebody walking in, Chun looked up. Sister stood at the threshold. She wore a new dress and had prettied herself, for her something unusual. As she came over and sat next to him, Chun noticed a faint scent of powder. There was something out of the ordinary in her expression. Chun gazed at her without uttering a word.

Sister glanced over at the book Chun was reading and said,

"Chun, would you like to have a little talk with me?"

Chun answered with his eyes and sat up straight.

"Chun, do you remember your brother-in-law's face?"

He nodded. Sister held out her right hand. On her palm lay a photo. Chun looked at it. It was a picture of Sister and Brother-in-law sitting side by side. Both wore student uniforms. Their two faces were smiling broadly. Sister looked twice as young and fresh as now.

"Remember the time the three of us went swimming?"

Sister asked as if talking to herself, her eyes glued to the picture.

"Yes."

Chun found it strange that she was suddenly asking such things about Brother-in-law. Feeling disinterested, he was about to return to the book he'd been reading when he abruptly froze. Sister had flopped onto the floor and began quietly sobbing. For a long time Chun just peered at her.

When he scraped together some courage, he cautiously laid his hand on Sister's shoulder.

"What's wrong, Sister, what is it?"

Seemingly oblivious to her brother's presence, she was now weeping violently, but still stifling the sound. Chun felt a pang in the bridge of his nose as sorrow swelled in his heart. Sister's sorrow had moved over into his own heart and forced him to feel for her.

They could hear someone outside the room but the door didn't open. In that position the two of them cried for the longest time, one with reason and the other out of compassion for the suffering of his flesh and blood. Finally, Sister ceased crying, wiped off Chun's face and hugged him tightly before releasing him. Expending a great effort, she smiled.

"Your sister is a fool, isn't she? I just felt like crying so I came to your room."

Chun felt much relieved, but he still said with feigned displeasure,

"What's all this? You are a grown-up, now don't you cry anymore."

"But grown-ups also have cause to cry, my dear."

She went through the motion of raking her knuckles over his head.

"Grown-ups sometimes feel like crying for no reason?"

"Certainly. When you're grown you'll understand all about it. When you're big, you should never make a weak woman like your sister cry."

"Why make women cry?"

"Well, that, too, you'll learn later."

Once more she seemed depressed. That night, though she cried, she looked like her old self for the first time in a long while. Watching her lively and boisterous old self, Chun's heart was warmed. He murmured to himself, "I like my sister."

She hung her head and was lost in thought about something.

After Sister left the room, Chun picked up the book once more but no longer felt like reading. Her blank stare hovered before his eyes, fixed motionless in one place. He tossed the book away and vacantly stared into space just as his sister had. He let his mind drift.

Drip, drip, drip, plop. Drip, drip, drip, plop. Outside the rain still was falling.

Soon after the rains end the apple trees will begin to bloom.

II

Gone is my love, vanished through the exploding autumn colors of the black forest.

Suddenly Tokko Chun awoke.

He had been dreaming, but the instant he awoke it was lost to memory. Just forgotten. To say "just forgotten" is strange. When awake, you may not recall the contents of a dream but you somehow know you were dreaming. It was certainly not a pleasant dream. In his head all the concrete specifics had eroded, all that remained were the echoes colored by the dream. These echoes were inadequate yet tantalizing. Though these feelings of incompleteness and fascination are in conflict, they coexisted in Chun's mind at that moment.

His room was ordinarily well illumined. Although windows opened to the south and east, it was not as bright as usual. It had rained the whole night through and on into the morning. His drinking bout with Kim Hahk seemed but a short while before. As always, Chun laid on his back and stared up at the ceiling. The pattern of the wallpaper overhead looked at once like leaves and also like a swarm of grasshoppers. That wasn't all. Upon looking up after closing your eyes for a spell, a multitude of spiders appeared to be creeping about. With pinkish backs and bright blue legs they were crawling everywhere. Chun scrunched the big toe of his left foot. He rubbed it with his other big toe. With his toenail he dug sharply into the wart, but it hurt not at all. As he diverted himself this way, he continued to ruminate and to project figures onto the ceiling. He remained captive to the dream. What sort of dream had it been? He was not even certain whether he had actually dreamt at all. No, there had been a dream. That is for sure. This certainty notwithstanding, the subject still evaded him. No matter how hard he struggled, he knew he wouldn't recall. It was a frequent feeling, but not even once had he managed to remember. That he remembered dreaming but not what he had dreamed, this arrested him in a troubling way. It irritated him, somehow. He felt like an innocent suspect unable to produce an alibi. Shall I rise? No, what is the point of getting up this early? Only then did he feel a bit relaxed. It was Sunday. Of all the days, Chun thought it the best. Because on Sunday morning you can sleep late. Not that one can't sleep in on other days, but that would not be sleeping late because it was Sunday. I. Tokko Chun. He thought: Aren't you a Sunday man? Content is the man who gets up late on Sundays, has a simple breakfast and then goes off to the local church, a bible tucked under his arm. Such a Sunday man would also be content to hurry his family to change clothes and put together a picnic lunch so as to hasten off to some old palace or resort. Or a Sunday man who meets a woman in some tearoom or at a park and indulges in lunch, in some harmless chatter and joking, and possibly takes the woman to a movie so they can feast their eyes on Western affluence. But none of these was Chun. For him, Sunday was a day to sleep in. A day with absolutely nothing to do. The sort of day on which the mere fact of having nothing to do made one glad. For a long while Chun had felt a plant covertly growing somewhere inside his body. Its shape was hidden to his eyes. Neither had he touched it. But as a man sooner or later becomes aware of a cancer multiplying in his body, so he in time noticed this growth inside him. Occasionally he entertained serious doubts about it. Was he at an advanced stage of psychosis? But unlike in the case of a physical malady, doesn't my ability to diagnose myself as possibly subject to a mental illness mean I've not yet reached total ruin? But ruin is not what I desire. Indeed, I desire to be happy. Except I have no idea what happiness would be like. Happiness. Does such a thing actually exist? If so, must a man be happy? Having a room of my own, like this, three meals a day, attending a university, having some pocket money, is this not a relatively high class life in this present society? Fragments, parts, knowledge of this and that, all lumped in my brain. Nonetheless remote from peace of mind or worldly success. But they say that in this age all classical paths to enlightenment are blocked. Earn money, spend it, enjoy sex, strive to age as slowly as possible, when old age inexorably arrives, inject artificial energy into the exhausted endocrine glands to prolong youth. . . . So what's the point? No, the very mentality of striving shows itself not to be the thinking of a corpse. That's all there is. And in the end, they die. To get excited is tiresome. This is democracy. The Anglo-saxon race has nerves as thick as rawhide. They chew time as if chewing the ligaments of cows. They do not run. Their life is a series of hurdles they repeat without irritation. A race like the Germans never dares to compete. A predisposition to neurasthenia, to entrancement, is a long way from realism. The fanatical faith of the Russians. Bone-marrow superstitions. Those are fools who always choose a flower in heaven over meat on the table, so teaches Western history. We. What on earth are we, after all? Living on grass, shitting thin coils, treated like dirt by sly neighbor children, receiving a windfall of freedom, grown into idiots. Without direction, the recurrence of aimless days. From one to ten, all we see and hear are symbols created, spent and distributed by Westerners. . . . Try as we might to stand up on our own, we lack the talent for it. That tough business skill ceaselessly to mass produce the new devices they have patented, and the capacity to revive over and over stories already exhausted to their cores. Western children are brilliant. What potent and amazing seeds they are. A race for which it is right to seek one's own benefit, at all costs to live well. The merciless greed to satiate oneself with happiness.

Knowing their state of things more fully, it's already too late to slip the yoke of history, struggle as you might. Neither you nor I are evil, consequently this is an age in which everyone is evil. Amidst all this, a man cannot enjoy glory, moreover, what would be the point? He remembered the parting words of Kim Hahk as he left the previous night with a serious look on his face, "perhaps what you said was right". No, what I said was not necessarily right. In revolution the power of will is supposed to puncture the antinomies of logic. I don't doubt it. But what if that will, like a rusted spring, fails to spring forth? Then what comes next? Revolution. Indeed. Revolution is the ultimate form of art, not in our age alone but always. But has not experiment already proven the barrenness of this art? The obsession to found a thousand year empire on this earth is certainly a Western notion. For us no such tradition existed, that is certain. An ego deeply buried in the species. They have been living for millennia lazy, squirming, helplessly dying only to return to the earth. Who could alter overnight this rhythm that connects even with the vegetation? Was Hahk suggesting a revolution? At the mere thought, Chun nearly laughed. Love and revolution would surely be worthy projects for the young. Revolution. Who is doing it for whom matters not at all. How fortunate the men must have been who lived in ages of faith, when hearts burned and eyes flashed with fire. The guy praised Yi Kwang-su. A likely sentiment for a layman. At any rate, Yi Kwang-su had something to adore. As the monk Yong-un put it: Is a lover the only love? The lover of Yi Kwang-su was the Korean race. But at present one hesitates openly to speak of "the race", for to do so is to invite criticism for being out of date. This society is bounded by cliffs on all sides, regardless of one's goals. And it is an age in which the strength of a few individuals counts for naught. No. I'm unconcerned about the age. In fact, I care nothing about the age. Nor do I care about the race. It's only that, living within it, I exploit it. It's not that I could not live without Korea. I'm not sure about the West, but I think I could live without much distress in such places as China, Japan, Vietnam or Mongolia. I would be able to love people there as much as I love my Korean neighbors, and I would hate people there no more than I hate my Korean neighbors. Unquestionably, we are residing in an inferior region in a filthy epoch. If only we could travel freely throughout Asia, how much richer our lives would be. What a stimulant for a modern poet, with an impoverished mind, to observe the descendants of Genghis Khan, of the mounted hordes that once menaced Europe. His poetry will be nourished, images revived, symbols brought down from the air to plant roots in *terra firma*. Going to the West has little attraction for me. In the first place, I lack confidence about the language. And the role of country bumpkin would inevitably fall to me. No need to go off and spend money just to play the fool. That's why I lack empathy for friends who are wildly ambitious to study in foreign lands. In three or four years, what could one hope to learn? At best, one would practice language skills at a high school level. The most that could be gained would be to grow familiar with their peculiar white-collared system, then return as a false prophet to the puzzled people at home. Oh well, it would be worth going if there were money. That's all. So? There is no "So?". At one time Tokko Chun had been enwrapped in a passionate obsession. In the period from high school to the freshman year of college he awakened to ego. Amidst the crowds he had discovered an especially charming self. At coming upon this self, prior to membership in the race, the nation or the family, he trembled with emotion. He was enraptured by the need to cultivate this ego, to polish it to a unique finish that would stand out from all others. For hours on end he would stand before the mirror, scrutinizing his own expressions. These hours were not unlike those spent by girls before their vanity mirrors. Perhaps he told himself he was not applying chemical make-up, but rather acquiring the skills of psychological make-up. But there was no difference. He read whatever came to hand. Books were to him what lipsticks and lotions were to girls. He undertook the work of adorning his inner visage under the plausible pretext of fooling himself. History, philosophy or what have you, he blended them all to embellish his inner face. Why did he read so frenetically? Perhaps it was due to loneliness. Loneliness? Perhaps.

That summer. As usual the apple blossoms appeared in the middle of May. In the orchard it was the busiest season. Chun helped break chicken manure out of sacks and load it into wheelbarrows for transportation from the barn to the orchard. Then the war broke out. It began quite undramatically. Initially, it arrived as a rumor. A month later, the war abruptly appeared right before all our eyes. From beyond the horizon, birds of black metal shrouded the sky over the harbor, assaulting the people and houses along the coast. Anti-aircraft guns screamed their replies, but no word came of planes being downed. From that day on a new and terrifying summer began, both for the city-dwellers and for Tokko Chun. In the wake of the black birds, sleeker silver bombers and fighters soon appeared daily in the city skies. It was a trauma without precedent since the founding of the city. The utterly malicious silver machines laid waste to the city from high overhead. At first their fire was targeted at a shipyard and kerosene factory alongside the harbor. Wood and metal debris were scattered about, burning, and a huge oil tank exploded, belching black smoke. Some said that the whole city would be engulfed in fire if all the oil tanks were bombed, but it never came to pass. Instead, an order of evacuation came. The mass evacuation was soon completed. But the city was not entirely dead thereafter, it still moved with life. People still trudged out in the morning, into a city that was crumbling more each day. For some reason, perhaps in part because they couldn't remove everything at once, the major government offices had not yet been evacuated. Though there were air raid sirens, the sound always came after planes were already overhead, a foolish, meek alarm. People acquired the habit of just ignoring the sirens, and retreated to underground shelters only upon hearing the first explosion. It was a sort of civil disobedience, evidencing popular distrust of the responsible authorities, but by then nobody could enforce the rules. The situation had come to that. Everyday war news was posted on the street. If these dispatches had been true, Korea would have been 9000 *ri* instead of 3000 *ri* in length, and the army of the American imperialists, having been decimated daily, would have had hardly any reserves left back home. Rumors of unknown origin were constantly circulated. For instance, American bombers never attack churches. Special devices in the airplanes were supposed to enable the crew to hear every word of conversations far below on the ground. The pilots had an uncanny knack of discriminating soldiers and civilians on the ground, and they only aimed at soldiers. These rumors jumping from mouth to mouth were without exception defeatist. Some of them were not entirely implausible. The Catholic church up on the hill was still intact. Its colorful stained glass shone more proudly than ever against the summer sky. The Christian faithful were vaguely anticipating imminent glory and in their clandestine prayers compared the city to Sodom and Gomorrah. Refugees from the city spent the summer orbiting in the outskirts of their decaying nucleus. They were like an army of ants climbing up and down as they devour a crab apple rotten at the core. Countless people died in a blink of time. There was no remedy. The food shortages were horrible. Nutrition was terrible. The silver sky machines that began by targeting only military facilities gradually moved on to indiscriminate attacks. Waves of bombers with shining silver wings rolled in through the bright July sky, destroying the cages where people lived in poverty. Then they vanished back to the South or else out to sea. People had by now resigned themselves to these raids as part of everyday existence. Astonishingly significant was the people's reaction to the daily migrations of these birds, which daily graced the skies delivering death and destruction as if by routine. The bombers they called "four engined machine" and the jet fighters "the shishshish". The former came literally from the number of engines and the latter from the sound of a jet streaking by, but in neither name is any nuance of hatred for the enemy aircraft detectable. Throughout the world, common people tend to deal with the direst tragedy with a naively resilient wit, but even if this is such a case, these reactions nonetheless reveal something important. In the coining of "shishshish" was embodied the sort of attitude a parent would feel toward a child sent home for bullying another child to tears. Nothing but trouble, you. . . . That kind of feeling, I mean. But in this case the troublesomeness was nothing less than one's house crumbling down, limbs blown off, workplace in conflagration. W City that summer was under sway of devils of despair and futility who quietly snickered at life as they stalked the streets. From the outset those in power avoided any human contact with the populace. Like in ancient times, when the tribal chiefs distributed used women to their subordinates, the government authorities acted from on high. Unsurprisingly, the people were untroubled at witnessing the state apparatus disintegrate before their eyes. Watching their own households and lives being annihilated, at the same time they saw ruin fall upon the comrades they hated. It was perhaps like the feeling people had under Japanese imperialism at the close of the Second World War, when they heard air raid sirens heralding an "attack of enemy planes". Such a bittersweet state was almost habitual for a people who lived their lives outside of politics.

Not all of these things had personally impacted Tokko Chun. One afternoon, toward the end of the usual twenty minute air raid, a bomb blast toppled the huge smokestack of the refinery, the road idol of Chun's imagination. After the bombing subsided, he felt an indescribable sorrow as he stared at the remnants of the smokestack base. It had been something precious to him. Since first becoming aware of the world, that tall white cement stack towering into the sky had to him been a friend with whom secrets could be shared. Chun sat in a chestnut tree on the edge of the orchard and watched the city smoke and smolder. The destruction to the city was so severe it was discernible from afar. The orderly lines of human construction were in disarray. If things went on like this, he didn't know what would happen with school, which normally ended in mid-July and recommenced in September. Secretly, he feared an emergency summons from school. Not that he was afraid to travel on the streets where bombs were falling, but he did dread more incomprehensible persecutions at the hands of his little comrades and the supervisor of the Boys Corps. In times like these, it was a blessing that Tokko Chun's family lived in a village on the outer fringes of the city. The "American Imperialists" seemed not at all interested in apples or chestnuts. Tokko Chun could spend his days observing the bleeding and destruction of the city from afar, as one might watch an epidemic peak from outside the walls of a fortress.

One day a representative from the People's Council of the village came and had a long talk with Brother. After he left, Brother and Mother talked into the night in the room where the radio was hidden. As he passed the door, Chun heard his mother say,

". . . nothing more to think about, safety comes first. . . ."

Chun wished the war would last for a long time. A permanent vacation would be delightful, he hoped he never would have to return to school at all. If that were possible, he felt he could even endure the grief of witnessing the destruction of the white smokestack. Stranded in this darkness, amidst the relentless rhythm of daily destruction reaching from the city to the village and into his own family, Chun felt the pleasure of escape from school but he also endured a boyish anguish at the suffering. To him this summer of unexpected changes was overwhelmingly full, more intense than any other summer of his life. After breakfast, he used to load his pockets with green apples from the orchard and head off to the chestnut trees with books tucked under his arm. At the time he was reading *How the Steel Was Tempered.* This famous Soviet novel was a kind of bildungsroman which follows a boy from the demise of Tsarist

Russia through the Revolution and the Civil War period, telling how through courage and resolution he was forged into a heroic party member. But the cruelty of the Tsarist regime and the fact he was a Communist party member were to Chun of no concern. The kind and good-humored nature of the boy protagonist that captivated the reader from the beginning, the vivid depiction of farm villages and cities on the path to ruin, and the foolish yet pure love of the hero were what fascinated him. It was nothing less than the Soviet version of *Sans Famille*. A story of a good and brave boy who conquered the world, becoming a courageous young man and winning a clever and beautiful bride. He read this same novel over and over again. This time, too, the result was the same. In this way he made everything his own—houses and forest, river and city, red brick mansions and school, clouds and sunlight, Cossacks of the Tsar and cellars of the workers, Greek Orthodox monks and convent schools—all the characters inhabiting the story. Reading line by line, over and over, all these were etched indelibly into his mind and his right to appropriate them was solidified. In this respect he was not without wealth. All the treasures and characters, rivers and mountains, he had accumulated inside his head made him indifferent to things in the outer world. Except for the radiant white smokestack. Such incidents as the annihilation of the Provincial People's Council building were of no importance. What the grown-ups felt at seeing their city reduced to rubble, an almost masochistic sense of inverted pleasure, was no more rational than how Tokko Chun felt. For the adults, too, shut their eyes to the destruction around them out of longing for that fairy tale to be true, that unverifiable tale about Korean flags flying in the Southern land of Dr. Syngman Rhee. The difference between the two attitudes is no more than that between *Sans Famille* and *How the Steel Was Tempered*. Through his reading, Tokko Chun discovered the primordial rhythm of life that vibrates beneath the phenomena. Both stories were the same. They differed only in that Remy wore the clothes of a

French farm boy while the hero of *How the Steel Was Tempered* wore the dress of a Russian peasant. Lying under the chestnut trees, he read. The Tsarist cavalry was galloping. Explosions could be heard. Looking up, flames and dark smoke could be seen rising over the distant city. The bombers were on schedule. He turned his face back to the book. The boy was walking up hill toward the villa of the Inspector of State Forests. In the sky over the city, B-29s were twisting their fat sleek limbs, dropping black metal catalysts of death. Below on the ground countless bones were crushed, and the city, creaven as any slave, bled from its wounds. Such things were of no account, in any event. The boy was walking up the path to the villa on that hot summer day. He was beautiful. But he was poor and the child of peasants. He is a strange youth who wonders whether God is not a liar. The B-29s were circling back for another bombing run. Like a pack of hounds attacking a wounded beast.

Fallen apples and green fruit thinned from over-burdened branches were collected to make hard cider. It could be sold at State-run restaurants or else paid as tax in kind. The baby green apples in Chun's pocket were surreptitiously lifted from a big earthen jar. That day also Chun was lying in the chestnut grove, chewing apples that already smelled of alcohol. The hero filled his book bag with ammunition to transport under cover. Not even the Tsarist police could imagine a boy's book bag containing such a cache. He carried cartridges to the revolutionary army. Little hero. A boy handling not books and flowers but bullets and mines as he grows up. It was an adventure of a certain boy in a remote land. Like all great literature, this novel had the power to outlive the age that produced it. What made this possible was precisely the accuracy with which the age was portrayed—although the subject was a child it was actually a narrative for adults. The time came for the bombers to appear, but none showed up on this day. Instead, from the direction of his house he heard Mother calling him. Chun looked that way. Mother stood in the front yard, waving to him. Beside her stood a man with a Lenin cap. He felt his heart sink. The image of the supervisor of the Boys Corps floated into his mind. He squinted, struggling to make out who the man was. No. This man was too short, a stranger. He was a Komsomol cadre from W City.

"Comrade student, come to school tomorrow. The streets are destroyed by the bastards' bombing and the casualties have increased. Komsomol and the Boys Corps will be mobilized, assigned to reconstruction and medical duties. You, comrade, must contact as many students as possible in this area and bring them with you to school. Understand?"

"We're to report directly to school, then?" Chun asked.

"That's right. Tomorrow morning at ten there will be a joint rally of Komsomol and the Boys Corps at the school. You must not miss the opportunity to contribute to our great national war."

The Komsomol man spoke in the tone of an orator, his eyes shining as if to persuade himself. His face was flushed quite red and his shoes caked with dust after the long walk from W City. Mother invited him in to the house and offered him some cider and potato cakes. After downing five fist-sized cakes, he reassured Mother that the casualties were not too numerous, and then he left. When he had gone, Mother spoke.

"Won't there be problems if you don't go?"

And so she talked over the matter with the little boy.

"Why?"

"Listen to you, what do they mean by calling out the children while it still goes on like that each day. . . ? The things they do. . . ."

Mother peered at W City off in the distance. What had happened today? Still no sign of the bombers. People could be seen moving in the streets alongside the harbor. The blinding white wall of the Fisherman's Cooperative stood out of the scene. That building was still standing. At such times, the city seemed still uncowed. Were the rubble cleared away, one might simply notice the open layout of the streets.

"A lot of houses are still there, I suppose."

Chun turned to Mother as he spoke.

"What?"

She was distracted by other cares, and looked at Chun in puzzlement. Without replying, Chun entertained the thought that Mother and Sister looked very much alike, especially the shapes of their mouths. He stepped down from the wooden floor and set off for the fields. Sister was out in the corn patch.

"I'm going to school tomorrow."

She straightened her waist and stood erect. After pushing the hair back off her forehead and tucking it under her kerchief, she asked,

"School?"

"Yeh, somebody came to tell us."

Chun told her about the Komsomol man. And he added the part about how he had eaten five potato cakes. It was his habit whenever he spoke to Sister to put things as humorously as he could. Mother seldom caught his wit and usually responded uncomprehendingly, so he no longer wasted it on her. Sister looked worried, however, and then said,

"Listen, don't you go."

"I shouldn't?"

"How do you intend to get there?"

"They said it was all right."

"Who said?"

"That guy. . . ."

"Oh, you. . . ."

Sister undid the kerchief from her head and shook it out. Then she walked back toward the house. It looked as though she was going to see Mother. Chun gazed at the city. His school was out of sight over the hill. He felt no fear. Besides he couldn't be the only one to stay away when everyone else reported to school. When the new term began there would certainly be a Boys Corps meeting to review activities over the summer break, and it would be unbearable to endure another session of self-criticism. The sharp looks of the Boys Corps supervisor were to Chun more terrifying than the airplanes of the American Imperialists. In a dark classroom lit only by candles, he'd been interrogated about why Father had gone to the South, where his brother-in-law had gone, what had they said to Chun before they left, and what had Chun thought about that? Didn't Chun think his own conduct had been influenced by bad petit bourgeois attitudes, etc., etc.—Chun winced at the mere thought of such interminable interrogations. There were only two students in the village that Chun needed to notify. Only two are my responsibility. If I contact them and bring them to school, the supervisor of the Boys Corps will be pleased. He pictured the tight-mouthed supervisor with his Lenin cap pulled slightly back on his head. Every time Chun encountered the Boys Corps supervisor he had a peculiar feeling. When that teacher first came to his school, Chun had liked him very much. He was in charge of Korean language, a handsome man with a gentle voice. One day he gave the students homework. The topic was "Spring". A few days later, Chun was summoned to the teachers' office. He took out Chun's composition and asked him a number of questions about it. To Chun his attitude seemed less like that of a Korean language teacher than like that of an Internal Security operative. As he answered he found his tongue stumbling. In the end, despite himself he disclosed everything the supervisor wanted to know. When the talk was over, the teacher's expression was icy. Suddenly, Chun was in a panic of terror. His composition was about spring rain, about soaked fruit trees, the white smokestack of the refinery and the sea shining in the distance. How could it possibly displease the teacher? It was naturally beyond Chun's power to understand how the young "comrade" was able to decode symptoms of a reactionary bourgeois family from a boyish composition. From then on Chun avoided the Boys Corps supervisor. Even though Korean language was his favorite subject, he restrained himself from raising his hand in class. When he knew the answers perfectly well he nonetheless learned to wear a dull, unknowing look on his face. The answers of other students Chun silently corrected to himself. He felt vexed whenever he recalled his good first impression of the teacher. In time the teacher became an enemy. He was the terrifying authority who ordered the Boys Corps members to put Chun on the platform of self-criticism.

After telling Mother, Chun set off for the house of a classmate who lived nearby. His friend wasn't home, but his mother came to the door. When Chun told her about the man's summons to school, his friend's mother seemed very surprised.

"Oh dear, what am I to do? He's been sick lately, running a high fever at night. He's been in bed unable to move these past few days. . . . Looks like malaria."

It sounded strange to Chun for someone with malaria to be having a fever.

"Still, he must go."

"How can he when he's sick? All right, you've done your part by giving us notice."

Chun was about to say something more but the woman had gone back inside the house. Uncertain what to do, he peered at the yellow face of a sunflower that stood in the corner of the front yard. He paused there for a while, hoping his friend might return, but he never appeared. Besides him, there were no other classmates in the vicinity. There was nothing left for him to do but to return home. When everybody was collected around the dinner table, Brother said,

"Chun, don't you go to school tomorrow."

". . . ."

"Do you hear?"

"But, how can I. . .?"

"What do you mean, how can you. . . . Do as I say. Understand?"

". . . ."

He looked at Mother and Sister.

"Do as your brother tells you. . . . My goodness, they must be out of their minds. . . ."

"Chun, do as your brother says."

Nobody could understand how Chun felt. Lately, Brother and Sister stayed in the room with the radio every night for hours. The two occasionally would look up, exchange glances and nod to one another. For Chun, that "Voice of the South" was no longer as great as it used to be. He used to like it because of the beautiful music and interesting stories but since the outbreak of the war the broadcasts had somehow come to resemble the messages from Pyongyang. By contrast, Brother and Sister seemed to be even more enthralled by the recent broadcasts. Chun sat on the outside edge of the floor near where Mother was ironing and looked toward the cityward horizon. The late July night full of shining stars engulfed the blacked-out city. In the dim starlight nothing could be seen except the form of nearby hills. Fireflies fluttered here and there, looking like tiny stars. He grasped his knees to his chest and sank into deep thought. I must go. Whatever happens, I have to go. Whatever happens I have to go. If I don't go. . . . No, I can't do that. He sighed.

"Chun. . . ."

He was startled. Mother had laid aside her ironing and was looking at him. In the feeble lamplight her face was not clearly visible. Chun flopped backwards until he was stretched out on the wooden floor. It was indeed a gorgeous starry night. Not a speck of a cloud marred the radiance of the bejewelled sky. Chun quietly shouted to himself—Wow! To peer at a starry sky was always a delight. Next to reading it was his favorite pastime.

It is daybreak. For over an hour he has been walking. The house is far behind now. He glanced back again and again. Brother might appear around the corner of the hill at any moment. He was closer now to the city than to his house. Like a child listening to a scary tale, he was torn in two each time he looked back, he both hoped and dreaded to see Mother or Brother approaching. After deliberating all night, he'd finally decided to sneak away from the house. Before vacation he used to go the distance to school by train, but they had ceased running since the war broke out. The road to the city and the train tracks for stretches ran parallel but often crossed each other. In the parts where they ran side by side, Chun forsook the road to walk the gravel bed of the tracks. It was a familiar path. When they missed the train, students always came this way to the city. He took out a potato cake and ate as he walked. Crammed in his pockets he had enough food to last until the next day. Even though he was travelling alone toward a war zone he was not frightened. He felt instead a warm sense of relief as he walked. He hadn't wanted to come down with malaria like his friend, and he felt a heavy weight lifted from his chest now that he had done his duty and feared no recriminations from the Boys Corps supervisor. He fumbled in his pocket for an apple, took one out and bit into it. The sweet and sour flavor was nice. Suddenly, Remy in *Sans Famille* came to mind. Then he remembered the boy hero of *How the Steel Was Tempered*. He was pleased at how his experience was resembling theirs. And in those characters he found a reasonable warrant for his own action. What the grown-ups say is not always right, for the heroes of those books sometimes disobeyed the orders of adults when what they were told was senseless. Gravel kicked before the toe of his shoe. Cosmos in bloom at random intervals along the road. All of these captured his mind afresh. Perhaps it was the crisp morning air, but then there might have been other causes besides. Until then Chun had lived only in the worlds of books. They were worlds peopled not by men but by the shadows of men. When he looked at grass or trees or flowers, they only made an impression on his mind if he could connect them with something he had read. As followers of Jesus see the world only through the Bible, and as "comrades" see history only through the history of the Bolshevik Party, so young Tokko Chun saw the world only as refracted through the characters encountered in his reading. This wasn't all bad, but neither was it all good. Escape, and the escape at dawn that day, depending on how one viewed it, was not insignificant, and the present episode might even have served as a sort of symbolic premonition of his future. By the time he reached the city one of his pockets was empty and the apples were all gone. As he entered the city Chun at last saw the face of the war up close. The concrete bridge that spanned the river on the outskirts near the convent—all that remained of it were the support pillars. In its place was a makeshift wooden structure. More than half of the grammar school was in ruins and fallen poplars that once lined the wall were strewn in the yard and in the street. The inspection platform was upside down and cast away from its normal position. Every other electric pole was either cracked at the base or completely down. As he approached the city center where his own school, Middle School No. 2, was located, the destruction became still more severe. At the core of the annihilation was the kerosene factory. Chunks of brick and roof tiles were heaped about charred columns. Seeing a once great building in such a state engendered disbelief. A few people occasionally popped out into the street from this or that alley, such were the signs of life. Tokko Chun felt he was wandering through a different, an unfamiliar city. That the buildings he knew no longer stood in their old places gave the city a strange face. That was unsurprising since a city is only buildings erected on the ground, and when those structures change or vanish, so does the city. The shock of seeing these city streets with his own eyes was as jarring as if all the trees in the orchard at home had disappeared overnight, denunding the earth. Never had he imagined anything like this when he laid in the chestnut grove watching from afar. Another shock awaited him upon his arrival at school. Only half of it was still standing. His classroom was in the destroyed part. He ran over and made his way into the ruins. One part of the building looked like it had been smashed by a giant hammer, and the contrast made the undamaged part seem especially erect. With its insides revealed, the structure appeared as unnatural as the anatomical diagrams in a physiology text. It resembled the stage of a theater, where only half of a house is constructed and walls are cut away. Though not at all awkward on a stage, to find his school in this condition made Chun's heart race. Scattered chairs, fallen blackboards, shattered windowpanes. He went over to the teachers' office. Nobody. It was bolted. He was utterly stupefied, as if a spell had been cast on him. On his way he had been immersed in a proud excitement at having snuck away in obedience to an official school order, but the empty ruins of the school kicked this crutch out from under his mind. Not knowing what to do, he flopped down on a fallen column. He had no watch, but he knew ten was still far off. At the latest it'd be around eight by now. He got up and walked about the intact side of the building, looking into the classrooms one by one. Some were padlocked, some open. He went into one of the open rooms. A thick layer of dust covered the floor and the desks. He stepped up onto the platform and looked into the teacher's desk. There was a chalkbox. He lifted a piece of chalk and scrawled "School" on the blackboard. Then he tried "Broken School". "Empty School". "Nothing". "No Teachers". "No Students Either". "War". "Bombs". "American Imperialists". (he went on doodling) "I have come to school as my Komsomol brother ordered, but nobody is here". "School". "School". "Streets". "Where has everybody gone?" "I am alone at school". "Boys Corps Supervisor". "Self-Criticism". "Petit Bourgeois". "Pioneers". "Boys Corps". "The Leadership". "Wall Posters". "Boys Corps Supervisor. . . ." He thought he heard someone. In a moment of confusion he picked up the eraser and rubbed out what he'd written. At the same time he listened. Before long the sound was gone. He descended from the platform and peeked out the door into the corridor. No one there. For a long while he waited, then stepped out into the hall. On his way out he checked the teachers' office once more but it was still locked. He walked into the street leaving the school behind. Bit by bit he was getting accustomed to the strangeness of the streets. In the distance people appeared and disappeared but there was not a single car to be seen. The sunlight was gradually growing hotter. Ambling along the deserted streets became more and more interesting. He turned into an alley and started walking as slowly as possible. He came to a movie theater with outdated posters out front. Its doors were flung open. In the big poster, a man was holding an accordion and gazing into an open field. Next to him was a woman with a kerchief on her head. Chun became startled when a woman came out of a house nearby, a basket on her head. That people were actually in these houses struck him as somehow strange. Almost all of them were empty. Suddenly he felt an impulse to walk into that house, but he couldn't. Someone might still be inside, though from all appearances it seemed an abandoned house. As he moved on, the urge to enter one of the houses became so strong he could no longer withstand it. He came upon the residence of one of his classmates. Why hadn't he thought of it until then? There might have been a mistake when he was told to come to school today. To confirm that the summons was for this day, he needed to locate another student from his school. He pushed open the gate of his friend's house and strode in. Nobody was home and all the doors were tightly shut. He called out his friend's name. No one answered. Plucking up his courage, he shoved open one of the doors. He peeked inside. The room was empty. Same with the adjacent room. The third room was padlocked from the outside. He gave up and left the house. It was broad daylight but the streets were as deserted as in the depths of night. The entire city, the homes and people, seemed bewitched by a magic sleep and only he, Tokko Chun, was able to walk about unaffected. Anyhow, there was no choice but to wait until the appointed time to assemble. Lightheartedly he walked along, chewing one of the remaining cakes. It wasn't so bad. In the beginning he felt awkward moving idly through the streets, but now he found it enjoyable. He crossed a main thoroughfare and approached the marketplace. It was open. Plenty of food and fruits were on sale. People still gathered there despite the incessant bombing to exchange the necessities of life. Unable immediately to evacuate all their household effects, they also had to return from time to time to check on their belongings. The number of people in the street was small, but there were always a few families returning to their houses. Chun walked through the alleys in which the fewest people were found. In front of a certain house he stopped. Flowers filled the front yard. He looked over the fence at the flowerbed. By stretching out his arm he could pick the flowers on the near side of the garden. But his hand refused to obey. The windows and door were all closed tight, even at this hour. He hesitated, looked back and forth between the flowerbed and the battened down house. All of a sudden, his hand shot over the fence. Just at that instant, a sound like metal being torn flashed overhead. Again and again the noise came. Air raid. The closed door swung open. A woman about his sister's age appeared. As she rushed out she grabbed Chun by the hand. He ran as the woman pulled him. Running behind and before them were people who had materialized out of nowhere. Jets were flying low with guns firing. By the time Chun and the woman reached the air raid shelter the air was filled with the rumble of bombers. Lots of people were already in the shelter. More swarmed in on their heels. The inside of the sickle-shaped shelter was pitch-dark. Chun and the woman were still holding hands. What sounded like a powerful torrent of rain was followed by deep 'thump', and the earth shook from far away. These sounds recurred at regular intervals. In the darkness, people seemed to be holding their breath in silence. The summer heat of late morning and the body heat of people packed closely together made the inside of the shelter stifling. The bombing sounds receded into the distance.

At that moment, he felt soft arms holding him tight. A hot cheek touched his own. Chun could hardly breathe, so great was his startled excitement. The smell of flesh. The sound of bombing began to approach once more. But to Chun's ears, that sound was barely audible. Hot skin touching his cheek. The strength of the arms embracing him. The soft pressure on his chest and shoulder made him unspeakably confused. The bombing went on. The howl of falling bombs and the concussions overhead seemed to have intensified. As the explosions grew more frequent, he struggled on the verge of fainting against the warm flesh pressing him tighter and tighter. The sound of a bomb blast. Hot air. Hot cheeks. Hot flesh. The sound of a bomb blast. Suddenly the earth shook very close by. In the darkness the people began murmuring all at once. Explosion. Once more the shelter shook. Pandemonium. Explosion. The odor of flesh. . . .

III

Let's crush the Communists, our mortal enemies.
Let's go and get our mortal enemy, Kim Il-sŏng.

Only after midday did the tiresome rain clear off. Chun went out to a nearby restaurant for an early lunch and came back. He had no plans for today. After eating he always had a strong urge for a smoke. Ordinarily, one mechanically takes out a cigarette and puts it in one's mouth, but once in a while it's not that simple. He had his first cigarette in the army, so he'd already been smoking for three or four years. After returning to college he kept smoking off and on. In fact, cigarettes played an important role in the life of a soldier. Of all places, he'd been assigned to a reconnaissance company of MBP Division. The place known as "OP" was a very cruel place, just right for a man like Tokko Chun. They said that men from the North were not supposed to be assigned to duty at OP, but somehow he had ended up there. When people said "shouting distance" they probably had such a situation in mind. It was right in front of your face. The other guys could be seen leaving their bunkers to do exercises on parallel bars. Maybe the bastards even called that a "physical training movement". Chun wore a bitter smile as he watched their bodies swinging between the wooden poles. Viewed through the gun battery field glasses their uniforms looked as shabby as usual. An ox cart rolled by on the supply road that ran down from the mountain and passed about a hundred meters from Chun's observation post. Why such a strategically vulnerable route was maintained he could not understand, but for the entire two years he was stationed there it was in constant use. On this long, tedious summer day, watching the ox cart pass below at a crawling pace made his heart suddenly sink with inexplicable sorrow. If an explanation were to be sought, it might turn out that the ox driver was an old schoolmate of his. But apart from any diagnosis of cause, this sorrow was of a dull and lethargic kind. There was absolutely nothing of excitement about it. It was more on the side of a sweet and tender lassitude. On such occasions, there is no substitute for a cigarette. You light one up and put it in your mouth. Happiness. You feel you are happy. You feel like singing the praises of an age that would erect an observation platform in the recesses of the mountains and permit such a lazy and useless man to enjoy such ecstasy. The ox cart creeping slowly. Sudden exhalation of smoke. You don't want to close your eyes. Eyes can be closed anywhere. But this place is too beautiful to shut your eyes on. Clouds lazily scaling the mountain peaks. Beneath the cascading heat, mountains punctuated by valleys overgrown with weeds. No trees. Both sides chopped them all down because they obstructed the view. Except for the grass, the seasonal change from spring to summer would have been undetectable. But not even the grass was entirely benign. Spies and surprise raids sometimes used the clumps of tall weeds for cover. At any rate, there was an unobstructed view of the ripening summer. The rations, all four kinds, were indescribably good. Though it was not war, the peculiar homicidal circumstances of war reigned. Chun couldn't help but be happy. Those guys regularly propagandized through loudspeakers. Dear soldiers. End American Imperialism. Treacherous regime of Syngman Rhee. Dear people of the South. Dear students and all intellectuals. In the North. . . . The same phrases always. Awfully dumb guys. Bears have only one talent, they say, what a way they have. Can't they come up with even a single fresh idea? Anyway, they are no longer words. They are winds. They are sunbeams. They are clouds. For they are vibration of air. For nobody tries to catch them. Compared to them, this side has a much higher intelligence quotient. Across the 38th Parallel in tears. Goodbye, Harbor. Matross Love. Como Valley in the Rain. A Prodigal Son is Weeping. The Way Home is the Way to Tears. Orphaned Brother and Sister. Myŏngdong Boogie-Woogie. Love in the Red-light District. From such colonial melodies down to GI sentimentalism like—Come on Over to My House. You Are My Sunshine. Oh, Carole. Tennessee Waltz. Darling, I Love You. Baby's Coming Home. These are far better than the bastards' empty screaming. They are a hundred times better than military music or hymns of construction. The bastards must have heard such fare until their eardrums turned to leather. We were told that a platoon leader had his head cut off not far from OP, but it is just not possible for a man to be on nerves' end twenty four hours a day and 365 days a year. In the blinding daylight with ample time like now, all one wants to do is admire life, especially one's own life. Dear God, if you ever existed, accept my praise. And this glorious spectacle. And this beautiful sky. And the abundant grass. And that fine sun. And postponed death. That is how one feels. Another thing, the cart. Such is an hour's work.

Cigarettes, therefore. Hwarang cigarettes. The tradition of the Hwarang lives on. The warrior Kwanch'ang at the Hwangsan battlefield. In the smoke of Hwarang cigarettes, the spirit of Shilla survives. Therefore, cigarettes. Straight over the hills is the road to W City. On the map, that's how it is. W City. A place of no return, now. He could only consider it a miracle that he emerged unharmed from the crumbled air raid shelter that day when it was hit by a bomb. Brother had gone in search of him and he was found in the corridor of the city hospital. Brother carried him straight home on his back. Though uninjured, he had lost consciousness for a long while.

After returning home, every night he had suffocating nightmares. He stayed in bed even after the fever was gone. The bombing in the city worsened day by day. For a while he buried himself under a quilt whenever he heard the sound of bombing. He stayed like that until the sound was gone. He saw a white face inside the dark blanket. The warm arm. Hot cheeks. The odor of flesh. They were same as Sister's yet different somehow. Whenever he covered himself with the quilt, they thought it was because he was frightened by the explosions. But the darkness under the blanket took him back to the darkness of the air raid shelter. His family tried to remove the covers when the sound of bombers died away. His clinging to the quilt at such times struck them as a reflex of fear. Such misunderstandings left him with a sense of guilt. As with everyone else, sex for him began as a guilty secret. No doubt it was fear. But the family couldn't have known it was not fear of tearing metal but fear of soft flesh. There was no way anyone could know that what made him quake was not the explosions that shook sky and earth, but the rush of hot blood he heard even when his eyes were tightly shut. Nobody knew that when he at last was able to leave his bed and sit once more under the chestnut trees and gaze at W City, he was no longer the same boy. Reading *Nana* he recognized parts that set his heart astir. When Nana stood nude before the mantel, warming herself in the presence of the Count, his heart fluttered. But he was separated from that universe as by a sheet of glass. What occurred in the air raid shelter was a physical experience. From the many-layered world of stories he had been pushed into this world. As he looked off at W City his eyes were as dim as fireflies. Yet they shone with the light of desire ignited within a boy. Peering at the city, the urge to rush back there flashed into his mind. The woman who held him tight could be dead. I might have survived thanks to her. She shielded me with her own body. Thus his young heart contrived a logic demanding that he discover whether she lived or died. But unlike before, he now lacked a pretext his family would accept. That the man had summoned him to school and that he feared the Boys Corps supervisor had made the prior escape understandable to everyone and also had fortified his courage. This time it was not possible. If he was to disappear again now. . . . He would either be whipped or treated as a boy with mental problems. He felt endlessly gloomy and impatient. In his memory, the image of the woman grew clearer with each passing day. The face was round. Light-skinned face. Striped dress. Dark eyebrows. Nicely shaped nose. White teeth. His memory and imagination through friendly exchanges projected a portrait of a tender young woman. Her face grew whiter. Her eyebrows grew more shapely. Her nose became almost aquiline. Her teeth were like pearls, shiny and lustrous. The lips tender and red. The bombing in the city was the sound of an approaching footstep tolling a new phase of history. But to Tokko Chun's ears the sound meant something entirely different. Sister and Brother still sat by the radio every night trading glances more significant than ever. To the grown-ups, the same tremors and explosions registered differently. September passed. Ragged clothes and military trucks from time to time passed along the village road. False rumors flourished anew. Early in the war there had been a rumor that Japs were fighting in the front of the American and South Korean ranks. This time, rumor had it that negroes were in the front ranks, and village wives and children swore that they were catching and devouring everyone in sight.

One day in early October. At last, people from the South appeared in the village. They were only passing through, rushing toward W City on trucks, singing military songs. They were excited. The villagers went outside bearing water and fruits. Everyone held an ROK flag in their hands. The soldiers were excited. People were impressed by the sleek GMC vehicles, the splendid uniforms and the clean and shiny weapons. The trucks frequently paused for the soldiers to accept the crates of apples and the water being offered. The villagers were surprised by the shiny boots of the soldiers and half boots of the officers. They seemed too expensive and imposing.

Brother was busy moving apple crates. Mother and Sister were carrying water. Trucks kept passing endlessly. The soldiers were excited. They were singing military songs at the tops of their voices from the trucks.

> Let's crush the Communists, our mortal enemies.
> Let's go and get our mortal enemy, Kim Il-sŏng.

The summer seemed reluctant to withdraw and a strong heat lingered. The songs of the victorious sounded high into the sky and the GMCs left big plumes of yellow dust behind as they sped off. As he stood among the crowd taking in the spectacle, Chun's mind was elsewhere. The Boys Corps supervisor has now been fired. W City. He longed to go see these rushing lines overflow the streets. Or so he told himself. As the true longing lodged itself in his innermost heart. It was an adolescent hypocrisy but not hypocrisy alone. He left the crowd and approached the road where the trucks were passing. None of his family was in sight. He walked on. Gaps in the lines of people along the road were constantly opening and closing and his behavior was inconspicuous. It was like a festival day, when nobody noticed the children moving among the grown-ups' legs. After a long walk he reached the next village. There the trucks were parked in a column for a break. Here, too, the soldiers were offered apples and water. The officers were resting inside a roadside farmhouse. Several pairs of shiny half boots sat in a row outside the wooden door. When he came closer to the kitchen of that house he saw steam rising from a big iron kettle and women passing to and fro within. Judging from the chicken feathers in one corner of the yard it looked like they had killed a hen. Behind another house he saw a circle of people gathered. He walked over to see what was up. One man held a rope tied to the nose of a huge bull and another stood beside him with a sledgehammer. Gotta do it with one blow, somebody standing there said. The man with the hammer spat in his palms and altered his grip on the tool.

The bull was flexing his hind legs and wailed Meaaah! In a flash, the long handle of the sledge-hammer traced a semi-circle through the air. One second. Three seconds. The front legs of the bull collapsed. The heavy body fell over to one side, raising a cloud of dust. That was it. Other men took over and with sharp blades cut open the belly from neck to loins. Another man pierced the throat. Blood streamed into a bucket below.

The man who was skinning the hide had finished the upper torso and was beginning on the flanks. By now, huge lumps of flesh covered with white membrane were piled on the spread skin. A man severed the hind legs at the knee joints, then went to work on the forelegs. The man who gathered the blood was about to hack off the head, and Chun was intending to walk away but his feet wouldn't move. The bull's head was taken off. A man picked it up with two hands and carried it away. Now they were about to remove the intestines. Chun left the scene and went over by the trucks. A man from his village was talking to a soldier.

"Any way I can get to the city?"

"See here, what do you mean going to the city at a time like this?"

"I heard that the People's Army fled and the city is empty, no?"

"You can't go, it's in the middle of a battle."

The man started to explain why he had to go to the city. He wanted a lift on the truck. The soldier half listened as he chewed an apple. Chun thought that if that man got a ride he would try to do the same. It was too far to walk from there to the city. Unlike ordinary times, the road was clogged with trucks and it would be difficult to pass through the convoys of troops. He decided to stay there and see what the reply would be. The soldiers scattered about the village returned one by one to their trucks along the road.

The vehicles started up and began to race their engines. How the talk ended was unclear, but the man from his village was now climbing up onto the truck. None of the soldiers stopped him. Chun hung his burning face and clambered up on the truck behind him. The soldiers just watched. The parade of trucks departed. They sped away trailing yellow-white dust. The confused state of things, the flux of the times, made it easier for Chun boldly to do what he ordinarily would never dare, but his aching desire to reach W City was what really drove him on. If he searched for a similar emotion in his past, the only remotely similar event was the time he walked all night to S Village just to borrow a book from his friend. As the vehicles made their way to W City every village gave them a similar welcome. The truck bore eight soldiers, the man from Chun's village and Chun. Apple crates lay in the truck. The whole way they munched apples and sang loudly.

> Gazing out on our boundless future,
> The nation's blood beating in our hearts
> Manly hearts broad and deep
> Forsaking life or death, ambition left behind.

Atop the speeding trucks this song they sang as if their throats would burst. This army song left a residue of indescribable loneliness in Tokko Chun's mind. The truck sped forward toward the next village, slicing through the rice fields on either side of the road. The youngest looking of the soldiers yelled,

"Hey, have a taste of this!"

Before finishing those words, he tossed an apple ahead. It struck an old farmer who was walking along the road with an A-frame on his back and bounced onto the ground. The fear stricken face of the old man looked up at the truck. Boistrous laughter emanated from the passing truck and several more apples rained down. The farmer turned away to avoid the projectiles. The moment the first apple was launched, Chun felt this heart skip a beat. Before he knew it the soldier had thrown two more and then the farmer was already far behind. Chun smiled. The carefree laughter of the soldiers he mimicked. He had snuck on the truck and felt a need to mirror their mood, outwardly at least. But his heart ached with sorrow and a loneliness infinitely deeper than what he felt at hearing the military song. A buzzing sound pervaded his skull. The truck ground to a halt as the one ahead of it stopped. There must have been some trouble with one of the vehicles in the rear. Two corpses lay right beside the truck Chun was on. They were bodies of People's Army troops. Side by side they lay, faces half buried in the earth of the rice field. The soles of their sneakers faced the truck.

"Those bastards died like pigs."

"Eat this, bastards!"

Apples showered the corpses from the trucks on the road. As apples landed in the mud and stuck, Tokko Chun grinned. To imitate the expressions of the men on the truck. The truck once more moved on, leaving a yellowish-white dustcloud behind. . . .

One jeep. Three passengers. Jeeps also frequently appear. Through the field glasses, the "comrades'" jeep looked drab and dull compared to ours. It moved about 100 meters from right to left then disappeared from view. Blinding sunlight reflected from the road. Heat haze. Birds chirping somewhere. Buzzing sounds of motors. Organization is a curious thing. Normally, it calls to mind the meshing gears of an enormous machine. Undoubtedly a faultless definition, that. But an organization invariably has a blindspot. Indispensable duties exist, but a space can always be found in which, if only one uses it properly, one can for the ego's sake construct a barrel of Diogenes. This was true in OP, as well. The antennae of both sides met at the place, one might say. The observations gained here mapped only the tip of the iceberg, still this configuration allowed conjectures about the immense volume of ice submerged beneath the water. But the single individuals here at work, all they do is repeat monotonous routines. Though the term "blindspot" raises echoes of the system's concern for efficiency, would it not be better to take a different approach aware of its positive potential? To picture perfection with no waste whatever is to depict hell. A logic of contradiction inheres in organization. For the organization to subsist, it must maintain inefficiency within it. Only then can ego escape suffocation. All work and no play makes Jack a dull boy. That is an illicit union of organization and ego. This illicit union is the logic of reality. You may speak grandly of "The Golden Mean", yet the meaning is the same. If you run it with a ruthless spirit then the machine breaks down and people get bruised. Come to think of, the plans laid after Liberation by the "comrades" in the North in many cases failed to grasp this reasoning. They ignored the fact that each individual ego constituting the organization possesses a blindspot capable of stalling the entire system. Hence, the atmosphere of their society is dull and ponderous. Two "comrades" are leaving their barracks. They are hanging on the parallel bars. This is their "physical training movement". "Movement", ha, ha. Dull boys, what in the world is with you? They say that as people age they come to understand the world and to exercise discretion, but in my case the further I go the darker the road grows. I can't make out what's what. It is not that I stand here at the 6th OP with manly heart, eyes glued to field glasses, forsaking life or death, leaving ambition behind. Idle thoughts and anguish are growing wildly in my mind like the weeds in the field over there. The sun of desire is boiling away. But the scene never alters. Like this field. Must it move? Must it move. . . . The sun high in the sky, the weeds lazily breathing, and I, Tokko Chun, scanning a hundred meters of road through my field glasses, shouldn't it do? Everytime he confronts the question what is to be done, confusion returns. What is to be done? The question presupposes a man must do something. But what must he do, what. . .? Ow, burned! He ground out the cigarette butt under his shoe. His relief for the next watch won't show up. "I'm sorry". Don't mention it, buddy. I love this duty. That's true, I wish there were a place like this in life, too. Men and horses. Enemy supply truck. One horse wagon with canvas top. Fifteen hundred thirty hours. That is all. If there were such a place in life, that would be what I would want. A life in which watching is all one does. An onlooker standing outside of life, unceasing desires all kept inside. Is that not a sort of participation, too? It is, in a way. Nonetheless. . . . Nonetheless. . . . It's all right. But don't I have to eat? Who'll feed me? Food. It was during the war that he first learned the importance of what they call "food".

The Father he met after coming South was not the same Father he remembered. In his memory, he imagined Father as a dignified man, a man with a good appearance yet quiet. Seeing his lean neck jutting out above the crumpled collar of a dyed U.N. jumpsuit, somehow Chun felt warmth for his Father. Father wept with abandon as he listened to Chun describe his solitary flight and how the rest of the family was left behind. When the U.N. forces pulled out, the whole city was turned inside out. People who until the day before never dreamt of leaving found themselves rushing to the wharves. A cargo ship out into the harbor to pick up refugees. Not just anybody was allowed aboard. Those who worked in the administration established after the arrival of the U.N. force had priority. In Chun's family, it was decided that Chun and Sister would seek refuge in the South. Everyone thought it would be temporary and they would be back. Brother took them to the wharf. Lacking connections, they had to give up the idea of boarding the vessel. Entirely by coincidence, Chun ran into a friend whose father worked at the Municipal Autonomous Council. Chun's friend pulled him into the line after getting permission from his father. Poor Sister pushed Chun along, telling him to go on ahead and that she would follow with another group. It seemed to her too much to ask protection for a second person. Chun looked up at his friend. Nothing was said. His friend's father looked stony and he kept looking away. The mother of his friend was busy scolding his friend's little sister. Nothing could be done. He boarded the ship with the crowd and it sailed out, leaving Sister behind. Telling this story to Father, Chun felt the shame of a guilty sinner. Two shameless men who ran away, leaving their family in peril of death. Thus began his life with Father. In Yŏungju Dong they built a tiny wooden shack and Father went out to the Kukje Market. He tried several small-scale businesses, but each time failed. When Chun inquired about Brother-in-law, Father spat out that he was a bastard, not a man. After coming South, he had married a different woman. Now that he had severed all ties with Sister, he was no Brother-in-law. Father's excuse for not succeeding in business was that he lacked capital. Chun wondered how such money could be gathered in the first place. The next year of their refugee existence, Chun entered school. It was a barracks-type building in the refugee quarter. Life was hard for the two of them. In retrospect, it was obvious that Father was constantly regretful about having fled to the South. If he had been left alone to live and work in the orchard up North, unconcerned about ideology and the like, he certainly would have chosen that life. But, of course, the "comrades" would not leave him alone, so he had to come South. Having been sent to school by his parents, left with the inheritance of the orchard property, and accorded the respect due a representative of the Residential Bureau, he was soft and weak, ill-suited to labor as a bread winner day-in day-out. Besides, South Korean society was in the process of changing into a new society entirely different from what existed before. A society in which money is everything. He had become a straggler in a society smelling of the gasoline of capitalism, a society with no tradition braking its change. The weakened father often attempted serious talks with his young son. He must have been lonely. One winter day, the father and son exchanged words as they walked along a windy street,

"Even Pusan is cold on a day like this, isn't it?"

"Because it's winter. . . ."

"Even in cold winter, if you're full you don't shiver. The cold is worse when you're hungry. Even if it's freezing, when there's plenty to eat it's not too cold."

Father gazed out to sea, and spoke in a kind of a moan, "Yeh. . . you're right. . . ."

They hadn't yet eaten breakfast that day. Cold and gloomy street of winter. Overcast sky. As they walked along on empty stomachs, they talked of the way cold aggravates hunger as if an important discovery had been made. One jeep, three passengers, fourteen hundred hours. Same jeep as before. The guy sitting in the front seat raised his hand to point in this direction. The jeep went out of sight. In adapting to circumstances even Tokko Chun had problems. His season of sexuality had begun. Despite the powerlessness of Father, sharing a life with Father helped by keeping him from being swept away into a phase of cold and naked sex. Otherwise, Chun's mental world would have followed a different path. Though nothing more than a barracks, lacking even a yard, still school was a school. Father dared not force Chun to work. In spite of everything he was a student, there was a house, even if a mere shack, and at home there was Father. When Chun entered college, Father drank some liquor for the first time in ages. If only you succeed, my suffering won't have been in vain. Such were Father's words. When Father died in the spring of his sophomore year, Chun became an adult. It was an icy despair scarcely captured by the word "sorrow". He had no money for the next term's tuition and so volunteered to enter the army. Life at the OP gave him a chance to rest and settle his mind. His life had been rooted in Father. He had been the source of nourishment—money and affection. With Father gone, he was drifting in the air. To put down new roots his isolated ego needed warm light and a shield from the wind. It was in this special place, with its still atmosphere, its sunlight, snow and wind, that he acquired the resolve and resignation for a new life. There was nothing extraordinary about this, of course. It was just a dull story of one more refugee, a youth with nobody to turn to, forced to stand on his own feet and raise himself from the bottom of life. To Tokko Chun, however, it was more momentous than the March 1st Independence Movement of 1919 or the June 25th outbreak of the Korean War. Those events were utterly beyond Chun's control, but this was his own affair. Mountain upon mountain. In the midst of this life, the harbor and streets of W City, the apple blossoms in May, and the old tin-roofed house back home, had become a new god in his heart. They had displaced characters from stories such as witches, Snow White, Cinderella, Son Oh-gong or Nana. They were the same in not being tangible parts of the real world, and also the same in being brighter and more beautiful than anything real. You could call this an improvement. A God dwelling on earth, though on the other side, had been substituted for a God dwelling in the sky, and thus the dream was that much nearer. Looked at differently, it was Tokko Chun's tragedy. The semi-normal state of life with his father, though not as advantaged as a life in a bourgeois family, had saved him from being swept away by sexuality, the idols of nostalgia now living in his heart had thrown up a wall between him and reality. His mind left him and journeyed over the barbed wire and back home, to the apple orchard, to the bombed out school, and to his air raid shelter Nana. Nostalgia, like love, brings crystallization. Scenes of his hometown returned trimmed in gold. The sun sets early on high ground. At one instant the sun hovers over the peak, and at the next everything descends into darkness. Insects cry in the grass. When the night is clear, the sky seems extremely close. The beauty of a starry night. Framed by the mountains on all sides, the sky becomes a dark pool of liquid. Fireflies. Tiny points of light fly over the pool. The lofty and pure impression received from the starry sky. For Tokko Chun, who'd never acquired the habit of praying, of speaking alone with God, each encounter with the starry sky made him more certain his ego existed. The certainty the subject feels in meeting another face to face, inverted, means that the subject exists as ego. The recognition that I existed was utterly incredible and overwhelming. Do I really exist? He felt sure of it gazing into the starry skies. Deep space filled by stars bigger than the earth, bigger than the sun, more stars than there are grains of sand on a shore of the sea. He felt a frigid loneliness. His eyes wandered to his neighbor. He sees another man as lonely as himself, possessor of the identical fate imposed on this yawning field. No man can love mankind from a disconnected state. What ties men to each other are the predestined conjunctions through which we endure loneliness in this infinite space. It is inexplicable. On the long, long journey of a wayfarer, the joy of a chance encounter with another man in a certain field. Is that not the last root sustaining the morality of human conduct? When the day arrives when all other roots have withered and rotted, still this universal feeling will remain. In this way, Tokko Chun's ego extended the hand of solidarity to his neighbor. His ego, the neighbor's ego, and the starry sky. Within the triangle joining these three points, he battled against loneliness. Like many another youth, Chun was obsessed with systematicity. The urge to explain the whole universe by a single principle. It must be an instinctual defense for an ego separated from its family, torn from its natural system, to fight against the circumstances that threaten the self with disintegration. To transcend tangential circumlocutions and speak simply, he loved the starry sky out of loneliness, and later he wanted human love, again from loneliness.

After life on the heights came to an end and Chun became a civilian once more, he was lost. He thought of the saying "there's always a way out", and the face of his brother-in-law floated into his mind. Since coming down to the South Chun had not met the man. Although no longer really his brother-in-law, Chun still remembered him as a handsome young man in the uniform of a student, sitting beneath the apple trees and talking to Sister oblivious to the fall of darkness. Naturally, he hesitated. His house was magnificient. The man who lived there was no longer the same man. Chun was turned away forthwith. Hahk had found a family for whom Chun could work as a tutor, and without this job he could never have paid his tuition. When he left the military, he'd been in a peculiar state of mind. I've just come from the front, where I served to protect the nation—such had been his melodramatic feeling, but not even a puppy was impressed. It was no surprise in a society with over a million discharged veterans. His brother-in-law's response had sown yet another malignant seed in him, a seed of distrust. Until then, as he moved from one tutor's job to another, Chun had been feeling more and more despair at his lot. His vague hope was to become a writer, but this ambition was formless, not something he would pursue at any cost, and not something he was ready to die for. He still greedily consumed novels, but he no longer experienced the intoxication of his boyhood. They were only lies and never reached his heart. He failed to perceive that the problem lay in his own emptiness inside, that the flame in his heart had gone out, and he went on searching for the novels beneath the novels he read. A man like a Sunday. A Sunday man every day of the week. He watched his own ego as if it were a spectacle. The sight of its writhing. Pathetic. Only if his divided self reunified could he feel enthusiastic about anything, but in this state he never managed to rise from his seat of skepticism and languor. Whenever his mind wandered back to W City and to the woman in the air raid shelter, he was transported back to his boyhood. The time he hitched a ride with the advancing troops. Apples. The bull in the midday heat, flesh spread on its hide as on an overcoat. The soldier throwing apples at the old man. The image of that soldier became an icon symbolizing what he'd later witnessed in the South. What sort of life does the woman lead now? What are supposed to be the most precious things, cherished deeply in one's heart, could they be so insipid? Viewed by another, they would seem no more than crumbs. But to me they are pearls, that is the problem. Touched there, it reverberates and hurts. My friend Hahk is a good guy. Too good to be stranded in Korea. But in some ways he is dense. Just like those "comrades". He is so lofty and great, he is a fool. Is he calling for a revolution? Does he think he can turn this land into a Utopia? Foolish bastard. Son of a bitch. Why build a Utopia here? Who asked him to? Who wants him to? This land is a land beyond redemption. Korea. Orphan of the world. An abandoned race. Jews of the East. My dear Mr. Kim Hahk, do you plan to become Jesus Christ? Judas, do you wish to boast of your work so others will do your work? Mr. Kim Hahk. It cannot be done, sir. These people are gutless and spineless. They neither get enraged nor do they weep. Why should a fine-spirited man like you waste his precious life? Don't you read the third section of the newspapers? The end met by a patriot who devoted the seventy years of his life to the Motherland. When I run into articles like that my skin crawls. Wondering what sort of miscalculations were made. Who will repay his wife, who met her husband only in dreams, or his children, deprived of decent schooling, not to mention the patriot himself? Do you call that rewarding, as well? Lies. The worst kind of lies. Perhaps our present pitiful state came about because we have been telling only lies. Upon meeting Kim Hahk, Chun, too, gets absorbed in the logic of youth and in a positive worldview. Had there been no Kim Hahk, Chun's life would have been far lonelier. To attack Hahk, to jeer and laugh at him, gave him a certain pleasure. Sitting together with his friend, Chun seemed a man content to spend his life in thought about the world. Hahk was taken in by this appearance of his friend. Once left alone, Tokko Chun instantly returned to his former condition. This shattered mind beyond consolation. This attitude of being sunk in a grey seat, viewing the world with hazy vision. He wanted to dispute Hahk's assertions, but at the same time the invitation to join his circle kept coming back into his thoughts. This bastard called "I".

Chun rose and went to the window. It was an old rundown Japanese-style house—the owner lived downstairs and he had the upstairs. His room was the only thing on the second floor. He had only taken the place because the rent was cheap. The rent of a thousand *hwan* was unbelievably low, even for a place away from the heart of the city. The landlord was a man in his fifties who had worked for the Railroad Bureau for thirty years. He lived with his wife and a daughter in the first year of high school. His three older daughters had been married off and he had no son. No telling how such people came to own such property, and the house was in a sorry state of repair. Besides the fact that the landlord's family was small, Chun loved the commanding view from upstairs. An American army base could be seen from the southern window and beyond was the Han River. The Army base stood out from a distance because of the barracks and other structures. It almost merited the word "beautiful". He could see a tennis court and liked to watch the white ball streaking back and forth. White lines chalked on the ground. White outfits. White net. White ball. The way they glided so swiftly suggested Korean chess pieces moving on their own without players. And beyond, the Han River flowing. Here, Chun learned that a river, too, has many faces. The trees and grass along the bank changing with the seasons were one source of change. In early spring the river's color was cold from the ice and snow. When the new plants put out their pale green buds and the sunlight showers down the water becomes a pale blue. It becomes as soft as a woolen scarf hung around a girl's neck as spring approaches. The river water in mid-summer. When the innumerable rays of light collide and ricochet on the river's surface, the water ripples like silk. When a ferry or children eager to swim or washerwomen come on the scene, of course, the impression alters yet again. Once frozen, the river is no longer a river. It is merely something within the mind. Surely a bridge stood there somewhere.... That tree over there, how did it look in the summer? Just as the river loses its form as the bank blurs into the shore, a tree bereft of leaves is no longer the same. The snow seldom stays on the branches. Winds whipping through the open air blow the snow away before it grows thick. On moonlit winter nights the Han River as seen through his window seemed utterly lonely. When stationed at the OP and here as well, what touched him most were the mountains and rivers of Korea. The mountains viewed from the OP, cut by deep ravines and yet naked of trees, were nevertheless not coarse. It was because of their coat of soft summer weeds, perhaps. If trees had clothed them, the only word apt for them would have been *Kŭmsugangsan* — "river and mountains embroidered in gold". Possibly this extreme beauty of nature was responsible for the people's ruin. When there was nothing else to do he thought such thoughts and smiled. His view of the Han River in winter, though lonely, was not so merciless as to make a soul quake with fear. Taking in these landscapes, the thought never occurs to you that the world is dark and beyond salvation. You feel there must be a way out, somewhere, in some corner. It is autumn, now. The view is just like a painting of a landscape. The photographic precision of oriental landscapes he found astonishing. They reproduce not the techniques of geniuses, but the rivers and mountains and clouds exactly as they are. Peaks jutting here and there through the dense mist, a tile-roofed house on the hillside, a villager bearing firewood on his back as he comes down the slope—this scene without more would make a painting. The country is ruined and so are the people, so why is nature so beautiful? An abyss of sorrow enveloped him like a mist. The feeling resembled the chill one might feel when singing the national anthem. It was displeasing to him. He disliked the pretension to loftiness. It would never amount to anything, anyhow. The sense of totality proper to a given age. What a spent force it becomes once that age has passed. But people are bound to go on living in their preordained bonds, are they not? Struggling for spiritual liberation, striving to escape the karmic chains, are these not the sources of suffering? So things truly are. Let us not attempt to attain nirvana. Living in chains. His heart pounded as though a great discovery had been made. That's right. Would it not be best to leave nirvana to Shakyamuni, to one individual, and for the rest of mankind to go on living and enduring suffering? The delight of suffering. The beauty of pain. How we Orientals have maligned this most beautiful sign of humankind. The law of cause and effect. Ah, the depth of the Buddhist canon. Now we are paying the price. Hahk's words of that night came to mind once more. There never existed circumstances in which revolution was possible. Revolution is supposed to overcome that impossibility by means of will. What was my rejoinder to that? Love and time. Love and time. But wait how long? When will that fire of the holy spirit ignite in our hearts? Will it come naturally if we wait? What if it arrives too late? Love and time. What could preserve us from self-deceptive evasion? The unenlightened multitudes? Obtuse history? These? No, the problem lies elsewhere. I have no such intention. I don't want to believe in truth. To believe in a truth that is identical for a thousand or ten thousand people, and to be pure enough to burn one's heart for that—this is no longer my lot. How has it come to this? How could I have turned out to be a man like this at my age? Is it this era that has castrated me? No. I don't mean to shift the responsibility onto the era. I will bear the responsibility for my own misfortune. If a man is unhappy even after attaining nirvana, only he can take responsibility for his own unhappiness. How much of human unhappiness is inevitable and how much is contingent? That problem he never learned to estimate, nor could he figure it out by himself. If Tokko Chun has one hope at this point, it is to return home someday. He did not intend to spend the rest of his life there. Even if he made it back, the sound of reed pipes would no longer be heard and raised to parched lips the reed would taste bitter. But that was precisely why he wished to go back, at least once. In order to blow that bitter reed pipe. If only he could sit once more under the chestnut trees, gazing at the blindingly white smokestack, a reed pipe at his dried lips. Oh, dear. Had not the smokestack already been destroyed then? Perhaps it had risen again? But if not what does it matter? That the white column no longer occupies that familiar space, is that not a bitter reed? But when will I make it back there? Love and time will permit it. The same fate that one summer day ten and more years ago released us from the Japanese might yet grant another miracle to us. Even thus would be good enough. If only it were possible to go back again. Then, mustn't I let

Brother, Sister and Mother know that the South where oranges ripen, the South they prayed to reach in so many nightly rituals had been revealed to my own eyes as a mirage, that the woman with the beautiful voice was a liar after all, and that the man Sister saw as the noblest in the world turned out to be a mean-spirited bastard. But will such a day ever come? We go on living like this. Like a perverse whore waiting for another rapist, we Koreans will forever wait for a lover. Love and time. The religion of Koreans. Ha, ha. Learned gentlemen who hoodwink and lie, though they know it is wrong, to save their wives and children from want—when they are the politicians, businessmen, newspaper publishers and educators, the murky water will never clear even in a hundred years. Therefore, revolution? No. Who would revolt for the sake of Koreans? If I must risk my precious life I'd choose a more endearing people. Tokko Chun, aren't you yourself a Korean? That is why I value myself so dearly, as befits a true Korean. I'll live on crouching alone like a dirty porcupine, though if I find a woman as base as myself I might not mind living together with her. Therefore, Mr. Kim Hahk, I like you and I dislike you. For you are making big waves in my life. You bring me sad illusions and impossible tasks. Mr. Kim Hahk, I do recognize your purity. But I am familiar with Korean physiology. Because I am a Korean myself. It will not work. It will not work out well. And that is not everything, either. How could it work out when the Western brats are sure to meddle? Kim Hahk, there is no way we could compete with their immense power. Wouldn't you like to live a life befitting a true Korean?

As he himself grew agitated, he violently jerked his head back against the chair and shut his eyes.

Music was heard from a theater nearby.

As the river flows and
Blossoms fall in the mountains,
Ah, the promises made,

Knotted with green grass
In the flow of Spring.
Sending our dreams and
Sending our hearts
Down into time,
Our flowering lives
Let's pass over the hill. . . .

IV

Answer youth's summons and the tribe weeps, Answer the tribe's summons and youth weeps.

The campus in the afternoon looks like a beach in the winter. Four members of the circle called "Imprisoned Age" were laying flat on their backs beneath two gingko trees that stood in a face-off behind the library. Nominally it was an editors' meeting to discuss the second issue of their circle's journal, but their posture suggested little concern with that business. So clear was the sky that the thin whisps of cirrus clouds high above were nearly invisible until one squinted to bring them into focus. It was about the time in autumn when one feels vaguely uneasy, oppressed by a sense that something has been forgotten. The aggravation was the sort one feels when struggling to recover a forgotten name.

"Kim Hahk. . . ."

". . . ."

Someone called Kim Hahk. There was no reply and nobody else opened their mouth. Gingko leaves were falling.

"Look here. . . ."

Kim Chŏng-do called as he turned toward Kim Hahk. Between the two lay Kim Myŏng-ho, stout with his eyes closed and double chin turned upwards.

"Yeh, Chŏng-do, whatcha want?"

Kim Hahk purposely exaggerated his hometown dialect.

Chŏng-do stared at the space over Kim Hahk's head for quite a while, then spoke as if he'd finally remembered, "Brother, what are we to do?"

He comically raised his tone at the end of his question.

"Well. . . ."

"Some answer that is, what do you mean by 'well'?"

"I mean 'well'. . . ."

"You mean to go on with 'wells'? Anybody know?"

Chŏng-do raised his own hand and looked around at the prostrate circle members. Oh Sŭng-ŭn, who had been lying at some distance from the others, raised his hand.

"You? Good."

A smile appeared on Sŭng-ŭn's face, a face aptly captured by his nickname of "hairy face".

"Is the word 'well' that hard to understand? Isn't it a good word? It's an excellent Korean word depicting the spirit of skepticism in a suspended judgment. Well. What a fine word it is. Either-or, upon reaching a dramatic peak the single word 'well' can anticlimactically dissipate tension, and the crisis is naturally resolved. I am a man who thinks this word 'well' encapsulates the boundlessly beautiful Golden Mean of Koreans. Well, I'm not all that sure about what I'm saying, either."

Chŏng-do listened quietly to the contorted opinion of his friend and then sighed. Hahk spoke,

"Let us, at least, not do that, O.K.? Such words come easy. For that was the fact. After Liberation every speech contained the phrase 'for thirty-six years. . .', isn't that true? Now nobody uses the phrase. It is useless to say it. To lament past humiliations, the wounds of history, is the easiest thing to do, but nothing good comes of it. The question lies in the time of the future. The future alone is time in its true sense, is it not? The past is not time. It is like a bill that's been paid. It's something nobody can do anything about now. Our problem is the problem of the future. To live like men, we must recognize this. Cruelty to self carried too far is no different than cowardice. That's what I mean. In my view, there's no need for us to feel any extreme inferiority due to the failings of our ancestors."

"Kim Hahk, did our sages not tell us that what you sow, you reap?"

"Nonsense. It may be true for crops, but man is neither a green bean nor a red bean. And history is no beanfield. Isn't that what distinguishes history from nature? In human history revolutions occur, but in nature there is only extinction. Possibly the most representative view of Korean history is found in *Chŏnggamnok* (prophetic texts of unknown authorship drawing on Taoism and geomancy, compiled in the Yi Dynasty around the 17th Century). The historical perspective that waits for someone, that is not what I'm criticising. This attitude of anticipating someone, the notion that 'He' will come and put the world right, completing history, is it not the essence of Christianity? They've been waiting thousands of years for the Messiah to return. They say man cannot live by bread alone, but they've been living, revolting and shedding blood for nothing else than bread. Their approach to waiting is different. The followers of *Chŏnggamnok* would just bathe and frolic in the valleys while awaiting the coming of Mr. Chŏng. The Christians, on the other hand, do good works while awaiting the Savior so they can be proud before the big man when he finally arrives. A crafty compromise, this, in a way—to love bread as well as God. What cunning fellows they are. This simple logic of hucksters has done us in, we of the rustic races who lead idyllic and simple lives, isn't that so? When you think it, we Koreans are the progeny of a stupid, stupid race indeed."

"Hahk is saying he adheres to the theory that history moves not inevitably but with a degree of freedom—that is not necessarily so. There are such things as blocks of circumstances that cannot be altered in the least. I mean situations that nobody can do anything about. Isn't our present state one such situation? Well, the present state of things is not terrible enough to stimulate a revolution, but without a revolution life is dull and hopeless, barely worth living and we feel ashamed, isn't that why this is an 'Imprisoned Age'? The condition of being imprisoned. The condition of being encaged in a prison. This is our predicament. We are imprisoned. Being imprisoned, there is someone who fills our mouths with enough food to survive. Just like prisoners. Prisoners are people for whom living is allowed but life is forbidden. Their freedom has been alienated. But since dying is not imminent they gradually become tamed by prison life. This is the scary part. Everyone feels Apocalypse is here, that the world is at an end, yet nobody wants a state of reckoning in which some will live and some die. Suppose we have here a flock of sheep. Driven to the right, they will bleat in a swarm to the right, and driven to the left they will bleat in a swarm to the left. These are animals, not humans. Only one road is allowed to us, all others are denied. Remember how one of the opposition National Assemblymen recently declared that reunification of North and South must be accomplished not by arms but by peaceful means? How was this received? They said it was a breach of state policy guidelines, a pro-communist pronouncement, sympathetic to the Northern puppets and so on. Speak only set expressions like a parrot. This is what the government requests. In our society it is still taboo to view politics pluralistically. The house where the President lives is clouded in mystery like a royal palace, and the people's only images of those who live inside are based on incoherent rumors. An example is the anecdote about how the President gave his man only 500 *hwan* and sent him to buy a gentleman's hat. And people say things like this: 'He's not at all a bad man, it's his treacherous courtiers who're bad'. Look at them saying 'treacherous courtiers'. Mark their use of a pre-modern term to describe presidential aids in a democratic nation. These voters say that the governmental man with the highest responsibility is infallible, thus if any errors occur the treacherous courtiers must be purged. The thought that 'Our President may be a scoundrel' never occurs to them, not even in their dreams, moreover, they are conditioned against the thought. By those 'treacherous courtiers'. I have doubts about general elections. That democracy in Korea has sunk to this rotten state is the fault of the election system. The voting franchise in the West was won after years of struggle, but in our case it came dirt cheap. That's why it is sold for a pair of rubber shoes or traded for a glass of rice wine. This is our tragedy. The tragedy of Western history was a bloody drama in which men wielding blood-stained axes hacked human rights from the claws of an aristocracy who fought to the death to retain the privileges they had hoarded. That was the tragedy in the West. The Western tragedy lay in the necessity to shed blood for the sake of something beautiful. The bloody love of Robespierre. The cruel love of Cromwell. Such were the tragedies in the West. The history of liberty is soaked in clotting blood. That blood still has a power to command and implore the inheritors. In our case, in place of blood, rice wine flows, and instead of human heads rolling, rubber shoes are tossed down. This is no tragedy. It cannot qualify as a drama. We are imprisoned and escape is unattainable. A case in point was Yŏngil-ŭl-gu in the last election. How could such a thing ever take place? The people who control this society, what on earth do they have in mind? A fetid atmosphere has now settled on us. To jar the minds of this age, sunk in the peace of evil, is beyond human power. As what's his name recently said, the only cures are love and time. What do you say, Kim Hahk?"

"Umm. . . . What you just said is good. That drama is lacking in our case is true. There is no strong faith as in 'give me this or death', so when freedom is taken away it is not sorely missed. That's why no rebellion occurs. Therefore the conclusion that drama is lacking. People who live in this prison, away from any hope of salvation, doubt whether this is the only place for us to live, and would not the path of intellectuals living in this age be to band together and destroy their prison. That it is base to live deprived of freedom, that it is base to distribute rubber shoes to voters while crowing about 'democracy', that such a condition is no longer endurable—is this not the way we feel? If we take the attitude that we can do nothing against what everyone else is doing, the vicious circle will go on. To evoke the spirit of tragedy in our heart of hearts and to communicate this spirit to others, even to one more individual, these are the things we must do."

At that moment Chŏng-do intervened in the discussion.

"Both of you are right. This reality of ours makes revolution out of the question. Revolutions traditionally erupted when completely rotten governments committed extreme atrocities. The reality we witness today is different from the French and Russian Revolutions in at least three ways. First, those two revolutions were both changes in the ruling class, that is, they were class revolutions. Citizens and workers displaced the aristocracy. Today, the reason no revolution is possible in our society is that class revolution is impossible. Because we are nominally a republican system, no privileged class is thought to exist. The sovereign power is supposed to reside in the people. On the level of ideology, the problem is already solved. The social system is so constituted that political corruption appears to be a matter of practical trial and error, never as an evil on the plane of ideology. In other words, the constitution is good but practice is deficient.

The second reason stems from the intimate connection between domestic and international politics. In the present age, bloodshed in Africa enrages French intellectuals and democracy defiled in Korea is a cause of worry in Washington. I mean no nation's politics unfolds in isolation, but rather with connections to the total universe. Taking Algeria as an example, that those who suppress the independence movement and those who urge immediate liberation are both French produces a curious complex. Also, the American government tacitly approves the corruption of Syngman Rhee's government, yet the Washington Post, an American newspaper, harshly criticizes the same Rhee regime. The Westerners hold two hands in the card game and play first from one and then from the other. Their good intentions, at any rate, are becoming poisonous to people in underdeveloped countries. America's affluence is no proof that Korea will inevitably become well-to-do, but in the name of the 'Free World' they create this illusion. Syngman Rhee was brought to us by America, and if we throw him out America will be displeased. Under the present threat from the North it would be very unsafe, thus even those with a reform programme plan to start with Dr. Rhee on their backs. In such circumstances, what kind of revolution could be expected? It may seem paradoxical, but American aid has spoiled us. There is a social mentality expecting that if we are in need, American aid will materialize, and that America will not permit Syngman Rhee to sell out the chastity of democracy. In this situation, despair is not engendered. I mean, there is no atmosphere of a cul-de-sac. As we sink into the bottomless mire, there is a single interminable breathing pipe that brings air all the way from the surface—this is our grotesque reality. We have the word 'despair' but despair itself is absent. For the French or Russians during their period of revolution, revolution was the only means of survival. The road was not either-or, but a single way, through revolution. It is not so for us. We have a breathing hole called America. Shall I give an example? An opposition National Assemblyman being pursued by the government, did he not seek sanctuary on a foreign ship docked in the harbor, didn't that happen? Many idealists despairing over reality here, have they not chosen the asylum called 'studying in America'? Perhaps you've heard how the intelligentsia in Tsarist Russia became students in France, however our situation is different from that. When they returned from Paris to Russia, they had become radical reformists, but when Koreans return from America they have become docile utilitarians. In this manner, the intellectuals who should play leading roles in setting fire to the souls of the people have been made into spiritual eunuchs.

The third reason is the partition of the nation. Attacking the government is allowed only within the limit that it does not jeopardize the national security and welfare, this is our situation. For we cannot allow any space to the Communists who constantly are watching for openings in the South. Thus, we may attempt to perform surgery on the bones only if the flesh is left untouched. Consequently, the bone and the flesh are rotting together. Even despair is impossible, such is our tragedy. Our age presents an insipid tragedy in which the classical drama of passion is not allowed. For what is revealed is so petty that one can scarcely recognize its cumulative importance for the situation. Twenty million people on board a rudderless ship, floating gradually toward a precipitous waterfall. But a huge television set up on the forecastle deck shows a stirring scene of a huge, well-constructed vessel cruising away in perfect trim. On the hull of that vessel is written 'U.S.A.' Those before the television superimpose 'R.O.K.' over those letters and enjoy the illusion that we are aboard that ship. In actuality, however, the propeller screw has stopped, the rudder is broken, the compass is shattered and the rats are moving up to higher decks as the holds slowly take on water."

The circle members were lying sprawled about but they listened intently to Chŏng-do. All felt a certain sorrow.

For quite a while no one spoke. At last, Hahk broke the silence.

"Chŏng-do, what you said could readily be misunderstood. We need to realize that although the grounds of despair may come from without, we ourselves are the ones who despair. However grotesque our reality may be, and however difficult it is to meet, these are no reasons to give up trying. Don't you remember how, near the end of the Japanese colonial period, Korean men of distinction blindly encouraged students to join the Japanese army? And some who gave such counsel were so respected that we still ask ourselves how *he* could have done such a thing. Their justification was supposed to be like this: It's now impossible to gain liberation by overthrowing the Japanese. Japan has become too powerful, and under these circumstances to preach rebellion to the people of Chosŏn means more harm and less gain. On the contrary, by assisting them we will be able to increase our share of the spoils, and when this war ends we will be rewarded for the blood shed by our sons. So, let us seek autonomy in this way, bit by bit. Dear million students, you are pure lambs to be sacrificed to history, give your lives for your people. This was supposedly their logic. They may be forgiven for their ignorance of the international political situation, but what sort of base and slavish logic was this? The ludicrous nonsense these men aimed at their own people, how noxious to the youth of that period it must have been. That reasoning, blindly followed, implied that we had to study the Japanese language more diligently than Korean and emulate their style of life until all thirty million of us become Japanese to the marrow. It would have been better for them to have shut their mouths, but those who spread such notions and led astray innocent souls were the so-called leaders of our country. Indeed, we are a luckless race. They say that even after a virgin has a baby she has things to say, but such an explanation of appearances is never as good as not having been pregnant at all. The state of affairs was indeed sad: those who began by composing our Declaration of Independence ended up lecturing at universities established by the invaders. We should never repeat such mistakes. For the present there is only one rule in the realm of politics: an eye for an eye and a tooth for a tooth. Either that or one should shut his mouth. How utterly absurd for a man like Lee Kwang-su to have urged the youth he loved so dearly to fight alongside our enemies. The excuses he published after Liberation—it would have been better if he hadn't tried to justify himself. He should have kept silent. Whether in the lives of individuals or of nations, those who succumb to temptation and commit errors should perform their penance internally. And those who have surmounted difficulties should be rewarded. Only then will justice be realized. After Liberation, when the political balance-sheet was drawn up, we were defrauded. Did not the tragedy commence when Syngman Rhee drew upon Japanese collaborators? Korea is such a strange country."

Oh Sŭng-ŭn took up the thread from there.

"There is plenty of evidence that Korea is uniquely situated. After the Second World War, nationalism swept all the so-called underdeveloped countries and even now it flows as the dominant trend, but in Korea there has been surprisingly little sign of it. For men to live hatred is needed no less than love. Here there is no hatred for anyone. Immediately after Liberation, 'Japanese Imperialism' served for a time as the focus of hatred, but that all ended with the coming of the Korean War. Even before June 25, 1950, anti-Japanese sentiment had already lost its power as a symbol of nationalist solidarity. In its place, we have 'the Reds'. How unspeakable it is that our antipathy toward our evil neighbors, toward those responsible for present travails, is so unfocused and inconsequential. What more can you say about someone who wears an idiotic grin after being raped? The psychology of individuals and that of groups are both formed in the same way. Resentment must be dissipated and desire quenched. If the trauma of a political rape is not properly treated then the people become politically frigid. They see only the dark side of politics and turn away. In other words, they live on, but without experiencing passion. Are we not like this at present? Everyone at this moment in control of Korean politics is an ex-con. They all, at any rate, at some point lived by compromising with the Japanese. The reason why patriots are so precious is that they exemplify humane rebellion for people reduced to a humiliated state by some sad twists of history. The sacrifices of patriots lay foundations allowing the people to regain courage and self-confidence. Between the two leaders, Kim Ku and Syngman Rhee, once the latter obtained political power, the journey down the road of moral degradation was underway. Had Kim Ku become President, we can at least say that he would have been direct and uncompromising in dealing with Japanese collaborators. I'm not saying that everyone who was pro-Japanese had to be sentenced to death. For in politics only the result matters. Whatever their motives might have been, they should be far removed from politics. I think such would have been the case if Kim Ku had attained power. You may talk about political ability, charisma and so on, but listen, but if the present decadance of this country is the fruit of political ability then we'd be better off without it. They say a wise man is never alone, therefore similar people would have gathered around such a leader. It would have been a bit bothersome with him always full of indignation, forcefeeding us patriotism in the Shanghai back-alley style. But would he not have been much better than this honorable Christian doctor who does nothing but lie? If a father is necessary, wouldn't you prefer a principled scholar, albeit a bit stubborn—how could you respect a fellow who breaches the dignity of his old age, constantly takes hormone supplements, and wears a silver tack stuck in his vest pocket? Whether Kim Ku was murdered by Syngman Rhee or by the Reds we don't know, but is not a world in which the perpetrator is out prancing the streets a bizarre world? What crazy bastard would ever think of sacrificing his life for others in such a world, even out of vainglory? Shit. Now that even the so-called educated bastards wag their tails for money, the small fry intellectuals like us only feel downcast after getting worked up with indignation."

Hahk was about to reply, but abruptly stopped. Everything seemed trivial all of a sudden. He felt that everything said to that point had been utterly useless. The thought that it had all been grumbling gibberish aimed at empty space pressed heavily on his heart and hardened his tongue. Words spat into the air. Words floating through space like dust. Gingko leaves shaped like golden fans dropping one after another.

It is winter. And... Hahk put his hand in his pocket, fumbling for a telegram sent from home. Why suddenly a message?

He didn't know how long he would need to stay, but now that he thought of returning home it occurred to him that the friends laying around him were the whole of his life in Seoul. Animals with similar scents stick together. They, too, need one another. Kim Myŏng-shik was from Seoul, but the others were all living away from home. Kim Chŏng-do was from Ch'unch'ŏn. Oh Sŭng-ŭn from Mokp'o, so they were in a strange place, too. Lately, the thought of being in a "strange place" pained him. Sometimes when he woke up in his boarding house in the middle of the night he missed his mother and his hometown. The circle occasionally gathered on campus like today, but normally they met in the rooms of the members in rotation.

As is often the case for youths lacking experience with women, there was a certain purity in their friendship. Upon assembling they would laugh boisterously and share a conversation that was more a sequence of monologues, and afterwards they felt they had accomplished something. Nobody tried to control the meeting or to steer the talk in a particular direction. That would have been impossible, anyway. They were a group of marionettes trying out their awkward logic, tossing opaque aphorisms to each other, and performing other mental acrobatics in order to allay an anxiety they themselves did not really understand. They were aware of it. This air in which they saw themselves as marionettes was perilous, full of risks and even a bit beautiful, but they knew it rested on falsehoods. They knew that even if they fell down they would not die. That the peril was not real, that the thrill was no more than an illusion, that the tension was merely egoistic anxiety and that the bit of beauty was narcissism—all this they knew deep in their hearts. That was why they at times felt their tongues grow rigid and were overcome by an indescribable emptiness. Those moments drove them even closer together. Falsehood has its own truth. Just as the acrobats who do dangerous stunts on high wires befriend each other.

Revolution. Blood. History. Politics. Freedom. This vocabulary enriched their conversations, but in their case it was doubtful whether these words were very different from words like "roses", "twilight", "live", "adventure", "mountain climbing". For they had no real power to take responsibility for the use of those ponderous terms—revolution, blood, history, politics, freedom. Their only power was over language. They lived not in the rhetoric of politics that moves the external world and impacts on reality but in the language of prisoners who constantly ruminate on their own echoes. In it, the more they struggle the further away reality appears to recede. The road spanning the ravine between language and reality was blocked. Being no better than shabby "children", they couldn't build their own bridge across the gorge. They had to use only the language of prisoners because it reflected the reality that contained them. Had there been in society a relative harmony between the world of young souls and the system of reality, they would have suffered less. Mind was high, reality low. To land was necessary, through whatever means.

The gingko trees with more than half of their leaves gone looked haggard, yet the unveiling of branches made their forms more distinctive. Sŭng-ŭn broke a long silence.

"Shall we go for drinks today? What do you say, Kim Hahk?"

"I said I have to go down today."

"So we'll have a farewell drink."

"What farewell drinks. . . ."

"At any rate. . . ."

"Enough, I have a suggestion."

". . . ."

"You don't seem to think badly of Kim Ku. Am I right?"

"Wasn't he a beloved terrorist?"

"Good. Then how about we all pay our respects at the tomb of Mr. Kim Ku?"

"Now?"

"Now. My place is near there so I could go straight home to pack and then be on my way."

Sŭng-ŭn looked at the other two. Rather than answer, they slowly began getting to their feet.

They walked out through the school gate and boarded a bus that had just pulled up. The exposed branches of the trees alongside the road stretched up like fingers toward the sky. Several electric lines ran between the fingers.

The fallen leaves whipped about on the asphalt like pieces of wastepaper. As always the street was a quiet street. Sŭng-ŭn nudged Hahk on his side and said,

"Look, the world seems like nothing's happening, doesn't it?"

Hahk was silent for a moment and then replied, "Well, perhaps there is really nothing going on."

Then, putting an elbow on the window base, he turned around.

They got out in front of Hyoch'ang Park and walked from there. Some students were visible walking across the campus down the hill.

"Mr. Oh Sŭng-ŭn, what do you think about love affairs?," Chŏng-do asked.

"Shouldn't raise such subjects when we are on the way to pay homage at a patriot's grave."

Sŭng-ŭn mildly reproached him. Chŏng-do chuckled. They arrived before the tomb of Kim Ku.

"I feel odd," said Sŭng-ŭn.

"Why?" asked Hahk.

"I feel awkward," Myŏng-shik said.

"What do you mean 'awkward' in front of a patriot's tomb?", Hahk said,

"Well, that's exactly what I mean."

"That's not what I meant," Sŭng-ŭn said.

"Then?" asked Myŏng-shik.

"I meant I felt a thrill."

"Thrill?" Hahk asked.

"We are now doing just the opposite of applauding as a Presidential motorcade passes by. We are now. . . . Aht! Get down!"

They all instantly hit the ground. At the same time they looked all about them.

"Ha, ha, ha. . . ."

Sŭng-ŭn was rolling on the grass, laughing. The other three squatted like idiots and watched him laugh.

"Ha, ha, I feel great. What are you doing, pissing? Lie down."

The three, realizing they had been fooled, laid down with their heads toward the tomb.

The four men lay there on the grass, contemplating the significance of their reaction to Sŭng-ŭn's trick. At last, Sŭng-ŭn said in a voice like a moan,

"To feel a thrill upon visiting a patriot's tomb will not do."

Far below where they were some little girls were jumping rope.

The late autumn sun had already set by the time Hahk arrived at Seoul Station. He went into the third class waiting room and looked for the window selling tickets for the Kyŏngbu line. The window was shut and no queue was in front. He glanced at his wristwatch. There were still two more hours to wait, he had arrived too early. As he turned around to walk out, he looked up at the electric clock on the facade of the building. It showed three minutes later than his watch.

He crossed the square and entered a tearoom that faced the station. The seated customers were sparse and the light was dim. He took a chair by the wall facing the counter and placed his trunk on an empty seat. At the counter sat a youngish woman, but she showed no sign of motion at the entrance of the customer. One of her arms was resting on a phonograph and she was staring vacantly at a spinning record. A feeble voice was singing a pop song.

> Holding the gift you gave me
> Deep in my heart
> I walk in a darkness
> Without sun or moon.

Hahk lit a cigarette and closed his eyes as he took a drag.

> The far away Bells of Nikolai
> Are sorrowful now,
> Don't you cry, owl,
> My heart is aching.

Hahk felt a chill, an indescribable light pleasure, run through his spine. Then he suddenly thought of Chun. The Bells of Nikolai. Come to think of it, Korean pop songs are full of absurd prattling. Nikolai is the name of a saint in the Russian Orthodox faith, and appears in a Russian novel. So the "Bells of Nikolai" must refer to a bell sounding for a mass at a Russian Orthodox church. Hahk didn't know whether there was a Russian Orthodox church in Korea. Probably not. Even if there is, if its profile is so low that its existence is doubtful, on the level of emotion it might as well not exist. One is curious what could have been in the mind of the songwriter who introduced such a reference into the lyrics. Probably he just borrowed the exotic sound of "Nikolai". Foreign words have such a strange power. One's native language is too intimate to allow any sense of alien material. Somehow foreign languages are resistant, like alter-ego. Hahk had experienced a similar feeling in classes in which he read texts in the foreign original. Once translated, there is nothing especially mysterious about the content, but while reading it in the alien original one somehow feels concrete. Could it be simply an inferiority complex? Probably that is partly so, but there must be another reason. At any rate, the pop songs he heard as he waited for the train's departure had an uncanny effect in his heart. An evening with the Bells of Nikolai. A woman who has lost her love is imploring an owl not to cry. (Why suddenly an owl?) Owl, then, don't you cry.

"What would you like?"

Hahk opened his eyes. The waitress was standing next to him.

"Coffee. . . is it good?"

She nodded, as if to say "of course" and returned to the counter.

Hahk automatically looked at his wristwatch. Ten minutes had passed. Whenever he took a train, he came to the station way too early for no reason. How he acquired the habit, he didn't recall. It grew out of a groundless concern that he might miss the train. Just today he had hurried to the station, turning down the suggestion to have a drink although there was time. He removed the telegram from his pocket and opened it.

"Hurry home. Father."

No way of knowing what the problem might be. Winter vacation was approaching, and he couldn't imagine what could have led his family to call him home in haste. He felt resentful toward his father for sending such a vague telegram. He could have said what it was about, even if very briefly. The waitress brought his coffee. As he slowly sipped that sweet chocolate-colored water he thought of home. Upon hearing he was from Kyŏngju, people sometimes said "Wow, that was Sŏrabŏl" (the ancient capital of the Shilla Dynasty) or "the site of Sŏkkul-am" (a famous Buddhist shrine). But to Hahk, born and raised in Kyŏngju, there was nothing special about it, it was just a country town. Besides, since Hahk came of age his family's wealth had been steadily declining. They couldn't really afford to send him to college. If his family actually had been impoverished, Hahk told himself, he could have put himself through school, but as it was, he just felt unspeakably guilty when he received money from home for his room and board. Because of this, he had arranged to begin a tutoring job the following semester. Kyōngju was no longer the place he knew in his childhood. Like all other cities since the war, there now was a military base, and lots of shops, tearooms and inns. It was now a dirty and disorderly country town. Once out of the city, of course, there is still old Kyōngju. But the pagodas, temples and royal tombs had not escaped the touch of modernity. The area around Pulkuk temple, now filled with restaurants, motels and hole-in-the-wall shops to ply the growing tourist trade, made him gloomy. T'oham mountain was still old T'oham mountain, but witnessing its dignity slipping away day by day, like a royal family deprived of the crown, drove him to reflect. At his age, he felt sorrier about the vulgarization of the beauty of his hometown than about the livelihood of the local poor being dependent on exploitation of historic sites. In this respect, his state of mind was not very different from that of the Luddites of old, English workers who destroyed newly invented machines, although he himself was not aware of this. Such reflections left him in a melancholy mood as he waited for the train to take him back home.

Another song was on the phonograph.

> Ah, the night of Shilla
> The bell of Pulkuk-sa I hear,
> Hey, stranger! Stop a minute.
> Let's sing a song
> "On the side of Kūm-o Mountain,
> 'Neath the still moonlight,
> A song of Shilla nights

The singer's voice trembled strangely as he sang. A curious technique that makes the listener feel out of breath. The Shilla we have found, the Shilla we still seek, is it like this? The song is perhaps more befitting in his hometown, where wooden shacks, hole-in-the-wall stores and barbed wire have become commonplace. Why has everything declined one level like this? Everything is degraded in this way. Everything.

The train left on time. Outside, the moon was out. The pale moon, waning just past full with an arc sharpening, floated incessantly before his eyes. Once out of the city, Hahk finally felt he was really on his way home. On the other side of the Han River, the brightly moonlit mountains and fields stretched far away to the horizon. His arm on the window, he insatiably drank in the passing scenes of the autumn night. Only a step outside the city there remained the unchanging face of Korea. The white natural highway running side by side with the train. Thatched roof houses. Thatched roofs, shrouded in thin mist, certainly looked beautiful in the moonlight. But living beneath those roofs would certainly be exhausting and unhappy. Am I right? Are they truly miserable? Yes, if people can be content with their lives only if they live under tile roofs. Even if they feel discontent, what if they know no other lives? Would it be right to awaken their souls and teach them higher wants?

That's right. They must awaken from sleep. There may be a moment of confusion, still they must wake up. To abandon simple and humble desires, to open one's eyes to more intense desires—this was the consistent ideal of the thinkers of the Enlightenment. No, the problem does not lie there. The question is, whether in the present age it is possible for the young to take as their goal in life the presumptuous task of awakening the desire of others. That is the problem. Chun spoke of love and time. Love and time. Love and time. The train is passing over an iron bridge trestle. Beautiful moonlight shatters on the surface of the water below.

Hahk inhaled deeply as he gazed at the river flowing toward the distant horizon. In Seoul the air is never this fresh, however deeply you breathe. Back in Seoul, he always felt anxious. There was nothing pressing to be done, yet his mind still flitted fretfully from this to that. It was the anxiety of a country bumpkin unable to put down new roots, perhaps.

When you really think about it, Seoul is a city of country bumpkins, not a city of Seoul natives. Not only Seoul, but all cities are like that. People migrate to the city from the country with a new strength and vanity in their hearts, and their tenacity is what makes the city fatten and diversify. In Hahk's case, he had left home to study in Seoul, but for those who earn their living with their hands Seoul was a giant marketplace, no more. These people are busy bluffing, cheating and ruining others, for the sake of money. They have no time to please their neighbors or to spruce up the neighborhoods in which they live. When you consider the growth of cities in the West, people stood up against the aristocracy, demanding new rights one at a time and finally acquiring an identity as citizens. Seoul, by contrast, is an ugly melange teeming with people who are neither this nor that. Whatever the reason for calling him home, now that he was on the train he felt a growing sense of relief.

The car was not crowded. The seat beside Hahk was empty. He decided to give up thinking about why he was summoned home, though his curiosity was strong.

Scenes on a night train are always similar. Little talk and a lot of people dozing off. The old man facing Hahk was sleeping with his head propped against the wall. The man to one side shut his eyes as soon as the train left Seoul Station. Hahk considered it fortunate. When seated beside someone who loves to talk you have to suffer a bit. He wanted to be alone. On boarding a bus or train, he always resolves to make use of the time. In the free time until reaching his destination, he planned to think as much as possible. Such plans always fail, however. The result often turns out to be that his meditations stay in a stationary orbit all the way from origin to destination. It was like getting on a train and running a race on board. Not a single original idea ever popped into his mind. One would think he would give up and just get some sleep during trips, but it never worked out that way. Each time, well, at least this time, but then again he yields to temptation. The only consequence is lost sleep. What is the reason? Perhaps it was the rhythm of the train, constantly the same. The train moved ahead, but for people on board there was only a tedious oscillation, perfect for inducing sleep. Even when the train runs exceedingly fast, those inside seldom can feel the speed. In this trains differ from automobiles. In the case of trains, there is no sense of speed. You don't feel yourself moving. Perhaps it is because the train is a society moving as a unit rather than individuals in motion. Just as people riding the earth do not feel the speed of its rotation. In this respect also, Communism fails. Happiness in which private possession is not allowed is not experienced as happiness. From group to ego, from ego to group. Human history moves like a pendulum between these polar extremities. It is our "circle" that has created an intermediate form between the two poles, a form neither group nor ego. The more such small groups arise in society, the better. It is easier to love ten people than to love a hundred, and easier to love five than ten. But to love only one person. . . to love only one person is harder than to love five people. Therefore, a circle. Such a unit coheres and lasts. After graduation, after taking jobs, and after aging, a circle will still meet. You gather secretly then, never putting an ad in the newspaper, and not even letting your family know of your membership. We'll meet quietly in inconspicuous places. By that time, everyone will have made some money, so we can even choose to meet in a decent place. When we gather there will be no special formalities, but we'll get consolation from one another. We'll show each other the basest of our wounds, ones hidden even from our wives, and trade devilish smiles. For instance, sex can be discussed without standing on ceremony. Only fools talk about dirty subjects with just anybody. We do it only among ourselves. Without getting excited (of course, we'll be past the age of getting aroused). And even at that age, we'll not have abandoned a secret ambition to bring goodness into this world. Innocence. We'll feel embarrassed at preserving innocence after living in the world. Just like those women in days gone by who after forty were ashamed that physical desire still glowed in them. Decent grey-haired men who still believe in the mystery of man, who after interminable debate remain undelivered and thus avoid the eyes of their wives and grown-up children, keep attending clandestine meetings of their circle. All their lives they have plotted, but nothing has come of their work. What sort of plot could it have been? A conspiracy to change the world. They dream of a strange rebellion. The work of changing the world. Why are men so crazed about revolution? Maybe we'll actually succeed in making a revolution. For history is filled with the snares of coincidence. Perhaps that is why we view this life with hate, with blood-stained smiles on our face, because we love it. In such times men simply go on living. In such times, perhaps even a man as meek as a lamb may turn into a ferocious tyrant. Or our future may turn out to be an age of prisoners, as in the name of our circle, "Imprisoned Age". That is more likely. An inescapable horizon. Nevertheless, our obsession will never become extinct. To all appearances we are quiet, sound people, but inside we are wildly inflamed. No one knows it. We do not scream. Often we joke and engage in banal chatter, to conceal our identity. We must ensure that nobody suspects us. Solitary exiles living behind masks of the ordinary, that is us. That is why among ourselves we grow still closer. Our vocations vary, yet each of us applies a common brand in our respective work. By doing so, we expand our domain in this world. But then, what about Tokko Chun, what kind of guy is he? Is he able to endure life all alone? How strong he must be to do that. By whatever means I must break his obstinate refusal to devote himself to any cause. Next time I see him, I will without fail bring him in.

He got up. He passed down the aisle, opened the door and went out. As he turned to the door on the left, he was some-one had beaten him to the steps. A person was perched on the bottom step, holding the handrails on both sides. It was a woman. Her hair flew behind her and her neck shone white. From where he stood, Hahk gazed at the woman's back. Bright moonlit scenes rapidly flitted by. Framed by the small space, the velocity seemed even faster. The woman's perch looked unsafe. What if someone shoved her from behind? As if to tame his wild fancy, he took a tight grip on the side of the train. The urge to push her off the train grew stronger and stronger. The hand with which he clutched the corner of the car quaked convulsively. The unsuspecting woman would readily roll off. The murder might not be discovered until after sunrise. By then I'll be at home. To locate the assailant would be impossible. First of all, the police will investigate the woman's relations with men. All the men acquainted with her will have alibis. The investigation hits a dead end. Any effort to identify all the passengers on the train would surely fail. For there would be no clues. The case would remain an open question, forever unsolved. Not a scintilla of evidence would exist. Shall I do it? A perfect crime, this. Why must I not do it? All it would require is a slight push with the right hand. That would end everything. Not to commit an absolutely perfect crime makes no sense. Let's push. Wait a second. What if? He looked back. He saw him-self standing there in silence, grinning. Ahhk!

Hahk raised his hand to cover his face.

"What's wrong?"

The man who had been sleeping the whole way was grip-ping Hahk by the arm.

"Seems like you've been having a nightmare."

Hahk stood up, shaking his head. He passed down the aisle, opened the door and went outside. Once there. he leaned back against the side of the car and looked down toward the landing. There was no one. Within that dark cube of space, the smoke and the diffuse metallic sound told him they were entering a tunnel.

Wiping the cold sweat from his brow, Hahk stood there mindlessly in that thick smoke.

V

Only heaven and I know, so why not do evil?
— Discoveries from Life

From mid-November, the weather grew wintery for the first time.

Tokko Chun bought a bag of roasted chestnuts at the corner of the alley and with the wind at his back headed home. As he pushed open the old wooden gate and approached the door, a low voice issued from the landlord's room. Normally he would have paid no heed, but that voice was somehow unusual. The voice had a melodious cadence, as if it were someone reading a book. As usual, he removed his shoes in the entry hall and held them in one hand as he stepped up onto the wooden floor. To reach the steps up to his place he had to pass by the landlord's room.

Only then, as he went past the room, did he say "Aha!" and nod to himself. A missionary had come. Today wasn't the first time. Chun hesitated a while, fingering the sack of chestnuts in his pocket, and then went on upstairs.

When he opened the door of his room, a warm darkness greeted him. The fire burning in the stove was seeping out, a white glow floating in the darkness.

Chun stood in the dark and peered at that dim radiance. For a moment the light saturated him with a curious sensation. Like a batter who has missed a swing, Chun never even considered switching on a lamp and just fumbled his way to a chair, his eyes glued to the light that brightened the space like a little bit of happiness. Suddenly the old days when he roasted chestnuts on the kitchen firepit at home rushed by in his head. The empty kitchen. The thought of reading comic books and chestnuts buried in the last remaining embers in the firepit, reading by that light. Brighter than this light. His eyes adjusted to the darkness, and he could make out the outline of the stove. Even the ashbox beneath. And also the very faintly lit ceiling. He listened carefully. Not a stire was heard from downstairs.

It is quiet. Chun shook his head in the darkness. Is this living? Suddenly, a nameless desolation fell over him. It was like the irresistable fatigue that sooner or later overtakes someone who has not slept for days. He raised his hand and touched his face. Then he felt his neck. They felt strange, as though they belonged to somebody else. In that state he sat in the dark for a long time.

Downstairs, a door was heard opening and closing. He removed his overcoat and stood still, the bag of chestnuts in his hand. He opened the door and went out to the hall. About halfway down the stairs he suddenly halted.

The door below opened and a guest started out. He stared at the face. She moved toward the front door, trailed by the landlord, his wife and their daughter, Yŏng-suk. Chun waited until they had returned from seeing the guest off and only then resumed slowly walking down the steps.

"It's getting so cold. . . . Is your stove heating all right?"

Yŏng-suk's father asked, peering over the top of his thick spectacles toward the room upstairs.

"It's burning fine."

Chun answered, putting the sack of chestnuts in Yŏng-suk's hand.

"Come on in."

As Yŏng-suk's mother invited Chun into the room, she closed a bible that had been open on the floor and pushed it into the corner.

"Shall I stop a minute before going back up?"

"Do come in. Even with a stove, still. . . ."

As urged, Chun sat down on the warmer side of the floor. Yŏng-suk put the chestnuts on a wooden platter and pushed it toward Chun.

"You've had a worship service?"

"Yes, we are learning a lot from Sister Kim Sun-im."

"I see. . . . A missionary?"

"Yes, but in our denomination we don't call them 'missionaries'. Men are known as 'brothers' and women 'sisters'."

"What denomination is it?"

"The church of the Kingdom of the Second Advent. We have awakened to the blessings of the Lord, all thanks to His high and deep grace."

"Kingdom of the Second Advent?"

"Realizing the truth brings happiness. It hasn't been long for us, but lately we feel grateful about everything. This is thanks to Sister Kim Sun-im. You should learn it, too. Soon, the battle of Armageddon will come."

"Armageddon?"

"Truly."

Yŏng-suk's mother retrieved the bible she had pushed off to one side, opened it on her lap and thumbed through the pages.

"Listen to this. 'And I saw, issuing from the mouth of the dragon, and from the mouth of the beast, and from the mouth of the false prophet, three foul spirits like frogs; for they are demonic spirits, performing signs, who go abroad to the kings of the whole world, to assemble them for battle on the great Day of God, the Almighty. "Lo! I am coming like a thief! Blessed is he who is awake, keeping his garments that he may not go naked and be seen exposed!" And they assembled them at the place which in Hebrew is called Armageddon. The seventh angel poured his bowl into the air, and a great voice came out of the temple, from the throne, saying,

'It is done!'

'And there were flashes of lightning, loud noises, peals of thunder and a great earthquake such as had never been since men were on the earth, so great was that earthquake. The great city was split into three parts, and the cities of the nations fell, and God remembered great Babylon, to make her drain the cup of the fury of his wrath. And every island fell away, and no mountains were to be found; and great hailstorms, heavy as a hundred-weight, dropped on men from heaven, until men cursed God for the plague of the hail, so fearful was that plague.' This is Armageddon. The end of the world will soon be here. God has been enraged by the sins of Babylon and He has said He will destroy the world, sparing only those who believe in His words. When that day comes, Jesus will return as a King with his army of angels, rooting out the evil powers, and build a new kingdom of the faithful."

Inside, Chun was astonished. It was the first time this woman had spoken at such length. She was a very quiet person, always some work in her hands. So thinking, he looked once more at her diminutive figure. Her eyes on her husband, she said in an admonitory tone,

"At first, my old man wouldn't lend his ears at all, but lately he's learned a great deal. All thanks to grace."

The old landlord nodded at his wife's words.

Chun picked up the bible and aimlessly flipped through it for a while, saying,

"I've enjoyed our talk."

Then Chun got up to leave.

"Why don't you stay a little longer?"

"No, I've warmed up pretty well now."

He left the room.

"Mr. Tokko, you, too, should have faith. Among the brothers there are lots of university students. Come with us to the next meeting."

Yŏng-suk's mother seemed to have been waiting a long

while for him to show some interest, and she continued her proselytizing up to the very last moment.

"Yes, one of these days. . . ."

Said Chun as he mounted the stairs.

When Chun came back into his room he hesitated to turn the lights on. He brought a chair and sat down right in front of the stove, his legs extended on either side. The odor of burning charcoal rasped the inside of his nostrils. Footfalls were heard outside on the steps, followed by the sound of Yŏng-suk's voice on the other side of the door,

"Sir!"

"Yes, come in." Chun even didn't get up from the chair. She opened the door and said,

"I was told to bring you some boiled potatoes. I'll leave them here. . . ."

Then she vanished downstairs. Chun got up and switched on the light.

The stove was near the southern window. One side of the window was sealed off for the winter. At one end of the room, a set of doors opened into a closet. A Japanese-style closet. Its floor was tatami, of course. Along the third wall stood a desk and a bookshelf twice its height. He removed his bedroll and quilt from the closet and spread them out on the floor. At the head of the bed he laid his pen, inkwell and diary, then climbed under the cover. The bedclothes were chilly after sitting all day long in the unheated closet. He pulled his knees up almost to his chin and pulled the quilt over his head. To an observer, this posture would seem silly, but it could not be helped. After curling up in that stuffy and tiring posture for a while, he started to warm up. Whenever he curled up that way he felt strange. A feeling of wretchedness, it may have been. To curl up against the cold was unremarkable, but not the feeling it always gave him. It was always the same, every winter. He felt like weeping. And now, the thought that weeping would be useless made him still lonelier. Family. He considered afresh this notion of "family". Into it man is born, in it he lives and dies, that's a family. Neither is dying the end of it. People speak of "the honor of the family". They also talk of "lineage". This "family" could not be more remote for Tokko Chun. Now that he had buried his father in the South, the mere thought of his family makes him start to disintegrate. Part of the family in W City, part under the earth on the outskirts of Seoul, and I, Tokko Chun, curled up in a second floor rented room. He tries to connect the three points into a triangle. The resulting form seems indestructibly solid and dark in color. Blood, memory, ideology and a bit of hatred—in other words, an indestructible abode built by time past. Retracing his ego, the book recording his family tree naturally falls to hand. Korean society at present is gradually moving away from a system in which family pedigree determines personal identity, yet in fixing the coordinates of one's ego, the normal method, whether one reaches it or not, still refers to an axis of bloodline, of status, on the one hand, and an axis of time, of generational distance, on the other. That modern Koreans wander aimlessly, bereft of confidence, is due to their inability to do the impossible, to locate themselves as individuals within the continuity of the total system. In the old days, acceptance of the family as the basic unit of the system could be interpreted as participation in an order of "values". For the essential principles of Confucianism constituted an ethos of the clan. Now, things are different. Not even a direct descendant of a Prime Minister to the Yi Dynasty is likely to entertain the conceit that his superiority is proved by his lineage. In the present world there is no hierarchy of nobles (*yangban*) and commoners (*sangnom*)—so the situation appears to common sense. But we presently lack any institution to replace the system based on families and clans. This is not to say that no system exists, but that nothing of similar power has yet ripened in the hearts of the people. Even for modern Koreans, the term "clan" strikes deep into the heart, but the term "nation" remains awkward. The term "race", which can be grasped as an extended clan or tribe, is far easier to swallow.

If after Liberation we had as a race pursued nationalism with single-minded zeal, instead of taking up the stupid battle between Democracy and Communism, a task assigned by others, then by now we would be much better off. That would have been the simplest way to command the sympathy of the populace, and the path easiest for them to comprehend. If such had occurred, then the old men would have acted with confidence and might have accomplished something. The new generation then would have seen the elders as a formidable wall and would have taken the position that rebellion was worthwhile. Thinking along these lines, Chun stretched his neck out from the blanket like a turtle. The bed was warmed up.

He shuddered.

Whenever he buried himself under the covers, a flood of thoughts swept through his mind, and without intending it, he recognized himself in those trains of thoughts.

The potatoes at the head of the bed. They look cold. They are good-sized with the soft insides breaking through the skin. He stuck out his right hand and picked one up. It was still warm. There was some sugar on a corner of the plate, too. He pressed the potato in his hand into the sugar and took a bite. The sweetness and delicacy of the taste were not bad at all.

The window was rattling. Seems the wind was picking up. Better reseal that side of the glass. Chun was lying parallel to the closet, his head to the south. For some reason it eased his mind to lay close to the closet, which held all his worldly possessions. From there he could get anything he liked out, without even getting up.

He thought about the day's events as he ate the potatoes. The student he was then tutoring was a senior in high school. His father said he would no longer need a tutor when he entered college in spring. The father was a high officer of a certain state enterprise, but the mother had recently told

Chun that her husband would have to resign before long. Chun was told to look for another position himself and that the family would also try to locate another tutoring job for him. They had been paying him thirty thousand *hwan* a month on top of paying his tuition, an arrangement envied by all Chun's friends. He had no idea what to do. When vacation is over, it will be February. A month will soon pass, entrance examinations are in March. Thus, the matter is urgent. Tuition for the coming semester is an imminent problem. When faced with such crises, he always feels lost. As though it were somebody else's affair, he distances himself from the difficulty and just lazes about. When this laziness had taken up residence in him he couldn't say. At all events, it must have been a long time ago. An incorrigible man, that's what I am. He sees himself as impossible. A Sunday man. An eternal Sunday man. A Sunday man who knows neither church nor recreation spots. Church. He picked up another potato from the plate and took a bite. Church. Why the thought of Jesus freaks always made him feel weird, he didn't know. Is politics unrelated to religion? There is no direct link between imperialism and Christianity. Naturally, we are natives. Our political system was not won by us through fighting. We have not even invented a screw fastener. Our situation is such that, to become an intellectual, we must know as many foreign languages as possible. The daily commodities we consume, whether spiritual or material, are without exception foreign products. Anyone who claims Lucky toothpaste or Haitai caramel are not foreign is a bit slow. Our ancestors thought salt was fine for brushing teeth and they loved their sticks of *yŏt* candy, in that sense Lucky toothpaste and Haitai caramel are foreign. What once was called "blocks of *yŏt*" is now called "caramel" and what once was called "tooth salt" has become "toothpaste". Are not all of our possessions Western transplants into Korea? The West. The world of science and Christendom, the notion—"give me the fulcrum and I will show you how to move the earth" and the idea of the eternal revolutionary—"what will it profit a man to gain the whole world if he loses his soul?" There is no connection between science and Christianity, either in genesis or in nature. They are two contradictory modes of thought, in complete discontinuity from each other. The history of the West can be summed up as a drama in which these two systems of thought repeatedly clashed. To borrow a Biblical parable, it is a wrestling match between God and man. Real drama only exists between God and man. Drama on the human plane, if it is to acquire true dramatic significance, must model itself on the "archtype" of a "wrestling match between God and man". There is nothing as simple as Western art. It reduces to innumerable variations on the same theme, endless permutations of one leitmotiv—"the wrestling match between God and man". They put meat on the paradigm of "settlement → wandering → homecoming", the basic theme of the Biblical story of the prodigal son. Aesthetics is simple. Western art always dances in 3/4 time. And not only in art. Hegel's philosophy reminds one of a collection of waltz music. Were he a composer, he would certainly have been a Johann Strauss. Thesis, antithesis, synthesis—thesis, antithesis, synthesis—thesis, antithesis. . . . This is the melody running at the very basis of Western culture. Whatever aspect of their culture we take, this melody is discernible in it. Eastern music is quite unfamiliar with this skeletal structure. Take traditional Korean music, for instance. The melodies of Korean classical music are elusive, with no end, no middle and not even a beginning. Here and there are indiscernible from there and here. An uncanny voice rising suddenly, then softly dying away. The delicate flavor of Korean classical music is nowhere to be found in Western music. Western painting emphatically reveals the life beneath it and Western symphonies merely communicate idealistic messages. There is no music as pedantic as symphonic music. One proof is that so-called "interpretation" is possible. No one has ever heard of an "interpretation" of traditional Korean music, and the concept is probably meaningless. The tradition of our music is sound without sound. Sound to reach the stage of no sound. The tradition of our art embodies not an aesthetics rooted in *logos* but an aesthetics rooted in Zen. This tradition thoroughly distrusts *logos* and analysis. Therefore, it is like water blended with water, wine blended with wine. Tokko Chun took out a sheet of paper and began to write.

> We are natives. Western history always dances in 3/4 time. The time I felt loneliest was when I learned of the conversions of Choi Nam-sŏn and Oh Kyŏng-ung. A seesaw with Christ on one end, Archimedes on the other—an amazing acrobatic display. Two Leviathans provided to mankind by the West—
>
> U.S.A. and U.S.S.R. We haven't even lived. Hegel, the great master of the waltz.
>
> Icarus and Bodhidharma. Come on down and wake up. The cure for history is history. It is said: There must be a hill to rub against—a true saying, indeed. Christianity as the "hill" of Western people. Shall we then find our hill in Sŏkkul-am or Paekma River. . . of that I'm not sure, that is, in other words, therefore. You shouldn't suppose that the survival of Korea depends on how Korean farmers survive, it lies rather in the survival of Korea itself. Is our hill then an actually existing place? It is where it is not (it is a fraud—no, it is not—yes, it is—and so on). If we accept Christianity as our hill, then we'll have another Liberation day, another August 15, but that would be all right. Not all engagement is better than all disengagement, in other words, not all female dogs are weaker than all male dogs, in other words, all female dogs are all male dogs, my god, let's stop. The bastards with good manners are snobs and the bastards with bad manners are sons of bitches. My

> love for Japan is boundless because they have humiliated us. The greatest tragedy in modern history may be that the Chinese were defeated by the Japanese in the Sino-Japanese War. Some Westerners assert that "the development of British capitalism did not stem from the occupation of India". The only reason the British stayed in India was to be able to say, "We would sooner lose India than Shakespeare". Anglo-Saxon—Christianity = (cut). (Manchester + Christ)—Christ = Stalin. (Chapter on the humble and simple formulae of political mathemathics). Western humanism did exist but there never existed any humanism in general. Were Prince Nekhludov the king of England, he would have insisted that Britain be a colony of Inida for four hundred years. Roses never bloom in a trash can. But Democracy blooms in the act of rape. And lotuses bloom in the mind, etc., etc.. A rumor circulates among mice that the cats of today are humanitarians. Some mischievious mouse theorized that the cats had proclaimed a moratorium on hunting lest the species of mice be extinguished, however the cats diagnosed this mouse as suffering from the aftereffects of a trauma in infancy, a trauma engendering a most twisted view of things. We are Arizona cowboys (the shameless worldview of backward Koreans).

Tokko Chun stopped writing. He picked up the last potato and popped it in his mouth. He reaches out his hand to open the closet door. The contents of the two shelves within were as many-colored as the wares of a sundries store. They were the possessions he had accumulated one by one over the last seven years of his drifting life. He pulled out a stack of university notebooks bound with rubber bands. They were diaries and notes. He often took them out and reread them. Occasionally, he comes across an anecdote that makes him question whether it actually could have happened. Certain phrases bring a bitter grin to his face. It is a record of a part of his life that is lost forever. He randomly reads this and that section of one notebook. As he picks up the notebook, something like a little card falls out. When he picks it up, he is startled. A membership card for the Workers' Party. It bears a picture of his brother-in-law. For a long time he stares in disbelief at the yellowed photo. The day he boarded the U.N. evacuation ship in W City he had been carrying his sister's bag. In the rush of packing they had mixed his things and his sister's. His brother-in-law's party membership card must have been in that bag. He thought it had been lost long ago, but it had just been buried in this old diary. As he looked at the card lying in the palm of his hand, a strange idea occurred to him. The first time he had discovered it, soon after arriving in the South, he had thought little of it. He merely assumed Sister kept it for the picture. But now, it struck Tokko Chun as a bit odd. Such a communist party card may mean life or death for a man. Why had she decided to bring that, out of all the pictures of him? One more time he gazed at the face in the photo. Though faded, he could see the face of a handsome man about Chun's present age. Bastard. He threw it on the floor. At that instant, a notion suddenly flashed through his mind. He gulped at the outrageousness of the idea. Was it possible? No. His sister was incapable of it. He moved under the covers, getting to his knees, and laid his chin between his hands. The thought that just occurred to him was frightening. But it wouldn't go away. Had Sister intended to take revenge? She must have heard how he made a life with another woman after coming South. That had been why she so often was gloomy, crying as she wasted away. Back then, the 38th Parallel had been a pervious borderline. People in the South heard news of relatives in the North and vice-versa. Chun remembered once reading a borrowed book entitled *A Demon of a Man.* It was published in Seoul after Liberation. Perhaps the father or brother of his friend had been visiting the South as smugglers. That was how it had been then. He must have been the only one in the family in the dark about what his brother-in-law had done. . . . Chun buried his face in the quilt and shut his eyes. He recalled the image of a woman, wandering on the waves of a screaming crowd, in her bag the party membership card of her treacherous lover, aiming to board a ship that would carry her to where the man was. She embarks by ship. After an exhausting journey she reaches the South. She meets her old lover. The faithless man is cold to her. She pleads. The man is increasingly irritated. She stares up at him. Instead of the man who once was her reason for living, her dream, she now sees a stranger so hateful she wants to kill him. A bright smile appears on her face. From her handbag she takes the party membership card and waves it before his eyes, from a good distance, of course, lest he snatch it away. The horrified face of the man at that moment. . . . Chun emitted a slight moan. He grasped his head with both hands. It is fiction. Fiction. It cannot be so. Not that kind-hearted sister of mine. No, kindness and love have no connection. Kind though Sister is, she is no fool.

He laid back down, his head on the pillow. His heart pounded violently. After a long while, he picked up the party card once more.

That party card with its tiny photography stimulated in him a complex train of thought. Back in the North, he had once seen a Soviet film called "Party Membership Card". A man and a woman in love. Childhood friends brought up in the same village. The man is an ardent young Komsomols member. In due time, he'll become a Communist party member and will marry his beautiful young love. Then, another man appears, a scion of a ruined bourgeois family, and a member of an anti-Soviet secret society. He approaches the woman, intending to use her to accomplish his mission. She is more and more charmed by this handsome saboteur, entranced by his rakish temperament. In the end, the woman falls into the clutches of the infiltrator. With the help of the woman's father, an important Communist party member, he rapidly ascends in the party. They are soon married. The infiltrator obtains the post of superintendent at a very important factory. One day, by sabotaging the power supply, he sets the factory afire. Fortunately, the fire is soon extinguished. As the investigation of its cause gets underway, the spy decides to flee. To escape, his party membership card is indispensable. The card is kept in a safe and his wife has the key. Only then does he reveal his true identity to his wife and plead for her to run away with him. In response to the saboteur's words, she pretends to retrieve the key from a drawer but instead pulls out a revolver and aims it at her husband. "Don't move!" With her free hand, she picks up the phone to summon the police. Pale as a sheet, the husband kneels down to plead for his life. I've loved you. That's the truth. How can you be so cruel when you recall our love? But the woman is unmoved. Now that I see you're an enemy of the party, you are no love or husband of mine any longer. Cornered, the spy rushes at her. Just then, the door is kicked in and a group of men rushes in. Agents from the NKVD. In the lead stands her old lover. The saboteur is arrested and the woman is returned at long last to the bosom of her childhood beau. That was the plot of the movie, more or less. To turn against a lover upon discovering their love was false is common enough, and in such cases the natural result is assumed to be sorrow and pain. In the film, however, there was no trace whatever of such sentimentalism. No sooner did the woman learn the man's identity than she had a revolver in her hand. Such was her reaction even though nothing in the movie proved that his love was false, only that he was a counterrevolutionary agent. It was like those old movies about Korean mothers who unflinchingly sent their sons to fight for the Japanese.

At that moment, Tokko Chun was swept up in recollections of those movies. If indeed Sister had made up her mind to execute that plan, she was much more human, was she not, than those automata, those mothers who smiled as they sent their sons off to die, or than the wife who picked up a revolver merely because her husband's political opinion differed from that of the government? The shock of guilt that first came over him was gradually dissipating and he was inclining more and more toward that thought. Sister probably wanted to come to the South. She really must have wanted to come. She had a purpose. She must have wanted to come here for a showdown, her whole heart invested in the plan, eager to face the victory or defeat of her life. Perhaps she didn't expect to win. Maybe she just wanted to encounter her fate face-to-face, with her own eyes. She probably never counted upon the card alone to decide things. It was no means to recover her love, nor would her pride have allowed that. Just to throw the card in his face, maybe that was all she wanted to do. But to do so, would that not have been to yield to evil? How often has evil prospered simply because people loathe shit? Shouldn't we dig holes to bury the shit? An eye for an eye, a tooth for a tooth, does this saying apply to human affection, too? When and where and how the holder of this card planned to use it is something that will never be known. The thoughts erupting in my head are not Sister's but my own. Once more he was astonished. If so, this card is mine. The decision whether to cast it straight or sideways is my decision. Chun stared into the eyes of the man in the photograph. It is in my hands. This card is still valid. What Sister would think of it does not matter. Again Chun moaned. The hand holding the card trembled. In view of Brother-in-law's present social position, this old piece of paper is as deadly as a poisoned arrow. If I wanted to, I could plant this arrow in him. Not necessarily in his heart. Wherever it touched would rot. Chun bit down hard on his lower lip. Any spot touched by this will rot. Brother-in-law will have to cut out that spot. For what? Why should I want to do it? To devour the piece of flesh he cuts out? He saw before his eyes the white, double-chinned face of his brother-in-law as he was a few years before. He had looked peaceful and content. That cold and gloomy expression he remembered from his childhood was gone. Does he suppose he has lived his life through? He thinks he is a success. Maybe he feels secure now, thinking he has finished wandering and has at last hit upon the path of good fortune. To open an unexpected pitfall in front of such a man. Chun felt no keen sympathy for those who had come South as refugees and remarried, once returning home seemed hopeless. That Sister and Brother-in-law were never formally married seemed of no consequence. Didn't they love one another? Besides, he lacked the excuse that he took another woman only after being exhausted by waiting. He hooked up with another woman immediately after coming South. The news before long filtered back home and that was why Sister had fallen ill. She wasted away, her youth forfeited. He recalled how her back quaked in his room that summer evening as she quietly wept. She so loved that bastard, that heartlessly inconstant bastard. Sister's generation still honestly believed in pure love.

He longed to see Sister again and his heart burned with hatred for that faithless bastard. Unconsiously, he was striving to incite himself to revenge and to justify the plan germinating in his mind. Chun thought of Raskolnikov, a character in the Russian novel *Crime and Punishment.* A pauper of a Russian student who murdered an old woman. In his eyes, the old hag didn't deserve to live. She was an old money-grubber, worth less to the world than a single flower. To rob money from such a monster is the right thing to do. If a youth like himself with good prospects (apart from poverty) could thus be freed from threats to his life, then the world would be better off. So he reasoned and murdered the old woman. Chun put a cigarette in his mouth and lit it. He took a deep drag. He was wound up. He exhaled the smoke. A drama was suddenly emerging from the monotonous routine of his existence. That's right. A drama. It wouldn't do to create a drama without any sins at all. I will do it. My case is less blunt than Raskolnikov's. I have sufficient provocation. I will threaten him and make him pay my tuition until I graduate. Were he a man, he would have done that anyway. Chun was the brother of the woman he once loved, after all. A man with a warm heart would never have refused to help Chun and his father, but he didn't even glance their way. He didn't come to Father's funeral. All those sorrows sunken in his memory floated to the surface in succession, stirring growing waves. Bloated with hatred he longed to ruin the man.

It is because such bastards live and command respect that society is in its present state. When such people are left alone there is no drama. A man who cheated a fellow man. A bastard who steps on those who trust him most is not human. Unlike Kim Hahk, I don't have a soul lofty enough to get inspired for the sake of the nation or the race. My nerves electrify when I see the person closest to me injured. And if everybody acted the same way, wouldn't justice surely be carried out? I'm not saying I'll kill him. What I'll do is threaten him, make him tremble with anxiety, and teach him that a life can be destroyed by a single rose thorn or shattered by a piece of paper smaller than a palm. Then I will take his money, because money is the most precious thing to a person who has lost his dreams. For him, the loss of money will bring pain. A man whose heart is as hard as a stone can be forced to weep only by taking away his money. Not just money for tuition but much more. It wouldn't be a bad idea to choose several serious students and provide them with tuition money. First, he would help Yŏng-suk, his landlord's daughter, who is in tears whenever her tuition comes due.

Chun grew so agitated as he hatched this grand plot that he felt dizzy. If the plot goes awry and some trouble develops, it will only affect me. Because I am all alone here. He pressed down the wart on his left foot. Remembering his aloneness made him feel strange. I am alone. Without a family I am free. God is dead. Therefore, man is free. So concluded the leading thinkers of the West. From their standpoints, what they urged was correct. For us, however, it is like this: I have no family, therefore I am free. This is our modern proclamation. Our God never lived in the Old or New Testaments but in our genealogy. Our idol is not a man who took sin upon himself and was crucified, but a genealogy in which one's very name expresses lineal and collateral relations in the clan. Thus, our God has been ancestry and family. That's why, whenever we are told about the stranger from Nazareth, we feel an inexplicable awkwardness, as if dealing with someone from a different clan. When they claim God is dead, that means only that God is dead for Westerners. The West is not the world, only a part of it. When Jesus was hung on the cross, the feeble-minded Governor washed his hands in an attempt to deny his complicity, but we never stood in his shoes. We were never present at the scene. Render unto Caesar that which is Caesar's—a moral atrocity committed by Westerners is their burden to bear alone. The meaning of "Israel" they expansively interpret, coming up with a new concept of "spiritual Israel". The move is from a species concept of Israel as a tribe or family linked by blood, to a genus concept of Israel as a spiritual collectivity, a group linked by soul. What an unseemly and fraudulent logic! We in the Orient have been deluded into seeing an historical synchronicity in the aesthetic universality of Christian symbols and allegories. A pathetic spiritual rape. Just as British capitalism alleviated its internal social contradictions, overcame crises and regained its vitality through well-managed colonialism, Christianity, encountering a cul-de-sac in the West, has alleviated its crises through so-called missionary work. Instead of directly facing their problems, they temporized by expanding their spatial domains. Because of this "double structure of symbols" saturating our society, problems keep circulating and suffering is canalised as melodrama, never attaining expression as tragedy. The language of the West has conquered us. When we accepted the language of an alien bloodline (thinking lightly of it as merely a language), we had in fact unwittingly accepted the history behind that language as well. Christ does not make us tremble. He is a stranger, totally unrelated to me. Therefore, between He and I there is no drama. We are characters in different scenarios. The meeting place for Orientals and Westerners should be a place where both sides humbly give up their lineages. The people who dispense independence and yet bind the liberated within commonwealths, what political geniuses they are. There is a saying that "only the dead lack recourse against wrongs", and, similarly, nobody ever breathed a word of contrition about the evils done by the West. It has become a taboo for us in the present situation. To demand repentance from them means confrontation of East and West. In this condition what freedom, what independence and what hope could there be? The West is Janus. It has two faces. Capitalism. Communism. There is no place for us. We are not main characters, merely extras. For us, there is no good or evil. Yet, for we Koreans, family comes first. A family is the only thing that we can truly love. A man with a family cannot behave recklessly. He cannot be too adventurous, nor can he gamble. But I, Tokko Chun, have no family. Therefore, I am nothing. I myself can choose. No, don't I have a family in the North? Mother, Sister and Brother and his family. To think of it was trying. It was true, he had a family. But could he call what he had a "family"? No, he had no family.

> Oh, this life, no returning home
> However much I miss it,
> Over the mountains and beyond the sky
> A thousand *ri* away.

He sniffed as he recalled these lyrics. How is it that Korean poetry never strikes close to one's heart, not even as close as a pop song? It is because poets have borrowed the verbal artifices of dissimulation. It cannot be helped, not in the future, either. Not until we find spiritual independence. Not until we return to the ego's home. For some reason a sequence of disconnected figures floated before his eyes. White neckline. Ample lips. A woman's face, a glance stolen on the way down the steps. Like someone. A woman once seen somewhere. He almost cried out. It's that woman! Explosion. The strange promenade that summer day, wandering the uninhabited streets. Empty houses. The woman who rushed outside just as he plucked a flower. The blast of bombs. Hot air. Hot cheek. Hot flesh. Explosion. In the darkness, people all at once jostling. Sound of screaming. Explosion. Odor of hot flesh. . . . Only then did he understand the source of the shock he felt at the sight of her. A mermaid swimming up to the surface of the deep sea of his memory, merging with another mermaid swimming there. He abruptly rose and walked over to the window. Looking outside, he saw not a single light, only a darkness pressing in at the very window. He went to the other window and peered out. Far away, streetlights were visible. He looked off into the distance beyond those lights. Countless ships were anchored in the harbor. In the night sky overhead a woman's face appeared. The more he gazed at it, the more it reverberated through the sky, like music. When it grew so loud it couldn't get any louder, it shot toward him like a meteor. Intoxicated by this beautiful fantasy, Tokko Chun pressed his forehead to the windowpane. The fresh coldness of the glass soaked into his skin. How could they be so identical? How? He mumbled to himself. The dream that had mysteriously crystallized in his heart like coral in the sea, it had come true. He had no idea what to do. Killing the sound of his steps, he paced back and forth between the two windows. Like an unpredictable tomorrow, the dark window made him uneasy. The city lights, looking like a distant harbor at night, had struck him as an unexpected pleasure and temptation. He heard a rattling sound. Swiftly, he turned toward the door. The noise instantly ceased.

His glance settled on the party card laying at the head of his bed. He grew increasingly confused as he recalled the evening's events. A man is bound to be startled when a clock, abandoned as broken, suddenly resumes its regular tick-tock. The clock inside Tokko Chun, long silenced by dust, had stirred, its gears rumbling into motion until it began ticking once more. He picked up the card. A passport to freedom, he quietly said to himself. The handsome, slightly gloomy man in the picture stared back at Chun. A woman who, carrying this picture, tried to board a ship to the land where the man was. The city at the climax of the bombing. A woman who caressed a boy in a dark air raid shelter. A woman with a white neck and ample lips who went house to house telling the story of a stranger who lived long ago in a distant land. The three women are waving to him now. Chun struggled desperately to read the messages sent by each woman's smiling eyes. Once more he turned about and walked to the other window. On the other side of the glass was dense darkness, nothing more. In the glass he saw his own face. Surprisingly enough, that face wore a bright expression. The three women gave new life to his inspiration, like three muses.

He didn't hurry his thoughts. Like an animal toying with its prey, he decided to cook the freedom before him very slowly. In his mind, he knew. Though it was not yet clear enough to be articulated in words, sooner or later he would construct the logic. He felt self-assured because in his hand he held a reliable miracle from which something more than language would resound.

Without any effort of thought, the figure of the woman came before his eyes. Even the bible tucked under her arm and the white hand gripping it. And even her gait as she moved toward the front door. He no longer felt ashamed about the desire that enveloped him like a hot flame at the first sight of the woman. He had a reason. The woman that summer day had been a grown-up with mature desire and he had been only a young boy. Now he himself was grown. But the woman stayed the same age. She had been waiting for him. He ran against the grain of time and returned to that summer.

In that summer much took place. His soul was pure and the world was a place worth living in. The black birds were bombing the city into oblivion. The city, incredibly, had prepared a place for Chun. To confront his evil nemesis, the Boys Corps supervisor, he had gone out into the shower of bombs in the streets. There was courage in that summer. And that courage was rewarded. Those flowers drinking plenty of sunlight in the quiet garden of an empty house. Until now, it had remained as something long ago. But then. . . .

The poor self-supporting student who returned to his boarding house submerged in worries about how to pay his spring tuition, he is now lost in endless reveries and excitement, and the depth of the night has been forgotten.

There is freedom for the poor.

VI

Be it even a place where an old father,
Too feeble to shake his drowsiness,
Props up his straw pillow. . . .

Hahk arrived home to discover that his father had returned from the edge of death, where he had been wandering until the day before.

"You needn't. . . have come. . . ."

The old man with sunken eyes smiled as he looked up at Hahk, who had sat down by the head of the bed.

"In order to die, I've got to want to die."

Though he was looking into the wasted face of his father, Hahk felt a bit relieved. His once ruddy complexion was as white as a sheet and his lips were too parched to belong to any human, yet in those words, "I've got to want to die", his father's unyielding spirit showed through and Hahk somehow knew he wouldn't die. He left the sickroom, and once he was alone with his older brother, he asked,

"When did you get here?"

"Yesterday."

His brother asked Hahk to sit down and then lay down flat on the floor. Looking at the Navy ensign's uniform hanging on the wall, Hahk asked,

"So you were able to come like this?"

"Um, hum. Because I was on base duty. Surprised, weren't you?"

"When? When I got the telegram? Nothing in the telegram to be surprised at. I couldn't even guess why it came."

"Soon the vacation will start, so it'll be all right."

"That's right."

His brother explained that Father had fallen ill about a fortnight before. When it worsened, the family thought he surely would die and hurriedly summoned the two of them. Since his arrival Father had slept well and the doctor said he should improve from then on.

"Father is still his old self."

"Why, what did he say?"

"Well, didn't you hear him a while ago?"

"Um, hum."

"Some confidence, isn't it?"

"I should say so."

"He really must have made up his mind that way, eh?"

"That can't be."

The brothers suddenly burst into laughter.

"Hush. We'll be in trouble if Mother hears us. She'll scold us for being disrespectful sons."

"Disrespectful. . . ."

"Well, you've been a filial son from the beginning."

"Watch out, you. . . ."

Though Hahk's brother was five years older than him, they were like close friends, maybe because there were only the two of them.

"How's your service going?"

"So-so. . . ."

"Don't you work on board ship?"

"Right now, I'm on shore duty."

"Alternate?"

"Yeh."

"Which is preferred?"

"By whom? Me?"

"Yes, you and others, too."

"You mean which do most people prefer—it's hard to say.

When sea duty lasts long enough you miss the shore and when you stay on shore long enough you miss the sea. That's how it is."

"Are you doing it for long?"

"Doing what for long?"

"I mean being in the military."

"It's only been two years since I was commissioned and that's something. I won't decide until my hitch is up."

"Sometimes I have a strange notion."

". . . ."

"I can't really see you in the Navy."

His brother laughed a little.

"Don't say such things."

"I'm sorry."

Hahk really did feel sorry. He lay down alongside his brother. The room was the one they had shared as boys. Back then, two short-legged desks stood on either side of the door but now they were gone. Brother used to read a lot of literature. There were moments when his brother had looked at him with a grave expression and at those times Hahk had felt separated from his brother's world, entirely alone. But even at those moments when his own brother seemed a stranger, he never lost his respect for him as a special person. He thought that one day his brother would become a great writer. On many occasions he had hinted at such an ambition. Often his brother, whose reading tastes were entirely different, gave Hahk lengthy sermons on the meaning of life, women and love. Even though these talks were hard to follow because filled with big words, the melancholy heat of his glances and his flowing eloquence easily overwhelmed Hahk. That this brother had volunteered for the Naval Academy had surprised him, and when he was commissioned as an ensign at graduation it made Hahk feel even more strange. One never knows what others think inside. Even between brothers that is so. That was how Hahk felt.

Although he was startled, now that his father's illness had

passed the crisis, the joy of seeing his brother and the peace of mind of being back home were precious to Hahk.

He looked at the chest of his brother lying beside him. It was deep and broad. Hahk turned over and said,

"Brother, let's have at it once."

He held out his right hand, proposing an arm-wrestling match. At first his brother just laughed, but at last he sat up and grasped Hahk's hand. Then, very cleanly, he drove Hahk's fist straight to the floor.

"Darn. One more time."

They tried several times more, but the result was the same.

"Strong, aren't you?"

His brother just smiled.

"After all you've done this. . . ."

Hahk made a gesture of rowing.

"Brother."

". . . ."

"Why did you go to the Naval Academy?"

Brother hesitated a moment, then said listlessly as he lay back down,

"To win at arm-wrestling. . . ."

Hahk felt dizzy. Then I'm a stupid bastard.

His brother was closing his eyes. Hahk got pillows, one for his brother and one for himself. They welcomed sleep.

The next day was fine late autumn weather.

When they checked on Father in the morning he looked even better than the day before. Upon seeing Brother, Father said,

"You stay one more day and then head back. No point. . . ."

He was glaring at Mother.

All the relatives who had assembled just in case were now gone and suddenly the house seemed empty.

Brother said to Hahk,

"Shall we go to Pulkuk-sa Temple today?"

The suggestion caught Hahk off balance and he was at a loss

to answer right away.

"It's been a year for me."

"All right, it's a nice day. . . ."

They left the house, saying they would be back by noon.

On the bus from town to the temple they didn't say anything.

Brother was intently looking out the window at passing scenery, like a tourist visiting Kyŏngju for the first time. They decided to get off the bus at the gate on the main road and walk up to Pulkuk-sa Temple. The weather was ideal for hiking up a mountain path. The wind flailing their faces, heated from the strenuous walk, was indescribably cool. The autumn leaves had not yet lost their color. The traffic on the path was not too heavy.

Blue sky and a sea of trees billowing below.

"How is Seoul?"

"Well, so-so. . . ."

After a long while, Brother abruptly said,

"Don't you worry about the tuition for next semester. I heard from Mother."

"Mother. . . ."

"Seems rather preoccupied. I'll pay."

Hahk paused and then answered,

"From now on I'll work as a tutor, I think."

"Really? Can you find a position so easily?"

"No, it's difficult. If it doesn't work out, I can lay off for a while."

"No, you can't do that. You don't understand. You have to study while you can. I, too. . . . I, too, once thought like that. A student has to study."

"I have no intention to get desperate about it when the situation doesn't allow it."

"That's the wrong attitude about it, I'd say. You say such things, but you harm nobody but yourself."

Their conversation ceased. They had reached Pulkuk-sa Temple. In the sunshine the stone steps looked especially bright. As he touched the rail along the steps, Brother said,

"I wonder why only this part was made of stone?"

"Stone is good."

"Of course."

He went on,

"When I was at sea I sometimes had a sudden urge to see Pulkuk-sa Temple. Not the family, but this temple, I mean."

"Was it some kind of nostalgia for tradition?"

"Well, anyway. . . ."

"You're after all a Korean. Longing for the mountains out at sea. Not like the physiology of Anglo-Saxons who boarded lone ships to loot the seas of the world and bring home the treasures of foreign lands."

"No, there's more to it than that. Even the Anglo-Saxons you mention, in old age they'd probably stick to their home pastures, take in a bit of fox-hunting, reading bibles beside their old wives. And they'd want to sleep at Westminster, if at all possible. They went to sea seeking adventure, battle and hatred, but what they wanted of their homeland was prosperity, peace and love."

"They did as they pleased."

"Indeed they did. Shall I tell you an interesting story?"

"What'd that be?"

"I'll tell you on the way up."

They came back out and headed up the trail to Sŏkkul-am.

"It's a story about a friend of mine. It happened during a port call at Yokohama when we were heading out for blue water training. It so happened that my friend and I pulled watch duty on board, while the rest of the crew went on shore liberty. People with no time at sea can't understand how painful that duty was. After mess, my friend and I talked as we trod around the deck. The harbor lights were glittering right in front of our eyes. When we came to the main gun battery he pulled me into the gunner's station. As I stood there mindlessly, our glances happened to meet. I was taken aback. There was a very peculiar look in his eyes. They were glassed over like the eyes of someone who'd been drinking.

"He may have noticed my questioning glance, for he said, 'Look, Ensign Kim, I'm feeling a temptation, now.' 'Temptation?' 'Um Hum.' 'From whom?' At the time, the image of a glamorous girl popped into my head. He said, 'From whom? You're asking who is tempting me?' Then he burst into laughter. I felt somewhat awkward and curtly said, 'What's so funny?' 'I'm sorry, it's just that what you said sounded so plausible. But the source of this temptation I don't know myself.' I was irritated by my friend's silliness and said, 'Are you an adolescent? Just reached puberty?' 'Ensign Kim, I'll tell you. Before supper, as I passed by here, an outrageous idea suddenly popped into my head. About this gun, I mean.' He was caressing the barrel of the cannon. 'What if I aimed this over there and fired away. . . .' He pointed toward Yokohama with his chin.

"At that moment I felt needle pricks all over my body. In the grip of a compulsion, I just stared at the countless harbor lights, unable to speak. As I stood there dumfounded, his words kept echoing in my ears like a magical murmur. 'How can I say how I felt when this idea occurred to me? Not even my first night with a woman was so intense. Frozen in this gunner's station, I stood here for the longest time, my eyes riveted to the city over there. My own hands frightened me. . . . my hands, quivering to act out the terrifying thought in my imagination. Plenty of ammunition. If my hands went to work only for one minute, that splendid night city would become a garden of carnage. Ah. . . the joy. The reward. Houses demolished, cars buried, and, that's right, people dead. Japs. Ensign Kim. . . .' He tapped me on the shoulder. 'What do you say, shall we do it together?'

"I was already half-drunk. There was a silence. Then he said, 'Scared?' 'No, but. . . .' 'Last time we landed here I saw the affluence of Japan that before I'd only heard about. What a peaceful and carefree country this is. This freedom. The joy overflowing on peoples' faces. They live well and we are bruised. . . . But that's something any Korean first visiting Japan would feel, so why did I, of all people, have this thought, the thought of firing the guns. Who was it who tempted me? Who do you think it was? The one who planted such an idea in my head?'

"That's the end of the story. We didn't fire the cannons at Yokohama, of course. Later, my friend was discharged due to bad health and now lives in the countryside. Since then I've often reflected on the strange excitement I felt upon hearing his outlandish notion."

Brother stopped walking and peered down the slope. Something disappeared swiftly into the brush. A squirrel.

Hahk thought his brother an odd fellow, after all. In the old days he had found him strange, and he still felt anxious, years later, at the inaccessibility of his brother's mind.

"It occurred to me that people's reasons for living are different indeed. Often money and power are thought of as man's primary desires, but those are just the most general forms of desire and there are countless others besides. Some desires are purely personal, others are not. Wanting to be rich or to possess a beautiful woman are personal desires, for the benefit reaches only as far as one person. But when a certain man feels an impulse to bombard a city harbor in a foreign country because that nation inflicted suffering on his own race, such a desire cannot be seen as purely personal. The entirety breathes in his desire. It was that totality who tempted him. In his case, the totality of the Korean people sought to avenge themselves through him. If he had fired upon Yokohama that night, many would have died. Including blameless Japanese. And children. Children who committed no crime. So my friend's act would have been wrong, an atrocity committed by an insane man. That is the difficulty. Once upon a time, one took revenge on the enemies of his parents, the enemies of his clan were his enemies, and a vendetta centuries old could be grounds for taking revenge on the offspring of blood foes. And yet, no one saw any injustice in the practice. Now, however, things have changed. With the passing of only one generation, no one remains to bear responsibility. Tough luck for the ones who'd been wronged. On the other hand, people in today's world are not oblivious to nation and race. Human groups are still the basis for changes in the world, but unlike in the old days, these groups are not organic continua, they have become inorganic entities. Thus, the strange compulsion my friend felt in Yokohama strikes one as a comic reaction in our present age. The epoch when race was a personal deity, a place to rely on, a mother's breast, in other words, the epoch of nationalism, is gone. From the Western standpoint, that is. Now, the race as a totalized person is gone, but it still lives in the mind of the people, and this is our difficulty. It would have been nice if it, too, had been eclipsed. But I've come to believe that as things presently stand to expect that would be unreasonable, and disadvantageous if it occurred. A man who attempts to leap ahead of his own age will bring unhappiness on himself. That I longed to see Pulkuk-sa Temple while at sea was not due to any chauvinistic conceit that it is the world's crowning artistic achievement. It only meant that, of all the places in the world, that particular place happened to be near my home, and what I had come to love was that coincidence. You may call it a love of fate. To be a Korean, that is my fate. You may call it destiny. Though it may be foolish not to change, to blindly obey the edicts of Providence, to be certain of one's point of departure, and if that point is an unhappy place, then compassionately to help the neighbor who shares that same place, that is the only way for us. Of course, as a student of political science, you should be better informed about theories in this field.

"Fundamentally, learning is something presumptively valid for all persons, all places and all times. But then such studies as political science do not necessarily seem to be so. Speaking of political science, what I am saying is that in the West they have a physical body of political history, but in our case it was given overnight like an oracle. In our learning, therefore, there is no harmony between logos and pathos. There is no subjective passion, only mechanical interpretation. I wonder if the attitude of Confucian scholars during the Yi Dynasty was not better? Nowadays people label it with one word, *sadae-juui*, the tributary mentality of 'serving the greater', but I wonder if they ever considered Confucian culture as a Chinese property. Perhaps they believed that the path to truth is a monopoly of no one, it belongs to all under heaven. They were, therefore, cosmopolitans. This phenomenon is no different from the case in which the Europeans long enjoyed the illusions that the Greeks were their ancestors and the Roman church their empire. Only they in the end met with nationalist revolts against the imperialism of Greece and Rome. When the European nations began to ask why Christ should favor Rome, why Rome rather than St. Petersburg, London or Berlin, that was when the promise of vitality and prosperity arose. And thus the age of imperialism lasted until the Second World War. From this process emerged democracy and communism, Western inheritances through and through. However, isn't the reality that the West has retained only the assets of this inheritance while the liabilities have been loaded onto our backs? Before we even had time to be skeptical about Chinese imperialism we were caught in the claws of Western imperialism. That time of skepticism, that historical opportunity, coincided with the Japanese occupation. Because we were under the bondage of others in that period, the chance to cultivate nationalism was lost. In our age, nationalism expresses merely negative nuances in terms of rebellion against Japan and lacks any positive aspect. For there was no nation. We had an other to rebel against but no other to love. That was the difference between Western nationalism and ours. The West had both colonies to tread upon and a motherland to love. We, by contrast, had a motherland to love but no colonies to exploit. So we are imprisoned in our own country. The motherland is divided in two, each part with its teeth locked on the other—a situation worse than this can scarcely be imagined. If you seek to diagnose the cause of this reality, you will discover the blood-stained face of Japanese imperialism, needless to say. I understand why that officer was obsessed by an impulse to bombard Yokohama."

"Should have fired the gun at that moment, right?"

They both burst out laughing. A young couple walking ahead of them looked back. They evidently thought the laughter was aimed at them.

"Those people, it's too bad."

"Why?"

"We must have spoiled their good mood."

"Well, the happy soon forget."

"Anything happy in your life?"

"No."

"Why not? No opportunities? In a place like Seoul there must be plenty, no?"

"Plenty of what? You mean chances?"

"Yeh."

"Not true. There are plenty of girls, but that doesn't necessarily mean plenty of opportunities. In this respect, too, the modern city is something of a monstrosity. The vast size and number of people often leads to a peculiar illusion. An illusion that you yourself have some connection with the crowds around you. But in fact, it is not at all like that. In my case, most of my life seems to be spent going back and forth between school and the boarding house. Apart from that, my only socializing is seeing a few friends. As it happens, most of my friends are from outside of Seoul, too."

"I see what you mean, now."

"So, it's like the sweets are only pictures."

"Then at least they strike you as sweets, eh?"

"Well, naturally. . . ."

Hahk grinned and went on,

"Maybe because I'm a country bumpkin, I lack the nerve. . . . For instance, back home if you meet a girl, you know or can easily find out what her family's like, whether she has sisters, and who her brothers are. So the prospects of success are readily gauged. But in a place like Seoul, even if impressed by a pretty face in a streetcar or bus or movie theater, what can you do about it? You can't just follow her and say, 'Excuse me, won't you please become my friend? I'm not a bad guy.' This just can't be done, so, after all, they are sweets in a picture."

"If everybody were like you, not a single man in the world would fall in love. There must be chances at events where male and female students both gather, no?"

"Somehow I never think of the women students at school in that light."

"You mean they are like sisters to you?"

"I hope not. It's hard to say, though. It's not that they lack mystery for me, maybe it's because there are so few of them in a male environment."

"Is it like how one feels about not picking flowers in a park?"

"Something like that."

"But there are lots of women's colleges, too, aren't there?"

"That's alien territory."

"They're out of reach, you mean?"

"That's right."

"Still, there must be some ways."

"Maybe. But I cannot play the role."

"What do you mean by 'the role'? You are very old-fashioned."

"Well, I don't know if I'm old-fashioned, but the mere thought of courtship makes my skin creep."

"A sheer idiot, that's what you are."

"But when Westerners fall in love in some movie or romance story, I don't feel that way. I find that strange."

"What's strange about it? It'll all work itself out naturally."

"Well, when it actually happens to me I don't know how it'll turn out, but right now I have no confidence at all. Love must indeed be something predestined."

"You're sure harping on fate often enough."

"How about you yourself?"

"Well, I have already graduated."

"Don't say that, consider yourself as my teacher. . . ."

"Courage. That's the only way."

"The only brave people in Korea are the hoodlums."

"Try to say that a little louder."

Brother pointed with his chin at the couple walking in front of them.

"It's not that I have any prejudice about it. I'm just not very smooth or resourceful."

"When it comes to love, advice is pointless. As you said, it's probably a matter of fate."

"Got to repair my fate."

"Repair it. . . ."

"Starting with you, brother."

Again they both broke into laughter. The young couple ahead of them had moved out of sight.

Though it was autumn sunlight, they were getting warm as they walked up the path. As children, the same path had often been their playground. Back then, their house was on the western slope of T'oham Mountain. For them, T'oham Mountain was a hill in thier back yard. It was just another mountain with no special meaning attached to it. The royal tombs and shrines scattered around the city were taken for granted. The awe and reverence outside visitors felt for these places had never been etched in their minds. But now, on the way up the path Brother had confessed that while at sea he had longed to return to this mountain. What could it be? Can we find salvation in our place of birth? At any rate, for the first time in a long while Hahk felt open to the world, as if relieved of a burden. They were still some distance from the mountain peak. Ahead, the winding path veered out of sight at each turn, then reappeared higher up, only to disappear once more. The forest was no longer a dense rising cloud as in summer, but a sparse coat of faded green, relived here and there by leaves of brilliant hues, the whole giving the slope an arid sort of beauty. How is it that beauty and filth coexist in this world?

Walking up the trail of crushed rock blended with larger pebbles, his everyday problems seemed far away. Were everything in this world of one nature, either all good or all evil, then no human suffering would exist. In antiquity, when our ancestors led simple and meager lives, the very same natural beauty we witness had a power of enlightenment. Even a hungry man could gaze upon this mountain and find consolation for his empty stomach. Even a man who failed in love could here discover nature's grand plan, and a man defeated in the struggle for power could stand here and contemplate human destiny. Nature was too sublime for human ambition. For those of us who have been taught that man's pride lies in his infinitely ambitious quests, however, T'oham Mountain itself is no longer the T'oham Mountain of old. How can this contradiction be resolved? Two sorts of paths in life. Struggle and resignation are in disharmony in our lives. An age with neither formality nor faith. The kind of psychology that sees everything as backward and out of date when one returns home from the bustling marketplace of the city. This must be surmounted. To overcome it requires more than a few minor changes. A and B are intertwined, B and C are codeterminate, and thus, no matter how desperate the crisis felt by individuals the conditions under which they live never change. In the end, therefore, one merely gnaws at one's own nerves. The world follows its own trajectory. That's why Chun says "love and time". Love and time. The problem is the love. This age, in which a young man who loves his own country fantasizes about bombarding an enemy city. An age in which youths find a visit to a patriot's tomb thrilling. An age in which ballot counting is done with lights off. In such an age, "to love" signifies doing what and by what means? Does it mean thinking about Pulkuk-sa Temple at sea? Loneliness frightened him. In Seoul, when he met with the members of the "Imprisoned Age" circle, it was possible in that atmosphere for him to believe he was living with a sense of certainty. But separated from them this way, he found himself alone, after all. No, he was not alone. He was the son of a father lying in a sickbed, the second son of a country landlord who had seen better times, and the native son of a country town growing more raucous with each passing day. He didn't yet have the courage to turn his back on all this and just occupy the space of Kim Hahk. Even his brother was like that. A man who at that age, himself not yet married, will underwrite his younger brother's tuition, is certainly not a cold-hearted city dweller. Whenever Kim Hahk thought of such things, he envied the situation of Tokko Chun. For him there was nobody in the way. Even if he has hardships, they concern him alone. Would such a man not enjoy a certain sense of liberty? In Hahk's attraction to Chun there was an admixture of envy for his freedom, perhaps. When he thought of Tokko Chun there was no need to consider extraneous things. Unlike when he encountered a woman, there was no question about relatives. Abstract logic learned from books, the subtle joys of being in the company of his circle, and the blood ties physically sensed when at home—among these three regions Kim Hahk's mind wandered. To him, T'oham Mountain, too, was a part of being home. The satisfactions he felt here made him uneasy somehow. It was like the unforeseen pleasure a man might feel in the presence of a woman other than his lover. When they reached Sŏkkulam it was past eleven. There was nobody to be seen in the garden beneath the temple, and only a couple of people were in the souvenir shop.

They wet their throats with spring water and walked up to the shrine. The carved guardians flanking the entrance stood in the same old places. Brother put his palms together and bowed to the image of Tathagata. Hahk did the same.

Even in summer, the interior of the temple grotto was like a refrigerator. The chilled air made one's body tense. Brother, who had walked around behind the granite Buddha, called out. Hahk looked where his brother was pointing with his finger. A chunk of flesh was gone from the back side of the Buddha and the hole had been patched with coarse concrete.

"Was it like this in the old days?"

"I'm not sure."

The patch was most unsightly.

"In the whole world, there's not another national treasure treated like this."

Brother's voice was angry.

"A decent family wouldn't accept such coarse work, even for the kitchen hearth."

"The other side is undamaged, isn't it?"

Said Hahk, as he inspected another Buddha carved in relief on the curved wall of the grotto. Some of the shrine's hollows were empty. The wall was formed in two levels, in the lower part Buddha figures were directly chiseled into the stone, and the upper had a series of hollows in which Buddha images could be displayed. Many of the compartments of the gallery were empty.

"I wonder what happened?"

"Probably gone out for some air."

Hahk laughed. The sound echoed through the grotto. Hahk inspected every relief of Buddha carved into the walls. They differed from the Tathagata in that all were standing figures of a very manlike god. One among the Buddhas had an aged face resembling a mischievous grandfather. None exhibited any arrogance. Simple and benign visages. National and unstrained posture. These icons of Buddha, incorruptible, had stood there for centuries guarding the Tathagata in their midst. They must have been carved by hands from this same village, and the forms bestowed from the workers' hearts must have come from figures of this land. Perhaps the Korean people of that time were as simple and natural as this.

"This one is the most beautiful here."

Hahk walked over to his brother. The figure he was praising was the third from the left as you entered. It was indeed beautiful. How could any man capture such tender beauty in stone? The copious body, lightly clad, seemed alive and breathing.

"Look at that charming instep."

Brother pointed at the Bodhisattva's naked foot perched on its stylobate.

"Nothing is as graceful as the limbs of Buddhist images. And even more so when the figure is female. The feet of Sŏrabŏl maidens. The artisan who carved this had the figure of his lover in mind."

"Do you think so, Brother?"

"Don't you?"

"Probably."

"In the old days we, too, did pretty well."

"Same could be said of every country, back then."

"Right. In the old days everything was fine."

"But now. . . ."

"Gone to hell."

"Still, the beauty of that Buddha remains unchanged, and humans are its offspring. No, there's nothing wrong with comparison itself. Man's life can assume many forms, the sad thing is we choose one and make it our idol."

Hahk said, his eyes upon the blue lips of his brother.

The way down was a lot faster. The fog was all burnt off and the clean contours of the mountain were fully revealed in the autumn sun. The sunlight striking the moist leaves no longer raised any mist. The air had lost its shimmer and the sky seemed boundlessly high. People in sunglasses and alpine hats occasionally passed on their way up the mountain.

"What are your plans after leaving the Navy?"

"I'm still thinking. . . ."

"Still?"

"Can't just make a reckless decision. It's not just anybody's life, it's my own, so I need to think it over carefully."

"You mean it'd be okay to decide rashly if it concerned others?"

"Got a point there, don't you?"

Upon returning home, they first paid a visit to Father's

room. Father was sitting up, about to eat some thin rice gruel.

"Do you feel all right?"

The tremor in Brother's voice showed how glad he was. Father stopped his spoon in mid-air and replied in a surly tone,

"I've decided to feel all right."

Mother winked at them. Brother hung his head and said, in an odd voice,

"I see."

Hahk barely managed to suppress a burst of laughter and followed his brother out of the room. Only when they reached their room did the brothers abandon themselves to hearty laughter. It was a carefree laughter. Mother soon came in and told them more details. She said that after they had left Father announced he was no longer ill, had his room cleaned and asked for his first real breakfast in some time.

The two brothers spent the afternoon calling on relatives. Since returning home, they had stayed close to the house, uncertain how Father's condition would develop.

Some of their relations were poor and some a bit better off. Most were farmers, and with the harvest just in, it was the gayest season of their year. As Hahk strode along a path atop one of the dikes between the rice paddies, the adjacent empty fields clothed only in dense stubble, he felt like he was sinking into a deep, transparent mire. It was not an unpleasant muck. Inside it was immensely peaceful, as still and certain as autumn air. By the time they returned home the pale moon, starting to wane after the 15th of the lunar month, was peeking over a ridge of T'oham Mountain.

They had walked pretty far that day, but neither of them was quick to fall asleep. When they lay down they just tossed and turned in the dark room. Milky moonlight shone through the rice-papered window. The wind sighed as it rushed through the bamboo grove on the hill behind the house. When that sound died a bit, the sound of crickets chirping reemerged.

Hahk remembered his dream in the train on the way home. An extremely unpleasant dream. Why had he dreamt that, of all things? Did it mean that somewhere, in some recess of his heart, there lurked a terrible desire to push a woman from a speeding train? Nervous exhaustion, that's what it was. The content of a dream is never controllable. You can't be responsible for such things. Still, why that of all dreams? Why of all dreams such a horrid dream, with another me standing behind me? I wonder which of the two was my real self? The I who wanted to commit the crime or the I who grinned at it? Such an eerie illusion of consciousness was a picture unbecoming this clear autumn night. It seemed an ugly stain on Nature on this clear autumn night. That his own head was besmirched by this stain distressed Hahk. Is it not possible to be as clear and clean as this night? Had my soul been torn and soiled by the time spent in a distant city? He turned toward his brother, who was lying with his back facing Hahk.

". . . ."

". . . ."

He tried to call to his brother, but his voice would not come out.

Brother told him not to worry about the tuition. Apparently, he had been saving his salary. To take that money to him seemed unjustifiable. Whatever work it might take, he had to support his own studying. That work would not be easy to find was obvious enough.

"Brother."

"Huh?"

Once he called, there was nothing to say.

"What is it, can't you sleep?"

"No."

Brother, his back still turned toward Hahk, said,

"Perhaps the night is too beautiful. It's better not to be too serious."

"About what?"

"About everything. . . . If you struggle too desperately for some goal, you will suffer."

Is that really why I hurt so, Hahk thought to himself.

"I grow more and more unsure of things."
"Do you know the poet Chŏng Chi-yong?"
"Just the name."
Brother cleared his throat and began to recite.

A place where a narrow brook,
Murmuring a tale of yore,
Wends off to the East,
To the reaches of an open field, and
The bespotted bull bellows on
With his lazy golden moos.

—— Not even in dreams could that
Place ever be forgotten now.

As ahes grow cold in the earthen hearth,
Out through the empty fields,
Hear the night wind gallop its steed,
A place where an old father
Too feeble to shake his drowsiness
Props up his straw pillow.

—— Not even in dreams could that
Place ever be forgotten now.

A place where my mind, born of the earth
Longs for the deep blue of heaven,
Pursuing an arrow recklessly shot,
Soaked through and through
In the grass so heavy with dew.

—— Not even in dreams could that
Place ever be forgetten now.

A place where my little sister stood,
Long hair streaming down,
Black as the waves of night

That dance on some mythical sea,
And my wife neither special nor pretty,
Barefoot the whole year round.

In the wake of the reapers, glening,
The scorching sun on their backs.

—— Not even in dreams could that
Place ever be forgotten now.

A place where the night sky teems with stars,
Toward a mystic sandcastle I step,
Humble roof o'er which cries
A frost raven in flight,
'Neath the faint lamplight
We gather and talk in a whisper.

—— Not even in dreams could that
Place ever be forgotten now.

The silence that follows upon things orderly is always unnatural. It is true of words. You speak to fill the void, but the more you speak the larger the void grows. A loud chirping erupted, as though the crickets had been waiting their turn. At that moment, even a chorus of insensient insects was a salvation. Hahk grasped at that salvation.

"Do you love your native place, Brother?"

"No, I've learned that my native place loves me."

"It does?"

"It does."

"Aren't you just toying with words?"

Brother sat up abruptly. Hahk felt tense, as if his heart was being constricted. Like a guilty child clinching his eyes shut beneath the menacing hand of his mother. Brother lay down once more.

"Angry?"

"No. I was just disappointed that you misunderstood me that badly."

"It's not that."

"I make no demands. Perhaps I'm the one who's in the wrong. People are like frogs, never recalling their time as tadpoles. Except. . . . I just wanted to say one must take care to mark well how far 'self' has been killed in one's desire. Our age is not the age of Yu Kwan-sun. This is an age in which the urge to bombard Yokohama appears only in a performance of marionettes. The fever of absorption in the totality meets with no sympathy in our time. Why should that be so? Why? The reasons may be various. I don't know them all myself, so we should cherish all the more what we can know with certainty, that's what I mean."

"There's a guy among my friends who says the same."

"Really?"

"It's cowardly."

"Cowardly? Then, are you saying you are doing something that makes you better than him?"

". . . ."

Nothing. Brother had pricked him at his most vulnerable spot. The difference between Tokko Chun and I at present is merely a difference of opinions. Only a difference of ideas. But what could we do? There is only one thing to be done. Revolution. Revolution is all there is. And it is impossible. For we inhabit a strange time, we are bound for utter ruin, yet our hands are tied so we cannot save ourselves. What is this? This unnatural mire in which not a single lotus blossom will grow.

From Father's room a cough was heard. The intended signal both brothers immediately understood. The affection contained in that weak sound. They shut their mouths and summoned sleep.

A night in their native place, a place where an old father, too feeble to shake his drowsiness, props up his straw pillows. For youths of a certain age, it could be pain that incites rebellion in them.

VII

Let us live out our lives with
our eyes
Never straying from the fields
of barley.

The year 1959 opened with an uproar over the so-called "December 24th Crisis". This incident, in which a contingent of warriors appeared on Christmas eve at the National Assembly and performed a truly wonderous feat, was indisputably a great landmark in the political history of Korea. To assume that all twenty million citizens felt indignation at this episode, or that there was a general atmosphere of panic would, however, be a mistake. Such was not the case.

The solar new year celebrations went ahead in the cities on January first, and the sun did not fail to rise, fresh as usual. People still ardently loved and went to their offices.

Some felt the age was rushing headlong into a cul-de-sac, yet there was no sign of a revolutionary eruption, two suns did not shine in the sky, blood-stained snow did not fall, no strange birds shrieked outside the Presidential residence at night—there appeared not a single one of the omens known by Koreans from long experience as portents of apocalypse. Instead, good auspices of a peaceful reign were colorfully embroidered in the newspapers—butterflies with wing markings like the Korean flag appeared in winter, an old man in Kangwŏn province dug up a mountain ginseng root as tall as a man. It is in history, mysterious and arcane, indeed, that the joys and sufferings of history's denizens lie. There is no need to quote members of the "Imprisoned Age" circle. Oppression alone is never enough to precipitate a great revolution. The hearts of the majority of the people must be filled with a sense that oppression has become unbearable. Unfortunately (or fortunately), however, the time is not yet ripe.

Various people have given excellent interpretations of this. But the heart of the matter is this: on Christmas eve a pack of muscle-bound men appeared and paraded their strength at the place where the representatives (or ostensible representatives) of the people had met to deliberate on matters of national interest. The incident was in truth an evil omen, a supernatural portent like an uncanny bird or snow the color of blood, yet it had no impact on the historical consciousness of our people.

If, for instance, the newspapers reported the discovery of a Herculean footprint on Samgak Mountain, or that Kyeryong Mountain had begun howling like a wolf, such would more likely be viewed as portents of Apocalypse. On these grounds, it is proper to say that we Koreans at our present stage are still a poetic people. A naive people, in other words. The cold hands of businessmen, contracting according to the profit margins they calculate by abacus, we do not recognize. We Koreans, with our touching poetic intuition, find it easier to credit old sayings like "even if the sky falls, there'll be a hole to get out" or "spiders pin no webs over the mouths of the living".

Speaking generally, the "age" has no real meaning for us. We sadly lack the capacity to divine whether a certain age has a special meaning, distinguishing it from all others, and even if we suspect it does we are at a loss to decipher it. Understanding time, in that sense, is like grasping a painting through the laws of perspective and the physics of color, but for us time is like a waterwheel endlessly cycling through the ten signs of the celestial calendar and the twelve signs of the hours. Indeed, are not good or ill luck, happiness or unhappiness like a waterwheel spinning round and round? Spring 1959. There is no sign of a revolution breaking out in this land. Nothing of the sort will come to pass until Kyeryong Mountain weeps.

Heavy snow is falling on an evening in late February.

The snow that day was indeed enchanting. Flakes the size of fists poured down. Though it would be a while before the sun set, the snowy winter afternoon in Seoul was dark and gloomy.

Tokko Chun left his boarding house and boarded a streetcar on the main street. There were few passengers. He took a seat by the window but when he tried to look out he found the view occluded by a layer of frozen snow on the glass. He turned away, crossed his arms and shut his eyes. He was on his way to see Brother-in-law.

The plot that had hatched in his mind a year before, on the night when he happened to discover the party card, had been forgotten for a long while. When he considered it the following morning in the broad daylight, it struck him as the mere reverie of an aspiring writer. It seemed he would never have the courage to carry it out. The greatest barrier was the stench of criminality attached to blackmailing someone. In order to justify the crime, that night he had even improvised a rather original philosophical theory, but it was no use.

He had painted his brother-in-law, whose name was Hyŏn Ho-sŭng, as a mean-spirited villain and tried to construct a logic in which harming him was no crime. But somehow it never sat well with him, deep down inside. He had certainly been agitated that night. Probably his feelings had been free of dissemblance that night. Nonetheless, by the next morning his hatred was ineffectual, virtually destroyed. The ground of its destruction is important. Either it meant Hyŏn Ho-sŭng was not an evil character or that, though he was a villain, Tokko Chun lacked courage. The latter was more likely. He had no intention whatever to return the party card to its owner.

As he ran about dealing with the problem of his tuition, his feelings toward this literary diversion had withered further until he was calmer. But the money was not to be had and time was running out. A few days remained until the tuition was due, but he saw no practical possibility of coming up with it.

It was then that the party card once more began to tempt him. To Hyōn Ho-Sūng the document was undoubtedly a dreadful thing. Among the well-informed, he was known to have made his fortune by means of special favors and privileged loans. He was also reputed to be one of the richer backers of a certain political party. Even so, he had never been implicated in a scandal and had never had his clean record sullied. Rumor had it that he had always been shrewd and meticulous. Were evidence produced revealing that he had been in the Workers Party, the repercussions would be profound. The matter of tuition was a trifle compared to what would happen then.

A mere thirty or forty thousand *hwan* would not do. It was the disproportion that made Chun pause. Nobody is surprised when one plants a gourd and gets another gourd, but if gold, silver and gems pour out of the gourd it makes one uneasy somehow. It was the cruelty of it, like killing a dog with an axe, that made him hesitate. But there was no way to get the money. Chun naturally found himself drifting toward a middle course. At any event, I'll look up Hyŏn Ho-sŭng, say hello to him again for the first time in a long while and ask his help. If he refuses. . . . I'll decide about it at that point. His mind thus made up, he sent a letter to Hyŏn.

Because he had put aside his earlier, more extreme thoughts in favor of a more moderate method he felt relatively calm, but a vague anxiety remained in a corner of his mind. If he refuses, what then? He hadn't made up his mind how to respond to that, and that was why he felt uneasy and seedy.

Chun arrived a few minutes early at the tearoom called "Rockefeller" where the meeting was to be. The interior of the the tearoom was spacious and few patrons were there. In view of Hyŏn's position, Chun had tried to choose a quiet place, and this was the one that came to mind. From the beginning, Chun had ruled out going to his house. So he had named

Rockefeller, a well-known high class tearoom. Looking around the sparsely occupied room, it seemed to him a suitable place to talk in secret.

He sipped hot coffee, undecided about how to begin his story. How often people rack their brains over the trivial is surprising. Chun was thinking about how to address Hyōn. In his head, Hyōn had always been "Brother-in-law". At this thought, Chun suddenly felt lonely. What Brother-in-law? Now, he is simply another man. A man from my hometown who once was my sister's lover. I just won't call him anything. Chun felt relieved that Korean is a language in which the subject can be omitted without awkwardness.

How shall I begin? "Please help me." Should I begin like that, abruptly? No, before that a few words of greeting will be exchanged. I'll wait for the proper moment and begin smoothly. Visualizing how Hyōn would react was like playing chess with an imaginary partner.

It was exactly the agreed hour. Chun automatically turned his eyes to the door. It did not move. As if nailed to the door, his glance did not stray. The door swung open. A woman with a red muffler walked in. After surveying the room, she went to the far side and sat down next to another woman about her age. Chun picked up his cup and finished his coffee. Perhaps he would be late. He lifted the newspaper the waitress had left. Inside accounts of the December 24th Crisis were still plastered everywhere. The death knell of democracy. The despotism of autocracy. The despotism of the majority party. The moribund condition of popular sovereignty. These phrases floated before his eyes. The despotism of the majority party. What a ludicrous phrase it is. Is democracy not majority rule? If something is approved by the majority, it is legal. Was the majority party not brought into being with the people's help? But the very same people now regard the majority party as a group of intolerable villains. This rotation. If you look only at the formal aspects of this rotation then no solution is forthcoming. The constitutive processes of the majority party are fraudulent. The reality that the majority party is made up of evil bastards stems from the fact that voting, the fountainhead of democratic rule, cannot be properly conducted. The guys in "Imprisoned Age" must be extremely upset these days. Even in his letter from Kyŏngju, Hahk went on and on about his fears for the country. The story about bombarding Yokohama wasn't bad. But wrong. Why couldn't they do it? Why could they not carry into action such an explosion of emotion? If they had. . . . No doubt. It surely would have made a big story. The incident would have shaken up the entire world. It would have been a case without precedent. But then. . . .

Fifteen minutes had passed and Hyŏn Ho-sŭng had not shown up. Chun began to feel fidgety. Each time the door opened his glance quickly homed in, but the man he awaited did not appear. Even the soft music began to seem unbearable to him. The newspaper was still in his hand but he was not reading. After all, it was an entirely one-sided appointment. Hyŏn might have had a conflicting engagement, and he never could have dreamt that Chun had in his possession something that could shake his whole life. But, Chun thought to himself, it had been a week since the letter was mailed. He had purposely allowed time for Hyŏn to notify him if he could not make the meeting. But nothing had been heard from Hyŏn. With the approach of the registration deadline, Chun's desperation made him more and more savage. Did Hyŏn Ho-sŭng mean to ignore him? He left a surge of rage in his heart. I'll wait a little longer, anyway. He slouched in his seat and leaned his head back. After an hour had passed, Tokko Chun left Rockefeller, his face pale and his brow furrowed. Hyŏn never showed.

The snow had ceased. Chun walked with a heavy gait through the darkening street, warm lights overhead. Judging from the still soft snow underfoot, it could not have been long since it stopped snowing. He stuck his hands in his pockets and just kept walking, staring at his feet. He didn't come. He didn't come. Even though the letter had implored him to come, still Hyŏn didn't show up. His heart felt indescribably empty. He expected no love from Hyŏn, of course, but that he had refused to meet without even knowing what he wanted to say, that pained Chun. In the whole breadth of the city, there was not a single soul to help him. They had come to the South in search of freedom. Father had already died, exhausted by life, and he himself was an Army veteran, in a time when many found tactful ways to avoid the draft. While at the observation post near the DMZ he had reflected on many things and in the end determined to confront life with optimism, to be a survivor by whatever means. There was no definite logic behind it. Freedom. Democracy. Things of that sort no longer had any power over his soul. Something larger than such things. Something that will outlive them. That was it. Life. The life instinct became for Tokko Chun a revelation. Life is worth living. Even without a home. Even without a father. Even if the motherland is corrupted. He had been taught that a man must live. Those clouds floating across the sky over the DMZ on summer days, they taught him that a man must live. The mysteriously beautiful night sky and the abundant weeds on that mountainside, they had taught him so. Upon returning to school, he had thrown himself desperately into whatever part-time jobs turned up, in order to go on living and studying. But he had no way to get the tuition for the coming semester. Up to that day, he had been rushing about, not even stopping to eat lunch, but nothing was going his way and even seemingly definite offers of positions in the end didn't pan out. There are times in one's life when one has no choice but to seek help from others, are there not? He needed such help now. That was why he sent the letter to Hyŏn Ho-sŭng. Since finding out the kind of man he had become, Chun had broken off contact with him. But when driven into a corner, desperation brings forth unexpected thoughts. That the party card was what brought Hyŏn into his mind made him feel a bit ashamed. The fantastic plot he concocted the night he came across the card had been plaguing him. Thoughts spawned in the depth of night can be bizarre. Whenever the notion popped into his mind he felt self-loathing. To extort another's money through blackmail is not a thought that a clear-minded person entertains. Even if the victim is a villain, blackmail is unforgivable. That his desperate circumstances led his thought to loiter at the threshold of despicable criminality was agonizing for him. At that very moment, the party card lay in the pocket of his jacket. Today he had planned to give it back to Hyŏn, but only after their talk was over. He had intended to put that square devil who had been tempting him into a bottle and return it to the hands of its owner. But Hyŏn had not come. Didn't respond at all. Was he as cold-hearted as that? Don't those who become successful and happy usually retain at least a shred of compassion?

Tokko Chun now felt utterly helpless. I am all alone in this vast city. It wasn't just the tuition, he lacked money even for next week's food and shelter.

Chun walked into a shabby drinking joint, a portable tent set up on the curb. He gulped down three large glasses in succession. When he emerged, he continued his aimless shambling. He didn't even bother to notice what streets he was walking down.

What am I to do? What am I to do? The same simple phrase kept spinning in his head. If I do that. . . . If I do that, then Hyŏn Ho-sŭng will taste pain. Hyŏn Ho-sŭng. Your heartlessness brought you misfortune. Don't blame me. I never intended to kill a dog with an axe. Think of it a result of your selfish soul. Chun abruptly halted. That's right. I'm not bad. The darkness before his eyes all at once lifted.

He was standing at the mouth of an alley opening onto a bright street. He turned and walked toward his place. I'll do it, he shouted inside. I'll do it. Mr. Hyŏn Ho-sŭng, you had no sympathy for me. I will show none to you, either. Between us only a bargain is left. Chun's head became still clearer. His step was now light. That's right. People ought to live like this.

To use everything in one's power is right. Thus you must have attained success, you must have gotten where you are today by coldly eliminating all superfluous emotions. It is your turn now to experience pain. Try the taste of suffering. Tokko Chun's heart was swelling. To get home from the main street he had a long walk up steep alleys. The white snow remained untouched except for a few sets of footprints here and there. As he went, he followed the track before him, one step at a time. Suddenly his eyes fixed upon the shadow of somebody walking in front of him. About ten meters ahead there was another person. As the gap between them closed, the person's back reminded Chun of someone. He felt a slight tremor in his heart. He quickened his pace and as he passed turned around to look at her. It was Kim Sun-im. Chun stopped. She recognized him, too.

Chun spoke.

"Ah, on your way there?"

She nodded with a faint smile.

"Let's go."

They began walking side by side. At another time Tokko Chun would have found the meeting opportune, but today was different. Leaving the footsteps to her, he walked through the unbroken ankle-deep snow without saying a word. He kept thinking he should say something to the woman, but when they reached the house he still had not spoken. Only after they were inside the gate did he say,

"Is God watching men's conduct from above?"

The abrupt question seemed to take her by surprise, but after a pause she answered.

"Of course."

Chun laughed. Then he added,

"Please don't misunderstand me. I was just thinking how nice it'd be if I could believe in such a God, too."

"God is a friend to those who suffer."

She looked Chun straight in the face. Her eyes he found calm and beautiful.

As he started up the steps to his room, Chun said,

"There are times when I, too, would like to hear God's story."

"I'll be happy to help you anytime if there's something I can do."

She entered the landlord's main room and Chun went upstairs. He pulled a chair in front of the stove and sat there rummaging in his pockets. The cigarette pack he took out was empty. He crumpled the empty pack and threw it toward the trashcan across the room. It bounced off the edge and fell on the floor. He cast a blank look at it. He gets up. Walks over and picks it up. Comes back to his seat, winds up, aims carefully and throws. He misses again. He vacantly stares at it. He walks over and picks it up. Comes back and pitches it once more. Again, failure. Picks it up again. After several tenacious attempts, the round wad of paper found its way into the trashcan. Suddenly his hands felt empty. He got up, and went to his desk and rifled through the drawers. He could not find any cigarette butts. Then he undertook a thorough search. Finally, he turned up a butt half the size of his little finger. It was a Pall Mall, though. He lit it and took a long drag. After savoring the butt until he burned his fingertips, his hands again felt empty.

What was empty was in actuality his mind.

He looked about. The room seemed especially shabby and desolate today. His fears about life and the wound from Hyŏn Ho-sŭng merged in his mind and crystallized into a question. What am I to do? What am I to do? His mind kept drilling him with the same question, what would he do?

Three days later, Tokko Chun was again waiting for Hyŏn Ho-sŭng at the same hour and the same place, Rockefeller. Five minutes after the appointed time, Hyŏn appeared. He had gained more weight since Chun saw him a few years before. He sat down in the seat across from Chun, who had stood to greet him with a bow. He took no trouble to conceal a grimace as he sat down.

"How have you been?"

There was no reply. Chun had lost the opening to proceed.

"I'm a busy man."

Hyōn's tone was quite abrasive. Chun slowly scrutinized Hyōn's face, not bad looking with its slight double-chin.

"Of course I realize that."

"What's this all about, then? You could have stated your business in the letter."

"It'd be rather awkward to write it down in a letter. . . ."

"You must be under some misunderstanding. I don't have to take such threats from you."

"Threat?"

"If not a threat, what was it? See here, I have no duty to help you. I mean, if you need pocket money, I could give it to you, but you have no reason to take it for granted. In that respect, your father, too, had some misapprehensions. I could have helped him, but such an attitude was. . . ."

"Stop talking about my father, please!"

Chun ferociously interrupted him.

"I have no intention to implore your compassion or to invoke morality. What I want is to make a deal with you."

Hyōn glared, as if to ask "what nonsense is this?"

"I have in my possession evidence that you belonged to the Workers Party."

Instantly, Hyōn's complexion lost its color.

"I will state it more simply. I have your North Korean party membership card. I'm asking you to purchase it."

Hyōn was unable to conceal his astonishment. Clutching the table with one hand, he leaned forward.

"I'm not certain I understand what you're saying, but. . . . Shall we move to a quieter place?"

The change in his attitude was astounding. Chun did not stir.

"This place is quiet enough. And I have no intention to raise my voice."

Hyŏn Ho-sŭng settled back in his seat and did his best to collect his dignity.

"Could you be more specific?"

"Not much to specify. A while back, while going through the things I brought South with me I chanced upon your party card. I'm now in need of money, so I'd like you to buy it from me. The number is 1134657. You know I'm not lying, don't you?"

"Do you have it with you now?"

"No. Three days ago when I came here I had it with me. But today I left it at home."

"Why?"

"In the first place, because it is a dangerous object. Secondly, I wanted to fix a price after gauging your attitude."

Hyŏn Ho-sŭng slouched in his seat and closed his eyes. He seemed calm but a muscle on his face was twitching. After a long silence he said,

"Let's move to another place. Even if we make a deal like you said, we can't talk calmly about such things in a place like this."

He got up composedly and with his eyes prodded the young man who was sitting there tensely coiled. Outside they caught a taxi and left that bustling street behind. Hyŏn took Chun to a very quiet, high class restaurant. They passed rooms from which voluble laughter was heard and were escorted to the most secluded room. They exchanged not a word until after drinks and food were brought in. When the woman serving them had left, Hyŏn filled Chun's glass. Chun did not object. Hyŏn filled his own glass and only then he opened his mouth.

"Chun. . . ."

A shiver ran up Chun's spine. Hyŏn's tone of voice had completely changed.

"Have a drink."

Chun remained frozen. Silently, Hyŏn downed three or four glasses in a row. Then, in a low voice, he began, "You may not believe what I'm going to say, but your sister is someone I'll never forget."

How could he try such a simplistic ploy? Chun could barely suppress the contempt surging up inside him.

"I found it hard indeed for a man to live. In the old days I, too, used to think a man earns in accordance with his effort. Wait a minute. . . . And I thought I would live to enjoy a fortune, if any would. Of course, others might find my position enviable, but whether a person is happy or unhappy is something others can never tell. My first misfortune was the loss of your sister. You might have a lot to say about it, but it couldn't be helped. I have no intention to make excuses about it. But I've discovered that man is a weak thing. I hope you understand that. At the time I came South, my idea was to bring her immediately. Who would've imagined then that the 38th Parallel would last so long? As I said a while ago, even when your father first came to me, things weren't going too well for me. Besides, I wonder if your father didn't have a stubborn pride. After that, between us there arose a subtle kind of barrier so I couldn't help him even if I'd wanted to. And I, for my part, wanted to steer clear of anything that'd remind me of your sister. That's the truth. It was painful for me to think of her. A man can have only so many truths in his life. And one's truth never alters. You just forget it and go on living. After that, it became possible to live with untruth. It was something I couldn't have imagined in the old days."

Chun sat there without responding. He had decided to regard his talk as if it were the sound of wind orrain, and not to take it seriously at all. Just sitting there was all he was going to do for Hyŏn. The bastard. In the span of less than an hour, you've become a warm-hearted sentimentalist, haven't you?

"I repeat, I'm not saying this to win your heart. I've often thought of you. But I didn't know your whereabouts. And when those moments pass, I forget about you for a long while. In the end, it's true I haven't done anything for you. I didn't quite understand what you said, since you haven't laid it out in detail, but I was sorry to hear it from you. As for me. . . ."

Chun smiled a bit.

"When you said specifics, you meant you haven't seen the thing yet. I'll show it to you, certainly I'm not proposing to make a deal without showing you the goods."

Hyŏn Ho-sŭng put down the glass just before it reached his mouth and bit into his lip. If true, there could be nothing more alarming than this. In his head he was busy searching for some reasonable sounding excuse. He tried very hard to endure the humiliation of having his ankle caught by a child. But it was such a terrifying matter that the humiliation was beside the point.

"So how did it come. . .?"

"It's as I said before. The most important thing is to verify whether I actually have it, no? I'd like to dispose of this matter simply. To listen to old stories is painful for both of us. If you say there was a certain truth, I'm willing to believe it. Truth that assumes no tangible form is indeed hard for another to understand, besides, I don't even want to understand it. I will tell you directly, no story will touch me. Please come to the same tearoom tomorrow."

Hyŏn's temples were twitching. He was staring into the space over Chun's head. Long ago. Old matters all past and gone suddenly returning. It probably is no lie. 1134657. An unmistakable number. When he left for the South, he had entrusted it to the woman, asking her to destroy it if he made it safely over the border. How could it possibly be in the hands of this bastard now?

Hyŏn could not help but boil with deep indignation at this undreamt of catastrophe. But it was not the sort of thing to be resolved by the inclinations of rage. If it is true I'll buy it, there's no alternative. What if the bastard had used it in some other way? The mere thought made him dizzy. It was fortunate it came up this way.

This time again Hyŏn was the first to get up from his seat. They left the place as they had entered, without exchanging a word. Hyŏn seemed very wary about the surroundings.

Chun took his leave from Hyŏn Ho-sŭng at the streetcar track. He wanted to get away from him as soon as possible. The day's work seemed to him to have turned out well enough. One cannot say that reason gives only good counsel to the passions. Sometimes, it takes the standpoint of an observer and pretends to ignore emotions. That was how Tokko Chun's mind presently was working. In the unending darkness looming before him he had found a road. It is the man who finds the road, but once found it often leads him. Whatever kind of road it turned out to be, Chun felt a balance in place of the emptiness in his mind. He had desperately longed for something to fill up that emptiness. If only he had an accomplice. He wished he had the excuse that he was doing it for somebody else's sake. As of now, he was undertaking it for himself. Something different. He thought of Kim Sun-im. Instead of taking the streetcar he decided to just walk. There was no reason to go home quickly with nothing to do there.

Chun paused in front of a newspaper office, where the news had been posted on a wallboard lit by a few tiny lamps. The December 24th Crisis was still the hottest item in the paper. He felt no interest in it whatever. Then he suddenly remembered that Hyŏn Ho-sŭng was among the powers in the ruling party. Hmm. He turned around and resumed walking. The ruling party hoodwinked the people as it held on to power by any and all illicit means. In other words, they were committing crimes on a massive scale each day. The Liberal Party was like a vast network of gangsters. It was just that the scale was so big nobody could catch them. Hyŏn Ho-sŭng belongs to that organization of gangsters. It is certain that he is a man without principles. He forgot his lover as soon as he was out of her sight, and there is no sincerity in his principles or his avowals. A former member of the Workers Party is now an influential member of the ruling Liberal Party and loaded with cash to boot. He is a man who lacked principles from the beginning. He plants himself on the strong side, whichever it may be. But, then, what about a man like me? I feel so uneasy about something like this. Is it due to conscience? Is stealing from a thief also thievery? Then. . . . Chun's thought kept hitting obstacles. Would he feel the same if he had acted out of righteous indignation? Chun smiled bitterly. Can't go on like this. The logic is simple. I'll be an evildoer. What's there to fear in becoming an evildoer if nobody finds out? God? I don't believe in God. Conscience? Are we to have a guilty conscience about the fate of cows or hens when we eat beef or chicken? Does conscience extend to things that are not even worthy of consideration on the part of conscience? If so, for whose sake? If for the sake of conscience itself, the right thing to do would be to announce the truth to the whole world. But in reality, to do that would be hard. It would be several times more troublesome than what he presently had in mind. He couldn't voluntarily choose such an inconvenient course. Besides, Chun hoped that the matter would go so smoothly that he would both evade recriminations of conscience and get the money, too. The matter did not work out that way, however. A conscience that bedevils the enemies of democracy. But that is meaningless, no more than an expression for the sake of expression.

Absorbed in his reveries of becoming an evildoer, Tokko Chun bumped several times into people walking in the opposite direction. He suddenly stopped. Kim Sun-im was standing in front of him. The coincidence of running into her just then made his heart flutter.

"Are you in a hurry?"

"No."

'Going. . . ."

"Yes."

"Then, I'll go that way myself."

Chun reversed direction and walked with her back the way he had come. His heart lightened. He decided to forget the things he had been wrestling with. He asked her what she thought about going somewhere to listen to some music. She nodded. They hadn't walked far when a suitable place appeared. As he went up the stairs side by side with her, Chun thought about making this woman his lover. It was a pleasant fantasy, certainly. He didn't see why it should be impossible.

As was usual in such places, the place was dimly lit and crowded.

"Do you like music?"

"Yes."

He was pleased that she had not spit out a snide reply, like "Is there anyone who hates it?"

"I've seen you often, but this is the first time we've met like this."

She smiled benignly.

"Has it been long since you gained your faith?"

"No, only since about a year ago."

"As I told you earlier, I am very interested myself."

It was a lie. He had not the slightest interest.

"Maybe the word 'interest' is not right."

"No. Everybody begins like that at first."

"Is there a way for a thing like me?"

"Why?"

Chun could not reply.

"Something I've found while evangelizing is that most people say something like that. As if some sort of qualifications are needed to have faith."

"Are you in school?"

"I quit after high school."

"Ah, I see. . . ."

Was she going to church to make up for missing out on school? He wondered. Then he carefully examined her face. He was no longer sure about his first impression of her that night. But then, the face of the woman that day of the bombing long ago was no longer clear in his memory. Since that time he had been in the habit of comparing every woman he saw with the woman on that summer day. For Chun, she was a kind of archtype. Actual women were gauged by their distance from that archtype. In a way, Tokko Chun had lost his psychic virginity on that day in the air raid shelter. The first sexual encounter between men and women is often determinative. The attitude with which sex is first approached, the method and atmosphere of it, predetermines one's attitude toward future sex. That being the case, Chun's first experience suited his temperament. It always vividly brought to mind the distant echo of exploding bombs and the stiflingly hot air. And the coincidental nature of the incident also satisfied him. That it had happened swiftly and passed like a dream satisfied his vanity. That summer day had in his mind become a sanctuary to which he could always return. The goddess image in that sanctuary could not be compared to the many women he had met on the road of his pilgrimage. Everyone has his own deity. Whether a deity is a registered god or not, it is nonetheless a god if it possesses the power to move one's soul with certainty.

Even the woman now sitting before his eyes had cost him a sleepless night due to an illusion that she resembled his archtype. A soft piano piece was quietly flowing. The woman was leaning slightly to one side. She was looking down at her clasped hands resting on her knee. It was a natural and unaffected pose. Chun immersed himself in a daydream. He remembered thinking of her earlier, after taking leave of Hyŏn. When a man commits a misdeed, he wants to have somebody stay at his side. Tokko Chun was now in need of such company. And the right person for that role was now sitting across from him. His mind, after endless wandering, came to rest at the closest place. I'll treat the other matter simply. There's absolutely no other way to get money. The anxiety driving him almost to insanity, without being aware of it he moaned.

"Not feeling well?"

The woman leaned forward and looked closely at Chun's face.

"No, I'm all right."

Chun forced a grin. Witnessing the concern on her white forehead, he suddenly felt desire.

"Will you teach me something about your religious creed?"

Tokko Chun spoke glibly, but the woman took it otherwise.

"Yes, I often visit Yŏng-suk's house, so just let me know when. . . ."

"What is Armageddon?"

He asked even though he knew from listening to Yŏng-suk's mother.

"In the Bible, it is the end of this world—they call it 'the Apocalypse'. The signs portending the Apocalypse are also recorded in the prophesies. So, when Apocalypse the day of doom, comes, there will be a great battle in order to destroy all the evil in this world. The name of that battlefield is said in the Bible to be Armageddon."

As he listened, Chun felt more and more wretched the more sincere she seemed.

"Is that Apocalypse coming now?"

"Yes. Present events exactly match the prophetic signs of the Apocalypse. So we call upon people to repent before the day when Jesus comes to judge. People think this only concerns others, but how could anything be more important than this? It's a question of either eternal life or death. To save even one more person, to lead them to Jesus, that is what we who have awakened must do."

The awakened. The word made Chun drunk. These people say they are awakened. What a beautiful word.

"Please help me to awaken, too."

"I will help you. The Bible tells us to gather our riches in the Kingdom of Heaven. Most of all, we must try our best to be awakened. I'm not an educated person, but I try my best to understand the truth of life."

"The truth of life. . . ."

This woman and Kim Hahk in a way were similar. Both are quick to spew big words out of their mouths, but so naively. Kim Sun-im. Even the name in nice. What would her body be like? Her body is probably beautiful, too. And she might even be a virgin. A rare treasure has appeared in front of me. Chun snuck a quick glance down at her breasts. Her sweater was smoothly swollen. A nice figure. Why should a beautiful girl like this suffer because of Armageddon? Or was it that she had other problems surfacing in this form? At any rate, her body looks great from here. Her neckline, white and round, was just right to awaken desire. Perhaps she hasn't yet really felt womanly desire. Naturally she didn't suspect he was mentally stripping her and looking her over. Far from it—in Tokko Chun she saw a suffering young man. The praises that Yŏng-suk's family sang of him came back to her mind. Looking at the handsome profile of this distressed young man, she wanted to do everything in her power to save his soul.

They sat for a long time without speaking. Only when the curfew approached did they rise from their seats. Slowly they walked down the dimly lit steps. Chun could barely control an urge to put his arm around her waist. What if he took a vast sum from Hyŏn and ran off with this woman to a foreign land? Fantasies were swarming like bacteria through his crazed head. Just then a streetcar pulled up. Pressing at the window of the empty streetcar she bowed to Tokko Chun as he stood in the street.

The streetcar pulled away with blue sparks popping from the line overhead. Chun remained standing there for a long time.

VIII

On a night of wind and snow,
Warm talk shared among friends.
The nation now in ruins,
The old men reside in the countryside.

Toward the end of his vacation, Kim Hahk met the man his brother had talked about. It was the greatest harvest of his visit home. After returning to his Navy duty, his brother had written telling him to see that man without fail. "... you will see that man is a strange being indeed, and that there are truly different men in the world. At any rate, go and see him. And then write to me, I'll introduce you by letter...." His brother described the man, named Hwang, as a sage.

Hwang lived in a small tile-roofed house on the outskirts of the city with a view of T'oham Mountain in the distance. Hahk felt his heart flutter for no apparent reason.

He folded his coat over his arm and opened the door of the room.

A man looked up from where he was sitting on the warm part of the floor, books spread out in his lap. Hahk swiftly looked over Hwang. Average height, slender build, tender and clear eyes. Brother had said he was sixty-one last year but he seemed much younger. Hahk fell in love with the man at first sight. It was a weird habit of his. Like a kind of wager on the face of a person. In his encounters with Tokko

Chun, the impression made by Chun's face had played an important role. Coming out of Chun's mouth, even unsound paradoxes seemed natural. In this world there are perhaps certain individuals who have the right to be corrupt, so Hahk thought. Hwang's case was the exact opposite. A man born destined to be lofty—that's how Hahk felt.

As he talked with Hwang, Hahk felt himself sinking into a deep joy he had never before experienced with anyone else.

". . . about Japan, I do not think in that way. . . ."

Hwang closed his eyes for a while and then continued.

"Generally, people say that the reason why Japan, unlike the other Oriental countries which were invaded by Westerners, retained its independence and also underwent the Meiji Restoration was because Japan was the only oriental country in which there developed a feudal system similar to those in the West, and hence that the foundation for a rapid transformation to Western capitalism was present in the feudal warrior and merchant classes. Or that being an island country afforded defensive advantages. Such are the reasons by which some explain it. But the Philippines and Indonesia are also insular countries and they remained culturally undeveloped and were among the first to be colonized. And no matter how clever the Japanese were or how strong their defenses, if the Great Powers of the West had then been determined to attack them could Japan possibly have repulsed them? As recently as the last Pacific War they surrendered in the face of Western technology, and Japan was incomparably weaker in the last days of the Ito Government. But neither England nor Russia acted. Why didn't they? Again people come up with reasons. At the time the Great Powers were preoccupied with the invasion of China or distracted by their domestic situations—those sorts of explanations. If so, then Japan's preservation of its independence can only be viewed as a coincidence, after all. When certain circumstances, considered in abstraction, entail a clearly inevitable set of consequences, yet things in actuality turn out otherwise, then all we can do is to label it a 'coincidence'. I would rather call it an 'original coincidence'. For instance, Genghis Khan became the greatest conqueror in history, but can we say that it was because the Mongol race was superior? If the man called Genghis Khan had never been born, then perhaps the Mongols would never have had a chance to play a major role in world history. The facts that the Mongol domains bordered China and that they thus could use all of continental China for a supply base may be cited as opportune conditions, but they change nothing. How could such a great and powerful nation have been conquered by barbarians from their border regions? Some may assert that they took advantage of the weakness of the declining Ming Dynasty. How could the nation of Zhang Fei and Gong Ming have grown so weak? To explain that, one would have to marshal all the facts and the narrative would never end. Explanation in terms of cause-and-effect, when all is said, follows a circular logic. I mean, one ends up only saying that something has become such and such because something else became such and such. When something turns out one way even though it might have been otherwise, doesn't that only mean that it turned out so because it turned out so? If we try to explain history in terms of cause-and-effect we come upon fundamental barriers, and these walls I like to call the 'original coincidences' of history. Viewed from this standpoint, the fact that Japan was never conquered gives them no reason to be conceited. It only meant that the Great Powers were all so busy subduing and devouring the elephant called 'China' that they cared little about the nearby Korean rabbit or the skinny Japanese monkey. History is a tragedy, and when one side succeeds that success usually rests on a sacrifice by the other side, even if neither side has committed any crime. This is not meant to belittle Japan, but a humble man should recognize the mystery in the accidents that turn the waterwheel of history, and become still humbler, instead of berating and assailing a neighboring country that throughout its long history has been innocent and good. What we must think about more than this, is the self-torture we've been inflicting on ourselves. That we ruined our nation at the end of the Yi Dynasty is certainly a shame. Nowadays it's fashionable to blame it on racial character, on factional strife or on the exploits of corrupt officials. But look here, where in history have factional strife and corrupt officials been absent? In Japan, too, during the same period there was bloody factional strife and a peasant rebellion. And British history, is it not drenched in the blood of horrible factional wars? Just because the War of the Roses had a beautiful name doesn't mean it wasn't war between factions. The wretched treatment of so-called 'serfs' under Western feudalism was no better than the fate of Korean people under any tyrant. Didn't the French Revolution break out because of such tyranny? But, once more, people will say that the French at least overthrew their tyrant and opened a new chapter in their history. Why, have we not done the same? Was not the Tonghak Rebellion just such a case? Those peasants who warred under the banner 'Man is Heaven' to destroy the tyrant and save the people, if they had been victorious how would Korea's destiny have changed? It probably would not have given rise to a parliament or a separation of powers, but under leaders burning with desire to realize *wangdonakto*, the oriental utopia of political justice, at least it might have been possible for this land to have been startled awake from a long sleep. That would have been nothing else than 'revitalizing reforms'. But the Tonghak leadership was annihilated by royalist forces and the Japanese army. Just as the Jews conspired with the imperial governor to capture and execute the long awaited 'savior'. To put it in our terms, in conspiracy with a foreign army we murdered the long awaited 'hero' who had descended the heavenly road to save the people. How wonderously things unfold, just like in a luckless household. Take the coup d'etat by Kim Ok-kyun and his faction, for instance. Why on earth should it have ended as it did? Unlike nowadays, in that period patriots resorting to such means could easily have altered the fate of the nation. But their rule ended. On the third day. Like a gourd rolling out of reach, the twilight of the Yi Dynasty was a series of heart-rending misfortunes unfolding before our eyes. It wasn't that no one lifted a finger until ruin was upon us, there was the Tonghak Rebellion, the regency of the Taewŏngun and the Kapshin Rebellion by military reformers. Arrows thus were shot close to the target but none struck it squarely. Why? Were shooting skills lacking or was a bad wind blowing? Why was skill lacking? Why did the wind blow? To explain, as before, we would have to give an interminable account of the muscular movements and climatic conditions of history. In the end, they didn't hit the target because they didn't hit the target. And this, again, must be attributed to an 'original coincidence'. Suppose we have a pair of dice here. Suppose these dice are a bit odd, that all six of their sides are alive and moving freely. Even when left to themselves, the dice flip this way or that. And suppose here is the hand of a giant who is playing a certain game. This hand lifts the moving dice and throws them time after time. If we let each side of a dice stand for one of the historical races and the giant's hand represent the laws of history, then which side turns up depends on a coincidence of two things: the random microscopic movements of the dice themselves and the random macroscopic movement of the giant's hand. When you look into the law of cause-and-effect, deep in that abyss you will, surprisingly, find this 'coincidence' smiling there. In Buddhism, this principle is called 'the void'. We cannot say that we need not try because it is nothingness. Both trying and not trying are aspects of karma, and karma is the void. Buddhist philosophy took a step beyond the aporias of cause-and-effect and saw this void. Coincidence, void, destiny, deity—all these mean the same thing, I believe. Thinking this way, I believe we must be humble even in our self-torture. Our race lacks desperate drive, and this is said to reflect an Oriental insensitivity to history, but in that there is both good and bad. With the Westerners wildly wreaking havoc, we have arrived at today in a bewildered and unthinking daze. But now that that historical phase is subsiding, we must learn to take a longer view of history and recognize the virtues both of waiting and of striving. The Korean race is inferior to no other race. Neither is it superior to any other. Listen to the melodies of traditional Korean music. Its style. Sweetness. Peacefulness. This not the music of a backward people full of vengeful spite at being treaded upon. They are songs of incomparably beautiful souls. Music is by no means the only example. Over there on T'oham Mountain, too, there is evidence, isn't there?"

Hwang cast a meaningful look at Hahk. His glance unsettled Hahk.

"I do not mean that Korea is therefore the best. I mean that Korea is not the worst. I mean that superiority and inferiority are not so easily defined. Young people nowadays are too hard on themselves. And too impatient."

"But, Sir, we have no other choice, do we? We are like animals locked in a cage—all sides are blocked. Here is a wall and over there is also a wall. Imprisoned, is that not what our generation is?"

"Why don't you struggle to destroy that prison? You are not the only ones to be imprisoned. It was the same with the generation that preceded you, and their predecessors as well. Where on earth was there ever a generation that wasn't imprisoned? Is that not why the Tonghak Rebellion, the Kapshin uprising, the March 1st Independence Movement and the Kwangju Student Incident took place? These days I'm afraid to read the newspapers. Student gangsters, student hoodlums, what not. . . . One can't expect every student to become a patriot as in the Enlightenment, but students nowadays have certainly gone too far. They search for no ideals and they have no dreams. They might say that this is no age for dreaming. . . but aren't the young the ones who are visionaries when there are no dreams? Instead of blaming the society, why not turn it to your advantage? If you're imprisoned, why not try to break out?"

"Are you advising a revolution, Sir?"

Hwang suddenly burst into loud laughter. Then, in a greatly relaxed tone, he went on.

"That's a very difficult question. In revolution there is something more important than to rebel. Without it, even after the revolution there is no way to consolidate control. What is it? New power. I mean people who can take over politics after the ouster of those formerly in power. Every revolution had such a new vanguard. Cromwell's Puritans, the men of Enlightenment in the French Revolution, the Bolsheviks in the Russian Revolution or the royalists in Japan's Meiji Restoration, these were the vanguards of each revolution. Those revolutions were possible only because the vanguards waited for the proper stage of social development, and they possessed ideologies capable of delegitimating the *ancien regimes* of their periods. In other words, a revolution is a trio, an ensemble of three instruments, an ideology, an elite and the populace. If one of the three is missing, a revolution can hardly succeed. But then what is the new ideology in Korea today? Is the reality before our eyes a product of the evil in the publicly-acknowledged ideology of this society? It is not. Whatever the origin of democracy, it is a great ideological value. Its persuasive power is universal. What is wrong with it, then? It is the political power controlling this democracy which is bad. Whatever words issue from their mouths, to them politics is a matter of personal power. This condition stems from the fact that there is no political tradition either in contemporary Korean parties or in the politicians themselves. They might vaguely feel the tradition of the most primitive struggle, of fighting against foreign enemies, but as you know, the revolutions accomplished in the West were not mere adventure stories about driving away foreign invaders. They were internal fights, wars with themselves. To fight for the independence of the race and to fight for the freedom of the people are two totally different things. After independence, even if a royalist regime is restored, there is no contradiction from the point of view of the race, is there? Not that the Korean patriots were such royalist types, but was not their foremost goal independence? Strictly speaking, then, we can say that not even once in our history have we expressed our opinion about democracy.

If the ruling ideology of a society is not something chosen through an historical resolution (namely, revolution) of that society, then how precarious it must be. The fragility of Korean democracy lies precisely in this. The democratic convictions of those who hold power are exceedingly theoretical. One often hears of Koreans who have long lived abroad yearning for the taste of hot peppers and soybean paste, but the same is not true of Korean democracy at present. Thus, politics for the people ends up being politics for the self. Blood has been shed for the race but never for democracy. You might ask what June 25, 1950 was all about, but wasn't it more like a foreign invasion? In any case, it was a defense, based on the instinct of national self-preservation, against a physical threat from outside Korean sovereign territory, but this is no commemorative oration, hence it cannot be put forward as a holy war for democracy. Revolution is not a battle against others, but a battle between us and ourselves. That's why revolution is beautiful, despite the flow of somber blood. It can be poetry. An easy way to test whether a revolution is authentic or phony is to write a poem about it. If the poem is awkward and hollow, then the revolution was phony. Just as love makes poets of the young, so revolution makes poets of the people. What I'm saying is that love of democracy has never cost Korean politicians any heart-rending suffering. They are like Kisaeng bitches, shameless courtesans who never have known true love. The notion that all that unites men and women is a pocketful of cash is in their marrow. No, they are still worse. Courtesans like Hwang Chin-i or Nongae lived for pure passion, but these people lack even that. Leaving aside the standing of those who came to politics from the Independence Movement with respect to the physiology of democracy, these very same 'nationalist' leaders who made their fortunes and obtained high offices by cooperating with foreign invaders in the country they were supposedly trying to liberate, these men who made the peasants weep are today the backbone of this society. How can we expect them to realize democracy when they've never grasped its meaning. Lastly, with condition as they presently are, for the people to stand watch over politics is simply out of the question. It'd be like asking a woman who's not pregnant to give birth, as the proverb goes. The people cannot deeply care for a democracy they have not themselves won. Moreover, we do not even know how to safeguard democracy. The political parties who speak for 'the people' are rotten, and that sounds nice, 'the people', but there is not much the people can do. This is our reality. The duty toward the noble cause is clear, but the ruling class lacks the will and the people lack the knowledge and the power to realize it in practice. Is there, then, a class in contemporary Korean society capable of replacing the old ruling class? There is not. The timbers of the house are rotten but there is no new lumber. That is why you are the hope of Korea. You are the seedlings. Though you've had no chance to choose democracy through revolution, and no such chance may arise in the future, you at least have been taught as you grew up that democracy is something natural, like air, and this will continue in the future. This is crucial. When your generation is in control, planted throughout the country, that is when Korea will make a great leap. Until then, time is needed. Right now you lack the ability to bring about a revolution, do you not? If you can't, you shouldn't. You must wait until the time is ripe. But will everything work out, if only we wait? When your generation becomes the backbone of society, is there any guarantee that you all will be incorruptible democrats? No. There is a saying that water downstream is clear only if it is clean upstream. Though you've been raised under the forms of democracy and schooled in its values, if your red hearts don't love truth, then all will have been in vain. There's no guarantee the same games won't be repeated, is there? That is the biggest problem. That is truly the biggest problem. A commitment to justice can never stem from calculation of self-interest. A resolution that it is worth dying for, that is what is needed. This is a problem that cannot be solved on the level of politics alone. In this respect also, we envy the West. In their societies, religion is still in good shape. The churches provide hidden foundations for society. It cannot be said that faith in democracy depends on Christianity, yet altruism and egalitarianism are rooted in the Christian spirit of charity and love. Undoubtedly, a conviction that to love man is to please God has been a fundamental tenet for leaders of their societies. We may speak of the evils of Western capitalism, imperialism, mechanized civilization and so on, but Christianity is the reason the West has never crumbled. Had Western civilization abandoned Christianity for rationalism, as was attempted at the time of French Revolution, then it would have been in ruins long ago. Fortunately, Christianity has survived in modern nations. From it, Western politics has received tangible and intangible aid. Ultimately, politics is something finite and incomplete. Whatever forms it may take, politics cannot maintain itself without some connection to the infinite. As a matter of fact, every state that ever appeared in history had behind it a religious edifice, a temple. The Egyptian dynasties and the progeny of the Sun-God. The Greek city-states and the gods of Olympus. The Jewish tribe and their Yahweh. Where there was politics, there was a God. The Arab race and Allah. The Indian dynasties and Brahman. The Chinese dynasties and Heaven. The Japanese dynasties and Amateras Oomikami. The Korean dynasties and Tangun. This multitude of gods, all of them were guardian deities of a nation or a tribe. Politics borrowed its authority from them. Most of these deities are dead.

Among these faiths, Christianity alone has prospered. In democratic societies, religion and politics are segregated, but the separation is merely an appearance. In earlier eras, politics borrowed authority directly from God, but in modern societies with popular sovereignty authority is supposed to stem from the people. But then there arises a dilemma: if power lies in the people, then ochlocracy, blind mob rule, must also be right. To evade this dilemma, a logic is contrived which flatteringly admits that 'the mind of the people is the mind of heaven', but only in order to invoke the authority of heaven directly. Thus, the divine authority that in the old days was said to be directly delegated from God to the state, in modern times is indirectly delegated to the state through individuals or the populace. The delegation now moves not downwards but upwards, and an additional circuit has been added to the process. This is democracy, is it not? In Western society, the church, the symbol of God, is alive and well. But we have no such thing. At the time when this village was most prosperous, we, too, had a faith, Buddhism. We berate the Confucianism of the Yi Dynasty, but the lofty integrity of the greatest scholars of that time was due to Confucianism. Buddhism and Confucianism were the foundation-stones upon which the Shilla, Koryŏ and Yi Dynasties were built. When these religious foundations eroded, the dynasties fell into ruin. When Shilla Buddhism fell into decline, it was taken over and revived by the Koryŏ rulers. And when Koryŏ Buddhism again became corrupted, Confucianism took its place in the Yi period. And when that, again, fell into decadence, Tonghak endeavored to replace it, but was suppressed. The names varied—Buddhism, Confucianism and Tonghak—but whatever the name, it was a label for an infinite personality. For centuries our nation also held aloft the sacred torch, the flame was extinguished only with Tonghak. It was then that the nation went under. And such has been our lamentable condition until today. At present, we are merely thumbing through technical manuals in the trackless and desolate desert of our souls. To reach an oasis in this desert, belief in the promise and love of God is absolutely necessary. The more hopeless our reality is, the truer this becomes. But then, our Gods are wasting their time in tedious tasks like entertaining tourists in Sŏkkul-am or occasionally attending ritual ceremonies honoring our ancestors. It is we who have brought this to pass. Our desert is a terrible spectacle, an expanse of dessicated minds, all that was left when the water of religion dried up. This is a truly frightening thing. Compared to it, other things are trivial. If we closely examine Western history, we discover one peculiarity. When the Roman church lost its political supremacy and throughout Europe the various races were forming nations, political movements exhibited a most intriguing feature. Originally, the people of Imperial Rome had worshiped many gods—before the rise of Christianity, Rome was governed purely on the basis of military force and law. After accepting Christianity, they transmitted their religion to the Germanic, Frankish, Slavic and Tatar tribes. When the Roman Empire was split into East and West, and, still later, even after Roman power was for practical purposes extinct, the Western world was obsessed by a strange complex. What I mean is that they entertained a peculiar illusion that they were still subject of a Roman Empire, as if the Empire still existed. There were two reasons for this, perhaps. First, Roman law had long been enforced alongside tribal customs, and this had created a consciousness that all Europe was one. The other reason, needless to say, was Christianity. When confronted by infidels, they sensed a commonality in their Christian faith. Europe, before racial nations were formed, was an extremely loose confederation, sharing the same Roman law and the same Catholic religion. The population all thought of themselves as subjects of this virtual confederation. That the German Emperor customarily took the title of ruler of the Holy Roman Empire, or that the Russian Tsars for generations claimed to rule the Eastern Roman Empire can be understood from this point of view. Nationalism first came into being with the formation of racial nations. It expressed a particularistic rather than a universal love. The important thing, however, is that this nationalism did not arise through a total divorce from Christianity or from Classical Greece and Rome, but rather through a direct appropriation of what formerly had been received through Rome. The Reformation, too, was in essence a matter of racial equality in religion. The translation of the Bible into the national tongues had this significance. It was not that the Bible had been abandoned. Why shouldn't one translate the Bible into his own language, why shouldn't prayers be uttered not only in Latin but in every language? Such were the protests. It became fashionable to exhume and study the myths and legends of local tradition, but this never reached the stage of restoring the racial religions that predated Christianity. Their memories of the ancient gods, though able to evoke poetic illusions, were too remote and dim to displace the Christianity that had so deeply saturated their being. Think of it. They had taken the flesh and blood of Christ every Sunday for more than a millenium, and the faith smeared into their bodies was no mere metaphor but a tangible truth. In other words, the Reformation signified that Christ who once stayed only in Rome had taken up residence in the capital of each nation. When the Western nationalist movements reached their crescendo, the people of each nation believed God had blessed them alone. To envision the once universal Christ as the guardian deity of the race, and thus to worship the nation favored by God's grace—such was their logic of patriotism. Just as the Jews saw themselves as 'the chosen people', all nations came to see themselves as 'chosen people'. The bad side of it was that these 'chosen people' were exclusionary—though to be 'chosen' was necessarily to exclude all others. From this standpoint, Europe in the modern age is spiritually degenerate and the 'Dark Ages' lies on this side of the medieval era. When the soul has fallen into darkness, you cannot claim there is 'Progress' simply because electrical lights have been devised. The Crusades of the Middle Ages aimed to preserve the Holy Land from the infidel, but after the industrial revolution, when the West crusaded into the Orient with guns, merchandise and Bibles, what did they aim to preserve? Unwarrantable thievery. But this was due not to any fault of the church, but to the fact that the state trod over the church and already wielded a greater power. The church, rather, exercised restraints on the selfishness of the race and on the violence inflicted on others. If there is anything still shared among Western societies, it is Christianity. It's no different with the Soviet Union. Communism is an absolute truth, and those who do not believe in it will perish. Because the Soviet Union is the first to have realized Communism, all other peoples must help the Soviet Union. What is the difference between this and the embarrassing missionary spirit of some fanatical sects of Christianity? In a way, Communism can be termed an 'inverted Christianity'. The confrontation between the Free World and the Communist World, and the confrontation between the Western and Eastern Roman Empires, these are battles between the positive and negative poles of Christianity. The fight, therefore, is not a fight against outsiders, but an internal war, a war between one and oneself, namely, an interminable revolution. Freedom, Communism, these are intrinsically Western propositions, unfinished problems of Western history. When Communism criticizes Western capitalism and denounces religion as an opiate in attacking imperialism, this can be taken as criticism of the hypocrisy and aggression of a Western Christian society that gives lip-service to love even as it commits atrocities against the heathen. I think of Communism as another reformation. Having witnessed the escapades of the West, the so-called democratic nations, in the Orient, for we the victims to denounce Communism, which has criticized imperialism, would be ludicrous. The problem arises with the subsequent steps of Communism. The more fairly we evaluate the ethical motives of the founders of Communism, the more disappointed we become in the subsequent unfolding of the situation. When Communism became linked with the people of the Russian nation, it lost the purity and universality it once had at the outset. Distinguished Westerners once sympathized with Communism. Why? Because they thought they perceived in Communism the true spiritual resurrection of Christianity. But their souls tasted the bitterest of disappointments. Why? Because Russian Communism lacked the resilience to separate Communism as a religion from the Soviet state, and rather adopted the line that Stalin's orders were always right, as if infallible assertions of a Roman Catholic pope. Consequently, today we confront an immensely powerful Slavic Empire that has colonized the neighboring nations in the name of Communism. These people have adopted the methods they themselves criticized, exploiting the consciences and passions of others like imposters. Thus have they erected a modern pan-Slavic empire, always ready to mold 'truth' to suit the interests of the Russian state. That is why we oppose Communism. Moreover, they linked Communism to a Slavic style of despotism, based on a merger of politics and religion. Therefore, their society has become suffocating. Dark. If it must be enforced, it is not truth. And so it has turned into a phenomenon worse than the capitalist social order it criticizes. Capitalistic society, by separating politics and religion, no longer held the state responsible for evil, and so became capable of institutionalizing a continuous criticism of the state. The dominant theme of Western history, you can say, then, is the history of Christianity.

"Ours is merely a walk-on role belatedly written into a script long since finished by the leading characters. From a subjective standpoint, at least, that is how things stand. Japan fought the Westerners in an attempt to construct a great empire. This afforded a chance to introduce a novel theme into a global history that up to then had been uniformly Christian. The historical value of the Japanese Empire depended, then, on how they developed this theme. But their attempt ended in a debacle. In the first place, they limited themselves by their choice of Shintoism, a creed appealing only to the Japanese race, as the religion on which to found their empire. Then they used terror to rule the vanquished domains, and in expanding their territory they employed the worst imperialistic methods just as the Western democrats had before them. How can one rule other races with a deity lacking universality and a politics devoid of justice? They only managed to degrade their Chinese neighbors, their undeniable cultural benefectors, into 'chinks' and Koreans, their friendly neighbors and cultural intermediaries, into 'gooks'. The Western powers may have come to the Orient and inflicted torture and indignities on the natives, but not even once had they done the same to other Europeans. For, except on the plane of politics, they were all fellow Christians. The Japanese had no such universalizing concept to deploy in dealing with other Oriental nations. If only they had propagated Buddhism, their hegemony might have extended from Japan to Korea, China, Southeast Asia and even into India. But they did not. Instead, they ruled this out from the very beginning. For their form of imperialism was one treating other races as mere tools for their use. All they had was the matriarchal goddess of their tribe—Amateras Oomikami. Their long-awaited opportunity elicited only this utterly inept response. Using this tribal religion, inferior to Christianity or Buddhism, as their vehicle, they conducted a vile symphony, beating the 'gooks' as if they were dried fish and kicking the 'chinks' as if they were pigs. And so they met ruin. The Mongols, though culturally backward, at least planted their seed in Europe before they fell, but what legacy did Japan leave on the continent besides broken wooden sandals? In this way, the opportunity to found a great Asiatic empire was not only abortive due to cultural inferiority, but the aftermath of the miscarriage was most traumatic as well. The communization of China and of half of Korea in all probability is due to Japan. Because of this failure, the pervasiveness of Christianity has been enlarged in our present world. That Japan committed violence on such a massive scale can be credited to the matriarchal faith of their tribe. The power of religion is that vast. There is nothing mysterious about it. For religion is a common language capable of welding human groups together. Don't you remember the saying that 'after Liberation, churches were everywhere'? The people are cunning and quick to see. They saw that Christianity rules the world, and so Christian churches proliferated. We should not forget what Christianity has contributed to our society. But the nature of this contribution, that is the problem. To us, since we were not barbarians, Christianity did not mean an education to a spiritual life we until then had never known. For the salvation of our souls, we already had a surpassingly sublime religion. Buddhism. What Christianity meant to us, therefore, was Enlightenment. For us, Christianity and the technological advances of the West had always been superimposed. When we accepted James Watt, the figure of Christ was superimposed on him. The rapid diffusion of Christianity throughout Korea was due to nonreligious factors, and its spread was further faciliated because our spiritual level was already high enough to accept spiritual appeals without resistance. The overwhelming technological superiority of the Machine Civilization left us astonished, feeling our tradition was inferior. Our defeats in technology and politics generated a kind of global skepticism, and this led to a loss of our identity. People therefore converted to the religion of those who invented this great technology. In other words, by becoming a 'Christian', they hoped to join the ranks of the 'Westerners'. As I said before, however, in the present structure of Western society, the church does not directly intervene in politics, and thus becoming a 'Christian' is by no means ever the same as becoming a 'citizen'. For the nation in reality is not the nation of Jehovah but of Caesar. Although we have many churches, what have they actually contributed to the spiritual amelioration of Korean society? Do Korean churches today actually wield the power of purification that Christianity exercises in the nations of the West? It is safe to say that the answer is no. Unending internal combat. Not revolution, but mere factional strife. Even violence. Is this not the spectacle presented by Korean churches today? For such a religion, not indigenous and so recently transplanted here, to so quickly have reached this stage of corruption, this indeed bodes ill for its future. Is it not true that, since the seeds of Christianity were first sown in the fields of the people, no flowers of any worth have bloomed? At this rate, we can scarcely expect that it will transform our wasteland into a fertile plain. Given that Christianity and modern science stem from different branches, and that we now see they can be separately assimilated, it is my opinion that the expansion of Christianity in oriental societies is already reaching a limit. Besides, as time passes in the present age, the established religions increasingly will encounter difficulties, and it cannot be expected that proselytization will grow any easier. Christianity's capacity to maintain its influence in Western society is based on the fact that for two thousand years the love of generations has been invested in the faith, and their descendants continue to receive dividends from that history. Some such investments failed, but others prospered and continue to pay dividends. This is evident in the transformations of theological dogma. Shortfalls in the theology of Augustine could be made up in the theology of Thomas Aquinas. That's why people say it's better to live persistently, holding to one path. Don't they say a family always moving from place to place will never gather any household property? If we Orientals are to achieve anything for ourselves, we must no longer permit the historical problems of the West to be foisted upon us. This is to reject a method of framing problems itself, the method presenting 'either-or' choices. Our own schema, too, is to be presented as a method of framing problems, this is a matter of tradition. Tradition imports not something old, but a structure of spirit passed down from ancient times that lives on in the present. Tradition appears not only in language but in every aspect of culture. Nevertheless, tradition is most distinctive in language, in thought. But that such expressions are lacking need not mean that there is no tradition. Because tradition is a structure of spirit it can readily resort to agencies other than language. Is music not such? For music truly is the purest framing of spirit. It's like an old family, in which family history leaves traces in household objects and in the carriage of the latest generation. It's like an unwritten constitution. It's of a nature such that even without linguistic expression it can be communicated either from mind to mind or in tangible media. Linguistified tradition, in other words, ideology, is essential when tradition is somehow cut off and must be revived. Similarly, when reconstructing a burnt down house, there is nothing more useful than the original blueprints. Even when all external evidence of a tradition has vanished, its embodiment still remains, namely, the race. As long as a single member of the race survives, he himself is evidence of the race. In the first place, there is his memory. If he happens to be a mute, there is still his glance, his movements, his build, his condition of health—all these will clarify the tradition. But this is no more than a metaphor and, in reality, worthless. Suppose we had no knowledge at all of the West, and before us stood a naked Western man and woman. Based solely on their appearances we could conjecture nothing about their culture—their laws, arts, faith or philosophy. To guess would be no more than a dream, at that point. But if they were clothed, educated and were carrying some sort of book, perhaps, things would be much easier. In the case of an animal, we can say that the body and the tradition are one. Animals indeed are incarnations of tradition but the same is not true of man. What is important is that a tradition takes time to grow and without time there is no tradition."

Hwang paused and smiled at Hahk.

Hahk hesitatingly said,

"Then, what you are saying is?"

"What is there, except for Buddhism? It is an immense trunk with two thousand years of roots. It may look weak at present, but it is not. It is a vast reservoir of power that may burst forth at any time if only an outlet is created. If Buddhism were a trivial religion, we could not obstinately insist on it, but since it is an incomparably noble and deep set of truths, is the conclusion not clear? Does a two thousand year investment count for nothing? Where can we find a weightier reason than this? Christianity did not originate in the West but after two thousand years it has become theirs. In the same way, Buddhism is ours. No, us. It is us. In Buddhism there is a term, 'karma'. I love this term. That we have been born Korean, and belong to the same race, that is karma. To be parents and siblings, that, too, is karma. The idea of karma explains human affection very well, such as why we feel closest to those nearest to us. There is no such nuance in Christianity. Because everyone is a child of God, its doctrine has no room for any preference for my parents, my brothers or my race. Therefore, in Christianity there is a perfect mathematical homogeneity of individuals. For Christianity assumes the viewpoint of God. But if you credit the doctrine of karma, no two people in the world are alike. Things are viewed from the perspective of an individual. Could there really be two individuals as identical as molecules of vapor? Brothers and sisters, if not parents, wives and children, neighbors, relatives, men from the same village, co-workers, men of the same race—individuals thus colored by karma, are these not specific truths? According to Buddhism, of course, love for others comes by breaking the chains of karma and merging with the void, in other words, by assuming the standpoint of the Absolute. Even if one attains enlightened comprehension of the void, however, a man's place in reality is the position of a man, not of God. When a man awakens to the truth, it does not mean he transcends humanity, rather he becomes a true human. As Shakyamuni took mortal form in this world to bring the law of Buddhism, so the awakened must remain in the human world in order to love man. In the *sutras* it is written that the bodhisattvas postponed their entry into nirvana in order to work for the salvation of mankind. Even bodhisattvas, you see, are bound by karma. Love is that concrete. In the Buddhist teaching, to love is always and everywhere to love those closest to you, not to love an abstract other. This in no way departs from the ideal of universal brotherhood. For to love all men you must begin by loving the person next to you. In Buddhism, love is concrete and practical in this way. I once read that a Western novelist said he could love mankind but not his vicious neighbor, and at the time I wondered if that did not stem directly from the abstract quality of Christianity. That his next door neighbor happened to be such a vicious person, is that too not karma? The Christian could only say that because he also in a child of God, you cannot avoid your duty. But if a man can only help one other person, is it not ludicrous for him to devote himself to a neighbor when someone in his own home is also in need? Considered abstractly, you might suppose that if you devote yourself to a person, it shouldn't matter whether the object is A or B. But doesn't this raise a danger of treating men not as individuals but as interchangeable objects? When truth lives for us in our native soil, in our neighbors, in our own bodies, what else must we search for? That Buddhism is within our reach, that is karma as well. Moreover, it is a karma entwined with us for two thousand years. To seek to untie the knots of this karma, what could be more natural for us? With a tyranny more dire than the ravages of a tiger now worsening day by day, there is no spiritual light to show people the way. What unspeakably terrible demonic dances await us in the coming darkness? Truly, I am afraid. If karma binds the race as it does the man, how did our race's burden come to be so heavy? There are men who suddenly awaken to the truth one morning at the sound of rain dripping from the eaves, but there are others who never escape the darkness even after wandering the five worlds and being reincarnated in every *kalpa*. In the same way, of the races inhabiting history, some seem always graced, like ships with the wind forever at their back.... The more time passes, the higher and thicker the mountains become, will we ever see a bright world? But my talk grows long."

Hwang abruptly ceased his discourse and calmly leaned against the wall, his eyes closed.

Woof.

Woof.

Woof.

From afar came the distinct sound of a dog barking.

The winter night had deepened.

"But then...."

Hwang, his voice much softer and calmer, added,

"The work of the world does not obey our will. When young, I, too, attempted many things. I wandered far, to Manchuria, to Siberia, to China. There was something wriggling inside me that forced me on. As I now reflect, I think it would have been happiest if I'd died then. And now, like this...."

Hwang rubbed his left knee and cheerlessly smiled.

"My body is now a burden.... My heart soars, but I am incapable of rushing about as I once did. You young people must be suffering, too, yet you have a future, you may see a good world. My sole pleasure now is to jabber with the young, thinking that I still have friends in this world. What I've said you should take in that vein. In an ineffable universe, all a man can do is struggle unceasingly. The world is far too mysterious rashly to judge outcomes. What is to be done? That is for you to decide. In the end, you live your own life. It's up to you. As for me.... I have no regrets about how I've lived. I'm content.... It's been interesting."

You live your own life. It had been interesting. Hahk was deeply immersed in thought, chewing his fingernails.

Woof.

Woof.
Woof.
Hwang extended his hand and tightly grasped Hahk's wrist.

IX

Living, that is nothing
Once a mind is made up,
But to make up a mind
Is no small matter.

It was something he felt every time he traveled to Japan, that the views from high in the sky were quite different from those in Korea. There, the rising and falling green of hills and mountains gives a soft, warm impression. Compared to those earlier scenes, the Korean landscape was like ragged heaps of stone. Despite the forbidding vistas spread below, Hyōn Hosūng felt more relaxed as he returned once more to Korea.

I'm a lucky man. Just because a man desperately tries, things don't necessarily work out. Luck is indispensable. Take the business just wrapped up, for instance. A project every big industrialist in the country was losing sleep over by luck fell into his lap. The support of Mr. P from the party was a determining factor, though. First visit to Japan in six months. A busy country, at any rate. A smile came to his lips as he recalled the entertainment provided the previous night by his hosts. That familiar warm movement coiling around his chest and legs. So hot and breathless, it's hard to believe it was just a job for money. As he recalled how the woman wailed in bed, the muscles around his mouth began to twitch. After the war a certain critic cynically described rehabilitated Japan as "a nation built on whoredom", but this was no news to Hyōn. He had become used to having "fun" whenever he traveled there. What was even better, with each trip his business had grown livelier, too. This time had been the same. That was why he wore a twitching hint of a grin on his face. It's luck, luck. Out of the blue, a face flashed into his mind. Light skin. Striking angular face. Melancholy eyes, seemingly interested in nothing. This impertinent face invading his mind at first left Hyŏn at a loss and then vexed him. The bastard. That little kid who used to run around in the fruit trees, when he popped up with that monstrous thing in his hand I nearly fainted. His position and his business precluded him from flatly telling him past was past and present was present. "Right Under Our Noses—Member of the Workers Party, Communist Party Member, etc., etc." And that would be the end of Hyŏn Ho-sŭng. He couldn't bear even to think of it. However. . . it would have been better if it hadn't happened, but it was lucky it had turned out as it did. Because the bastard is in my hands, now. When he had first coaxed him to come and live in his house, he never expected the offer would be accepted. For him, it had just been a tactic for dealing with the unyielding youth. That was why he had been surprised when Chun took him up on it. Still more surprising was the fact that Chun didn't offer to cough up the card. But by then, Hyŏn was not overly concerned about that. He had been captured and was in the house. As time passed, there would be a way, he thought. As it happened, that too worked out well enough. So mused Hyŏn Ho-sŭng. Everyone, when face to face with imminent danger, tends as far as possible to downplay the risks. Hyŏn, too, had done so. He was unaware how much he really hated Tokko Chun inside. In fact, he had told himself that perhaps he had gone too far, that in view of the old days he probably should have taken in at least one of them, and maybe Chun was taking revenge for such treatment. In this way he had tried to fit Chun's conduct into a simple psychological scheme. True, Chun's attitude after he came into the house had eased his mind. He had behaved very naturally, exhibiting none of the symptoms Hyōn had feared. Hyōn had been surprised at the youth's inscrutable character, but nonetheless relieved. His own performance had been so convincing his wife had noticed no grounds for concern. The sudden appearance of Chun's image in Hyōn's head, then, though irksome no doubt, elicited neither desperation nor intense hatred. Was it lingering affection from the old days? He sometimes wondered.

"What are you thinking about?"

Only then did he looked back at his sister-in-law.

"Nothing much. . . . How do you feel?"

"Nothing unusual."

"That's hard to believe. . . . How many years has it been?"

"Four years."

"Already. . . ."

On this trip to Japan he had met his sister-in-law in Tokyo as planned. She was on her way home after four years in America. Her clothes and cosmetics were a bit more extravagant and her personality, too, seemed more fastidious. They had scarcely spoken since boarding the plane. He looked at her eyes. The eyeshadow made them appear unusually sunken. You still look down on me, don't you? Just like before. Why don't you remember that the bread you ate for four years in America was bought with my money? At any rate, I'm past the point of quibbling with you. The airplane slowly descended, twisting through the gentle skies of early spring. The cabin began to bustle.

A ship that's dropped anchor is at peace. At sea is where a ship belongs. On an unknown voyage with charts or without. In a storm. Under the scalding sun. At the North Pole in a blizzard. A ship must work, breathing, sweating and struggling. A fight in peril of death with a whale. Transporting cargo to a port in a faraway land. Carrying as well passengers with diverse dreams, ambitions and sorrows. On such a voyage one may drop anchor in a safe harbor, but those are not the only times anchor is dropped. For ships are of many sorts. A warship anchored in a channel, restlessly lying in wait for the enemy with bated breath. A pirate ship ambushing a merchant vessel. A wounded ship crawling home. A cargo carrier awaiting a berth to unload, feet bound. A splendid freighter owned by a bankrupt company. For each of these, dropping anchor means something different.

Opening his eyes after his Sunday nap, a habit not abandoned when he moved to this house, Tokko Chun looked up at the ceiling from where he lay. Unconsciously, he expected the same pattern to be there. The crawling red-backed spiders. A great army of locusts, enough to cover an autumn field. The hindquarters of sheep being driven away. Hindquarters... weren't there, of course. Instead, expensive ceiling tiles, with tiny acoustic holes, spread over the soft, whitish space.

Two months since he moved into the house of Hyŏn Hosŭng. Life in this house had not worked out as he initially thought it would. Living under the same roof, two men with a mutual animosity. A stream of dark emotion. Subtle knots of psychodrama. A strange atmosphere enveloping the whole house. These expectations had filled Chun's imagination, but none became reality. Not a single thing in the life of the house had changed with his appearance. In the first place, Hyŏn himself left Chun no opportunities. And only two people in the house knew why Tokko Chun was there—Hyŏn and Chun. Hence the roles of accomplices they played well. As for Chun, he had come to feel a certain sense of being anchored since arriving there. What sort of place he had chosen for anchorage and how it had happened were irrelevant. A young man with no place in society had all at once acquired a way of living and a "family" requiring constant reaction and confrontation. He felt a sense of security at having tied himself down at fixed coordinates. Simultaneously, Tokko Chun had decided that he would never allow himself to feel any love for the system of coordinates he had joined. To preserve such an ethics of heartlessness, he had concocted a philosophy of the family. The notion that people have freedom because God is dead, for Koreans that is nonsense. That's why the good guys in American cowboy movies seem so awkward to us. From his theory he had derived a modern manifesto: family has disintegrated (or vanished), therefore we are free. Holding fast to this proposition as to a cross, he saw himself at the beginning as directing a drama of congealed heartlessness on this sumptuous stage. After two months in the house, however, his behavior was far from being guided by this philosophy of heartlessness. He had been surprised at first that he was able to live each day without the slightest resistance. Laziness. A laziness for which moral censure is too bothersome even to think about, that made him live as he did. Laziness, the worst vice of all. He had dropped anchor over this tumor growing within him. He felt a certain elation and peace. No more worrying about meals for me. No more worries about tuition. All my time is like Sunday. I have earned time. Time free of tension and time to be endlessly lazy, namely, freedom. My time is spent in reveries in which the conclusion need not be hurried. And I'll write a novel. A great novel. Great? No, it need not be great. I'll just write. Whenever I'm bored. A novel will bring me another freedom. For I am a god while I'm writing a novel. In so doing, I'll become a god. Just a minute, wait. Wouldn't it be a foul god? If it is a god who lives off the bread of vile capitalists. That's all right. Nowadays, it's the only way to become a god. Perhaps there is also Kim Hahk's way to become a god. But that's not for me. I will leave that for the good people to do. . . .

He finished a cigarette and got out of bed. He put on his pants and shirt and went out of the room. He walked straight to the door at the end of the hall and knocked. After the second knock there was an answer. He opened the door. Smell of paint. The protagonist of the room turned her face back to her canvas.

Tokko Chun walked over to a spongy chair in the corner and sat down to watch her paint. The fairly large canvas was painted to look like floes of lava, dark blue and grey with red clotted here and there. Clad in a jumpsuit, the woman went on working as if totally unaware of her guest's presence. It was the brightest room in the house. Canvas wrapped in paper stood against the walls all around. Several canvases had been hung.

After a while the woman, Yi Yu-jõng, put down the brush and turned around.

"I'm sorry."

"No. . . it's all right, please go on."

"I'm through."

She took a seat herself and took a pack of Kents from her pocket, took a cigarette out for herself and offered the pack to Chun. He pulled one out and lit her cigarette.

Yu-jõng savored the smoke, taking care lest her paint-stained fingers touch her lips.

"It won't be long now."

Her exhibition at the gallery would be opening at the end of the month. As she inhaled, she nodded.

"How is America?"

Briefly uncertain about the intent of his question, she looked at him. He pointed with his chin to her painting.

"I mean, is that the latest style over there?"

Only then did she understand.

"No, it's not. Generally speaking, the conventionalist and avant-garde groups are of about equal prominence."

"Not too different from here, then. But is avant-garde the perennial opposition party over there, too?"

"Opposition party?"

"I mean, can they never form the mainstream of the art world?"

"Well, how do you divide mainstream and non-mainstream. . .? Since the fine arts has no core to its movements, the exhibitions are very numerous, and each group has its own distinctive characteristics, it's hard to say anything clearcut."

She paused and then asked,

"Don't you have any intention to go to America?"

"To study Korea literature in America, isn't that a bit much?"

"I beg your pardon?"

"My major is Korean literature."

"Really?"

She winked at him.

"Of course, there's no law that prohibits Korean literature students from studying abroad. Perhaps they might go to study linguistics or comparative literature."

"You're right there."

"No need to feel sorry for me. Besides, I'm not interested in going to America to study just because everybody else does, if that's what you mean."

"Why?"

"If studying abroad means traveling to a developed country to learn their arts and sciences, to learn about their way of life, then study abroad is pointless for a major like mine, and especially unnecessary if it is learning about their lifestyles. For what our whole race is doing these days is no different from studying abroad. What we see, what we hear, how we act, it's all American culture, isn't it? Why spend money to go there when you experience it sitting right here?"

"A nationalist."

"No, that's the problem. I'm not a nationalist."

"Then?"

"I'm nothing."

"You mean you don't even have any attachment to your own field of study?"

"It's not that, either. Korean literature is not a bad field for becoming a nationalist, but somehow it hasn't worked out that way."

"Why?"

"Because I have no confidence."

"Confidence?"

"See here, I've now chosen not *Romeo and Juliet* but *Ch'un-*

hyang-jŏn. But then, will there come a day when *Ch'un-hyang-jŏn* rather than *Romeo and Juliet* is the love story *par excellence* for people all over the world? No, that day is unlikely to come. You may call this infantile, but it is so only for those who are in a position to be free of such infantile things. For those standing on the other side, it is quite a painful thing. For a people like us, who have always been on the losing side politically, we cannot naively separate arts and culture from life and put forward pleasantries such as 'art for art's sake'. Thus, Korean prodigies all studied law in the old days. After Liberation, law was displaced by science and engineering, no? In this respect, as a race we lag behind the age. In any society, artists are a species who choose an empty name, a vocation without substance. But for them to sustain their suffering, they must have spiritual pride. I mean the secret of one's soul, a spiritual joy one wouldn't trade for the whole world. I'm unable to feel that. I find it in the biographies of Western artists, in their insanity. If along the way a masterpiece should emerge, you get spiritual satisfaction as well as reputation and money. And also accepted into high society. Four years in America didn't turn you into an American, so you know very well that the Korean art world is miserable. Lately I've acquired the habit of drawing analogies between art and politics, and I've been asked by some friends of mine to join their party because they think I have political sense. But our condition is hopeless. For instance, take Modernism in Korean literary circles. Irresponsible epigones. Without even being aware of cultural currents, they are slavish mimics. Nonsense they don't understand themselves. They call it 'avant-garde'. Vanguard for what? Resistance against whom? Antitheses without theses. That is the climate of our art. It's the worst of all exotic tastes. Exotic hobbies evoke nostalgia for those lands. A longing to go and see those places and a nostalgia for the land and the people that produced that art. What then becomes of the people who've been to America or France? Instead of reflecting on their identities as Koreans, more people satisfy themselves with citizenship in other countries. The artists who return from overseas come as propagandists of French or American literature, not as artists dedicated to love and serve Korean literature. Isn't that why things are presently as they are? They probably couldn't help themselves. That overwhelming energy. That pressure of a vast tradition. That fine-meshed net of the traditional system. To expect them to withstand all these and remain Korean would be unreasonable. Just as it would be unreasonable to expect today's Korean politics to expel foreign influences and be independent, a beautiful flowerbed of democracy. That's why I keep analogizing art to politics. How could they be so alike? How so identical? How is it that the problems of Korean politics display the same *gestalt* as the problems of Korean culture? They are exactly the same. What business have we with Christ? Yet, haven't we misapprehended Christ as the symbol of our life—through Dostoevski, Tolstoi, Kafka, Bach and through Raphael. We are like athletes playing a game with rules laid down by others. How could it be possible for us to express an authenticity or beauty of our own? We are like comic actors scratching others' legs and leaving our own legs to itch. But do we scratch at all well? The audience bursts into laughter and we grin, feeling awkward. This is why humanism in Korean literature is not heartfelt and why the acting in modern Korean films is too pitiful to watch. We watch and laugh. But once we realize it is a self-portrait, that laughter instantly freezes. The characters portrayed in historical dramas, however, how natural they are. At least they look natural. Because they are dramas acted in accordance with our own rules. I'm not saying that humanism is impossible in Korea, but without indigenous symbols, without the voice of tradition and without trained elocution, the actors are merely dressed up in foreign clothes so it becomes awkward, like a translated play. It is the same if we try to resist. Resistance should mean the transformation of tradition into a weapon, not that we take up new weapons. Otherwise, it would be not antithesis but rupture. Is there any chance for Ch'un-hyang to prevail? Will a future come in which Korean culture ousts Western culture? I doubt it. Sooner or later, Ch'un-hyang will have her hair done in a permanent, be driven around by automobile and, in the end, dance to jazz. At last, even her love for Yi Mong-ryong will in a terrible catastrophe be spoiled by lassitude. This is the general trend. For anyone with the initiative to inquire, the outcome of the game is clear. In such circumstances, there are two attitudes a man can take. One can be an observer, or else a Don Quixote."

"How about you?"

"The former, a mere observer."

"That's awfully cowardly, isn't it?"

Chun laughed.

"If not cowardly, then what? It's a personal thing. Things would be different if I felt sure I'd been called to alter the predominant trend. I don't feel that way. All I've done is pulled myself back from a game that doesn't excite me. To satisfy my pride a little, at least."

"How can anyone pretend to remove himself from his own life? That I can't understand. Today's cultural patterns. . . ."

"I say it's not only culture. . . ."

"Well, what if the pattern of life, including culture, is Western in form, still isn't it foolish stubbornness to surrender your life because of that?"

"If pride is immaterial. . . ."

"What is pride? It's an inferiority complex. Based on my experience in America, I'd say that the culture over there has a healthy tendency to discount such sentiments. If you are capable, being a foreigner is no great handicap. You can make a contract with anyone if the terms are agreeable. It's the same in the arts. There are lots of Europeans in the field of fine arts."

"You're talking about something entirely different. What difference is there when an European comes to America? Didn't America model itself on Europe? So the fact that an European feels at home in America has nothing whatever to do with our situation. I could understand if you'd said that as a business woman, but as an artist? Weren't artists originally shamans giving expression to divine will? When your own gods are dead, isn't it demeaning to worship an alien deity?"

"What do you mean by 'my gods'?"

"I mean our gods, the spirit of the house, the spirit of the hearth, the mountain spirit. . . ."

She laughed out loud.

"Interesting."

"Really? It's all thanks to your homecoming. Nothing like a home where the flowers bloom and birds sing, don't they say?"

"I was really glad to find a friend here when I returned. We'll be good friends."

"If possible. . . ."

"Oh, my. . . ."

She glared at Chun.

"Do you have a hobby?"

Chun thought for a moment and said,

"Well, no. A hobby that requires thought is not a hobby. But, if you insist. . . ."

"What is it?"

"Do you really want to know?"

"Enough. You'll probably say something nasty."

"Right you are."

Chun rose and started out of the room.

"Do you have something to do this evening?" asked Yi Yu-jŏng as Chun headed out the door.

"I always have nothing to do."

She giggled and said,

"I'll buy you dinner."

She turned back to the canvas and Chun closed the door.

Chun walked past his door and down the steps, entering the billiard room. As usual, the room was under the cold dominion of red and white balls. He picked up a cue and hit a white ball to the far corner of the table. The crack of the cue on the ball echoed especially sharply. Banking first this way, then that. . .? This billiard game resembles human behavior. When the target you want to hit is right before your eyes, you must carom here and there before you strike it. When a lion encounters prey in the jungle, he takes the shortest route to accomplish his goal. Man is different. Feigning disinterest, walking on all sides of it, then he sneakily snatches the objective. He pulled the cue ball into the corner and attempted a difficult shot. He missed. Going around the table, he aimed and stroked again. Clack! As she said, now there was a friend he could talk to. And an artist, so much the better. If a woman goes into literature or the like, she either becomes a fool or grows more and more masculine. In the case of women, the more instinctual the artistic medium, the better. For instance, painting, music or dance. He remembered Kim Sun-im. He had not seen her even once since leaving the boarding house. The last time they met. That night. . . . He shook his head to squelch a certain thought. The detours one must take to cross paths with a person. Clack! He half-sat on the billiard table and sent a ball careening away. He had never frequented the billiard parlors on the streets. It wasn't until he had come to this house that he had learned to play. A pleasant feeling it was to daydream as he followed the cold smooth balls rolling over the soft surface. Turning the corners of the table with cue in hand, in fact he was following whatever orb of thought then occupied his mind. That at least helped him to avoid confusuion. He selected one and with it struck another, never allowing the countless other egos to scatter. There is no solution, of course. It's a constant circulation on the same level surface. But there is movement, at least. Movement that fills the emptiness of time. And there is form. Pulled too much. Should have put more spin on it in this direction. At any rate, to be offered salvation is frightening. And next? What would come afterwards? What about the boredom that comes after salvation? My god, it would be better not to be saved. Freedom? Freedom with nothing to do. Time without responsibility. Laziness without being glared at by morality. That's all there is. And it's mine. The hours of reverie enjoyed in the orchard as a boy. The time to be immersed in the illusions of those summer days. The laziness taught by the clouds over the 38th Parallel. Until when? Until then. As long as it lasts. Then, the next chapter. Yi Yu-jŏng. An artist, after all, wouldn't be too boring. A nice character has appeared. On a boring stage. Sooner or later, I'll shoot toward her. "Me". Since she is in motion, too, it may not be simple. In any case, the rate of hitting bulls-eyes is higher in the human game than in billiards. For these orbs gravitate together. They lock teeth on one another and don't let go. Lock teeth on one another? Shouldn't play dirty. Clean and inorganic, like these balls. How is being clean different from being inorganic? What's the difference between a Zen master's excrement and a mechanical automaton? The residue that remains when pathos is extracted from conduct. So then, after all, we are ahead. For we produced that condition a thousand years ago. There's no law saying it can only be expressed in a glittering machine. Truth incarnate, with wrinkled skin and drooping testicles. To live for truth, feeling nothing. Whipped by the wind of the truth. But not fitting the endless "movement" engendered by the Westerners. Beatniks love Zen, I'm told. Bodhidharmas on motorcycles. Zen masters dancing to jazz. Interesting fellows they are. But can't get along with those guys. For that would be indecent. Stubbornness is all right, but not indecency. We do not rebel for victory. For there will be no victory for us. The myth of Sisyphus. When it rolls down, once again you roll it back up. Don't make me laugh. I mean, why not put a block under it? If he'd nailed the stone down that way and laid down beside it to think over the meaning of life, then wouldn't he have awakened to the truth? He would have been able to figure out what to do with the next task. We are like laborers called out to push up a stone the Westerners had rolled down. What's more, we aren't even allowed to lay hands on the stone, we can only push Sisyphus's butt. There are some people who miscomprehend this. And so they rack their brains wondering why the stone feels mushy or why a smell of farts is in the air. A myth based on a misunderstanding. The Westerners may be Sisyphuses, but we are not. We are something like "Sisyphus's ass-pushers". So our sufferings do not find expression in the lofty ordeals of Sisyphus. Rather, we always look bewildered, awkward, embarrassed, uncertain and indecesive. Waiting for an opportunity to take our hands off the ass and run away. This is our self-portrait. It is from a persistent misunderstanding of this that well-intentioned enthusiasm stems. Scratching someone else's legs. Pushing the ass of Sisyphus. Dear fellow countrymen. Dear beloved race. We are not heroes. We are not Sisyphuses. But some girls keep saying we are Sisyphuses. Thus they torture their fellow countrymen even more. Like a student's overambitious parents. Like parents who completely forget their own failures in school. I can't stand those shitasses. So I remain a spectator. Our stone. There is no such thing. It's only a delusion we have. The stone we thought had been assigned to us was in fact just Sisyphus's ass. Of course, that ass is our destiny. (Aha!) When that ass flops down, it'll be the end of us. But the situation doesn't change a bit, whether we put our hands on it or not. Because he didn't accept his fate with us in mind. What's more, if we put our hands the wrong way, he might find it ticklish and kick back. A picture of being kicked while pushing an ass. A picture of a dog glaring up at the fence where a chased chicken came to roost, at least that's comic, but in our case. . . . Then, what is to be done? What is to be done? There is nothing. Nothing. Perhaps professional orators speak of national policies, but in reality there is nothing to be done. Isn't that why present conditions are like this? What, then? Am I saying what, then? To meet ruin. Rapidly to meet ruin. The sooner the better. Thereafter, if there really is a god of the abode, a good will, then he'll grant some kind of miracle. From there it would be Chapter 1, Lesson 1. Pushing up the ass of Sisyphus is shameful for the neighbors, too. Therefore, I choose. Once done, it's over. Because it merely shows that the chooser was not squeamish. The others who don't choose can only observe. The coming of ruin. Without unseemly writhing or struggling, just observe the coming of ruin. That is the highest virtue possible for our generation. That is our melody. Our song is no hymn to victory, but an elegy of fall. There are some dense people who insist on misunderstanding this. There are people, too, who knowingly will dissemble in speech or writing for a pittance. Sisyphus is François Sisyphus or George Sisyphus or Ivan Sisyphus. The symbol of mankind's fate. Don't you lie. As Madame Laurent says: "Humanity, how many crimes have been committed in your name?" So goodbye sincerity. Enough. Did I not already decide to cease these excuses? It makes no difference. I have purchased freedom. This exquisite laziness. With a cool-headed plan and a cold heart I will. . . . This laziness. Pull back like this. . . wait. It's a difficult shot. Once more he sat on the edge of the billiard table and stroked. One, two, three, he shot the ball.

"I see. Well, I haven't seen him since school started."

"Me, neither. I didn't even see him when he moved out."

"So not even the landlord knows where he's moved?"

"So they say."

"How could he. . . ."

He almost said "How could the bastard. . . ." but caught himself. Hahk had gone to Chun's boarding house and was now leaving with Kim Sun-im, whom he had run into there. Chun indeed had vanished like a wind. But who was this woman?

"So, you are. . .?"

Hahk hesitated, searching for the right word.

"I'm a friend of the landlord's family, from their church."

"I see. I think I heard about you before."

Kim Sun-im smiled shyly. She wondered what had been said about her. They were already at the main street. Hahk seemed uncertain whether they should go their separate ways. The woman asked,

"If you're not in a hurry. . . some tea, perhaps. . . ."

"Shall we?"

Hahk, too, felt empty after finding his friend gone.

After walking a bit further down the street they entered a tearoom. Once seated across from each other, they introduced themselves.

"I'm Kim Hahk."

"My name is Kim Sun-im."

Under the fluorescent light, Kim Hahk scanned her slightly gaunt face. So this was the missionary woman Chun talked about. He remembered Chun saying "She's beautiful".

The waitress brought them tea. Kim Sun-im sipped her tea and after thinking for a moment asked,

"Are you two at the same school?"

"No."

Answered Hahk, thinking the woman had stopped him to find out more about Chun.

"I'll see him soon and when I do I'll tell him I ran into you."

At those words, Kim Sun-im raised no objection and just hung her head. A thought flashed through Hahk's mind as he noticed her gentle expression. Well. . . because it was him. . . lest the woman misunderstand, he hurriedly collected himself and said,

"Chun said you are a very enthusiastic believer."

At this, too, Kim Sun-im just smiled. A good-hearted woman, Hahk thought to himself. This time he asked,

"If you have time, would you like to see a movie?"

Having said this, Hahk blushed a little, wondering if he hadn't been too forward. But Sun-im immediately replied,

"Yes."

She got up from her seat first. Imagining her carefree response was due to Chun's position between them, Hahk thought once more about the disloyal friend who had left him in such a peculiar role. They asked the waitress for a newspaper and looked through it. There wasn't much worth seeing at the movie theaters nearby. So they agreed to go downtown, though it was rather far.

As they rode on the bus, Hahk felt a little strange. It was the first time he'd taken a woman to a movie. That she was "a friend's girl" lessened the awkwardness a little. He thought she probably felt the same way.

It was almost rush hour and the bus was packed. Hahk regretted not taking the more expensive, less crowded kind of bus. Sun-im stood very close to him and he gazed down at her hair, gathered into an unpretentious ponytail. When they reached the theater the prior showing had not let out. They bought tickets and waited in the lobby by the projection room. High ceiling and shiny floor. Even in such surroundings she looked beautiful. Chun is a lucky bastard. But what could have happened to him? Seated beside her as they waited for the next show, Hahk wondered about his friend's sudden move. Had he found a new job? Since he moved elsewhere, it seemed likely he had taken a new tutoring position. As far as he knew, Chun hadn't quit his old job. Even if he had, how could he. . .? Hahk had hoped to tell him about Hwang today. Being resentful didn't help matters, but he still thought Chun had gone too far. There are different kinds of friendships. In some cases, one side pulls and the other is pulled. In others, both sides are composed. Even at first glance, the friendship between Hahk and Tokko Chun was like the relationship of a man who clings to a woman who is cool to him. But Hahk was not the sort to attend to such subtleties, nor was Chun, so their friendship had gone ahead. In any human relation, there are always undercurrents invisible from outside.

Sun-im was thinking of the night when she last met Chun. When they had met by chance on the street and gone to a music hall. To think of that night made her head spin and her heart pound. He is. . . . He is. . . . She couldn't decide just what kind of man he was. Once he was out of sight, she found it hard to imagine his face. Compared to him, Kim Hahk made a much clearer impression. A good man. His face, with unkempt hair falling over his forehead, and his shyness made her feel secure. Though she didn't reflect on it, deep down she was crediting Chun for having such a good friend. Though it was their first meeting, she had revealed her concerns to Hahk with almost embarrassing candor because she felt him a trustworthy man. A bell rang to mark the end of the previous show. People poured out. The two of them rose and went in to find seats.

"Seems like Westerners no longer have any qualms at all about remarriage."

Chun invited Yi Yu-jŏng to say what she thought of the film they had just seen.

"That was my impression, too. They really seem to believe that love is all that matters."

"Sounds like a nice place for women to live."

"Are you envious?"

Chun erupted into laughter.

"Not in the least. I approve whole-heartedly. It's a matter of taste, so no one can say it should be this or that way."

They crossed the street and walked into a hotel grille.

"Which side are you on, tastewise?"

"Me?"

Slicing his meat, he said,

"As for my taste. . . . Do you really want to know?"

"Why is it so difficult to say? That's why I don't like Korean men. They're never open and straight-forward. And always evasive."

"Ha, ha. Since I'm not a typical Korean man, don't be so disappointed. As far as my taste is concerned, I believe women should be virtuous and men free."

"An evil sort of taste."

"You are right."

"That's not a matter of taste, just something long practiced in this society, isn't it? In other words, you're sticking to the conventional point of view."

"No, there's a difference."

"What's different about it?"

She snapped at him.

"The difference is. . . ."

He swallowed a bite of meat and went on,

"The difference is this. In Korea, too, it's been a long while since social ethics crumbled. A new type of woman has appeared, but I hope that experiment soon is over and we return to *Ch'unhyang-jōn.*"

"And the man?"

"As always, free. . . ."

"Barbarism."

"Well, didn't I warn you? But you insisted on hearing it."

"Is that your true opinion really?"

"I'm lying. Because it'd be a loss."

"Loss?"

"Think about it. If every woman in the world were virtuous, there'd be no room for Casanovas. It'd be like poking yourself in the eye."

"You speak as if you were a notorious Casanova. . . with traces of pimples not yet gone. . . ."

She gazed into the young man's handsome face. There were no acne scars, of course.

"I don't know, but maybe a dog biting for the first time bites harder."

"Goodness, what do you mean by that?"

"I'm sorry. The conversation's taken a wrong turn."

But Chun detected in her expression no hint of displeasure. A detour. Only humans have raised sex to the level of a game. What for animals is an exercise in physiology. Miss Yi Yu-jōng. Certainly. Of course, if I frankly tell you. . . .

"Can I ask you one question?"

"Go ahead."

". . . no, I'd better not."

Chun hung his head down, stabbing a chunk of meat with his fork. Yu-jōng looked at the young man, smiling brightly. A cute pet. Brother-in-law prepared a nice gift. She recalled the time Brother-in-law had stayed in her house after coming to the South. Hyŏn Ho-sŭng had been young and handsome then, but not arrogant like this youth. He had been ingratiating to her father and sister and to herself as a would-be sister-in-law. This young man's situation is a bit different, of course. For Hyŏn supposedly is indebted to his family back in the North. She had really been delighted to find Chun in a house that otherwise would have been boring. She found it easy to be carefree with Chun because he was younger than she, in fact, still quite young. So people rationalize their behavior. Her eyes on the young man as he quietly raised a piece of meat to his mouth, she thought about a certain evening in Boston several months before. The memory oppressed her. She turned her eyes to the window.

The woman's silence made Tokko Chun look up at her. This woman is...? Yu-jŏng's face, turned toward the window, looked very lonely.

X

I am unoccupied,
Therefore I am.

Even the sunlight filtering through the leaves to the grass is already altered. No longer like the thin, pale light of spring, it pours forth in abundance.

It is May.

Tokko Chun had moved a chair out under the cherry trees in the back yard and was enjoying the brilliant early summer afternoon. High overhead the window of his room and the gigantic picture window of Yu-jŏng's studio were shining like polished shields. When the breeze occasionally picked up, an indescribably fresh smell of green filled his lungs, spreading throughout his entire being.

The garden was at its climax. The sweet pungent scents of cherry and fir, of roses in one corner and of perennial herbs, all these aromas blended together to make that fragrance. Peace.

Chun was so content with the freshness of the moment that he wriggled and wistfully sighed, like a delighted child. Burying himself in the garden made him forget he was in the heart of the city. Not a speck of a cloud was in the sky. As far as he could see, sunlight saturated the deep blue summer sky. Birds were singing in the trees. Chun closed his eyes and listened to the chirps. He couldn't tell how many species of birds were singing. Only the incessant chirping sound, as resilient as that of a rubber whistle. Interminable chatter at the same level. Cheep, cheep, ka-ta-ru, ka-ta-ru, ka-ta-ru. . . . It was the first time he had enjoyed such pleasant air and sunlight since his duty at the OP in the Demilitarized Zone. Come to think of it, the birds he remembered from the OP were mainly mountain pheasants and crows, there hadn't been many little songbirds. Of course, at the OP the state of nature was more like nature. It was strange, however. The arrangement of plants in a couple thousand square yards alongside this brick building somehow more deeply impressed upon him the abundance of nature. He felt the trunk of the cherry tree. Cool strength in his palm. The dense leaves rustled wildly in the breeze, diffusing the sun's rays.

A colony of ants was swarming over a path across the lawn. The tiny thin-waisted spots were bustling back and forth. They could only be black shining spots. Not one of the ants was bearing a load. Yet they were moving to and fro most busily. Were they running relay races? He had never heard of such a thing. They are saints. Since the first seed came into being, they have been doing the same work without a trace of doubt.

A thought had often occurred to him since he had come to live in this house. In the old days, poor artists were usually fed by the influential and powerful families. They would offer shabby rooms letting the artists stay as long as they liked. And when the master occasionally had leisure from political affairs, they would be invited to the main house to discuss life and nature over wine and tasty morsels. Though their food and clothing might have been inferior to their masters', in the realm of spirit there was no high or low, nor would the masters have claimed as much. Though unable to raise themselves to high ranks in the worldly hierarchy, these dependents nonetheless elevated themselves. They were not hangers-on who flattered the powerful to seek patronage, but people who had awakened to transience. And still less like flatterers were those who kept moving, never eating and sleeping in the same house. The drifting bohemians of the feudal age. Wanderers of the spirit. These men of the medieval age should not be confused with the numerous scholars who grew disheartened after being ejected from high magistracies. The men who regarded official status and pleasure as drifting clouds, who lived quietly in the bosom of mysterious life with nowhere to unburden their hearts before they died, they must have been true artists. They may have left behind not a single line of writing. These ancestors of ours loved absence more than presence and rarity more than abundance, thus from their own standpoint it is hard to deem them failures. Chun compared himself to such men. In the West things had seemingly been the same. Most of the scholars and artists of the Middle Ages wore the dark monkish cassock, and the drifting minstrels often found succor under the towers of the nobles' castles. Besides, these fellows were bolder, at times stealthily dallying with the wives of the very lords who had sheltered them. Such were the arts in olden times. Monks were by no means ashamed of their shaved pates, nor did artists grovel for their daily bread. Although reduced to a low social status, they had the pride of the unworldly, or the obstinacy of the artisan temperament. The works they produced were dedicated to aristocratic patrons, to the only class then empowered to enjoy art. With the coming of the modern age, however, the situation has greatly changed. Among the greatest changes were the printing press, sound recording and film. The revolution in instruments of communication, the so-called mass media, fundamentally altered the situation. As a result, the arts once relished by a very limited class now reach the hands of the masses. Can you imagine the strange scene of every household using Koryŏ green celadon or Yi white celadon instead of Western aluminum pots and pans? In an age in which everyone can read the classics, sit and listen to the performances of virtuosos, and watch famous actors for a paltry sum, in this modern age everyone has become an aristocrat. By these same means, patronage of artists has also broadened. Art is no longer created for a single individual, and artists no longer can act like pampered children, as in the old days. Now the artist himself must solve the problems of bread and freedom.

Chun was thinking he had shielded himself from such a state. That one must concoct so many stories to justify his present situation is evidence that the situation is far from normal. It wasn't that Chun entirely lacked excuses, of course. He was writing a novel now. But up to then he had more than once started over. He always began with enormous passion, but as he wrote his thought began to change and he became displeased with what he wrote. Unlike in the old days, a false appearance has arisen that every individual is entitled to influence politics. In the present age, a man's acts are inevitably intertwined with politics. At least in one's head. But a danger always follows here. Nothing is more paradoxical than politics. At the same time it is most fundamental and most superficial. To make a wager on politics is the highest form of action, but with one misstep it can fall into the lowest form of action. The hottest and most beautiful moment of politics—revolution therefore attracts the heart of an artist. Milton, Heine, Byron, Hugo, Gorki, Aragon, Sartre —the secret of these hearts lies here. But when we read poetry like the political satires of Heine we cannot help but feel, shall we say, a certain sorrow. The political enemies he so passionately mocked, and the ideals he so ardently championed, how empty they now seem. To contemporary readers they must have been incendiary poems, but with the passage of time they have no more power of ignition than old and stale dynamite. The life of such dynamite is tied to the newspapers on the dates of its composition. Obsolete news is no news. The instant an artist steps into history he always loses something. It is still worse when this derives from the good motives of one who cannot be indifferent to neighbors' misfortunes. Some may content such works at least leave behind the value of a record. But that, too, is an anachronistic point of view. It might be plausible if works of literature and land tenure documents were the only records of an age. But for us, the people of later ages, it would be pitiful to rely on fiction in order to relive the experiences of the past. Our readings of the novels of Balzac does not depend on the texts alone. Only by reference to knowledge beyond literature, to all our knowledge about French history, economics, social climate and religion, is the appreciation of Balzac's novels made possible. This vast expanse of background information ulterior to literature, compressed between the lines of the novel, is indispensable material. An appreciative interpretation of a novel is an illicit cohabitation based on a promise (a promise which need not be explained to contemporaries). How fast the world flows. How quickly the problems change. If a writer competes with the newspapers, defeat is certain from the outset. Should he then shun history? The deportment of Goethe, supposedly so imperturbable midst the storms of revolution, is nauseating. We cannot turn away from politics because we know it affects roses, winds, clouds and lovers' hearts. Politics lies nearby, in the closest quarters, in the heart of evil. In our predicament we don't need to take the trouble, like some happy people, to travel to the jungles of Vietnam or to wander about Algeria in order to "act". From the opening of this century to today, Western literature displays a very curious profile. Their artists leave behind the evils at home to pursue exotic hobbies in Africa, Vietnam, Spain and Cuba. Thanks to their unwillingness to see that the evil lies within them, the snows of Kilimanjaro, the bulls and the sharks, all have paid dearly. If there is any merit to these fortunate idlers, who proudly loitered about with grave expressions, it is that in time they came to doubt themselves. We understand what their problem was. A century from now, however, it will be very hard to help the French understand why such a melodramatic tragedy had to be performed in order to appreciate the historic sites of Vietnam. Even the politics unfolding before our eyes is not ours. The conceptions are not ours. In such circumstances, politics does not tempt the artist. It is as unfamiliar as a mannequin. Or, should we rather devote ourselves in eternity to this tumultuous age? Or, should we abandon the competition with the newspapers, lock ourselves in a secret room, without all the extra-literary apparatus, and stare at a retort containing the elements of the human spirit, doing research to discover a greater explosive? Though this might not immediately kill an enemy soldier, wouldn't it earn you a draft exemption for the sake of greater weaponry? But what if the motherland loses the war before the new weapon is perfected? Lose the war? Even if the motherland is defeated, the men will remain. Moreover, for the last few centuries of our history, there has been nothing deserving the name of "motherland", so it wouldn't be much of a loss. To withdraw from participation in history, this is the only road to take. Tokko Chun himself was also leaning in this direction. Here, too, there was a difficulty, however. It was none other than the problem of language. Language as a literary medium is not a pure substance. It is an animal that has evolved in history, in a climate and on a soil. Experimentation with this. To think of language as a laboratory guinea pig, to be carved up and disemboweled, bones disarticulated and flesh flayed—no matter how eager the scientist may be to pursue this task, "life" retreats from him a step at a time. There is a limit to purity in literature. Other methods using bolder lines can be employed. In this regard, Chun found Kafka attractive. A method that does not completely dissect the object, but strips away only the colors of mundane significance. By these means, one is able to keep all the canons of modernism and at the same time create a world that is the complete opposite of the ordinary. Kafka's world is a questioning of tradition and order. His astonishment at first reading Kafka. That literature could possibly call forth such a world, had been his thought. Man's loneliness in a world in which God is lost. The world of dreams. The last symptoms of the disintegration of the bourgeois spirit. This was readily translatable. Kafka exhausted the symbolic resources of literature. If pushed past that point, language could not cope with such extremity. To call a stone "stone" and a flower "flower", and at the same time make them not a stone and not a flower, that is the fiction of Kafka. Even if it is surrealism, the surrealism of Kafka differs from the liquifying trend that countenances the blending of images. In Kafka's world a chair is a chair. But in this case a chair is a Sphinx-like riddle. Each scene of his novels is free of leaps. But in combination and as a whole, his fiction is one riddle. This is a most extraordinary method of "questioning". Conventional novels, too, are in essence riddles. For instance, from a novel of Balzac, as clear and distinct as a realistic painting, can we say we have acquired anything "absolute"? Despite the fact that the details are so considerately explicated, it tells us nothing. Within the bounds of description, the contents of a novel are mere indices of something beyond language, say life, if we can call it "life". Isn't it this essential semiotic transcendence in language that makes possible not only translation but also correspondence among artistic genres? In conventional fiction, if a novelist methodically takes the skepticism of the reader as his subject-matter, he may manage to construct a Sphinx face, but this need not mean the self-conscious questioning of the writer himself is expressed. The fundamental difference between conventional and avant-garde modes of art depends on the attitude of the creator and not on the surface technique or the choice of subject-matter. Nothing is new under the sun. There are only new viewpoints. At any rate, Kafka was a great master, indeed. But when he tried to follow the master's method, Chun again found himself astonished. Why? Because he realized that one Kafka was enough. In a Kafkaesque world, a strict priority of claims must be observed. Even were one to write a novel more Kafkaesque than Kafka's own, it would be a mere superfluity. In this respect, all geniuses attain a place like that of Jesus Christ in Christian theology. An event that occurs but once. A singular insertion of the Absolute into history. Christ came only once. With that the work was done. The name of the hero of the New Testament had been decided. If a man attempts to imitate Jesus Christ in everything he does, he may become a disciple but he will never become a "lord". An incident for which repetition is meaningless. History records the names of the fortunate, but omits the names of their innumerable epigones.

Tokko Chun had been popping into Yi Yu-jŏng's studio anytime he felt like it. From her work and from reading on painting and art history, he could see that art and literature had taken surprisingly similar paths. Generally, her paintings could be divided into two classes. One sort were designs in a style similar to Mondrian. The other used forms to convey untold stories, like Chirico or Dali. She seemed to oscillate between the two styles. Tokko Chun envied her being a painter. She was experimenting to see with her own eyes the very same problems that perplexed he himself. While working on an abstract design, if suddenly inspired she would jump to the narrative universe of Chirico, and vice-versa. By contrast, in Chun's case the drafts erased in his head were far more voluminous than his manuscripts. Like a student doing practice sketches on a slate. In painting he preferred Mondrian to Chirico. Because Mondrian is purer. The figures of Chirico or Dali, who raggedly expose the preconceptions of everydayness, he found less attractive than the canvases of Mondrian, which exhibit a perfect form of gambling. The world of Mondrian, however, can never be recreated in literature. Especially in prose, it is impossible to create an unconditional geometric universality.

More often than not, Tokko Chun's novels thus crumbled with their prologues. For they were not dramas staged in real time with natural lighting and pleasing costumes. They always commenced with a certain picture flashing through his head. Being (or trying to be) a novelist, his conceptualization was painterly. Ways to connect the sequence of screens were needed. Modern painting standing alone is meaningless. It moves only when bound to the history of art. Time thus intervenes in painting as well. There is neither a purely spatial nor a purely temporal art. Art requires a synthesis of time and space, and so Tokko Chun's novel displayed one scene and then stopped, like a frozen movie projector. He could set it in motion, of course. But unlike the readers of *Ch'unh-yang-jŏn* who always already know the next scene by heart, he was too sensitive to shame to follow the accepted formula. One must be a genius or else devoid of honor, but he was neither. That was the source of his impatience. A thought constantly glowered at him from the bottom of his consciousness. To parry moral self-castigation at being a base creature, a thief of the bread of another man, he needed to be a genius. He didn't know, of course, how much of his impatience stemmed from an authentic desire to create and how much from such practical concerns. Safe to say that both factors were at work.

He had felt nothing upon meeting Kim Hahk a few days before and hearing that the spring issue of "Imprisoned Age" was coming out and that Hahk planned to go to his hometown that summer to do social work, a survey of some kind. Whenever he met Hahk, Chun's mind seemed to him unusually calm and composed. By himself, he wavered before "either-or", but in Hahk's presence he was always firmly decisive. He found himself defending the position opposing Kim Hahk, in other words.

Hahk also had talked about Kim Sun-im. It was a story he had no desire to hear. What, then, had been the shock he had felt at seeing her that winter night? The desire the night they listened to music, and the incident at their last meeting. Perhaps it was lust. No, not perhaps. It was lust. Worse still, it was an irresponsible passion, bursting forth from a passing moment of bewildered urgency. When he recalled her now, all that remained in his heart was an inarticulate aversion.

The feeling was strong enough to transfer itself to Kim Hahk as he spoke of her.

Hahk also said the survey he would be doing was intended to size up political awareness in his native province in anticipation of the next presidential election. While listening to him and peering at his face, a face showing nothing but goodness, he had lost himself in thought. This guy certainly is blocked up inside. He's no fool, but neither is he conceited. Still, he thinks the destiny of Korea is on his shoulders, he actually believes it. Chun suddenly recalled the man Hwang whom Hahk had talked about. Hahk had praised him to the skies. When he grows old, Hahk will be like him.

Soft hands cover his eyes from behind.

"No need to look, is there?"

Said Chun without stirring.

The hands over his eyes stayed where they were. At that instant, Chun felt desire. A sudden impulse to caress the one standing behind. He wriggled his fingers. Yu-jŏng must have been alerted, for she stepped back and then came around in front of him.

She was not clad in the jumpsuit she normally wore when painting. Her pale blue blouse looked impeccable in the sunlight. She sat down on the grass not far from where he was.

"You seem to be in a great mood."

She had received accolades at her private exhibition the month before. That was what he had in mind.

"Stop teasing me."

"How can you say that when I was congratulating you?"

"Because you are not a person capable of praising anybody else."

"Now, what is that supposed to mean?"

"I mean you are bad."

Chun struck his forehead with his palm and hung his head for a moment.

"I'll consider that a compliment."

"That's why you're bad."

Chun nodded, laughing.

"Since you've said it, I wish you'd go a step further."

"?"

"And say I'm not even good at being bad."

"Now, that needs explaining, go ahead."

"Ha, ha, I will. The age is too far gone for an individual to become evil. A frightening era. A time in which it's not only impossible to do good, but also to do evil. In all prior ages there was a name evildoers could quietly invoke in the depths of night. The name of the demonic familiar who aided their dark tasks. In this horrible age in which we've been stranded, there is not even a devil to contract with. Traitors to the race. Communists. Could these possibly be domons? No. They are not demons. Suppose they are capable of killing us, still they are no demons. Even if they are murdering us, we can still say, 'I'm being killed by you, but I fear you not.' What makes us tremble can only be an icy voice issuing from somewhere deeper below. An age lacking even a legitimate devil. In such an age, we cannot even do evil. This is the explanation."

"The explanation is even harder to understand."

Chun nodded.

"It's true. And, you know, I often feel regret these days."

"Why?"

"I wish I'd become a painter."

"My, what a pity that a genius of a painter has. . . ."

"That's what I say."

"Why not give it a try?"

"You can't mean it."

"In America there's a grandmother who became famous after starting to paint on the far side of fifty."

"Then I've plenty of time left."

"You're like a tree frog, contradicting for the sake of contradiction."

Chun guffawed, wondering how he could break her of the habit of talking down to him just because she was older. But what he said was something completely different.

"I always feel indebted to you."

Yi Yu-jŏng just glanced at him with a smile, as if wondering what cute trick would be coming next.

"I mean, having the chance to chat with you is one of the things that makes life worth living. Our salon."

"With just the two of us?"

"To say 'just the two of us' makes me feel a bit strange."

"You shouldn't, I'm like an elder sister."

"An elder sister. . . ."

"The age difference, think of it."

"Impossible."

"Why?"

"It must not be like that in America."

Yi Yu-jŏng's expression hardened a bit.

"There, age is no problem. . . ."

"Enough."

She calmly rose and steered their talk elsewhere.

"I'm thinking of going to the seaside this summer. If you don't have other plans would you like to go with me?"

"To the beach?"

"Should go somewhere in midsummer, no?"

Chun recalled Hahk's proposal that he join him on his trip to his native province.

"Well, we can make up our minds then. Will you paint there, too?"

"I'll take along my things. But why, should I not?"

"It's not that, but your paintings don't need sketches from life, do they?"

"You say that only because you don't really understand. You can say such things because all you see is the completed work. Sketches are necessary. Suppose I depict the sea as a blue triangle. Beforehand there's a process of drawing what I see, of deleting and remolding."

"I'll buy that."

"Impertinent."

She pretended to hit him on the head and then strode off into the house.

Once alone, he stretched himself and then sank back into thought. As he'd said to her, he did envy the happiness of painters. Given the opportunity to start over, if he had the talent he thought he'd choose to go into painting. To create a schematic diagram of existence with the variety of phenomena reduced to the elements of color and form. When all is aid, it was an urge toward system. He started reading this and that but soon abandoned each thing he picked up. Thinking he had at last grasped something perfect, he would pass a sleepless night, but then he'd find himself back where he'd started. At one point he bought a copy of the *I Ching* and read it. Its author experienced a similar obsession, perhaps. A desire to arrange the entire manifold of phenomena into the simplest possible formulae. That's probably been it. But the price for creating such formulae is a loss of ego. The ego disappears, drowned in the sea of generality. That is no solution. It is a regression. An ecstatic confluence of the ego and the general, that alone is salvation. To fight against the loss of the ego, under any name. To save the ego that disintegrates in modern society. Must we go to the village of Salyŏul, like Yi Kwang-su? For Ho-sŭng to have gone was right enough. But not an artist. Because artists have chosen paper, not earth. The artist's duty is not to toil with one's hands but to arrest the wreckage of the ego. And there is no one method that completely discharges this duty. To think so would be to cheat oneself. After all, do I love in order to save someone from something? No such thing. For me, wrting a novel is simply writing. For the sake of art. No, when I can love no one, how can art be anything to me? A way to open a path to love?

Deeply absorbed in thought, Chun sat for a long while in the garden, drenched in the afternoon sun of early summer. He looked at the woman's face. She was smiling shyly. It seemed to him a beautiful smile. Casually, he drew closer to her. She avoided his eyes and fingered the bible in her hand.

He laid his hands on her shoulders. She lurched back, startled. The woman's face was fear stricken. Undeterred, he pressed forward again to touch her. He held her in his arms. She struggled in his embrace. Her elbow struck him in the lip. The acute pain stunned him. With both hands he covered his mouth. With one blow, his swollen desire was tamed. His hands still on his mouth, he didn't lift his head. It wasn't due to the pain. As if a thousand pound stone hung from his neck, he hadn't the strength to look up. He said "I'm sorry. Please go," still without looking at her.

He never saw how here complexion changed. At last, Kim Sun-im opened the door quietly and walked out. Once she was gone he squatted down on the floor and wept. It couldn't have been his aching lip. The tears just kept flowing down. A few days later, Hyōn Ho-sūng had proposed that he come and stay at his house. That night he went back to his room and after thinking all night about it, decided to accept the offer. And all night through he somehow kept returning to the pain in his lip a few nights before. When Kim Hahk had spoken of her, Chun had felt only repulsion. It wasn't that he blamed her, of course, but it wasn't self-reproach either. He didn't even want to think about the quarrel in the room that night, a quarrel that could have been with anybody. Every reminder of the incident brought the pain back to his lip. A reflex, apparently unintentional on her part. Her movement, like that of someone on a crowded bus who steps on a stranger's foot, was scarcely a gesture of refusal. Had that elbow not smashed into his lip, he wouldn't have heeded her resistance. For that it is how such things go. Of that he was sure. Nevertheless, the wound of the episode never left him. And countless images he had projected onto her quietly vanished. The face of the woman in the air raid shelter that he once had merged with her face. Explosion. Smell of flesh. Sunlight on a summer day. The boy's throbbing heart as he gazed from the chestnut grove down at the city in the distance. All these images clouding in a shell around the nucleus of that summer day, all were decomposing since that incident. Perhaps I took up Hyōn's offer to avoid running into her again. Even this sort of nonsense he once told himself, he now recalled. As time passed, the thought of it evoked a laugh laong with the pain. Even now his memory did not begrudge her her beauty. She might have been a good lover. And might have saved me to boot. Because she had God. Maybe she was an angel dispatched to me. Shouldn't have gotten upset and broken it off just because the angel inadvertantly elbowed me. That was the comedy of it. Probably I was embarrassed by the abruptness of my desire at that moment of impatience. Embarrassed, hurt, angered, ha, ha, ha. And the lip still hurts all the same. And if you follow these passions further you run into a wind. A wind no longer explicable. He fumbled in the darkness and switched on the lamp next to the bed. Then he sat there on the bed for a while. The shaded lamp cast a sphere of pale light centered on the nightstand where it sat.

At last, he got up and walked across to the desk. Sitting down, he rummaged about. He pulled open a drawer, removed a bundle of notebooks and began to read. Written in one was this:

Back alleys of Shanghai. Winter in Harbin. Window. Russian ballet school (chimney and X). Winter and stove. In the mountains. Prisoner. Escape. Winter in Beijing. College dormitory. (A couple drumsful of sperm) Sunflowers. Intellectuals in China. Tortue. Flowers. Opium. Frontier. City people. Time in fleet white clouds. Blood. Whorehouses. Flesh. Under the roof of Tokyo. Colonial people. Two sorts of paths. Right and left. Attic room desire. Despair of Chosōn intellectuals under colonialism. The temperature of the land. Sex, action and motion. Skin of machines. Face of politics. New human being. New religion. U.S.A. Pointillism. Abstraction. Kafka's testicles. Minimal human being. Eerieness of films. Eating and sex. Spring and autumn. Waltz. Ocean. Home of seabirds. Meaning of race. Glory of ignoramuses.

Genius's secret room. Tuberculosis hospital. Don Juan. Tokyo. Harbin. City A. Winter. Suburb. Exodus from the West. Spy. Korea. Club. Crime. Against whom? Pattern of pilgrimage. Hair and bastard. Life of struggle and life of resignation. Recovering the capital stakes of a lifetime. Shylock. Revolution. Revolution. Pure passions of liars. Burning passion. Icon of the hero. Faith. Rape. Evil and good. Sexual organs of philosophy. Schopenhauer and Nietzsche. Monad. Monad. Monad. Monadology. Monad. Explosion Flowers. Escape from the baseness of cosmopolitans. Those who want to live, live. (A lie. The best die and the worst live.) Three types. God and man and nature. War and peace. Nuclei of romance. Describe a group of masculine symbols ♂ surrounding a female symbol ♀. Western vices. Blizzard. Dreams. Impatience for Utopia. The problem of the ego and the problem of the group. Thirst. Winter atmosphere. Introduction of characters. Young man A. Whore D. Scarlett O'Hara. Ego as bodysized portal to nothingness. Once inside, disarmament prohibited. Our hands, let them not unlatch the door for nameless visitors, and our lips, let them not summon the nameless.

He felt a sight exaltation while reading these notes, notes in his own hand. It had been quite a while since he wrote them, and his packets of thought seemed locked in some secret code that had to be deciphered. Some parts were quite beyond him. The countless sperm ejaculated by the penis of his mind. The residue of many nights of masturbation by a poor and wretched soul. He looked around the room. It was a nice room, even without comparing it to the upstairs room at the boarding house. The sheets looked cleaner under the pale lamplight. Good quality carpet underfoot. Furniture that had cost a considerable sum. But the changed surroundings did not make him feel less miserable. The tumor within him was still spreading. Was his peace of mind something Chun had invented to deceive himself, merely a means to repress his awareness that he had stolen another's bread? No, the tumor was an atrophy of the nerves, an adaptation to deaden the pain of the pinpricks of morality. He no longer even hated Hyŏn Ho-sŭng. At first, it even gave him a certain pleasure to live under the same roof in such an abnormal situation. But things didn't turn out that way. Since he had first come there, introduced by Hyŏn as a son of an old friend in the North to whom he owed much, Hyŏn had actually behaved as though this were true. Just like a man who eventually deceives himself into believing his own lies. At least that's how Chun saw him. Chun felt the meaninglessness of his own tension. Hyŏn was almost always busy. He was absorbed in his business, but when home he always took a plausible, though not overly inquisitive, interest in Chun's well being. The performance was so outstanding that Chun couldn't believe the actor was the same man who had been flustered at the outset. The scenario planned by Tokko Chun thus fell flat. Peace. Rotten peace. Shameless mind, nonetheless. Even if the incident with Kim Sun-im had never taken place, he probably would have broken it off Chun couldn't say how sincere her faith might be. But her faith, her greatest possession, would have come between the two of them. He had not the least intention to urge her to become like him. Besides, what if she took his salvation upon herself as a calling? That would have been likely. What if she insisted on "awakening" him to "the truth"? How could he possibly explain to her that he didn't want the truth? A woman like Kim Sun-im is the same kind of person as Kim Hahk. With people who are blocked within, it's better to leave them as they are than to try to change them. They are specially graced people. They are the sort who come into this world and leave behind them beauty and goodness. If there was a Kim Sun-im without faith. . . ? She would have been ideal. But one cannot snatch an apple out of a child's hand. Kim Hahk and her as a possible couple. It would be becoming. He smiled at his own ingenuity. It might turn out so. He got up from the desk and went over to the window. The curtain he pulled aside. The garden below was cold and still, devoid of the afternoon's charm. The leaves of the cherry trees from time to time glimmered under the stars. Beyond the trees lights shone here and there along the streets. Why this? What is it? To fall down rotting with both eyes open wide. What if this shameful urge is renounced? No. That, too, is impossible. Shall I call someone's name? This warm and fresh May night. He touched his forehead on the windowpane. The patch of skin felt cool as if exposed to the air. Another tomorrow. The day after tomorrow. And the next day. Plenty of time for me. With the coming of tomorrow, the day after or some future day, will joy come into my life? He shook his head. He remembered his mother, brother, sister and cousins back home. Did they still live in the same house? He couldn't picture a day of reunion. That would not happen in ten or twenty years. Everyone thought we would be back soon the day we boarded the ship from W City. We all thought we were just following a temporary retreat after a reversal in the fighting and that we would soon return home. And that was how he kept thinking for the first few years of refugee life. Kim Hahk had asked him to come along to his hometown that summer. Going home. What a classically nostalgic expression. Returning somewhere most happily after sweating for your bread. That's the life most in harmony with reason. A younger brother, student at a country school, will probably be at the station to welcome you. No sooner do you step off the train than you become a native again. It's only natural, for it's the place where he grew up with so much snow, rain, wind and thunder. Being away can never extinguish the memories. Plenty of passers-by would exchange greetings. When did you get here? Just got off the train. Ah, that's right, feel the peace. He's come home. . . . Things like these. Kim Hahk has them. Homecomings. Going back home. A basic gestalt of life. A strange land. A drifter's existence. Coming home after a long journey through wind and frost.

Even a man dying the death of a stranger in the hinterlands will, in his last flickering moment, see his mother before his eyes. And where else would she be standing but under the chestnut tree back home? Kim Hahk has that home. But I do not. It may be long before I can go back. But would I be truly happy if only I could go there? In that fruit orchard could I find my dream and my peace (oh, that sweet dream like an apple blossom in May). Could I call forth the idol of the road from the white smokestack that once gave me such joy? The fallen apples on the ground, would they still be as sweet? The soaring steeple of the Catholic Church, would it still surprise me? No, it wouldn't be like that. Buried there, too, is the memory of the unrelenting communist insistence that these orchards were the economic basis for the pro-Japanese and the petty bourgeoisie. Now I understand the sorrow of a young woman who quietly buried herself in work until her face grew dark under the May apple blossoms. The factory smokestack was already shattered then, and have I not since discovered it was never anything like a road idol and that it grew out of filthy and terrifying things? Once you have learned that the cross on the steeple of that Catholic Church is a torture instrument freely chosen by a good-hearted man long ago in a distant land, and that he has been up there weeping for two thousand years, how could it mean the same thing it did in the old days? Home was already dead in his soul. He thinks of a man buried on the outskirts of this city. Father. A father forced to witness his young son's discovery that the cold is harder to endure when you're hungry. Home was buried with him. He was alone. He was merely a homeless animal, one who had strayed too far to believe. A man who had come to feel his home was within himself. And a man with only a silent wind inside. Was it merely an instinctual compensation in a man who had lost his home? No. It was a lie I created in order to snatch the bread of Hyōn Ho-sūng. It wasn't an act of revenge for my sister and it wasn't out of hatred for his viciousness. It was merely a crafty design I came up with to park my exhausted body and corrupted soul in a hygienic space. But, for what? Because delving into the soil from which that tumor sprouted, that desolate windswept soil, was still a task of value and one I couldn't abandon. Until the hour when the Motherland and my neighbors woo meet ruin. Because I gambled everything on a total dissection of my own ego. No, rather I was bound to gamble. My Motherland and neighbors surely weren't my creations. Their problems will be minded by people like Kim Hahk. When Hahk and his group come into power, they won't arrest me and put me on a trial. Because he is my friend. At least I didn't steal from a poor widow. I at least have that excuse. He stepped away from the window. His face was reflected in the glass. Slowly he scrutinized it. The man in the glass was staring back at him. The man was asking, who am I? You must tell me that. I don't know, that manner of speaking is nonsense. I'm not leaving your sight without an answer. Why because I love you. Could one who loves do this? Such love I don't want. Whether you want it or not you have no choice. Wherever you go I'm there. It won't do for you to forget me even in your most self-absorbed moments. I'm right behind you. You don't exist. You are my shadow. Don't try to resist, for you know only too well that is untrue. Everything is due to love. That alone is true. I'm not asking you to answer at once. There is time, except no time to be wasted. We can also compromise, can we not? As long as we shut our mouths, nobody knows, is it not right? I, too, know what you're saying but there is precedent, is there not, and it has failed every time, has it not?

Tokko Chun turned around. The man in the glass did the same. Chun found the conversation familiar. But it never occurred to him that he would go insane one day. Without intervention of a third power, he didn't think he would be the loser in this battle. Though pained and afraid, he would not go crazy. I do my own work under the eye of my keeper. Should it be impossible to resolve this confrontation, the only way left is to go the whole way.

When he turned around once more the man in the glass was grinning. It was a smile of friendship among men.

XI

Beware falling ill with the history of spirit,
For your skull will never bear it.

One evening Tokko Chun was reading an out-of-date issue of *Atlantic Monthly* in his room. As he read that special issue devoted to Africa, many things came into Chun's mind. African social problems were touched on in the features and there were pieces introducing African sculpture. It also contained a short story by an indigenous writer. One article on the rapid decline of African wild-life populations left him with mixed feelings. In this, along with the other pieces, Chun saw "The New Africa". In the Africa inside his head, lions and elephants often paraded by, and rifle-toting white explorers in pith helmets walked about with natives bearing spears and bows before and behind. But according to this periodical, whites didn't spend all their time hunting, nor were the natives all bare-footed safari guides. It was not the Africa of Stanley and Livingstone or of Hemingway and Schweitzer, but the Africa of Africans. The image was of a traditional society with its own history, governing itself as it suffers invasions of Western civilization. The old and the new. Attachment and resolution. Family systems in disintegration and the loneliness of city dwellers. A society of people wandering between traditional religion and Christianity. Chun felt a certain shame. The image of Africa in his head was one reflected from the eyes of Westerners. The images projected by movies, novels and newspapers were that irresponsible and that devoid of understanding. But in that brief story written by an African writer there was love. It was a love rooted in a space inaccessible to travelers. The hero was none other than Tokko Chun himself. There was an empathy spanning two continents. He felt a sense of contemporaneity never captured in Western novels about Africa. In the eight page spread on African sculpture, one photograph appeared side by side with Picasso's work "The Dancer" and a note called the reader's attention to the astounding similarity. Had Picasso seen these sculptures or could it have been mere coincidence? On every page he saw indubitable archtypes of 20th century western paintings. He seemed to remember similar judgments in his reading on art history a few days before. In Africa these are conventional. In the West, the same style becomes avant-garde. He read the magazine commentary, in which the writer said that Picasso, Braques, Vlaminck and Matisse derived their colors, their composition and their visions from black art. But what sort of paintings were being done by modern Africans? Are they, in an inversion, getting their colors, their perspective and their vision from Da Vinci and Rubens? It's a comedy. A rather sad comedy, though. But still more distasteful was the fact that he, a Korean man, had been surprised at these African art objects from the standpoint of Western art history. As if he were himself a Westerner. This curious detour of consciousness. It is not my fault, of course. It was not my crime when several centuries before Westerners brought artifacts back from Africa to display in their museums and to be happened on later by Picasso and his ilk. And according to the writer, in recent times this precious African folk art has been vanishing. Today such art objects are reproduced for the European market, but uniformly with coarsened skill so that beauty no longer lives in them. Originally, such sculpture was created to be deposited in tombs or as masks for religious rituals, not for idle aesthetic contemplation. Since the coming of European culture, with indigenous folkways and religion gradually disappearing, the original uses of this art disappeared as well. What the artisans now produce for souvenir shops is shoddy and virtually worthless. An African who adheres to the Western style of oil painting feels insulted when advised to extend native traditions. To preserve existing creations is naturally a priority, but when newborn African nations open museums of art they are in the situation of having to repurchase their native art from abroad. Etc., etc.

The article about wildlife on the verge of extinction was interesting as well.

. . . before the arrival of the Europeans, Africa was a paradise for wild animals. In the first place, the human population was much less dense. Traffic was more locally confined and people lived in small ensembles, leaving vast ranges to the wildlife. The number of animals taken was never a threat to their perpetuation. The situation changed with the advent of the Europeans. With the growth of the human population, the space taken over by man expanded. The European demand for such things as ivory and skins led poachers to indulge in reckless extermination of beasts. And they clear cut jungles and killed animals to eradicate disease carrying flies. If this continues, mankind will soon forfeit an invaluable inheritance. The animals of Africa are the property not only of Africans but of mankind. To preserve them is the responsibility of everyone. National parks and wildlife preserves have been established, but those very enclaves are unhesitatingly pillaged by local poachers. The really pitiful thing is that it is so difficult to persuade the Africans themselves of the need to conserve this endowment of nature. They think of wildlife as only a spectacle for Western hunters and tourists, and consider the dedication of wildlife preserves as an odd sort of colonialist system. A nationalistic attitude toward their patrimonial resources is not to be expected from them.

Eight out of ten of them are still leading traditional lives in the jungles and forests. If the political leaders, tribal chiefs and students do not recognize the importance of the matter, then future prospects will remain quite bleak. The day that the giraffes, zebras, lions and antelopes no longer roam the acacia-spotted slopes of Kilimanjaro—on that day the charm of old Africa will disappear forever.

Tokko Chun laid the magazine on his knee and looked out through the open window into the garden. In his imagination he popped up the plot of vegetation outside, luxuriant "nature" for the middle of a crowded city. It seemed acacia were plentiful in Africa. Africa, then. A running herd of giraffes, shaking their ladder-like necks as they weave between the acacias shining under the equatorial sun. The genius of camouflage—the scuttle of zebras. The deafening sound of a roar, without a doubt from an unseen king of the jungle. A rare spectacle, indeed. No wonder the writer finds it deplorable that the memories in his album are disappearing. He could easily understand the motives of the writer. After all, the problem depends on the individual's position. A giraffe is a giraffe, to be sure. An individual's attitude toward the giraffe will vary depending on one's point of view. The writer and African political leaders will find it easier to preserve the giraffes than to preserve another inheritance of nature, the African race itself. For giraffes are no spectacle on an empty stomach. Repeatedly to admonish hungry Africans about their duty to protect cultural treasures is useless. But then, after all, it is the Westerners who love culture and are concerned about the preservation of natural beauty. Perhaps their concern for the natural inheritance led them to do away with the African slave trade. Humanism, in other words. Their recent decolonization of Africa, too, is consistent with the dedication of a vast scenic preserve. Wonderful gentlemen they are. Bestowing medicine, bestowing disease. Beating and caressing. A drama, so to speak. In the contradiction there is dramatic conflict. They know one must do ill in order to do good. And how paradoxical for Picasso to have pirated African sculpture. For his creativity rested on a destruction of tradition. Therefore. Mondrian, after all, was honest. There is no evidence that Africans invented geometry. To lament the extinction of African art and to lament the extinction of African wildlife. The melody is the same. Nostalgia for old Africa. Had Hemingway realized this, he would perhaps have made a generous donation.

And there is not much difference between Africans and Koreans. They are alike in that both are natives. Yellow negroes. That is our self-portrait. Soon Westerners will come and advise us to add shamanistic exorcism, the historical philosophy of *Chŏnggamnok*, and *T'ojŏngbigyŏl* divination to the regular humanities curriculum in the universities. Because it is our duty to maintain and develop our yellow negro culture. There is very little difference, in fact, between Jehovah and Master Chŏng as historical spirits of the abode. Except that ours was never dialectical and from the earliest times has always worked directly in the style of a bolt from the blue. In other words, ours has "style". After all, revelation is always supposed to be in the style of a bolt from blue, no? There is not much difference.

The only difference is that we never loaded our fabulous truths onto a fleet of ships or flocked in force to foreign lands to pick fights and peddle snake oil. To be detected. In that lies the difference between a hunter and a ferocious beast. A hunter detected is no longer a hunter. The only way to overcome our collective inferiority complex toward Westerners is for us to do the detecting this time. It may take time. Consequently, the present generation cannot help being despondent. If there exists a man who is not, then that man is—a fine specimen of a gentleman. Still, how can you possibly give up on your own life? So Yu-jŏng asked. Certainly. Because living without committing suicide in itself is a commendable life. To sleep until a new sun dawns? No. The sun rises with a mind of its own, so it is an unhappy metaphor for human affairs. Well, let's see, then. That's right. In order to stand, don't you first have to sit? To sit up, don't you first have to belying down? Naturally. He set the magazine on the chair and went over and lay down on the bed. How to refuse to be a native? How not to become a giraffe? How not to become inhabitants of a reservation? What is to be doen? There is no chance that *Ch'unhyang-jōn* will win. Should I then scratch someone else's legs? No. Don't the wonderful Western people love even the natural resources of others? They are indeed men of the future. Exemplary citizens of the world. But. Only conquerors enjoy such leeway. And so it should be, but it is something beyond us. If so. Revolution. The task of changing the situation. Revolution. Come the revolution, will this suffering vanish? After the revolution, after we become the Switzerland of the Orient, what if I lost my lover? A utopia of the Orient, what good would it do me then? That's right. My problem is not of that kind. Whatever may become of Korea, in truth I don't care in my heart of hearts. This age in which we live. We are deluded in an age in which a life of classical order is yet unestablished. Thus poets are made into revolutionaries. What if a revolutionary loses his lover? What good is his government to him? What will it profit you to gain the whole world if your own soul cannot be saved? In this age must you gain the world to save your soul? Something fishy here, somehow. To gain the whole world, for we ourselves to become Westerners without delay, is that salvation? But we cannot become Westerners, either. By the time we've become Western, the West will have become something else. It would be the same thing all over again. Instead of endlessly pursuing that illusion, let's just flop down where we are. At least I. Let's think out some entirely different solution. Let's find a way to reverse the endless race between Achilles and the Tortoises. This Tortoise, in other words, should just sit down. Let the other Tortoises keep up the chase. Kim Hahk and his sort. Some Tortoises should sit down and ponder. Like me. So don't ask me with a glare why I'm not running.

This is long-term business. Not to be in the lead is all right. I needn't if I don't want to. So now I'm lying down. I do not run. I don't enlighten the rural hamlets and I don't do social surveys. Because my ruin is more painful than the ruin of Salyōul village. For Salyōul to meet ruin, does that not mean your own ruin? No. Even if I meet ruin, the villagers of Salyōul will not. Not in the coming world, at least. And Salyōul will not fall. For people like Kim Hahk will, by whatever means, protect it. My phase comes after that. Am I shirking? That's correct. I am shirking. I reject the idea that political vice can be overcome with the love of the ego. It can be overcome only by "time". Because time is the love of history. Devote the love of the ego only to the ego, whether your own or another's. I disbelieve the lie that the love of an ego can be devoted to a nation, a tribe, politics or history. An ego can only love another ego. Cursed be the pervert who declared "Italy is my lover." Cursed be those masked polygamists. A human can love only one other human. One who can love more than one human—that can only be God. But then, God is dead. A situation in which one can love more than one person—that can only be a family. But then, I have no family. Therefore I am free. Damn it. I am back where I began, after all. He rolled over onto his stomach and clutched his head between his hands. There was a time when the young could attain happiness by shedding their own blood for the sake of one great human. There was a time when people found life's reward in sitting in a dark room in some back alley of a foreign metropolis, conspiring to assassinate prominent leaders of an enemy state. Some people on a safari through a foreign jungle were once able to find a symbol of life in the promenade of a passing leopard. They were elated. They had a goal. But what on earth are we? Natives, weak animals already detected. Urchins drafted into the factional fight between George and Ivan. Not all fights are the same. If a fight breaks out from sheer rage, an inevitable life or death struggle, that is one thing. But if all you do in a fight is dark between the legs of your master and pinch the enemy's calves, there is no dignity in that. A lie. A lie. And again these suffocating layers of lies. A man who despairs of improving society and prefers just to live in a hygienic milieu. The idea that to Westerners we are merely yellow negroes. All of these things. An age never free from the gaze of self and others in which one blushes even to lift a finger. Castrated swine who invoke the banner of democracy in place of the philosophy of Confucius and Mencius. The pitiful sovereign people who vote for those swine. People who infallibly send not friends but enemies to the National Assembly. People who barter their souls for a cup of rice wine and a pair of rubber shoes. There can be no excuses for that. Nevertheless, false prophets put the people on a pedestal. Even though all of this emanated from their ugly soul. And still false prophets put the people on a pedestal. In order to extort petty sums from them. When the enraged prophets of Israel thundered to their people, how deep the despair whence their voices issued. Have we ever had such prophets? Plenty have shed tears avowing love for the people, but not one has gnashed his teeth and wailed his hatred of the people. People pawing the air in the miasmal swamps, applying cosmetics instead of medicine to each other's wounds. What a misfortune to open your eyes in the midst of this. This mire beyond your power or mine. So stop trying so desperately and pick up a handful of mud. Rub it on your face. Rub it on your neck. And then roll. In doing so, become like everyone else. That is love. To meet ruin together, when you cannot save them, is that not love? We awoke to find ourselves natives. In the old days, when the Westerners came to Africa they hunted elephants for ivory and they shipped the natives to America in chains for use as slaves. We are now negroes driven out to hunt in our own locale. To catch bears. What I saw in the North was the same. A tributary mentality, serving the greater without a speck of self-respect. A man lives within politics, and when that politics, both North and South, is a comedy of scratching somebody else's leg, what is someone living in such a world to do? Here, to think of a nation or a race is like fishing from a treetop. No. I nearly made a blunder. As if excusing myself for not being a patriot on account of the times. That's not it. I dislike patriots. By whatever means, I must steer clear of the path that leads to becoming a patriot. At least I'll not become a patriot. For to become a patriot is to become a beater for the hunt. Because unable to become a hunter? No. Because hunting gives me no pleasure.

He got out of bed. Stepping down onto the wooden floor, he staggered a bit. To liberate myself from all Karma was my resolution. I believed it possible because I had no family. When I accepted Hyōn's offer and came to his house, it was to experiment at that. The anticipated drama did not unfold. The only thing clear now is that he bought me. I was to endure this vice with a cold heart. I'm not regretting it now, of course. But I cannot control the world around me that has me making excuses at every opportunity. But still I can't ignore things. Like a monk who can't overcome his lingering attachment to this life. And listening to the noise it puts forth, and trying to identify what the noise is all about. What has Africa to do with me? I know that those most precious to me are themselves in a strange domain. In this situation, what's left for me to be concerned with? Should I stop reading entirely? Because reading breeds confusion. In the Bible there is no mention of Jesus Christ reading a book. God reads no books. Neither do the saints. Shall I stop going to school as well? In that way I would imprison myself completely. Then I could be free inside this room. Freedom. I become a god. Isn't my present life enough of an imprisonment? Still, I keep peeping out. An outside surely devoid of anything. I listen to the murmuring from the marketplace known as "living." Resting his elbow on the windowsill, he looked across the garden to the main part of the house. Over there were living people. Living. Why is the word so unfamiliar? How can I begin living? At any rate, I attend school, eat three meals a day, and those meals even require a grand acting performance, does this not deserve to be called "living"? Perhaps. I may be to greedy, and that's the problem. Does it come from my sense that the whole world's problems are on my shoulders? I don't think that way, but why this stifling feeling? Sometimes I run into Hyōn Ho-sūng as he rushes out of the house. At such times I feel a kind of respect. Because I see that he is living. A man who is diligent in anything exudes a certain dignity. Perhaps it is the armpit odor of "living". Is it some primitive longing for mobility? What could be done that most perfectly would preserve that primitive dessein? Unless it has the purity of a Mondrian, I wouldn't want to do it. In order not to be deluded.

There are such moments, of course. Moments of sudden longing for trivial things. Moments when the heart overflows with ineffeable joy after turning a certain corner. When the postman delivers a letter some evening. When I see a white-bearded old man sitting calmly in a tiny shop below a sign saying "Bean Sprouts". Those are the moments when I feel joy. I feel alive, with a faith as good as mint notes straight from the bank. But they are only moments. I cannot hold on to those mint banknotes forever. With that money I have to purchase time. Those precious moments I spend, receiving time as the change. It is an exchange of gold coins for copper. That is living. This exchange is beyond my power to comprehend and therefore I am sad. Am I, who rejects this circulating currency, to become a counterfeiter?

He abruptly stopped and held his head in his hands. A sound of whirring gears is heard inside his head. Long, long ago artists painted only special people and special landscapes. As for portraits, the subjects were always Taoist sages or the Buddha and his disciples. In the West, they painted Greek gods and heroes, or else Christ and his disciples. The subjects of art were preselected. The word "art" meant depiction of such preselected subjects. To depict the ego recognized as preeminent among all egos was art. It was the same with landscapes. Nobody painted their own garden, garlic or green onions, mackerel or scabbard fish. Only scenes with a special ego were considered art. Hence landscapes always showed a Garden of Eden with an evil serpent crawling by, or an enchanted Arcadia, or else the four gracious plants: plum, orchid, chrysanthemum and bamboo. When an artist painted an apple on a table one day, a new age began. One day when a certain Italian began speaking not of goddesses but of simple women gathered to gossip, a new age began. Artists from then on acquired freedom. They gained the freedom to paint beggars, neighbors' wives, maids, peddlers, soldiers (not generals), woodcutters, fishermen, drivers, whores (not Venus) and idlers. They gained the freedom to paint apples (not of Eden, but bought at a fruit stand), whales (not Job's, but one chased by a whaling ship) and pigs. There is no longer such a thing as a special ego. The age of gods and heroes, goddesses and queens, is gone. We now live in an age when everyone is a god. I'm a god and you are a goddess. I'm Apollo and you're Venus. An age in which all of us have high opinions of ourselves. Everyone enjoys the right of succession to the throne. Of course, there are differences among egos. But the difference is quantitative, not qualitative. It is not a difference of bloodline and rank but of address and occupation. The equality of egos thus has become like sweets in a picture. Because a princess without maidservants is no longer a princess. In the modern age, then, the ego divides itself like an amoeba. One becomes a maidservant and another a princess. The age in which we live in is an age of Onanism. An age in which a lonely and crazed ego performs a self-coronation witnessed only by the self in a secret room in the depth of the night. The next morning, off to the office with a briefcase and sack lunch, in this age of delusion. Therefore, writers also rack their brains to create a prince without pedigree. But could it be possible? For citizens of a metropolis, sickened by trivial concerns and dizzy with boiling lust, how could it be possible to gild the fantasy of

Ulysses? But there is no other way. Because the castle has been demolished. Now there is no name to call, for God is dead. A name you can call. It can only be your own name. It's no use to make the sign of the cross. Because God is dead. Knock. It shall not be opened. Because within God has already expired. But such a rational explanation is possible only for Westerners. For us natives, matters are still more complicated. For us the myth contains not the apple of Eden but just an ordinary apple. As our myth we had to accept an apple liberated from the coordinates of myth. Like the wife of a native chief who apes the dress of a missionary's wife, unaware it is long since out of style. The missionary speaks: "Jesus Christ is not a Westerner but an Oriental". Aha. So what? Like a merciless man who, having stolen the love of another, returns her after she's borne a dozen children, saying "Wasn't she originally your lover?" How painful not to be among those austere people who never attend to fashion, and who can gaze tenderly at an old lover who's cut the umbilical cord a dozen times? Cursed is the fate of those who must know the history of culture.

There was a knock at the door.

He walked over and opened it.

Yi Yu-jŏng stood outside, dressed to go out. Only then did it dawn on him.

"Oh, I forgot."

"What do you mean you forgot? Aren't you going?"

She looked inside and said,

"I'll wait, hurry down."

"Be down in a minute. . . ."

Said Chun, walking past the bed toward the closet.

When they reached the university, it was almost time for the performance to begin. They got out of the taxi at the gate and walked up a steep gravel path toward the brightly lit auditorium.

The big auditorium was already full of people. In the middle of the floor had been erected a stage about a meter high. The stage was set as an interior with abstract backdrops that merely suggested the contours of a room. On all four sides of the stage were stairs for entry and exit of the players. It was a theater-in-the-round production of the drama circle of that university. At last the play began.

It was a tragedy adopted from a Greek myth, but Tokko Chun was more interested in the stage design than in the action of the play. He had heard about round stages but this was the first one he had actually seen.

The actors waited in the audience for their appearances and when their scenes were over exited from the stage back into the audience. Every time this occurred the audience stirred and these distractions dissipated the dramatic tension on stage. There were even light ripples of laughter.

Whether intentionally or not, the lighting never changed from the beginning to the close. For people accustomed to being seated in a pitch black audience, eyes locked on a matchbox with one wall cut away, the set up was awkwardly unfamiliar. Not only Tokko Chun, but the entire audience seemed to feel that way. A play with no backstage. Following the story of a sorrowful destiny in a faraway land and a remote time as it unfolded on the stage, Chun found himself carried away by various thoughts. Their intention was to return to the simplest form of drama and to bring forth a deeper empathy between stage and audience, but that the desired effect had been achieved was doubtful. Whenever a foreigner in ancient costume suddenly appeared in the aisle to mount the stage or a radiantly dressed princess descended the stairs into the seats he felt uneasy. Was this bourgeois taste? Did it stem from a bourgeois inability to find any plausibility in a noble princess, having just shed tragic tears, coming down to sit beside commoners? Was it the inferiority complex of a plebeian, a *sangnom*, who feels that even in human sorrow there is a hierarchy of status? The notion that when a woman of royal blood feels sorrow, she should be surrounded by marble and diamonds, and when she collapses, it must be onto a settee of pure gold, is this not most undramatic? That a beggar should weep for the sorrow of a prince and a prince should feel compassion for a beggar's distress, isn't this where the value of drama lies? No, I cannot reduce it to that. In the first place, the choice of this play for their repertory was not good. Unsurprisingly, stage and audience were in disharmony. Not only were they experimenting with an unfamiliar form of production, they chose translated material for the content. If they had chosen a drama by a Korean playwright it would have come off a little better. With content so remote from our experience, to introduce such a stage design made it seem like a game. Even if art is like playing a game, it should totally absorb you in the moments when you enjoy it. That's it. The core of avant-garde aesthetics probably lies down this line. Theater-in-the-round supposedly was born in the earliest phase of classical drama, hence it is not avant-garde in the temporal sense. Yet, as the ancient art of Africa has become avant-garde, so the resort to the round stage should be seen not as a return to tradition but as an avant-garde phenomenon. We should not forget that the relics excavated from the ground are newer than anything else for us. Only then can we confront and climb over our ancestors. Theater-in-the-round, consequently, should not be treated as a recovery of an ancient form but as an innovative experiment. A man deprived of all background, a man with no dressing room to which he can retreat, is this not an image of the modern man? A man for whom it is impossible to invoke the god of destiny or to express his sorrow through poetry, is that not a modern man? But the hero on that stage does so. He does not despair. He tears his heart apart, but still he calls out to the god of fate and tries to impart a rhythm to his speech. He believes in the order of fate and in the utility of poetry. Hence his words ring false. And that is why the audience laughs. An atmosphere befitting a stage without walls. A change of direction is needed to move the denizens of modernity gathered here. To begin with the content, they should have forsaken the world of gods and heroes for the world of plain citizens. They should have chosen the tragedy of a contemporary man who must rise early and go to work at a lumber company after performing the secret ritual of a king the night before. For our present tragedy is a tragedy in which people who having nothing in common with tragic heroes are nonetheless cast in such roles. Only then could the actors be greeted warmly when they descend into the audience. There should be no room for a sullen response from an audience unable to identify with the heart of the high nobility. Only then would this form of drama live. Though this form has nothing left to hide, even if one wanted to conceal something, it can still be used to depict scenes in the empty-minds of modern men who must endure a dramatic existence.

On the stage the princess was weeping. If her crying is to leave us stricken, she must first renounce her status. And then she should abandon her logical, rhythmic lines and speak desperate lines in a confused and uneven style. We cannot unconditionally trust the tears of others. For all we know they might be singing inside. Drama alone can simulate reality. Because actual people appear. In this sense, drama is the lowest form of art. For, with one misstep, it is no longer art but reality. But fiction is not the same. Fiction must use not real substance but shadows—language. When real things disintegrate language must maintain control, a painfully difficult task. The more honest the attempt, the harder it is. When reality itself has become too confused and turbulent, language cannot properly perform its function. The language of our age, bereft of rhythm, cannot even dissemble. A nation living its life as if everyone is a player in a translated play. So everyone is unbecoming. The king looks like a peddler, the princess resembles a whore, the prince has the face of an urchin, the peddler speaks like a poet, the whore retains her chastity, and the urchin philosophizes. A nation in such a predicament and still everyone is bad mouthing each other's acting. How could a scenario be composed in such a place?

The princess was exiting with her face covered. Where is she going? The prince with a confidence as ample as his broad shoulders is nowhere to be seen. In whose embrace will you unburden that sorrow of yours? Beware of a man with a clam and quiet face. For he might be contemplating suicide. This world is full of animals with wounds of their own. The medicinal herbs used to treat those wounds are used up and the seed is dried up. All we have left is our tongues. We all sit in our attic rooms, licking our bleeding wounds, and scrounging some sleep for the morrow. Prophets always hold back the final word to preserve their own lives, but they closely attend to the number of listeners mobilized for their public orations.

Wherever you may go, there is no solution.

The prince on the stage unsheathes his sword.

It probably would be useless. Your sword would not even slice through the neck of a cat. Dear lofty Greek prince. Do you have any idea how Korean cats cry? Do please sheathe that sword of misunderstanding. Nobody at all fears such a thing. Instead, try brandishing a fistful of cash. Rain will fall from a cloudless sky and Ch'unghyang will take off her skirt. Even if the sword had been forged in heaven, occupying the best of Vulcan's apprentices for three years, it would still be useless. Because that sword is too artistic to cut the throat of a sow fattened by an old mother for the wedding of her only son. If you had come out wearing a kitchen knife on your belt, perhaps the audience would have been a bit impressed. But then, some people are more incorrigible still. People who mistake a kitchen knife for the godly sword of Vulcan. The chief gatekeepers of mighty Realism. Tribal chieftains in command of the arts, perched high on the back of scrawny donkeys, tridents in their hands. Compared to them, dear prince, you are exalted. Your sword undoubtedly is of fine lineage, and you too are of impeccable ancestry, born from the Milky Way of sperm launched in some velvet bed deep within a palace. But why on earth have you appeared in this college auditorium? Do you know who founded this college? Do you know how much the trustees of this college are now suffering? Do you know that the admission cut line has been raised substantially this year? Not likely. Then why in god's name have you come here and saddened us? On the plane from Greece, did you even once utter the name "Korea"? Perhaps you were irritated to notice that the ass of the stewardess was in no way inferior to your sister's. Surely. Besides, why have you come all the way here when you can play in your own land? That's the pity of it. The king snatches the sword and rushes at the adulterous queen. The white neck of the queen. But. Just a minute. Is it really possible for a human to love only one other ego? Consider, please, how she must have felt as your ego happily made its rounds through the cells of your concubines. Consider that her faithlessness is her love, and it was because she loved you that she clamped a lowly slave between her thighs. Shouldn't her unfaithfulness, therefore, be your glory? You should remember that love revives like a phoenix. You must know the affinities of the traveler, departing some tavern only to be drawn on by new charms and kindnesses to the next village. Isn't love something like this? Therefore, admire her honest vagina. Think once again of the magnificent physiology of that dark cave. Do not feel ashamed to hear that your esteemed mother, too, commited adultery. Your mother did know love. Love. Repent. And love once more.

The play was hobbling toward the final catastrophe. The adulterous queen was lamenting the death of her son.

Who would deny that sorrow? There is one embarrassing thing in your lament, however. ". . . would not exchange for the lives of a thousand men. . . ." For you, it is the truth. But in the present age one who talks that way gets arrested. Perhaps you could get by with "more precious than my own life". After all, you are a woman from a kingdom founded on slavery. But you are truly sincere. I wonder if you do not misunderstand, for in this age candor is no longer a virtue. The covert smile at the corner of your mouth when your son died. If anyone had seen it. After all. After all, you are a woman. Wise as a serpent. Death. You must have been imagining your reunion with your son in the underworld.

On the stage the queen was drinking poison. Her white throat. The play was over. The spectators shook hands with the foreign royal family dressed in fabulous costumes.

Chun and Yu-jŏng walked out amidst a crowd through the school gate.

"How did you like it? You were watching quite intensely. . . ."

Said Yu-jŏng, holding Chun's arm.

"I was busy acting myself. . . ."

"Acting? Now are you shifting to the calling of playwright?"

Chun laughed out loud at her misunderstanding.

"In my opinion they should have put on an original Korean work instead of a translated play."

"Maybe it was difficult for students to choose."

"Perhaps. At any rate, it was interesting. Are there a lot of such theaters-in-the-round in American?"

"Yes, I've seen some."

"It might be mistaken for a strip-show stage. They used it as an experiment, of course, but when there's not much of a theater-going public anyway, using an unfamiliar set up like that turned out to be too much of aleap, didn't it?"

"Someone I know was the art director and sent me the tickets. What did you think of the sets? Quite bold, don't you think?"

"Well, there's nothing wrong with boldness, but I can't say I approve without reservation. If the scenery employs abstract expressionism, then the production should follow similar lines, no, rather I mean the two should complement each other. It shouldn't be like a man riding a bicycle wearing an old traditional-style *kat* on his head."

"You are most severe."

"It's a fact, not my severity. Koreans are peculiar in feeling anything Western to be modern, even things classical. And if something is Korean, however contemporary it may be, it strikes them as classical, I mean, old-fashioned. So it's better to use original Korean creations, if possible."

"Do you plan to write plays?"

"Why do you ask?"

"I could sell your work for you."

"Well, you've no need to trouble yourself on my account."

"Very humble, aren't you?"

"Ha, ha, ha. This is somewhat different, but occasionally you do happen to read a newspaper piece about drama. I mean on the offical "Drama Day", for instance. Invariably such articles deplore the stagnation of Korean drama and call for some sort of major remedial steps to be taken. Every time I read such things I feel strange. The ambience of such columns always has a moralistic breath, like that of a world-deploring missionary at a revival gathering of some kind. As if the ruin of drama portends the ruin of the whole nation. Quite unnecessary, isn't it? Because drama is an art medium requiring production facilities, it's understandable that it needs cooperation and protection from society, but that doesn't mean it has any special rights. Even in the West, drama has long since ceased to be the principal form of art. Still less could we expect calls for government funding to bring a golden age of drama in nations where the tradition of drama never prospered. The problem lies elsewhere. The people who once made up the audiences of Shakespeare are now sitting in movie theaters, and that's why it can't be helped. We are lagging behind in everything. If there had been a man two centuries ago who proclaimed drama to be the art of the people, then now. . . . Enough of this. It's not that I have anything against drama."

"At any rate, there's not a single thing you don't find fault with. It's a good thing you didn't become a revolutionist."

"My God, don't say such a murderous thing. Unless you

want me to vanish without a trace."

"How cowardly for a man!"

"How can you say that after being away in America? Cowards are cowards. What do you mean by saying 'cowardly for a man'? Do you imagine a man is all rock and sinew? It's because only images like that are put forth that drama fails."

"My, who are you angry at now?"

"Pardon me, I got carried away. Why don't you treat me to a drink, instead?"

"What do you mean, 'instead'?"

She seemed in a good mood, however. When they reached a hotel, standing on a streetcorner with a blue lit sign overhead, they went into the bar for a drink. Yu-jŏng matched Chun drink for drink.

The dimly lit interior was filled with smoke and the plump liquor bottles adorning the bar were falling down drunk. The white collar of the waiter. The thick make-up of the waitress. The late night atmosphere of the bar made him feel drunk.

"Had enough?"

"Out of money?"

"You're always like that."

She glared at Chun as though she thought him hateful and gestured to the bar for another drink. Chun downed it in one gulp.

"What do you think you're doing?"

Yu-jŏng turned a wide-eyed stare upon him.

"Just a little more. Let's go after three more drinks."

"Will you be all right?"

"Out of money?"

She tut-tutted.

About the time they reached home the last curfew warning siren was heard. They got out of the taxi and went in through the small door cut into the main gate. The rooms where Chun and Yu-jŏng lived were in a back wing set off from the main part of the house. Just then, something dark came rushing at them out of the night.

"Shhh! Beth, shhh!"

Yu-jŏng waved the dog away and walked on through the back yard, arm in arm with Chun. Chun leaned on the woman, pretending to stagger.

"Don't pretend you're drunk." She said, pushing Chun's arm away.

After they walked in the house and arrived outside Yu-jŏng's room, Chun put his arms around her.

"Don't. Shhhh!"

Suddenly recognizing the voice that had just hushed the dog, Chun became a dog. He held her head between his hands and pressed his lips to her forehead. The smell of the woman's hair and the odor of whisky stung his nose. She didn't move. He tilted her chin up and sucked her lips. Leaning against the door with arms at her sides, she surrendered her lips to the man. The plump whisky bottles spilled over in Chun's head. Pulling her neck toward him, he tried to stick his tongue between her teeth. But that dense wall of ivory would not open. The woman stood up straight and gently pushed his chest away.

"Now, go and sleep."

This time she took Chun's head in her hands and touched her lips to the tip of his nose.

She turned around quickly, opened the door and went in. A click sound was heard. Chun stood vacantly outside the door. After a long while, clutching his spinning head between his hands, he walked upstairs, one step at a time. Murmuring to himself, I'm a dog. I'm a dog. . . .

XII

Oh, bucolic fields!
Oh, local magistrate!

Once out of the city streets the bus began to accelerate. His elbow propped up on the open window, Tokko Chun was looking outside. It was a journey that commenced with a sudden impulse, but now that he was underway a strange thought engrossed him. It was something like a sense of relief at having finally taken up something long planned. The place called P township was a little past Anyang. Before his father died he had told him of a man, a relative of Chun's through his paternal grandfather, who lived in a village of that district. Tokko Chun's grandfather had left that area for W City near the end of the Yi Dynasty. His family had long lived in P township. After coming South, Chun's father often fretted about not having gone there even once. He kept putting off the visit until things were going better, but in the end never accomplished his wish. The man in this village and Chun's grandfather had been especially close cousins, both being only sons. So for Chun's father, coming South meant not a refugee's flight to an alien land, but a kind of homecoming. Once in the South, however, every day made him more deeply aware of his impotence and every failure made it more difficult for him to reach his ancestral home. When one speaks of going home it always brings to mind a glorious homecoming. Reduced to poverty, his father's mind wandered further from home. It was a place his father had never even seen, and he didn't even know whether that old man was still alive. But the descendants of the old man might be there, his father had once said, and it had seemed that to visit the place was a duty in his father's mind. After forgetting all this for a long while, when Chun suddenly remembered he there and then had vowed to pay a visit. Now, on a bus approaching the place, his heart was buoyant. As if he was carrying out a long-standing intention. Would he still be alive? Even if he was gone, there would be his children. No. Not necessarily. The whole family might have moved away. If they were still living in the same place, at one fell swoop Chun would have a grandfather, uncles and countless cousins four or five times removed. The mere thought was incredible, like a lie. I'm like an adventurer with a marine chart handed down for generations who goes out in search of treasure buried by pirates. This is an adventure, needless to say. A quest for a multitude who share his blood-line. What are blood ties if not a myth? A procession of genes extending down through thousands of years. The words "generations of the clan" have a nice ring. They refer not to a mosaic of the Chinese characters in the names of relatives in particular clans, but to a steady parade of vessels on a long sea voyage, a line of procreative cells sharing similar traits. The position one occupied in this order, that determined our worth. As long as one had a place in the generations of the clans, one's position in the universe was solid. Reflecting on the sunlight and dew needed for a lone wildflower to bloom will engender a philosophical poem. And can there be any comparison when you reflect on man? The ancients who revered ancestry were doubtless poets. The continuation of innumerable Tokko. ♂♂♂♂♂♂. . . . That is history, it is the universe, it is mystery. The moment of carefully opening the precious book of genealogy beneath an oil lamp. A world of poetic vision would have opened before their eyes. It cannot be said that it was always bound to self-interested calculations. They must have felt the mystery of life in a sense broader than sustenance. That they themselves took pride in the achievements of their ancestors was both the most universal meaning of the classics and also the means by which tradition was continuously carried forward. Thence came their morality, their joy and their sorrows. Thence came forth their destiny. Thence issued everything for them. A gigantic living form continuing unbroken for hundreds of thousands of years, that was the mammoth shape of life. A dinosaur with limbs stretching endlessly across centuries and centuries. That's it. A family tree is a huge, huge dinosaur. Its head lies in a distant prehistoric age, its shoulders somewhere around the era of Three Kingdoms, and its tail an infinite serpentine "S". An individual within his genealogy is like a cell in the body of the dinosaur. In this immense body one breathes, eats, grows and then sleeps. It is not dying, it is sleeping. Our ancestors could never die. They just journeyed to the other world to be with their own ancestors. And if they became worried about their living descendants, they might visit at any moment. And if some narrow-minded descendant on such occasions slighted the ancestor, then the spirit would take revenge through some vulnerable target, inflicting a pinch of pain. Then a shaman would be brought to help discover which ancestor in which generation was enraged, and the spirit would quietly withdraw only after being mollified with sumptuous offerings. Inhabitants of mischief-filled myths, to be sure. We lived in an age of myth in which the living and the dead traveled without hindrance to one another's worlds. The life of the Greeks was forever under the sway of the love, jealousy, greed, estrangement and fighting among the Olympian dieties. And our ancestors lived the life, too. Official rank, vocation, love and hatred, all these were ruled by genealogy. The brilliant Golden Age of genealogical order and astrological divination. Even Father still lived in that epoch. Home must have held an unshakable place in his heart. This visit would be a belated gesture of filial piety, one never performed while his parents were alive. And from then on, he wondered, would he have a homecoming befitting the traditional worldview? The vicissitudes of man's fate all turn on the vagaries of time. To discover people whose blood is the blood in my own veins. Whether I will be able to love them is a question subsequently to be answered. To discover characters who had never once appeared in my life. Because one alone can never act out a drama. Hmm. So I'll be a solitary hero in search of my counterparts in this drama. Ahh. How sad the drama in which one character must search for another. That's it. It's worth a try to write a scenario along these lines. Or, shouldn't I? Isn't it quicker to live than to draft a script?

"Go straight up that road."

The bus conductress lifted her hand and pointed at a newly-finished road branching off from the expressway.

Chun stood there until the bus vanished around a mountain, and then he began to walk. It was close to noon and the sun was hot but the walk was not fatiguing. Now that he was approaching his destination his heart was fluttering violently. He hadn't felt that way since first plotting against Hyŏn Hosŭng. He follishly marveled at the miraculous presence of such bucolic fields so close to Seoul, and contentedly kept walking, clouds of yellow dust rising behind his heels. Mountain peaks were spread far and near before him, and when he turned about the highway seemed a belt of mist passing through this blue space. The mountains were sparsely wooded but most of the area was pasturage. Trees were even rarer here than in the area of the OP. Still, these mountains gave the impression of being real mountains. Solidly covered with soft summer grass, the smaller domed hills reminded him of tombs. Even so, they didn't make him feel grim. They might, in fact, have been tombs. These mountain fields must have been the site of countless tombs, though all are now indiscernible. In the old days before there were public cemeteries, people must have buried their dead wherever they liked. The flesh and bone rots and turns into earth. Washed by the rain, the soil moves down into the fields. There are planted the grain and vegetables to be eaten. Soaks into the wells, too. Becomes the fertilizer for mountain trees, trees cut to build houses and for firewood. Thus we have lived, eating our ancestors, drinking them and burning them to stay warm. Ancestors never die, they live forever. No one can die. There is only a metamorphosis, constantly recurrent.

The township hall was at the mouth of the village, beside the grammar school. The building had translucent windows and was shaped like a post office, with the entrance protruding from the middle of the front wall. Upon pushing upon the door and entering, on one side were compartments behind wooden bars and on the other seven or eight desks, all unoccupied. Within, across from the door, was a man eating his lunch. It was lunch hour.

The man who was eating lifted his head and looked over at the visitor.

"Well, I've come to get some information from the census registry."

"Census registry?"

The clerk gulped down a mouthful of rice and took a sip of water from his cup. Then he said,

"Everyone's out for lunch. They'll be back before long."

"Thank you."

Without responding further the clerk turned back to his lunchbox.

Chun left the township office and walked over to a hill behind the school. There he sat down under a good-sized pine tree. Low ridges diagnoally converged there from three directions, the fourth side toward the highway was open. On a hill facing the hill where Chun was sitting there stood a tin-roofed church. A stream wandered through the middle of the village with an incongruously straight cement bridge cast over it. In sight there were about forty or fifty dwellings. Beyond the hill there must be other villages, invisible from here. After looking for a while there was nothing left to see in this smallish hamlet. He smiled to himself, remembering he'd told the clerk he was there on business concerning the census registry. Because it was, after all, certainly business concerning the census registry. He rose and walked down the side road alongside the school. Bored with just sitting, he decided to have a look around the village. Leading to the bridge was a road scarcely wide enough for two cars to pass. This road and the stream divided the village into quadrants. A bit further on he came upon a tearoom. It was a two-story building. The two-floors together were barely as tall as a normal single story house. The signboard outside read "Greenhouse Tearoom" although the downstairs was a stationery shop. On one side of the building a flight of stairs led upstairs. He walks up the dusty steps. Tables were packed like sardines into the small room, and even so they number less than ten. He takes a seat and counts the tables. Nine. At one is sitting a group of customers who look like school teachers and at another an old farmer is sitting alone. Just then he realizes why the tearoom is called "Greenhouse". It is certainly hot. In fact, it would have been better named "Steambath". He can't just walk back out so he orders a soda water. It doesn't taste cool in those sticky hot surroundings. A limp wet breeze occasionally crawls through the open window. This. . . is too much. For the first time since arriving in the village he feels speechless. While sitting on the hill looking about he hadn't felt at all like this. A popular jazz song is wheezing and puffing from an old crank-type phonograph on the counter. The other customers were also just sitting there with blank expressions. The group looking like school teachers got up. They exchange pleasantries as they paid the waitress and then left. The school can be seen through the windows on the left. So they are. The just departed group can be seen on the road leading toward the school gate. The tearoom is unbearably hot. He pays the waitress. She takes the money with one hand as she pops a piece of ice in her mouth with the other.

He comes down the steps. It's much cooler out on the street. Buys a straw hat at the stationer's and puts it on. Feels very cool. He comes upon a little tavern. In the streetside window is a cooked pig's head. A sudden sensation of nausea, for the whitish nostrils of the pig seem about the flare alive. In front of the shop, a couple of drunks are flirting with a young woman. Next was the police station. Nobody on watch out front and the inside is clearly visible through the open door. A policeman with his shirt off is washing his face. A yellowish mongrel sits watching the man wash. A barnlike building with a sign reading "Cotton Gin". Liveliest place so far. From the dark interior issues a whitish dust along with a sound like "tŏl-k'ŏ-dŏng, tŏl-k'ŏ-dŏng". In the shade under the eaves a man in knee-length pants with his navel exposed is taking a nap. Beside him a woman with a kerchief around her head is flopped down, breast-feeding the baby on her lap. Big breasts with blue veins standing out. He steps by and looks inside the building for a minute. The machine with its barrellike wooden cover is running "tŏl-k'ŏ-dŏng, tŏl-k'ŏ-dŏng", its leather belt gripping and slipping. On the far side of the machine are three men bent over their work as if it were an old watermill. The clapboards of the walls, nailed up in a haphazard fashion, tremble with each turn of the motor. The monotonous sound of "tŏl-k'ŏ-dŏng". The shaking walls. The shadows working in darkness at the mill. The man slumbering soundly. The woman seemingly content to leave her nipple in the baby's mouth forever. He moves on, feeling that if he stayed any longer he too would have to lie down in the shade. The sun was getting worse. Clouds of dust rise from his toes with each step. The straw hat he wears does little good. He doesn't intend to stop walking, though. Looks at his wristwatch. Still time before lunch hour is up. No cause to hurry. He decides to make the whole circuit of the hamlet and then go back. Besides, his mood isn't bad. The tired, monotonous drone of "tŏl-k'ŏ-dŏng". Boiling sunlight. Still, this weary pleasure. A weary joy pervading every last cell of his body. Thinking is bothersome. Simply weary. Good. Keep on walking. Shoes now caked all over with dust. A man passes shouldering a huge earthen jar on an A-frame. he leaves in his wake a strong smell of rice wine. Probably on his way to that tavern. Crossing the bridge. Church standing on the steep hillside. On both sides of the road leading up to it, cosmos are growing. A tiny building with a tin roof. To one side is a lattice belfry and behind that, a dog pen. A mixed-breed dog, his forelegs sticking out of the pen, looks up, alerted. He does not bark even once, and it seems that in three years as a church dog he must have learned love. A peek into the church. On the far side of the off-white wooden floor stands a pulpit and behind it a religious painting is hanging. Going around to the backyard, he sees a tile-roofed house standing off by itself. There is a ledge for storing food urns and a solitary canna. The outer door is open but the screen is closed so he has no way of knowing whether anyone is inside. None of his business, so he turns around and heads back out front. By the dog pen he squats down. The dog stares back listlessly, his tongue hanging out. Thick saliva strings down. He is chained. Where could he possibly go, anyway? Chun rises and walks down the hill. He looks at his watch. Still not much time has passed. He comes back down the road again and happens upon a small Confucian school. Compared to this, the church was very neat and new. The grounds are spacious but the building is very run down. The earthen wall around it in places has caved in like a sick donkey's sides. The tile roof of the main structure is like a mugwort field, covered with green moss and weeds. Somebody was living in the wing that jutted out diagonally to one side, for a pair of men's rubber shoes were sitting on the steps. Here again, however, the door screen is closed and nothing of the inside can be seen. Weeds grow abundantly all over the yard, bespeaking a long period of neglect. The June midday sun is the only thing filling the wide yard. Peering over the earthen wall, he feels like a man exploring a ruin.

Most of the blue and red paint of the building had long since peeled away, and the woodgrain, darkly weathered by wind and rain, clearly tolled the state of decay. Speaking of red and blue, the primary colors in which we paint our buildings are anything but beautiful. Each time he sees pillars and gateposts painted in those crude colors he gets nauseated. How could people who enjoyed the clear sounds and cool melodies of traditional Korean music possibly have chosen such colors? It was absolutely beyond him. Thus, its weather-beaten and peeled condition made it look far more graceful. This massive, solidtimbered building was definitely more dignified than the church he had just seen. Would my ancestors, too, have strolled in leisure about this yard? The thought of it filled his heart. Truly. It was an uncontrollable feeling. After all, a man, an ordinary man, feels most secure in the embrace of tradition. This yard must once have bustled with people, and whenever something took place on the central political stage the local scholars must have dispatched memorials or petitions to the throne. The local Confucian academy must have been a kind of pressure group. Perhaps they were more than blind followers. With the passage of time, moss overtakes everything. There must have been nameless saints who, out of blind love for Confucianism, never strayed a step from the orthodox path. Such men would have sat down here, feeling despondent or indignant about developments in the distant capital of the kingdom. It might have been issues of protocol concerning a royal funeral or questions of ritual for the wedding of the crown prince. Disputations *pro et contra.* "According to the texts of the sages. . ." and so on, so they would have said, stroking their beards. The underlying causes, whatever they might be, were of little consequence. For them, political obstinacy was necessary, and their conviction that it had fallen to them to set right the morality of the world merits respect. They had a sort of single-minded devotion to order. It must have been their form of the love of truth. In their own way did they not repulse the Japs in 1592, at the time of Hideyoshi's invasion? If "repulse" is too strong, at least they didn't roll over and play dead. In the war of that year many were cowards but many endeared themselves to us, as well. Without obligingly dragging out Admiral Yi Sun-shin, there were many instances of manliness. That it was not the high officials but the low-ranking Confucian scholars, not the rich but those who had been brutally thrashed, who were bravest before the sword—was this perhaps evidence of the hidden power of Confucianism? Oops! Almost made another blunder. I never intended to concern myself with the administration of justice in this old ruined citadel. Looks at his watch. Now, shall I slowly head back?

Turning the corner of the earthen wall he walked down the road. The cotton gin was still droning "tŏl-k'ŏ-dŏng", like an old man in convulsions, but the man and woman were no longer there. Maybe she was a distant cousin of mine. Passing by the police station, inside he saw a white-collared man thumbing through documents. He considered how to put his questions to the clerk. Because his inquiries come out of the blue, he feels a bit uncomfortable. The fact is, this is the domicile of my grandfather and I've come to find out if any of his relations are still living. Could you please check the registry for me? I'll put it that way.

At the tavern with the pig's head, a young woman was flirting with a man, her arms around his waist. He passes the tearoom and walks into the township office. This time there is a man behind every desk. He asked for the man in charge of the census registry and put his question as he had planned. After listening to Chun, the clerk stared at him as if to say "Wow, what have we here!" Feeling sick at his stomach, Chun awaited a reply.

"No way of knowing."

That was supposed to be an answer.

"What do you mean?"

"What you are asking is to look into documents from several decades ago, but we only have documents dating back to the

Korean War. The old ones were all burnt during the war."

The net on which he stood, delicate as a spiderweb but which he had reckoned strong, quietly began to give way. The clerk's explanation was brief but sufficient. His arm resting on the counter, Tokko Chun vacantly looked at the clerk, unable immediately to speak. Perhaps sympathizing with Chun's disappointment, the clerk shifted to a much gentler tone, saying,

"You'll learn nothing here. As far as I know, there's nobody at all named Tokko in our township."

"None?"

"Nobody."

"Isn't there any other way? I know for sure that he once lived here. . . ."

"Well. . . . Why do you need to know? You don't need such documents to obtain a reregistration certificate."

"Reregistration?"

"Yes, if you notify the registry where you presently live, they will certify your permanent residence there as legal."

"It's not that. I just wanted to locate some relatives this way."

As Chun said "relatives" a blush came over his face. Until now, he had no such word in his dictionary.

"You might try this, then. Go straight out this road and there'll be a Confucian school. There's an old man there who knows about this village from way back."

Chun's ears pricked up.

"Ah, you don't say. I'll go there and try to see him, then. Thanks very much."

As he walked out he felt every eye in the room trained on the back of his head. The distance to the door, though only a few steps, seemed far, and by the time he made it outside he felt a little giddy.

He turned back again the way he had come, heading for the Confucian school.

So, they were all burned up during the war. Probably they

were. The sandcastle within him continued to erode. Why didn't it occur to me before? But then, I didn't start out with any certainty of finding him. Never know, might find out more from the old man. Still clutching at a thread of hope, Chun passed through the gate of the Confucian school.

On the stone step the shoes he had seen before were still there. He stood before the drawn screen and let his presence be known, but there was no response from inside. Chun put one knee on the wooden floorboard and slowly pulled the screen open.

Inside the room, a white-haired old man was asleep, his head resting on a wooden pillow. Chun closed the screen again and sat there on the edge of the floor. He waited, hoping the man would awaken before very long. Off to one side, near the corner of the earthen wall, was a semblance of a flowerbed, with a couple of sunflowers, crepe myrtles and balsamine. The sunflowers alone stood tall amidst the other crippled-looking flowers. A kingly dragonfly sat on the tip of a sunflower leaf, then hovered up for an instant only to return once more to the same dangling perch. There wasn't even a sound of breathing from the old man. Loneliness and stillness suddenly took command of Chun's heart. Pure sorrow. Emptiness. Then, something resembling joy. A certain course of evil—his heart pounded with a masochistic urge. He sat in that state of mind for a long time. The tumor that had long been growing within him once more had brought forth a murky stench. It was a wind from the nameless void yawning on the far side. Yet again he had fallen victim to those symptoms, symptoms he had hoped to leave behind him.

How could he sleep so long? The old man would not wake up. Was he going to pass away directly? He once more opened the screen and looked in. Not a sound.

"Grandfather."

He called softly.

"Grandfather."

The body that had been lying there like a corpse stirred a little. Again he called, a bit louder. The old man's head slowly turned toward him and for the first time Chun could see his face clearly. As people do when just roused from sleep, he looked blankly at Chun for a few moments. Then he slowly sat up.

"Who are you?"

The old man asked, his voice raspy with phlegm.

Chun half-bowed and said,

"Well, I was wondering if I might ask you a few questions. . . ."

The old man moved closer to the door. With one hand he pounded himself on the back as he waited for Chun to go on.

"Do sit down."

As invited, Chun sat on the edge of the floor across from the old man.

"Well, my grandfather used to live in this village. Toward the end of the Yi Dynasty he moved up to the North. There he passed away. During the last war, my father and I came down South. For some time I'd been meaning to pay a visit here, and it kept being put off, but now I've finally come. I couldn't learn anything from the township office because the census records from before the war were all burned up. They told me I might be able to find out something if I asked you. After waiting while you were sleeping. . . ."

Chun stammered.

"Humm. End of the Yi Dynasty. . . ."

The old man looked at Chun for a while and then said,

"It's difficult. If it was the end of the Yi Dynasty, I was barely starting to school. Well, what was you grandfather's name?"

Chun gave him the name.

"Tokko?"

The old man shook his head decisively.

"I don't know. It's an uncommon name but it doesn't ring a bell, so I can't say. Wait a minute, how old was your grandfather when he left?"

"Well. . . perhaps. . . ."

Chun made a rough guess at the age.

"An adult. So he wouldn't have had anything to do with us snot-nosed kids. . . . Are you sure this is the village?"

"Yes, this is the place."

"Hmmm."

The old man took out a pouch of tobacco and loaded his long-stemmed pipe. Chun hesitated, wondering whether he should take out the cigarettes from his pocket, but in the end decided not to.

"It's going to be difficult. I'm the oldest man in this village, I was born here, and everyone older than me has either passed away or moved off. . . . A rare name like Tokko, yet I can't recollect, so it seems unlikely anybody else would know about it. Besides, it was so long ago. . . ."

The old man took a puff on his pipe and said,

"These days there are only a few families who've lived here as far back as that. And most families are headed by younger people. Well, is your father still alive?"

"He's passed away."

The old man nodded.

"Then are you alone now?"

"Yes."

The old man tut-tutted.

"Bad times these are. Can't travel back and forth in our own land."

The old man lamented with a sigh and, turning his eyes to the yard, gently exhaled some smoke.

Chun said nothing and closely watched the old man. If this was how things would turn out, the matter was over. Perhaps a barren heart leads a mind down strange paths, for now Chun began scrutinizing the old man's face, trying to judge his character from his physiognomy. It was something Chun had felt when the old man first turned to face him a while before—and the more he peered at him the more he saw a noble's face. Broad forehead, solid chin, sharp bridge of the nose, short-cropped white hair and white-specked eyebrows slightly turning down over the eyes—all these features contributed to his dignified air. But his most distinctive feature was his beard. It was no common goat beard. His long white whiskers flowed from thick sideburns in a wave down to a slightly upturned point. Whenever he spoke, slightly yellowed but even teeth could be seen behind his mustache. For a moment Chun felt stunned by the beauty radiating from the old man's face. He probably doesn't have a soul to match this face. But what, then, was this phenomenal beauty? Such a face. That calm and stoical expression. A face with no trace of animality, a face like a memoire of one who enjoyed life. Enjoyed, indeed. It seemed most unlikely that an Yi prime minister would still be alive, and this old man, merely one of the countryside literati, probably had experienced more sorrows than joys in his long life. Why else would he be caring for an old Confucian school in an advanced stage of decay? Cast out by the world because his learning was out of date, he still lived his life full of righteous indignation. Cross-eyed life. A life spent contemplating an irrelevant eternity. Marionette. But even so, that face. Was that how one who grasps a kind of perfection ends up? Impossible. Was not Socrates strong proof to the contrary? In what sense is one's face really a function of one's soul? Oblivious to Tokko Chun's impertinent reveries, the old man displayed his kindness one last time.

"Wait a minute. Let me think. . . ."

The old man stood up and went to the other room. He came back with an armful of dust-covered books.

"Take these out there and dust them off, please."

Chun carried the bundle out into the yard, brushed the dust off, and brought them back.

"These are old documents, indeed."

The books the old man was looking through were old records of the Confucian school, things like membership rolls and lists of patrons who had donated money for renovation. The old man checked through some and gave others to Chun for him to look through. Since they were lists of names, it didn't take long to run through the pages. The family name "Tokko" appeared nowhere.

"Hmm. . . . I'm truly sorry."

Murmuring in that sympathetic tone peculiar to the elderly, the old man replaced the books and came back.

"It can't be helped. Besides, it was so long ago. I didn't come with any great hope of success. . . . I'm sorry to have troubled you."

The old man shook his head.

"It's only natural for a descendant to do his filial duty. . . ."

At these words,Chun felt his face heat up.

"Perhaps there may be some other way."

Such was Chun's reply. His business concluded, it was time for him to leave but it seemed unnatural abruptly to depart.

"The place seems really run down."

Chun said, looking at the main building, in an attempt to fill the silence. The old man just nodded. The gesture was far more eloquent than gratuitous explanations.

The shadow of the sunflower meanwhile had grown longer.

He got up and bid the old man farewell.

"It's too bad, you could have stayed a while and taken a meal with me, if you wished."

The old man said, coming out to the gate to see Chun off.

When he reached the cotton gin Chun looked back. The old man still stood at the gate with his eyes on Chun.

As he came to the pig's head tavern, Chun turned and entered on a sudden impulse. Inside there was no one. In a loud voice he called out for the proprietor. Through the kitchen door appeared the woman he had earlier seen outside embracing a man. He asked for a bottle of *chŏngchong*, but she said they were out. He settled for a bottle of *yakchu* rice wine and bought some beef. Then he headed back to the

Confucian school. There was no sign of the old man in the room.

After some time, the old man appeared around the corner of the main building. Chun gave him the wine and beef, telling him it was his pleasure, and started to leave. The old man asked him to leave his address, saying he would check around and inform Chun if he learned anything. Chun wrote down his boarding house address and gave it to the old man.

The time he spent waiting for the bus by the side of the expressway was incredibly boring. During the half hour he waited the only vehicles to pass were two cargo trucks. There was no railroad line or army post nearby, so he imagined it was always like this. Sitting under a roadside zelkova tree, in the direction of the village the view was blocked by ridges on either side and all you could see was a stretch of the stream, a few houses here and there, and the church.

The bus arrived, raising a dusty wind. He took a seat and one last time took a look toward the village. A day's voyage was ending without profit. Treasure island had no written coordinates. He had just gone to look for it because the thought popped into his head. It was no more of a treasure than that. Nevertheless, for him it had been a valuable voyage.

On the bus ride back he closed his eyes and reflected on the events in the village that day. The name Tokko had been utterly unfamiliar to the clerk at the township office and to the old man, too. Tokko. But then, however eagerly you may thumb through the history books, no generals or statesmen named Tokko are to be found. Nowadays, they say Kim and Yi are the most commonplace family names, but in old times the mere fact one bore the name Kim or Yi was enough to entitle one to the protection of the local community. Since his family name was neither of these, the Tokko family tree evidently was nothing very splendid. Even if it once had been great, of course, it hadn't amounted to anything, but for it to vanish without a trace was a bit too much. I wonder what the Tokko name derives from. When I have a chance I better look it up. At any rate, it had not been a waste. A faint sound of "tŏl-k'ŏ-dŏng, tŏl-k'ŏ-dŏng" still echoed somewhere in the back of his mind. Comparing the full day just ended with the day he might have spent at a music hall or a movie made him feel better. Wait a second. I didn't stop and see the post office. Unlikely there hadn't been one. He checked his mental map of the village. But no likely building came to mind. He hazily seemed to recall a mailbox out front of the township office, but he wasn't certain. No. There wasn't one, was there? As he repeated the task of inserting and deleting a mute red postbox in front of the tin-roofed building, the bus had already come to the Han River bridge.

"You seem to be enjoying yourself."

Yi Yu-jŏng said insincerely, as she sat in a wicker chair drinking juice.

"I sure am. . . ."

Chun pulled up a chair across from her and took out a cigarette. Now that he thought of it, he had not smoked all day.

"Everything is fun. To make a lotus bloom in the mud, to grow a chrysanthemum in a manure heap, or to paint a halo over a whore's head, such is the work of a poet."

"How sublime."

"Don't be such a cynic. Try at least to hold on to the virtue of humility."

"Seeing the tan on your face, I bet you've been on a picnic. Am I not right?"

"I've gone on a Western voyage."

"Western voyage?"

"With a response like that, how could you do a painting of genius? Is there another Western voyage besides *The Chronicle of the Western Voyage* undertaken by Son Oh-gong?"

"Goodness lord, he's philosophizing again."

"Don't be that way. As a race we've always loved empty

theory and idle talk. Go ahead, talk forever. Don't hold precious words inside where they'll rot, spit them out. Surely, no one else has said anything very great. It is the brazen with eyes clenched who always succeed. Everything in sight, nail it down with words. Then it'll be yours. Don't screw shut the mouth your ancestors left you. Speak. If you won't open the barn door, at least let the poor of Korea open their mouths. Whoops! I'm making another blunder."

Yu-jōng bummed a cigarette from Chun and inquired,

"To whom is this addressed?"

"To myself, all of it."

After taking a drag, she said,

"By the way, I'm starting a business."

At that abrupt announcement, this time it was Chun who asked,

"Starting an art gallery?"

Yu-jōng laughed, blowing smoke out as well, and said,

"Not a bad guess, but wrong. Nobody in their right mind would open a gallery in this country. There are only a handful of old paintings, no active market for them, so galleries have to try to deal in modern works that are unknown quantities. How can you do business without merchandise? In such circumstances, how can you open a gallery?"

"Hmmm. So that's how it is. Then what are you doing?"

"I told you to guess."

"I give up."

"I'm opening a commercial art firm."

"You mean interior design?"

"Designs, signboards and landscaping, among other things."

Chun stared at Yu-jōng.

"What's wrong?"

"Nothing, I'm just impressed."

"Impressed, are you kidding?"

"I mean it, really. The sort of courage that links art to money, I find it commendable."

"Money is part of it, but in the present situation it won't

be a big operation. It'll just be like moving my studio onto the street."

"Popularizing art?"

"No. It's convenient for meeting people and will let me earn a little on the side, don't you think?"

Chun nodded.

"I suppose so. Applied art. Sounds good. Applied literature should be developed, too, don't you think?"

"There's no such thing, is there?"

"Sure there is. You must be blind. Movie scripts, radio drama, newspaper ads, journalistic articles, what are these if not applied literature? You can distinguish pure and applied literature, can't you?"

"Criteria?"

"Far from clear. Literature that is pure is pure literature, and literature that is applied is applied literature."

"There you go again."

"Enough of that. Are you starting soon?"

"No. I'm thinking of working out the details this fall."

Yu-jōng paused for a while and then added,

"By the way, my sister asked me which resort we should go to for our vacation this summer. I told her I would discuss it with you first."

The word "resort" at once brought "country" to mind, and P township popped into Chun's mind. The rumbling cotton gin, the pig's head, the policeman washing his face, the Confucian school—all these scenes rushed through his head like a preview at the movies.

Realizing Yu-jōng had fixed a stare upon him, Chun tried to cover his discomfort with a laugh but it didn't come off well.

"Something seems strange. Sure nothing happened to you today?"

"Why, do I look it?"

"You do."

He did not respond at once and turned his eyes to the window. The leaves of the old cherry trees were floating in the twilight outside like whitish clumps of cotton. He finally decides to say nothing. For some reason, he feels reluctant to talk of the day's journey. Not that he had found any salvation. Do I lack courage, after all? In whom can I transplant this shapeless tumor growing within me? Oh, grief. I cannot even give you a shape. You've long dwelt in the heart of my heart. You are an arrow lodged, a bird not flying. Your sad cries and painful gestures I keep. I found no neighbor to whom I could return you. I tell you in confidence, you are loathsome to happiness. Have you purposely taken over my soul? Grief, my bride. For you, oh, my bride, I have closed my window and ceased my laughter. The day my youth ended you too died. But no stone gate stands at your tomb. Oh, grief, you who spread your wings over the pyre. Your phoenix and my tears. The sweet sorrow of Chŏng Chi-yong's verse resounded in him like twilight. Have I not hated to caress sorrow this way? Have I not struggled to escape becoming a serpent devouring its own tail? But my teeth close on nothing but wind. Even in that village, sunk in drowsy exhaustion, wind was all I chewed. Though my wish was to bite and rip the flesh of Hyŏn, all I managed was to scratch his wallet a bit. Nor did I succeed in sinking my teeth into Kim Sun-im, Christ's woman. Are these teeth of mine real? Are they no more than false teeth that deceive others but not myself? Are they teeth set in a locked jaw, like those of the cooked pig displayed in the window of that tavern? A set of teeth. Shhh! Beth. Shhh! Yu-jŏng's teeth were locked tight that night when we returned from the play at the theather-in-the-round. My tongue was powerless against that rejection. The wind on the far side of the tumor within me. That's it. That summer day when those silver birds bombed the city, that was when the tumor germinated. Like a grain of sand insinuating itself in an oyster, that woman implanted an incurable tumor within me. A grain of sand more lethal for me than the city, the bombing or the motherland. Can it be called a pearl? No. An incapacity to beautify in that way, this is my malady. It is a tumor. A tumor. It is a dense tumor eating into the flesh. It doesn't boil up and burst out, it just aches. To forget this pain, I bared my teeth and went in search of prey. Even at the OP, I constantly tried to grind up everything, the tedium of air and sunlight, the enemy I saw through my field glasses. But in fact I was consuming my own flesh. I merely deluded myself when I imagined I'd bitten Kim Hahk, Kim Sun-im and Hyŏn Ho-sŭng. All I had done was rip and eat my own flesh. There has been a mistake somewhere. And Yi Yu-jŏng.

Chun looked over at her.

Yu-jŏng was sitting well across the room and only her silhouette could be seen in the already darkened room. There was a faint halo around that dark human shape. That tender shadow. That shadow. . . .

Like a wave rushing onto rocks, a heart is rushing there with a roar. The first wave broke against the solid wall of teeth and shattered into foam, and now, the heart has built once more.

In this age, is an adventure more real the nearer it is? No. Was it not so in all ages? In all ages.

XIII

Count Dracula's Genealogy

Gloomy patches of clouds rushed swiftly across the dark blue sky. A thunderstorm was about to break as twilight came one early summer evening. A carriage rolled through the gate of an old castle.

An old lady and a young maiden climbed down from the carriage. The old lady guided the girl to a room, admonishing her never to enter the wing of the castle beginning at the end of the corridor. When the old lady was gone and she was alone, the maiden went to the window and looked out. The sun was down and the last glint of twilight had flown. Through the dark air the spacious courtyard and the watch-towers soaring here and there looked as mysterious as scenes in a painting. She was a student on her way to a distant convent school. At the kind invitation of the old lady, whom she had happened to meet at a roadside inn, she was spending the night in this castle. After eating dinner and talking a while with the old lady, she returned to her room, thinking it strange that there was no sign of people in this huge castle. Since her arrival she had seen no one but the old lady and the servant at dinner. Only two people in this big castle? After pondering this for a while, the maiden was overcome by naive curiosity. She stealthily opened the door and went out into the corridor.

To the right and up a flight of steps was the old lady's room. She walked the opposite way. It was the direction she had been warned not to go. She traversed the corridor on tiptoe and entered the forbidden wing. By chance the moon was full, and the blue rays of moonlight pouring in through huge windows set in the wall were enough to illumine her path. It was at that moment. She abruptly halted. The door of a room a few steps ahead was slightly ajar and there was a light from within. Her heart began pounding violently. She approached the door that was leaking light, as if she were being pulled toward it. Then, putting her eyes to the crack, she looked inside. She was aghast. In the room was a young man, standing with his wrists and ankles in chains. He had dragged his chains out into the middle of the room but they allowed him to go no further. He was dressed in fine clothes and leather boots, his hair neatly combed. His face was noble in its features but there was a slight cast of blue to his complexion. It was at that moment.

"I know someone is out there! Hello! Open the door, please! Save me, please!"

Shouted the man in the room.

The young maiden was frozen stiff.

"Open the door just for a minute! Please, hear me out! Nothing to be afraid of. See how I'm chained, see?"

She made up her mind and opened the door. She then took one step in.

"Oh, who are you?"

"I am a traveler passing through, a guest here for tonight."

"I see."

The man nodded and stared at her piercingly. She felt dizzy, as if sucked into that gaze.

"What did my mother tell you?"

"What?"

"The old lady, she's my mother. She's the one who locks me up like this."

"Oh, dear!"

"She didn't want to hand the castle and estate over to me so she chained me up here. I've been in this suffocating room for years already. Whether it rains or snows, whether spring or summer comes. . . it's spring now, isn't it?"

"It's early summer."

"Oh, then the roses will soon bloom. Dear maiden, if this goes on I'll surely go mad and die. I can no longer endure this horrible loneliness. Please unchain me, please save me."

"Ah, what am I to do?"

Asked the maiden, clasping her hands with tears of compassion in her eyes.

"If you go to my mother's room, you'll find a small chest on her dresser. The key is in it."

"All right."

She walked back to the main hall of the castle. Her heart raced with fear, but not only with fear. The thought that her fearless help was needed to restore the castle to the rightful heir gave her courage. She stole the key then, as the young nobleman had ordered, went to the back of the room and looked outside. From there she could see the balcony of the room where he was imprisoned. The young man was outside the door waiting, his chains trailing behind him. She aimed and threw the key. The little piece of metal flew in an arc and landed at the man's feet. The man bends down and picks up the key. He puts it in the lock. His feet are now free. Then both wrists. The man looks up and raises both arms. The Prince of Evil has been freed. Dracula, the Lord of Darkness, runs fleetly up the steps, his cape flying behind. The first victim is his mother. The loud and lusty laughter of the son of evil echoing through the night of the castle. The son who has sucked his mother's blood. A young maiden who had safely arrived at school without suspecting a thing, Dracula, who had followed her—when he appears before her it is always as a well-bred young nobleman. The maiden becomes his unwitting accomplice. The pursuit of a theology professor who had sensed it. The successive victims. The last scene. A fight inside a windmill. In the nick of time, the professor turns the blade of the windmill and casts a shadow of the cross on the Prince of Evil. Dracula staggers and falls to the ground. . . .

A bell sounded and the lights were turned on.

Tokko Chun left the movie theater, following the surge of the crowd. Outside it was raining.

He walked along beneath storefront awnings. When he came to a music hall he opened the door and stepped in. He looked for an empty seat and sat down. The theater, down the street from his college, was a place he often frequented. For a low price they screened films several years old. Today, as usual, he had no reason to hurry home so he had gone to the movie. The customers were mostly students. The films were ones that after a few years came back to Seoul following a first-run in the premier theaters and after release in the provinces. It wouldn't have mattered if they were several decades old instead of a few years. He just liked the hours he spent sitting there idly, watching the trivial tossing and turning on the screen. Besides the tickets were cheap. Of course, now Tokko Chun no longer needed to worry about the cost of admission. He didn't know what to do with his excess pocket money. But he still had the habit from the days when he had to walk to save streetcar fare of ducking in places just to rest. His clothing, food and shelter were incomparably better now, but the state of his mind had not improved a bit. It was still like that old, run down, third-class movie house.

The hall was packed with customers, probably because of the rain. The sound of people jabbering, their hot breaths and the wailing jazz all blended into the atmosphere of a steamy and deafening cavern.

Students pinched by poverty, worried about tuition, watching third-run movies, listening to jazz and drinking watery coffee in a dim cavé. The sound of rain wafts in during the interludes when the music stops. The door opens and some people come in. His seat was away from and below the entrance, so he sees only the legs entering and leaving. The high heels are wet. They pass by. Again the door opens. A pair of high heels and men's shoes beneath tight pants. It's been a while since he last came to a music hall. The music a place like this provides is not for enjoyment but rather a wall of sound to keep private conversations private. So there is a whirl of noise, choppy music and murmuring voices flowing together against the vague thumping of bass rhythms. Squirming mud flowing into an enclosed cave. Sinking into that mud. Here is another feeling entirely different from the taste of chasing an ego by aiming a slick ball on a level surface. Mire sinking endlessly. Then, suddenly, spewing up. The gloomy drumbeat, the lazy and gloomy drumbeat, lazy and monotonous... single melodic line. Harsh woman's voice. Without you, there is no world your heart is my home come to me... "You'll stay in school, won't you?" "Well. . . ." "Any plans after graduation?" "No special plan. . . ." "Think about it. . . ." "Your thesis was excellent" "Not really. . . ." "You don't look healthy, got to take care of yourself even when you're studying. . . ." no sir it is because of too much masturbation weren't you like that sir? hoarse voice without you there is no world I really don't know you're saying that again I told you not to worry still Mr. Yi I trust your sincerity two coffees and one tea listen don't put too much sugar in one coffee give it here that order slip why do you keep omitting it's not that it is to discover the microscopic truth of human behavior in small groups is American sociology becoming bacteriology at any rate American society is a society with a future it's moving with relatively little prejudice little prejudice? when they refuse to sit beside nigger boys that is their business don't be too severe in every society there is prejudice at any rate they are trying to solve the problem rationally are they not the problem that can't be solved in this world good-bye it's still raining isn't it shall we stay a little longer my who told you to leave give it to me have a sense of shame shame how is it gonna be it's a new semester I mean it's September yes it's fine so stifling here go if you can at any rate wouldn't it be better than here I intend to go on to the master's course you sure you're not going to settle there? well I'll have to go and see but still it might be better here to live there with a halo over you seems to be lonely here that goes without saying I've read plays by Tennessee Williams don't think so narrow-mindedly the guy with a bad lot will be begging even in heaven without you there is no world truly I cannot forget I cannot forget you... sit over here will you lend it to me for a day I'll return it soon Confucius said those who lend books are idiots don't use stale talk he said it because then there was no libraries only a private library can it be saved salvation? when the cure is prepared the sickbed is changed then once more the cure and the disease begin their hide and seek must you become great? why? what for? can't you just live as a nobody? listen idiot I have to be great because I don't want to be great this age we live in I love I'm crazy about you without you.... it's not enough mother I'm sorry you may make what you will of what I say I understand really if only we could communicate without talking it's necessary to be stingy with words after all it's the same whether you say it or not rhetoric is silver silence is silver too therefore talk at all events silence is bad rather than being fallen upon without making a sound screaming and biting look who's that it's Descartes isn't it it is wonder why the hell they put it here why do you go to school stifling stifling are you a patriot? you bastard you're talking nonsense again well it's because I'm not a patriot shall I kidnap you to the north? well now that Korean residents abroad are proclaiming they don't trust the government how can it be stopped? in the eyes of Japanese kids it means the south is a government and the north is also a government because of the Japanese kids we've been bruised at a time when absorption in making a modern nation is necessary without you there is no world... there's a seat over there isn't there a little bit more that's right shall we go which way? I have somewhere to stop in then see you tomorrow if there is a new election won't the Liberal Party win ha ha ha you know very well the names of the politicians well if you read the papers it's natural I never read the first page while you're not reading the country falls into ruin ruin? then that's something else again it's not something else no citizen of a democratic society should be like that cut the nonsense so you mean I should read those half-assed bastards' rantings and that filthy gossip I'd rather see the nation in ruins can't be helped after all this is not a society that moves under our power I'm crazy about you without you. . . .

The rain had stopped.

Chun hesitated for a minute, then decided to pay a visit to the boarding house for the first time in a long while.

Yŏng-suk's mother was cooking something on a burner in the yard and cleaning vegetables as she sat on the edge of the wooden floor. She welcomed him with delight,

"Oh my, Mr. Tokko!"

"Everyone doing well?"

"Same as always. . . . You should have stopped by once in a while."

"I know, I just. . . ."

Chun sat on the edge of the wooden floor as invited.

"Give these to Yŏng-suk."

"You didn't have to."

"They're exercise books for Yŏng-suk."

He pushed the bundle of books he had bought at a bookstore on the way toward Yŏng-suk's mother.

"Stay for a while. No need to hurry. You can have dinner with us before you go."

"May I?"

"Certainly. My husband and Yŏng-suk will be home before long. Please go on up."

She added, pointing upstairs.

"Since you left the room's been empty."

"Nobody's taken it?"

"No. There's been no suitable tenant. So when the brothers have worship meetings they use that room. . . . By the way, sister Kim Sun-im is coming today."

"She still comes these days?"

"Yes. She's such a kind girl. . . ."

Yŏng-suk's mother gauged Chun's demeanor with a glance and went on,

"She always talks about you. And when we pray she never fails to mention your name. . . ."

"I see. . . ."

"You don't meet a girl like her everyday, that's for sure."

"Nobody there now, right?"

Sensing the direction of the conversation, Chun walked toward the stairs, pointing up to the room.

"Yes. Go on up. Open the window for a cool breeze and take a nap. Meantime, I'll make dinner. . . ."

Chun walked up those familiar stairs. There was no furniture in the room but it was very clean. He opened the window and sat on the sill. Yŏng-suk's mother looked up and nodded. He got up and opened the closet. It was empty as well, except for a frame used for embroidery. Chun took off his jacket and laid down on his back.

Someone seemed to be calling his name. Undecided whether to get up, his eyes opened. It was blindingly bright. The light was on. He abruptly sat up.

"Are you awake?"

It was the voice he had heard in his dream. For a second he thought he was still dreaming. It wasn't until the figure of Kim Sun-im appeared in the door that he felt completely awake.

"Ah, have you been calling long?"

"No."

"Come on in."

Kim Sun-im sat down with her back to the other window. She looked especially fresh in her white blouse and navy blue skirt. She talked of this and that church matter, as if to someone she regularly saw. The thoughts he had once built around her suddenly rushed back to him. And the woman now before his eyes looked as pure and beautiful as she ever did. Her face again reminded him of someone, he tried to think who it could be. Somehow the old man at the Confucian school in P township came to mind. What resemblance could there be between the two faces? Listening to her speak, he felt his heart gradually soften. Her personality seemed able to bring out a calm good will in others. He felt gently pulled toward her, his heart overflowing, like a heart seeking a return to repose after long wanderings in the channels of some maze.

"Please come down you two. Let's have dinner."

At the sound of Yōng-suk's mother calling from downstairs they both rose.

It was at that moment. Chun stepped back, emitting a cry. Kim Sun-im looked into the man's fear-stricken face.

"What's wrong?"

She asked, startled.

"Well. . . all of a sudden. . . ."

Chun stood motionless for a long while, his hand on his forehead. His face was very pale.

"Aren't you feeling well?"

"No, I was a little. . . I'm all right now."

Chun said, his eyes still cast down, and walked downstairs in front of her.

After dinner was over, Chun whiled away an hour there and then left.

Yi Yu-jōng wasn't back yet. As soon as he entered his room, Chun collapsed on his bed with his clothes on. Earlier, Kim Sun-im's face had reminded him of the young maiden in that film. And at the same moment, Chun saw. . . a man's face reflected from the windowpane behind her. The pale face of Dracula. Chun lit a cigarette, went over and sat in a chair. He tried to laugh, but it was no use. Dracula. Vampire. In his head, those sombre scenes from the movie matinee again flashed by. He suddenly realized the beauty of that eerie tale. Dracula the vampire sucks blood from the throats of his victims with his sharp fangs. The victims become vampires themselves and wander in search of other victims. They are not cannibals. They have no hunger for flesh and bones, they only suck blood. Their thirst for blood is not gluttonous, they only take a taste from the wounds. Their manner of sucking blood thus is more a symbolic ritual than a biological act. By this act, yet another comrade is made. If the focus is on the act of sucking blood, the story becomes nothing special. For, viewed that way, Dracula differs not at all from the countless vampires flying through the summer skies—mosquitoes. That's it. The young man in chains was lonely. Freed from his chains, he wanders the dark streets in search of his lover. In the film, his victims followed him, concealed him and loved him. The victims did not hate him. Dracula merely knocked at the window of the lonely heart. Beckoning for them to leave behind the prison of common-sense. Then he throws them the key. It is a drama of men who have lost God. He cannot love God. It is a tragedy of men who have lost their appetite for the blood one can drink at church every Sunday for a paltry sum of money. He has a taste only for human blood. Sacred blood injures his mouth. That fluid of dissimulation nauseates him. The blood of God, like some corpse's liquid gore, destroys his heart. He declared war on God. God, who has a church and an army, tries to hunt him down and imprison him. Day—in the hours when the sun of common-sense shines he is powerless. Night—in the hours of revolt, used by the revolutionaries of all epochs, he acts. Though the genesis of the Dracula image is uncertain, it may be an image of an ancient folk deity whose throne has been seized by the Christian god. If so, is the image not our own? The theology professor pursuing Dracula seemed as detestable as a secret police agent chasing a revolutionary. In the movie, the theologian kills Dracula at the end. Slaughter of an awakened soul. He is the Pope's assassin who has crushed everyone who over the centuries ever dared oppose the church. In a drama in which Dracula is clearly the villain and the theologian plainly the hero, what sort of psychology does it take to take the side of Dracula this way? Simple. It's because I am Dracula. Love. Love of God. Blood that is the blood of nobody. The vampire who refrains from injuring his neighbors is law abiding, but the one who demands real blood is a devil. One must not covet real blood in place of false blood. The legend of Dracula is a legend of revolt against the Church. It is a threat to the teaching that prohibits any demand for real blood. But why, then, was I so startled? When Kim sun-im's face looked like that of the maiden in the movie and my own reflection looked like Dracula, why was I so startled? When I don't believe in Christ and hence don't consider Dracula a devil. Besides, the visage mirrored in the window was as seemly as that Dracula put forward when appearing before the maiden. The fangs were not even showing. But then. . . why did I jump back? At that instant, my mind was peaceful. I was feeling that she looked lovable. When a man is in love does he resemble Dracula? Sucking each other's blood is merely a symbol. That's it. It was, my hesitation was, compassion. It was a mind not wishing to injure her peace. It has been two thousand years since the blood of God dried up, and in the present age sacred blood is as plentiful as if it poured from water faucets, but still there are those who need the lie. To take away their false peace, to drive them into the night of endless wandering, can a right to do so be justified? No. One must not snatch a flower from the hand of a child. Even if it is an artificial flower. Kim Hahk and his sort may insist that we must. That's what politicians are. They hand out yet another artificial flower. Kim Hahk will suffer a bit because he is a good-hearted kid. Chun felt a burden lifted from his heart.

He got up and walked to the window. As usual, a man was there looking at him. He was smiling. True. Shouldn't bite just anyone out of loneliness. The man grinned. Not biting the one you want to bite. As long as I endure this enigma, no one will discover my identity. Escaping banishment by pretending to drink the repulsive holy blood at the church of common-sense. Lingering emotions surrounding Kim Sun-im were at long last being put to rest. It seemed obvious that his love for Kim Sun-im had to be dealt with that way. Chun felt at once sorrowful and proud.

He went down to Yi Yu-jŏng's room. She was almost finished changing her clothes.

"I'm ready, you can come in now."

"Aren't you busy?"

"Polite, aren't you?"

"Ha, ha."

"You're looking very innocent just now."

"As you wish."

"Shall we listen to some music?"

Chun nodded.

"Mozart."

A violin sonata was softly flowing forth.

"Well, Karl Barth said. . . ."

"Yes?"

". . . he once said that if he went to heaven he would first ask after Mozart and only later inquire about Augustine, Aquinas and Luther."

"It's a bit strange for an avant-garde artist to like Mozart."

"Well, I can't keep up with avant-garde music. I'm willing to compromise when it comes to music."

"Perhaps avant-garde composers would say they are willing to compromise when it comes to art."

"Sometimes I think that artists don't want a mass following. Once popularized, any avant-garde art tries to flee. Art history bears this out, too."

"You can't simply say they do it solely to distinguish themselves from others. In art, there is something that transcends individuals."

"What social significance could there be in Mozart?"

"It could be his faith in harmony. Doesn't that make him an unquestionable conservative? Music scares me. Only a saint like Confucius or a shepherd boy playing his pipes, whether highest or lowest, only those who've attained a certain composure have earned the right to enjoy music. For those in between music is no answer."

"To view music as an answer is wrong. It interprets nothing. So, there is no answer."

"When it comes to music, many people seem unable to rid themselves of superstition. Even Picasso never receives unconditional trust."

"No, he doesn't. In a way, Picasso was a man who oscillated wildly. Like a clock's pendulum, he swang—first one way, then another. Some works, his drawings for example, exhibit a rigorous balance like Greek sculpture, but other times he smashed objects into bits. He constructed an epic poem of war and peace. . . ."

"So he battered the critics from behind."

"He's the kind of artist who can't be fully judged until after his death."

"A wise approach, perhaps. Instinctively, he knows the ins and outs of his own era. He knows he would publicly disgrace himself if his pronouncements were too conclusive."

"As long as he is sincere, an artist cannot be publicly disgraced, can he?"

"That may be true in music and painting, such as they are, but it's not necessarily the case in literature."

"Literature's not the same?"

"Literature the same?"

"Yes."

"But literature can never become music."

"You needn't be pessimistic. They say nothing is impossible for a genius, don't they?"

"But then, I am no genius."

"My, I thought you were."

"I'm sorry."

As she walked home, Kim Sun-im was thinking of Tokko Chun. Save the man. From somewhere a voice seemed to be telling her that. After her unexpected meeting with Chun he remained, as always, a riddle to her. A while before when he had acted so strangely upstairs she had been anticipating something else. The embarrassment she caused him on that other night long before had often made her feel deep regret. To her, Chun seemed a lost little lamb who had wandered from the fold of the Lord's heart, doomed to repeat vain wanderings. How good it would be if only she could help him find hope in the words of the Lord and be reborn. After he moved away she thought she would never see him again and running into him again seemed somehow providential. It meant the Lord had not abandoned this poor soul and would receive him into His flock. I, too, want to know the truth. He had once said that, the winter before. It would be a simple matter. All he had to do was to leave it all to the Lord. All he must do is believe that everything in this world belongs to the Lord, and that our bodies and souls as well were created to please the Lord. One should never try to compete with the Lord. I have to convince him that anyone can be saved, as long as they don't suffer from the pride afflicting those who think they have mastered the wisdom of the world. But why is it that he shows so little sign of really wanting to learn? Maybe he thinks I have nothing to teach him. It is because he doesn't understand that I'm merely a servant of the Lord and he has no cause to feel uneasy about me. Dear Lord. Dear Father in heaven, full of grace, Who has vouchsafed light to this poor woman. Come to me, Holy Spirit. Help me to become a better servant, to work harder for the Lord, and to accomplish the Lord's will on this earth. Help me to save at least one more poor lamb before the coming of the end, let the Holy Spirit work through this body of little faith, and lead me not into temptation. Guide me to live not for myself but for our Lord. Though the whole world goes the way of Sodom and Gomorrah, make me your trumpeter to wake the people from their sleep, to protect the army of your worshipers, and be always with me. Lord always be with us, for we are weak, and we fear we may take into our own barns the sacrifices due to you. Fill my soul with courage and with love for my neighbors as you did the righteous prophets. Give me the wisdom to face those who are wise. With Your words, the greatest wisdom of all wisdom, they can be turned, and only for Your glory.

She went on silently praying as she walked the dark path to the streetcar track. Then she remembered that snowy night the previous winter when she had met Chun on that street.

Emerging from Yu-jŏng's room, Chun started back to his room but changed his mind and went to the billiard room. As always, it was kept by the four balls. He picked up the cue and began a solitaire game. The pride he had been feeling a while before seemed to have subsided. He struck a ball. Clack! Slightly mishit. Once more. Sensing someone watching him, he quickly looked back.

No one was there.

Along the wall were three chairs. He had an odd feeling that someone had just before been sitting there. He shook his head violently. I must be strong. To hold on to my own ego, at least. If only I can endure this godless loneliness with a cool demeanor and a hint of a smile. If only I can endure the loneliness of having lost my ancestors, then I might catch sight of a new sun. In my generation. If I don't drop dead. Imperturbable nerves and tight-fisted out of greed. Trying not to love because I love. Sure. No doubt about it. In order to escape detection by the secret operatives of the heathen interrogation office, until the exiled Dracula has been restored. Kim Sun-im. I seemed to have liked the girl. An angel. How could such a seed exist in this society? As if to belie the fact that a filthy war ravaged this land. How could such a woman be living in this filthy city? Happy, blessed, cute, color-blind. People who see in a rotting corpse only the possibility of a divine miracle. Shall I cling to her? Shall I? No. I shouldn't do that.

He stood up straight and smoothed his hair back with one hand. A man who had uncovered the inverted moral of the Dracula legend ought not harm a girl like Sun-im. A man who has lost the shock absorber called "God". A car that has lost the brake called "family" must steer clear of flowerbeds. I must be strong. Nonetheless, his heart was empty. Her gentle eyes. Her roundish chin floated before him. If he extended his hand, she would be pulled along. It had been easy to gauge her heart in the sincerity she showed in talking of church matters. Would he still refrain from reaching out with his hand? What could that be?

For a long while Chun stood with his cue poised to strike the ball, but he didn't move. If she is to my liking, shouldn't I have her? For whose sake am I saving face? No, I shouldn't do it. Why? Because of conscience? It's not conscience. In the first place, it would be troublesome. Are you avoiding a fight? It's useless to tempt me. I can't compete with a child. That's all. Sure, sure. You're not doing it because the formalities create trouble, so don't deceive yourself into thinking it's out of benevolence. Say what you will. Just as two fighters of uneven weights are never matched, so this is a purely formal matter of procedure. I have not the least intention to paint a mustache of plausible morality on my conduct. If I forbear from robbing a widow, it is not out of sympathy. It is because it would mean trouble. So it has nothing to do with compassion? Ha, ha, you may think so. They say compassion leads to love, and it is unlikely such sentiments will be found in me, but wait a minute, I'll try to come up with an answer you'll accept, let me think, perhaps it is like. . . .

The cue was shaking in his hand and his forehead was drenched with sweat. His face pale, he stared at the ball.

All of a sudden he raised his glance from the ball and looked at the window. A man's face reflected on the pane. With all his might he threw the cue at the man. It missed the target and struck the windowsill, making an enormous noise. When Yu-jŏng rushed over and opened the door, Chun was bent over with his forehead pressed to the table.

"What's the matter?"

She put her hand on his shoulder and looked down at his

face. After a long time, Chun raised his head.

"What's the matter? Goodness, look at the sweat."

Chun grinned.

"I'm sorry. Couldn't hit the shot. . . ."

With suspicious eyes, she looked over at the cue laying on the floor.

"No matter how I tried, I couldn't hit it right. . . ."

Chun pointed with his chin to the ball. After scouring his face with her gaze, Yu-jŏng just shrugged. Perched on the side of the billiard table, Chun calmly asked,

"Was it very loud? You must have wondered what it was, eh?"

Still looking suspiciously at him, she sat on the table beside him and said,

"Has anything happened?"

"What?"

"I won't pry, but I'm here if you want to talk about anything."

"With that look on your face, you remind me of a dormitory house mother."

"That's not nice. You should start taking seriously what others say."

You, too, Miss Yi Yu-jŏng. . . .

"An outburst like that makes me feel like I have to make a false confession."

She did not reply.

After watching Chun go up the stairs, Yu-jŏng returned to her room and sat in a chair. Staring down at her hands clasped on her knee, she was submerged in thought. Compared to when she first came back home, she was now fairly well settled and the dissonant feelings from her long sojourn abroad had mostly been controlled. After all, the attraction of coming home is that you can return to being yourself. The people around her had no idea what she had experienced over there. In her life abroad she came upon a wall that would never be overcome in her generation. A knot that cannot be untied by the talent or resolution of an individual. This she had learned from a painful experience. Her resentment toward the other had faded away. There is no law saying it can never work out, but an affair with a foreigner has extra burdens. In my case, unfortunately, the burden was too heavy.

The feeling of relief after having wept. Lately, she thinks too about being able to laugh again. The business of becoming an adult means nothing else, it means one has experienced falling down. Even after falling down you can get back up. If you just stumble, it's not difficult to get up and brush yourself off. If the fall was serious, it might take several months, you might even need a false leg, but you'll be able to stand again. In the beginning, Tokko Chun in her eyes was merely a cute little child. She hadn't even thought much of what happened that night after they came home from the bar. But lately she had felt a little confused. She tut-tutted to herself, recalling what he had said about the age difference not mattering. There was something hollow in his talk. When he dealt with her, at least, he went out of his way to be outrageous and to feign calmness. All she knew was that he was from the same place up north as her brother-in-law, but somehow he didn't seem to show any particular concern about living in somebody else's house. She walked to the mirror, tilted her head and looked at her face. From the tip of her nose down to her upper lip, she was prodest of that part. She rubbed her eyebrows with her fingers. For some reason she felt gay. After trying a few ballet steps she took off her clothes and laid down in bed.

She thought she heard a thud upstairs and carefully listened. It wasn't repeated.

She pulled the sheet up and rolled over. The clock on the desk began to chime with a clear tone. Eleven. She rolled over again and murmured. A strange kid. . . .

What was all that fuss about, as if I had belatedly discovered the devil of orthodoxy. Men are known to err so let's not be too fastidious. That there is no orthodoxy. That his family tree was incinerated. That he has no home to return to. Aren't these incontestable facts? So many people out there. The ones with true courage are the ones who despise the people who stand with phony genealogies under their arms, peddling sacred blood as if it were cold barley tea. They are not the fearsome ones. They will eventually face ruin, will they not? The underground resistance avoids secret agents not because they are criminals but out of convenience. That we still find it shocking is probably due to immemorial custom. We inadvertantly get hoodwinked by the commonsense trick of painting the dark hue of negation onto everything opposed to the preexisting order. I reject the image of the criminal. I am not a criminal. Because I do not recognize their law. It is useless to try to capture me with the crucifix of common sense. I will not fall, not even in the crossfire of their gazes. I stand firm and smile. And I will not beg for love. Neither will I steal. What I took from Hyŏn Ho-sŭng, I took fair and square. Because money was necessary for an isolated fight. With that money I bought time. Instead of human blood I drank time.

Chun lit a cigarette and walked to the window. Mirrored in the glass was his old friend. At the sight of that face Chun felt a bit ashamed. My one and only friend. His most trustworthy ally, he was sorry he had been suspicious of him even for a moment. The only way is for the two of us to deal with of everything. We must not be taken in by importunate tricks and temptations. The man in the glass nodded his assent and took a puff. Chun was relieved by that relaxed gesture. When you cannot get love you must be content with time. Like a man with nothing to do. As though it bothered you not in the least. I wonder how Dracula ever became a vampire anyway? There was no explanation of that in the movie. As often happens in folk tales, he just appeared without further ado. Chun compared Dracula and Faust. Perhaps Dracula also began as a heavy reader. A bachelor in a huge castle, all he did was read books. Like Faust, he must have voraciously consumed works of philosophy, alchemy, literature and theology to boot. There was no answer, however. In a dark study reeking of old tomes, there came a moment when a certain notion flashed into his head. Am I not God himself? At that instant he trembled. Why must it not be so? However much you call out to God, there is no answer. Though He had promised to come again to this world, no news had ever come. He must not possess the power to do so. Waiting for Him is useless. I alone am the only thing certain. That's true. God exists, does He not? But the one existence I can prove with certainty is myself. Therefore, I am God. After a sleepless night full of fear and excitement, in the end he made up his mind. If I am God, I must have disciples. He chose to become Lord. Thus began nocturnal proselytization. For in the light of day lurked the eyes of the clerics who had already appropriated the world. The enemy propaganda admonished all to bolt their doors at night, saying devils were about. Faust made a compromise but Dracula did not. After his separate peace with the enemy camp, Faust was granted a peerage, but Dracula was slain. How symbolic for him to be burned to ashes in the shadow of the cross. Dracula, too, died nailed on cross. On that cross of Calvary, signifying false common sense and a squalid, ignoble peace. Thus he became the Lord. Discarding the raiments of rulership, His crown, His army of angels, His trumpet and His punishments, He allowed Himself to be slain in the form of an insurgent, stigmatized by a judgment of treason, a pack of secret agents on his heels, torture, and a supplication of love. He has become the hero of a black New Testament. Dark Lord Dracula of the Black New Testament. The Post-New Testament Lord Dracula. Quite satisfied with this notion he had concocted, Tokko Chun forgot about the question that had been taunting him not long before: Why shouldn't I love, if I love? But. He stopped abruptly. What the hell am I doing now? What has Christ to do with me? What has Dracula to do with me? Am I to sing and dance in accordance with other's rules? I've been acting in a translated drama. Damn. I nearly made another blunder.

He laughed uproariously. And became quite cheerful. I will

not become a Don Quixote, I will not become a native woman aping a missionary's wife. Weren't these my resolutions? This damn world we live in is full of traps. And then I almost did it. Not one chance in a million. So long, drama. I decline to be in that script. Like an animal escaped from a trap, he moved lightly and cheerfully as he took off his clothes to sleep. There was a thud when he leapt onto the bed. After tossing and turning a few times he quieted down. He was already asleep snoring lightly. Very peaceful was the sound of his breathing.

XIV

To the barley fields. . . .

One rainy evening in the summer of 1959, Kim Hahk paid a visit to his friend Tokko Chun, bringing with him a bottle of Chillo soju and a couple of dried cuttlefish. As he veered into the quiet alley, he muttered to himself, "Well, this guy sure picked an odd corner for his nest". Hahk peered up at the high stone walls of his friend's new abode, walls he had often passed by without paying them any heed. He was in. Judging from his beaming face, a rarity for him, he must have been bored to tears.

"Welcome."

"You mean it?"

"Sure. What's this?"

Hahk opened the bundle a little to show him. Chun let out a raucous laugh.

"When you graduate you should work for Chillo Ltd."

"I'm planning to."

This time both laughed in unison. Chun took the things his friend had brought and put them on the desk, offering him the chair by the window as he himself sat down on the bed. All smiles, he asked his friend,

"How are things?"

"So-so."

"Wait a second. . . ."

"Why?"

"Well, I'm going to get some food."

"No need."

"Just sit there."

Chun got up, pushed his friend's shoulder down, and said,

"It's been some time, so we ought to have a good meal."

He walked out of the room. After the door closed and his friend was out of sight, Hahk leaned forward, stretched his legs and looked around the room. He seemed to have been writing, for clean paper and manuscript pages are spread all over the desk and crumpled papers are scattered over the floor. Several books lay here and there at the head of the bed. The sheets seem freshly changed. It is a brass single bed. One cabinet at the foot of the bed. On the left as you enter the room there is a bookcase. Even with all this furniture the room is spacious, it would be thought a very large room in a Korean style house. Thinking such thoughts, Hahk turns around and looks out the window. But rain is flowing down the glass and all he can see is his own face peering back at him with only darkness beyond. He listens intently. Not a sound. Perhaps because the house is so big and the rain not heavy. The trickles of water on the windowpane were the only sign it was raining. He heard the door open and the owner of the room returned.

Chun set a tray of peanuts and spiced radishes on the low table between the bed and the desk where Hahk was sitting. Then he sat down on the bed.

"Have a drink now."

"No, guests first."

Chun filled Hahk's glass and then filled his own and lift it, saying,

"To whom shall we drink?"

Hahk thought for a moment and then said,

"To His Excellency the President."

"Good. To His Excellency the President."

They both drained the glasses in one gulp. This time Chun

made the proposal,

"To the July night."

"Good. To the July night."

"Ahhh. Should have roasted some of this cuttlefish."

"Unroasted has a taste of its own."

"With *soju* this is the best."

Chewing a cuttlefish tentacle, Chun asked,

"So, how are the Cabinet ministers?"

"What?"

"I mean your future members of the Cabinet."

"Oh, I see. By the way, here's the latest issue."

His glass in one hand, Hahk pulled a copy of "Imprisoned Age" out of a manila envelope he had laid on the desk and handed it to Chun.

Chun took the magazine and slowly flipped through the pages. When he got to an article by Kim Hahk he read aloud, from time to time taking a sip from his glass.

—Had the Shanghai Provisional Government constituted the first Cabinet after Liberation the situation would have been much improved. They would have taken over administrative powers without an election, founding their authority on the nights of Shanghai and on Heunggu Park. Because nations are born of myth, they first of all would have thoroughly purged all pro-Japanese elements. The Special Committee on Civil Enemies would have become the Office for Interrogation of Treasonous Collaborators, and the balance-sheet would have been rigorously drawn up and the old accounts closed. The Thought Police, the judiciary, the local magistrates and the petty officials of the colonial administration, all would have instantly made themselves scarce without uttering a word. Such a political catharsis would have immensely benefited the mental hygiene of the people. Throughout the country, shamanistic shrines would be dedicated to patriots. The Hero of Harbin Railway Station, the Rider of Ch'ŏngsan-ri, the Don Quixote of Seoul Station and the Joan of Arc of Ch'ŏnan. . . these tribal martyrs, shining like radiant stars, would have ceased their restless wanderings and have partaken of the sumptuous offerings. And the site of the Chosŏn Shinto Temple would without a doubt have become the Westminster of Korea. Though the administration would be unskilled, because they would be tactlessly honest there would be no lies. And the whole nation would have mirthfully laughed to read in the papers how, on a tour of the country, the ruling party Chairman had thrashed a corrupt township mayor with a long pipe. A plan would have been laid down for conservation of historic sites and excavation of antiquities to polish what we have and dig up what is buried, and the project of restoring the "racial face" that had been shattered into pieces would have been undertaken in high spirits. Thus, Kaneshiro Sendatze would once more become Kim Sŏn-dal. Liberation Army officers would have become the founders of the National Defense Army and would have instituted somewhat archaic but impeccably patriotic traditions derived from Hwangpo Military Academy in China. And the history of the struggles of the Liberation Army would have been a mandatory subject for all students at the military academy. At every opportunity they would have claimed Manchuria as Korean territory, urging the leaders in the North, because they were on its border, to recover the lost territory and transfer it to United Nations protection pending consolidation upon reunification of North and South, thereby making Kim Il-sŏng piss in his pants. As for Japan, they would have established a policy of resuming diplomatic relations only after thirty-six years, the duration of the prior Japanese annexation. And a law would have been enacted prescribing that all official functions and ceremonies should begin with everyone present grinding their teeth three times toward the East. Once up-stream had been cleared, down-stream would have been clear, too, and the social morals would have resembled an autumn sky. Important leaders, including the Chairman, would have worn traditional *hanbok*, not Western suits, and content with simple sustenance, they would have been impervious to bribery.

Once a decade had passed in this way, the black-eyes inflicted by the Japanese kids would have healed, and long stupefied heads would have begun to work once more. Our pals up North, naturally, would not have dared to play with fire. As they say, the heart desires but the limbs quake. By that time, friends would have returned one by one after studying abroad and would be dropping hints about modernization, economic nationalism or existentialism, subjects the older generation would feel insecure to dispute, gradually insinuating that the time had come for the older generation to.... There would have been no resort to filthy tactics. A plan would have been announced for the first general election after Liberation and a Constituent Assembly formed. Candidacies of collaborators, who if they had been men would voluntarily have renounced for life any position of responsibility, would have been prohibited as an exception. In addition, the Chairman and all of the major officials associated with him would have declined to run for elective office. A new Constitution in place, with the accession of a young and competent government the age of myth would have come to an end and an age of practical professionals would have begun. The reception of foreign civilization would have been judicious and work would have been earnestly and diligently done. Concerning education, it would have been engraved on people's minds from the very start that schooling is preparation for earning a living, and the state would have seen to it that no one with only a high school education ever went hungry. No vain ambitions would have been pressed into the hearts of the people and they would have awakened to the truths that haste makes waste and that hard work is never wasted. With a tradition of disdaining bribery strictly observed, high officials would have received no special gains and only the industrious would have accumulated property. And.... The more of these fruitless suppositions I put forth, the more my heart swells with grief. I have been here and there asking questions, but all I am told is stay healthy, study hard and become a great man. Suddenly I realized. I am a student. . . .

"Hmm. Quite good!"

"I tried to imitate your style."

"It's a fine yellowprint."

"Yellowprint?"

"The word 'blueprint' is for the future, so this is a yellowprint."

"Because it's about missed opportunities?"

"That's right."

"Worth reading?"

"I said it was quite good. Now, let's drink another to the lost yellowprint."

Chun put down his glass and with his hand on his forehead remained quiet for a while. Then he looked up and continued,

"The last line is excellent."

"You think so?"

"The fact that we are, after all, students."

"The fact that we have no political power."

"To speak plainly, it means we are still children."

"Look, I didn't intend it to be taken so literally."

"Then?"

"I meant the problem is, despite the fact we're students, we must suffer."

"Proposing revolution?"

"Don't keep talking like that."

"No, I'm not being cynical. That we suffer is needless to say, but what do you suggest we do? I already know what you'll say. You'll call for more social participation, for people to form political discussion groups and to spend their vacations doing volunteer social work."

"Yes, to act for reform by all possible means."

Hahk emphasized each word as he chewed a cuttlefish tentacle.

"It's good work. That's why it's not a revolution. It's work within time. It's faithful. If it's not a revolution, after all, but a reformation, then the participation of others mustn't be forced. Unlike in a revolution, where either-or choices are posed, in a case where one struggles in pregiven circumstances the path has not just two but innumerable branches. Is it not so? To decide whether society is better served by a narrow-minded man who spends a month in the summer teaching math to children in the countryside, or by the same man spending that month in self-scrutiny, would be a difficult decision to make. As you said, we are merely students. Politically, I mean in the broad sense, politically we are impotent. In the case of dealing with foreign oppressors, the position of the students was much simpler. But now, in a situation where the nation is our own, we are at a great disadvantage. So I say time is the only solution. There is no other way but for you all to do well when you become the Cabinet. To do well when the time comes, shouldn't you be studying hard now? Stay healthy, study hard and become a great man is right then, isn't it?"

Hahk shook his head.

"I doubt if the country will last until we become great men. Are you telling me we still should just sit and aim at A's?"

"The conversation keeps going in circles. What do you propose, then?"

"I have nothing to propose."

"Then, it means there's not that much difference between you and me, after all."

"So you interpret it, but there is at least the difference that I'm still uselessly eating myself up, telling myself, even if. . . ."

"So very self-righteous patriots are. Just as men's faces differ, so does sincerity from man to man."

"And your sincerity is. . .?"

"To become anything but a patriot."

"You mean, then, you wouldn't join with revolutionary conspirators?"

"Never."

"That's not what you just said, is it?"

Hahk's voice was growing louder.

"You mean a revolution in which ideologues band together to form a party and seize political power by violent means, right?"

Hahk smiled and said,

"Isn't that what a revolution is?"

"That's why I don't like it. Listen, revolution is putting a new myth into practice, isn't it? Can you think of a myth that instantly could take the place of democracy? There is none. And if that's true, it means there'll be no revolution, just a violent shift of political power, a change in personnel. In my opinion, mere replacement of people, without a new religion being founded, is a dangerous thing. It's a different situation from the one in your article. It would be one thing if there were a person or a group with a mythical halo, like the men with what you called the authority of Shanghai, but in our society at present there is nobody like that left. We either devoured them or else they've been beaten down. I don't mean to say there is no way at all to change present conditions."

Hahk scrutinized Chun's face and asked,

"And that is?"

"One day, if twenty million people, school children aside, suddenly feel humiliated enough to all join together in an insurrection, on that day I'll be in their ranks."

"Frightful."

". . . sorry."

Breaking into a grin, Hahk struck a match and lit a cigarette. Chun smiled back, and said,

"Our talks are bound to end in a stalemate. Shall we change the subject?"

"We have no choice, do we?"

"Shall I get something more to drink?"

"No, I'm drunk."

"You can sleep here and go tomorrow."

"No, I'm heading down home tomorrow."

"Really? The rain is. . . ."

He rose and opened the window. The rain had grown thinner, almost like mist.

"I can go, it'll be all right if I catch a taxi."

Chun sat back down.

"Going home for vacation. . . after all, for you vacation is better."

"I'm sorry."

They both laughed.

"If you have nowhere to go over the vacation you should come."

"Well, as I said last time, it looks like I'll be going somewhere with the family that lives here. I could go with them for a while and then break away to visit you. Perhaps I will trouble you."

"Do as you wish. Anytime. It'll be your first visit to Kyŏngju, won't it?"

"I've never been there."

"It's worth seeing at least once."

"Well, I'd like to go. Singing 'Nights of Shilla'."

"But that's for the others."

"They say you only appreciate home when you're away."

"It's true, I think. I'm sorry it's no consolation to you. . . ."

Glimpsing a tint in his friend's eyes, Hahk made a bow.

"Well, it's no fault of yours, is it? When all is said and done, home is good, isn't it?"

"Nothing that great about it, it's just home."

"Let's say you're walking on the streets of Kyŏngju, watching the people go by and thinking about the sorts of work their ancestors did and how they lived in ancient Sŏrabŏl, wouldn't it be interesting?"

"A rediscovery of the ancestral home?"

"Something like that. Because we are all homeless. A home is a home, but if it's a place like Kyŏngju, it gives you something to be nostalgic about."

"It's not that either, Seoul is a strange place for me, too, but being home doesn't make me feel calm and at peace. . . though my brother says he misses Pulkuk-sa Temple when he's out at sea. . . ."

"It's because you're still young."

"Maybe you're right."

"Said Hahk, taking Chun's remark lightly, and then suddenly remembering, he went on,

"Oh, yea, Miss Kim Sun-im. . . ."

Chun's expression at once stiffened. Feeling a bit awkward, Hahk continued,

"Have you seen her?"

"Yes, not long ago."

"Makes a good impression, doesn't she?"

"Think so? Good luck to you."

"Nonsense."

"No, really, I'm nothing to her."

"Still, when I see her, she always asks about you."

An embarrassed smile came to Chun's face. To Hahk it seemed funny that he was so naive when it came to women.

"You never know, do you? She might turn out to be an angel sent to save your corrupted soul."

Chun looked down and didn't reply. Thinking of Sun-im's face, Hahk continued his teasing,

"Well, it's only natural for a happy man to have no interest in revolution. . . ."

Hahk stopped short, for he saw a strange look come over his friend's lowered face. Chun gripping the corner of the bed with both hands, biting his lips like a man in pain. Suddenly feeling sober, Hahk froze. Only after a long pause, Chun looked up and said,

"I really must be drunk, eh?"

He forced an unnatural smile. Hahk checked his watch and got to his feet. Without rising, Chun looked up at him and asked "Why?" Then he motioned for his friend to sit back down. Hahk put his forehead to the window and peered outside.

"Better go while the rain is still light like this."

Hahk's tone was cheerful. Chun then got up as well and,

recovering his normal voice, said,

"It's still early, isn't it? It's not even ten yet. . . ."

"No, it's getting late. I have to leave early tomorrow. . . and I'm feeling drunk, too."

Hahk picked up the manila envelope.

Chun loaned a raincoat to his friend and the two of them went downstairs. In the front hall, they ran into Yi Yu-jōng returning home.

After seeing Hahk to the main street and watching him head off home by taxi, Chun felt discontented. Not because of what Hahk had said, but because his own attitude had made his friend uncomfortable.

"Just passing by?"

Hearing this, he stopped, stepped back a few steps and opened Yu-jōng's door. She had put on a comfortable robe and had some music on.

"Let's have a little talk before you go."

Looking at Chun sitting in a chair across from her, she smiled broadly. Chun closed his eyes. He felt sobered up, perhaps from being outside in the wind.

"Did you drink a lot?"

"No. But we're not very formidable drinkers."

He got up, picked up a water pitcher from the shelf and downed two glasses in a row.

"A powerful thirst."

Yu-jōng teased him without cracking a smile.

"Can't even drink in peace with you around."

Chun retorted, affecting a surely voice. Yu-jōng lowered the volume of the music and turned back around.

"You don't even know what alcohol tastes like."

She said, her lips in a pout.

"Too many painful things to do without the taste of alcohol."

". . . ."

Yu-jōng just gazed at him.

"I often feel like drinking myself into the mud, but I don't."

"Why not?"

"There's nothing really worth getting drunk over."

"Because you're only a kid."

"Kid?"

"Are you grown up?"

Chun nailed his eyes to the floor and to himself moaned "ai, ai". At last, he lifted his head and changed the subject, asking,

"Got any cigarettes?"

Yu-jŏng put a cigarette in his mouth and lit a match for him. Chun looked up at her. Against the pale color of her clothes, her tangled hair looked alluring.

Emptied by just the right intake of alcohol, his head sucked the music in. Once pulled in, the music shattered and was swept away, and new sounds kept on flowing in. Any drunker than this and there would have been no music, no anything. The strings flew lightly by, stopping and soaring, like a May morning breeze at the seashore. He put out the cigarette and looked at Yu-jŏng. Her eyes were on the newspaper in her hands but she didn't seem to be reading.

"Music is like a door between the worlds of drunkenness and sobriety."

Yu-jŏng nodded.

"I've been afraid to open that door and go to the other side. That's why music always left me cold. But now. . . ."

Chun shut his eyes. The fresh May sea breeze was even more invigorating. Yu-jŏng saw a look of simple joy shining on his face. As his expression grew tenderer, a faint smile was engraved on the young man's lips. She thought of a drop of paint falling into a cup of clear water.

There was a sound from the phonograph as the record finished. The rustle of feathers as an eagle lights on a branch, Chun muttered to himself.

"The thing on the far side of music."

This time Yu-jŏng picked up his words and said,

"Alcohol, you mean?"

"Yes."

"But liquor's not the only thing."

"And. . .?"

"The man."

Chun made no reply.

Out on the ocean the seagulls are playing hide-and-seek with the waves. The bright sea of spring becomes the burning ocean of summer, and on those waters fall the cold shadows of far wandering birds, and soon the snow is slashing down. An ocean of ice. A polar bear slips into a hole and dies. Again, wind. Only the wind remains, futilely blowing on, with no spring or fall.

Chun got up.

"I better go and get some sleep."

"Good night, baby."

Chun's eyes came to rest on the skin peeking out from the open neck of her robe. It looked white and warm.

Gathering the front of her robe with one hand, with the other she held Chun's hand. She accompanied him to the door and then turned around. He looked back at her.

Chun opened the door and left. He walked toward the door. About a step before reaching the door he halted. The chains on his hands and feet held him back. He clenched his fists and tried to pull himself forward. Only an excruciating pain in his wrists, the chains won't budge. He tries to move his feet. They're the same. Just then, from somewhere comes a voice. It's a woman. Come over here. You must leave that room. Who could it be? The voice is unfamiliar. Come over here. You must leave that room. Who are you? Me? You know every well. I don't know, who are you? What did you say, you know me? I don't doubt it. He tries to say no, but his voice won't come out.

Chun opened his eyes. He felt thirsty. He sat up in bed and drank water from a bottle sitting on the headboard. He laid back down again but couldn't sleep right away. Remembering how he couldn't speak in his dream, he tried to speak, "I. . . I. . . ." He turned and tossed about, trying to get back to sleep, but he was completely awake. He rolled over on his stomach and turned on the radio. You are now listening to a night broadcast from Seoul, Republic of Korea, to the people of the North. Next, some music. Aloha-e softly flowed out. The sweet music that suddenly rolled forth captivated him. It was the same voice he had once heard long before. I know who you are. I know very well. I heard your voice ages ago in that house with an apple orchard overlooking a white factory smokestack. It's true, you presided over us. A secret ritual conducted in the depth of the night before the radio with the emblem of a little dog sitting. Excited with bated breath. Feeling the deepest sympathy. Dear beloved people of the North. Today, the hour you've been awaiting has come once more. Yesterday in your provinces the following occurred. In P'yŏngyang. . . . In Ch'ŏngjin. . . . In Wŏnsan. . . . The poetry of my boyhood. We imagined it was you who sent the silver birds to drop death from the fleecy clouds of the summer sky. The swift metal birds suddenly came soaring from the horizon and toppled the looming giant. Dear people of the North, today there was an exhibition of children's art at Kyŏngbok Palace in Seoul. The precocious talents of our children, the new buds of our flowering race. . . . Countless citizens. . . . His Excellency the President. . . . His Excellency the President. . . . Chun was climbing the rope ladder of an LST. Over the rail and through the haze, W City looked fresh and crisp like a city seen for the first time. For some reason, he felt no fear. What you have all longed for in your dreams. Sure, because it is where your beautiful voice is. Because it is the place where father and brother-in-law are. What's more, the boy knew about the adventures of Remy. Because it is the land of Dr. Syngman Rhee. It was at the refugee camp, when he saw the thick lips of a black guard on the other side ofthe wire fence, it was then that he first opened his eyes in an alien world. There they were, father and son, walking side-by-side down the street through the wind off the harbor, remarking how hunger is worse on an empty stomach. There was an afternoon when, walking a lonely path with apple blossoms overhead, he learned to his surprise that one could love again. Riding alone in the hearse carrying his father to his grave, and in the street the children went on playing games. From then on, he was convinced children are vicious and cruel little beasts. Then there was the night when he happened on the party membership card in an old bundle he had been lugging wherever he went, the night when he had hatched the plot and tried to subdue his fearful pleasure. All these things had issued from this beautiful voice. Walking through the city after people were evacuated, I understood nothing. The meaning of the flower blooming in the yard of that house I didn't understand. I didn't grasp the significance of that suffocating embrace as the air raid shelter shook from the bomb blasts. Now, I understand. They all were one. That summer sky. Clouds. Birds of silver. Blood spilt on the ground. Deserted streets. City ablaze. Cruel children. They all were one. Kim Hahk solves all such things simply. Saying they are evils of politics. Could that be all? That humans go astray and stumble, is it only because one old man governs badly? I have chosen another path. I have decided to rely only on the hatred my own heart can trust. But did I take revenge on Hyŏn Ho-sŭng for my sister's sake? That's untrue. I merely plotted for myself. But. But. That's right. I chose to become a villain. To be free. To exchange that uncommon freedom for money. To exchange that money for time. To exchange that time for freedom. But something in this circulation went wrong somewhere. Why didn't I tempt Kim Sun-im? What's the grand revenge in taking over an upstairs room in a huge mansion and eating three meals a day? I was cheating. I cunningly arranged extenuating circumstances, matter suitable to be presented to a court. My evil design was to commit a crime without becoming a criminal. Trying to commit a murder without getting blood on your hands? Is that possible? To take the side neither of God nor the Devil? But I have no god to betray. For me, drama was impossible. To surpass the impossible, is that revolution? The impossible?

Chun abruptly got out of bed onto the floor. He paced back and forth across the room, clutching his head. The impossible? That's it. To become God myself. That's the only way. But. Isn't it a translated drama? It's a lie. Do it not in the name of Judas or Dracula, but in one's own name. Not invoking Faust, but signing the name Tokko Chun. That you use a pseudonym, trying to elude your own name, that's proof of cowardice. To pretend you are above corruption just because you don't contract in another's name is merely a malicious evasion of risks. No, I took risks. I extorted money by threatening a Workers Party member. I must be a pain to Hyŏn Ho-sŭng. I'm content extracting money from him. I don't care for melodrama. I just wanted to rest in my own cave, caressing the incurable tumor growing within me. That's a lie. To Hyŏn, you are no more important than Beth. He doesn't even have to deal with you, does he? He merely throws bones to you. Such a coward, you don't even dare to look up on the master's table. You're a contemptible bastard, like a robber who robs with the law in mind. I am not, I am not.

He walked to the window and looked into the glass. The pale man was watching him. He spoke coldly. Live honestly. Very honestly. I mean, get out of this house. I didn't know you were such a fool. Then, then.... It wasn't that I lacked courage. I just had no taste for melodrama. It wasn't that I chose moderation. I just didn't want to reenact Don Quixote. If necessary I'll act. Don't you realize that the only way left in this age is to lunge toward the windmill, fully aware you are Don Quixote? Don't you realize you must become a Judas without a Christ? You are looking down on the common people. You'll only have a love affair with a princess. If you're God, everyone else is God, too. Don't be conceited and imagine you are alone in the drama.

Moaning, he sat down on the edge of the bed. This has been the midnight broadcast to everyone in the North. So long until next time at this hour. And... the national anthem. Chun listened, as if it were the first time he had heard it in a long while. When the national anthem ended, the room suddenly was saturated by the night. He moved the radio dial this way and that. At one point, a strange voice came forth. Two, two, three, five, four, six. Eight, three, three, six, six, six. It was a woman's voice calling out numbers three at a time. The calling went on. The dry female voice seemed interested only in precision. 356 777. 948 333. 547 666. 123 355. 388 444 444. Inside Chun's head, exactly the same thing took place as happened earlier when he was listening to music. It was a secret message transmitted in code from the North to spies in the South. 999 333. 753 555. 311 222. 148 077. 888 444. 699 233. 666 222. 444 444. Inside his head, until then so chaotic and incoherent, a hot wind was blowing and the only sound was that of waves periodically beating the shore. Like a spy decoding signs bearing no relation to the cipher book in the transmission room. For him, this secret code was infinitely deep and free. Like Hyon's party membership card. How could I have thought I was threatening Hyŏn for having been a Communist Party member? Why did I whisper that I was taking revenge because he was once my brother-in-law? Why did I think of that party card only as a savings account passbook? An incomprehensible thing. I'll consider it an invitation card sent to me from a domain I hesitated to enter. Who dispatched the invitation is of no consequence. The important thing is that I've been invited. I'll accept the invitation. What if it is cowardly to put off ringing the bell until I know the name of the one who invited me?

The window suddenly brightened and a crack of thunder soon followed. Chun got up and opened the window. The wind blew rain into the room.

The rain kept up its muffled moaning and each flash of lightning revealed countless arrow-like streaks of pale rain.

He closed the window, picked up the pair of trousers he had tossed on the bed, put them on and fastened his belt. 333 444. 444 444. The woman was still calling out the numbers. Chun opened the door and walked down the hall.

He slowly descended the stairs. At the landing where the stairs turned, he sat down. The ceiling light shone on his back, sending an uneven shadow down the stairs.

Chun peered down at the shadow. It looked as if his double had fallen down there. He felt a certain strength surging into his heart. All at once his heart began to pound. Hot blood rushed to his temples. But he didn't immediately get up. He wanted to calm down a bit. Passion may be needed to reach a decision, but once resolved there's no call for excitement when one puts it into practice. He tried to imagine her heavy body. His throat was parched. He gulped dryly. He clutched his throat tightly with both hands. Suddenly he felt a sense of shame. He stayed like that for quite a while, lost in thought. He kept gulping dryly and his face burned, but he couldn't make up his mind. The lightning kept flashing, and each time a blue light pulsed through the windows. He smoothed his hair down and got up. There was a thin smile on his lips. Without making a sound, he slowly went down the stairs and walked along the corridor. Upon arriving in front of Yu-jŏng's room he paused, then firmly grasped the doorknob, turned it and pulled. The door noiselessly opened. As the door closed behind, his figure vanished from sight.